Gerard Doan

The Horse's Rescue

Gerard Doan

The Horse's Rescue

ISBN/EAN: 9783744662925

Printed in Europe, USA, Canada, Australia, Japan

Cover: Foto ©Andreas Hilbeck / pixelio.de

More available books at **www.hansebooks.com**

Gerard Stout

THE
HORSE'S RESCUE.

BY

GERARD DOAN,
FOR FORTY-ONE YEARS A WORKER ON THE HORSE.

"I don't go much on religion,
For I never have had any show,
But I've got a mighty tight grip on
The few things that I know."

NEW YORK:
PUBLISHED BY THE AUTHOR.
1882.

INTRODUCTORY.

Of course all scientific men of advanced and developed minds well know it is necessary to have references in order to introduce any great science with success; and at this day it requires noted men, men of good standing, men of honor, men that have been tried, men that are located and well established, in order for references to carry any influence with them. There have been all kinds of humbugs, as they are called by some. The people have been duped in so many ways that it has become almost impossible to introduce a good thing; and after reading this work through you will be convinced of that fact. In this work there has been but a very small part told. The financiering necessary in order to make a center or focus of this great science, and to get it introduced in some great center of science, where we could get reliable and scientific men for references—men that were known all over the world nearly—for this science extends round the wide world, everywhere the horse has ever had his feet ironed. After many years of hard labor this was accomplished. This firm is known as D. M. Osborn & Co., with which the well-known inventors and scientific men are connected, Cyrenus Wheeler, Mr. Kirby, and O. H. Burdick. Such men as these are not going to give themselves away by allowing their names to be used to back up any science without knowing what they are about. They all have had and seen this work done and watched the result, and many others in Auburn city. This is where this great center of science is located of D. M. Osborn & Co.; this is where the great center of this horse science is now well established, and this is to be one of the great centers; this, too, must, like all other businesses, in order to be successful, be systematized and introduced on the principles of science. I could give you scores of names to back this work up—some are many miles away, and some hundreds, where I have worked and my brothers in different places on the horse. That is not necessary, as Auburn city is to be the center. I will give you a few men's names that will be worth more than a score of some, and here they are.

After you read this work carefully through, and look at your horse, you can easily see how this all is. I could get hundreds of names to put in this work, if it was the biggest humbug that was ever written, by asking them. To prove this work to be a valuable one, test it; then you will know; you always will be in the dark unless you do. The trouble is and always has been that nearly all have learned this science out of selfish motives; they would keep it all to themselves in order to make money fast out of it. This is not my intention. I want all to know how this work is done. I will show and teach all mankind. If I would not be willing to do this, this book is wrongly named. This book is the teacher. I do not know as I can work on the horse much more. My health is failing fast; persecution and abuse have had something

to do with its failing. I will go back to my boyhood
days and show you where I and all others must begin.

The first mechanical work I ever did in my life
Was to make a sled out of shingles, my tool was a jackknife.
With a rickety knife I bored the runners through,
It was all the tool I had, 'twas the best that I could do.

The next job for me to see what luck I would have to make
A small bundle of ax-helves I would undertake;
Of course these were all small children's toys—
I was just like all other children and little boys.

I made small ships, sloops, and every kind of boat;
In my mother's rainwater trough I set them afloat;
After a while I traded off some of my toys,
And got a gimlet of one of the neighbors' boys.

Then I must make a sled that would be of use of boards
With this gimlet the holes through the runners I bored;
There must be more tools added to my kit,
I cannot make the holes large enough with this gimlet bit.

These holes in these runners must bigger be,
Or it will not be strong enough to hold up me;
These holes must be made bigger by running a hot iron through—
It must be made strong enough to hold up two.

After making several sleds in this way
They did not suit. They had to be repaired every day.
They were poor and rickety things at the best—
Were soon all in pieces, but a few days they'd last.

On this sled business there must be some improvement made;
Some of us boys will get hurt with these sleds, I am afraid.
They must have the beams cut in the top like a dove's tail,
And a board put all over the top and all solid nail.

This proved safer and a great deal better to be,
Now two could ride in safety, sometimes three.
I had learned quite a good deal at the sleigh-making trade
When this improvement on my sleighs I had made.

The next improvement was frame with pin beams,
Like those you see drawn around with ox teams.
Next I made with mortise and tenon, beam, and knee,
Quite a sleigh maker I was getting to be.

Wagons and carts I made and improved in this way,
And some had to be repaired nearly every day.
If any of these wagons or sleighs should happen to break
They would come to me for repairs or new ones I must make.

I had quite a business in that line and trade;
I made the girls and boys happy—no charges I made.
It was plenty pay enough for me them to see.
After I had got their work done, how happy they would be!

There were trades of other kinds I was learning too—
Of my mother I learned to knit, mend, and sew.
My mother has got feather tick pillows I made the first I learned to
sew,
Them I made for her over forty-five years ago.

Shirts, pants, vests, and all kinds in that line of trade,
When I was a small boy I repaired and new I made;
Pants and vest I cut and other garments, and made them too,
To cut and make a coat that I never tried to do.

To know how to do this work has been of use to me—
I could mend my own clothes no matter where I would be;
I have been where I have mended other's while to bed they had to go,
For this reason—they themselves did not know how to sew.

The cap trade I took up—I had lots of little brothers; they did a
surround.
I must make them some caps. For foundation I used old straw hats'
crown.
The first I made was round on top, covered with green,
Cut goring with a button on top. It was the funniest cap ever was
seen.

The next cap I made the foundation on top was flat.
Of course I had to make my work to fit that.
The cloth that I made it of was dark blue,
That was a nicer color, and the style was better too.

These caps the front piece was made of old boot legs,
Each one covered with the same cloth it was made.
These caps were both lined with different colors too;
They were very good caps—it was then the best I could do.

The shoemakers trade I must try that work to do.
No lasts I had; them first I will have to make too.
The children's feet all vary in many different degree,
And I must hav a pair that will fit me.

In an old woodshed these lasts were made
With an ax and an old jackknife blade;
With my gimlet I bored the holes through
To make a place to pull the last out of the shoe.

A string I tied in the hole to pull out the last,
For sometimes I would get my shoes all pegged fast.
I got along very well for a while in this way;
I would like to hav a hook to pull the last—sometime I may.

My pegging awl and pegs them I all made
When I commenced first to work at the shoemaker's trade,
After my kit and stock all rigged I had got,
In my father's old kitchen I opened my shop.

My father had a large family. There was always leather round,
Go up garret at any time there it could be found,
With five or six little brothers all gathered around me,
How this work was going to be done they all wanted to see.

Through the course of the day I had made some progress at this
        trade—
I had repaired several pair of shoes—no charges I made;
As we sat in front of the old fireplace in a half circle round,
My father was a chopper. He came in with his ax and with us sat
        down.

My father was as hard working man as ever you see,
He soon had his lap full of children—two on each knee.
After working all day in the woods in the cold,
All the evening this lap full of children he would hold.

The children gathered round him, showed him the work I had done.
He said to me, If you can do as well as that you had better keep on.
This of course encouraged and very much pleased me,
My work was being appreciated by him, I could see.

My father was a good farmer—all kinds of that work he understood—
And all the work he did he always did good.
His word could always be relied on no matter where he would be;
An honester, kinder-hearted man no man ever see.

My father never tried much mechanical work to do—
Make beetles, his ox sleds with wood he could shoe.
To dress a beef or hog, and all work of that kind,
No better man for that in the country could they find.

He always had something every day to do,
No matter how cold, how much the snow and wind blew.
For him to work there was never a day too cold,
And this he kept up until he was very old.

He kept right on one steady course, you can see,
As provider for his family no better could be.
Through cold winds and drifting snow, out all day in the cold,
Nights in this half circle a lap full of children he would hold.

I was next oldest of this large family of boys;
I had plenty of work all of the time to keep them in toys;
There was eleven boys in this family grew up to be men;
Seven boys first, then two girls, then boys again.

There were two boys that died when they were quite young.
I assure you to support this family, some work had to be done.
A truer and better man in a family than my father could not be;
How he carried this heavy load has always puzzled me.

It was all done by hard knocks, the sweat of the brow;
If you want to know how it was done, ask him; he can tell you how.
My father was a large, powerful, strong-built man;
To do better work, and more in a day, very few can.

He supported his own family, and helped others too,
And this, wherever he could, he was always ready to do.

I have seen him on trees chopping, that was four feet through;
All alone, coat, vest, and hat off, no matter how hard the wind blew.

And this, too, after he had got to be quite old.
I never heard him say, I cannot go to the woods to-day, it is too
    cold.
Day after day to the woods to chop he would go,
And his hair had got to be now as white as the snow.

And at night he would by this old fireplace sit down,
With his children help form a half circle around.
First there must be a big back-log put on,
And that too he almost invariably done.

I have thought what fools on this earth some folks must be;
Such a man as that his worth they cannot see.
He would work early and late, and it was not for gold;
He would suffer himself to feed and shelter others from the cold

My poor father passed away many years ago.
Whether he will be rewarded in the next life I do not know.
I would as lief take his chance as any man I ever see.
To be a better man than he was I can't see how it could be.

The course he took, it always seemed right to me;
And never in life did he and I ever disagree.
We did business together for a very long time;
A more honorable, honest man no man can find.

To forget my father, that will be impossible to be.
His life must always be stamped indelible with me;
And after I pass from this life, if him I do not see,
In the next life, heaven will be no heaven to me.

When I was a small boy, to help my father I would try;
I would make him some ax-helves, them he all had to buy.
I made a lot, put them up garret in a barrel to dry;
There is no telling what a boy can do if he will try.

My father used up many ax-helves, you must know;
There was many ways they would give, and sometimes by a misblow.
This stock of ax-helves I did not show him or have them around;
They were not dry yet, in a short time them I see he had found.

Them I see were going to be of use and help to him,
Then making ax-helves I went at it again.
Of these I kept on hand a small supply,
While my helves could be found in the barrel no helves would he buy.

Somewhere about this time I went to learn the blacksmith trade:
At that time I was about fourteen years of age,
To go to work at that business my father opposed it some;
That is very hard business, I am afraid you are too young.

I was very anxious to learn a trade, some place to find
To learn the blacksmith trade, I had not thought of, that was not the
       kind.
The carpenter's trade, when I was a boy, was what I wanted to learn.
It is curious sometimes how quick our course is turned.
•
At this at first I commenced on a very small scale.
The first thing I tried to make was a horse nail.
Small hammers, jewsharps, hooks to catch the trout, I made,
Repaired old gun-locks, put in tubes and jackknife blades.

Of this kind of work I always had some on hand to do.
In order to learn this trade I must always be trying something new.
To make a gun, that, too, I must try and see if could make.
I got along very well, all but the mainspring, that would break.

Several locks for this gun I made, all new;
The mainspring would break, the very best I could do.
How many springs I made, of course I do not know;
There was a great many : every time I tried them, ching they would go.

I learned in springs the temper must very low be.
After making and breaking many you can see,
And the steel varies to a very great degree.
That, too, I did not know at that time; that bothered me.

I did learn after a long time these springs to make,
And could do it very quick, and they would not break.
No receipt can be laid down that is good for tempering steel;
In all degrees steel varies quite a great deal.

Many different kinds of mechanical work I have tried to do;
The art of taking likenesses, that I have worked at too.

At the time when the chemicals we all made,
I did not work at that long, I did not like that trade.

For many reasons, of them I will give you a few;
They all wanted me to make handsome pictures, that I could not do.
There always would be a lot standing or sitting around;
Find fault with these pictures they would, or the background.

They all wanted a handsome picture, all the same, young and old.
A good likeness of themselves was quite hard to be sold.
No matter how dark the sitter was, they all must be white;
To suit them they must be nearly burned up with the light.

Then they must all be painted, and colored up, too;
Unless they were daubed in this way they would not do.
I got tired of taking good pictures to spoil in this way,
About that kind of business I shall have no more to say.

A carriage I can make; iron, paint, stripe, and trim it, too.
Houses I have painted and worked on; some I have built new.
The mason trade, I never did much of that kind.
To be a good mason, it wants some practice, I find.

I have plastered and laid quite a good deal of stone wall;
To build a chimney of brick, that stuck me the worst of all.
To build a nice chimney, it is quite a knack to do;
To have the brick all lie level and carry it up true.

To build only one brick chimney in my life did I try,
And that was all daubed and winding before it was two feet high.
I could not keep it true, do the best I could do,
So I plastered it inside and out; the smoke could get through.

To know how to do this work has always been of use to me.
There was always some work to do, no matter where I would be.
It all kept me busy, and I was learning, too.
What does a man amount to with nothing to do?

Nearly all of these trades I dropped off, one by one;
Some I dropped off many years ago, when I was quite young.
The horses' feet nearly all of my life I have worked on,
And at that yet I have not got done.

Nearly all kinds of saws, them I have worked on, too;
To make a saw, that I never tried to do.
I have filed, set, gummed, and re-teethed some new;
Circulars to work on is quite a science, and keep them true.

Not much work did I ever do at the harness trade,
Only repair; once a bridle, martingales, circingle I made.
At the machinist business, that, too, I have turned my hand;
The principles to do that work on I quite well understand.

If you want to make a machine, and have it good work do,
From the center you must work, and make all true.
One great center you must have, that you ought to know,
And all must run in harmony, or to pieces it will go.

It is the same with the horse, if you will look you can see,
For him to move well, in harmony of action all must be.
On him for many years I have spent nearly all of my time,
For he needs help, he is a great sufferer, I find.

There are a great many kinds of work I have done and understook.
Of course I had learned something before I could write a book.
The science on the horse is all I ever perfect made,
And to do that I had to leave behind every other trade.

On them, others have sailed far in advance of me in their line;
For this reason, my time has been spent on the horse, you find.;
A man cannot carry along so many trades and excel,
If he perfects only one in life he will do very well.

To write poetry is quite a science, too, I find;
To make all run smooth, and make all rhyme,
Five parts have got to be carrried at the same time;
Compose, spell, write, convey, and make all rhyme.

After writing awhile I think at that I can do well;
What bothers me the most is to all words spell.
There are so many things that all have the same name,
If I do not spell them all right, I ought not to be to blame.

My main object in writing this book is the horse to rescue;
And if you will read it, and study the horse, that it will do;
And after you have learned this science no man can fool you
Much on stiff horses; if they do it will be only on a few.

SCIENTIFIC WORKS OF GERARD DOAN ON THE HORSE.

By experience and experimenting for forty-one years, by practical work as a horseshoer, by studying the natural horse and all of the changes from the natural to the unnatural, and their effect in all of the different changes, I find the noble animal, man's and woman's favorite, in a suffering and deformed condition, which I shall explain in this work, and stand ready to demonstrate and teach to seekers after knowledge and the truth.

Everything is a mystery until it comes to light; then it becomes a common thing when understood, like the telegraph, and all things, man being a progressive being. The seekers after knowledge get it; that is the way this great discovery was made, through great mental and practical labor, and with but little help or reward. A large part of my hard-earned money has been used to perfect this work, but it is the long-winded horse that wins the race. Right here, I will say, I will introduce the principles laid down in this book or die a pauper. They are all facts, and have been demonstrated hundreds of times by J. J. Doan, of Auburn city, Cayuga Co., N. Y., and by Oliver Doan, of the same place. They are skillful operators. The horses are all, or nearly all, that have been shod one year, changed from natural, more or less, some way; it being the natural consequence, it not being natural for the horse to have his feet ironed. When the horse gets stiff or lame, he is called by the ignorant, foundered. They think or talk that they had watered or fed them to warm, or fed them too much. All the argument they can bring is, he was stiff after they had fed or watered him. Almost all men water and feed their horses three times a day, and it must be soon after the feed if ever they get stiff. This word "founder" has been in use for hundreds of years, and, for all of that, it has no meaning; it does not tell how and where the animal is affected, only he is lame and stiff, he is incurable. So say the ignorant pretenders to great wisdom on the horse. This stiffness is classed in four different kinds of founder—water, grain, plank, and chest founder. Some said they are affected one way and some in another; all disagree, and none cure or remove the cause. I differ with them all. I have long known what ailed these horses, and can remove the cause, and will explain it all in this work, and produce plenty of honest and scientific men that have had and seen it done; and, as strange as it may appear, it requires no medicine to do this wonderful work. Remove the cause, and nature repairs the damages. This work is confined to the feet, tracing cause to effect and effect to cause.

I might as well say here what removing the cause does. It lets nature have a chance to repair damages; it does its work very quick; it cures water, grain, chest, and plank founder; perished shoulders; it straightens

the leg, called the tip-knee; straightens cocked ankles,
cures corns, coffin-joint lamenesses, the ambler, shuffler,
spring-halt; horses that hop behind when speeding; the
single-footer. These names are known and understood
by horsemen. It removes all air puffs from the
horse, and makes him the perfect natural horse.
These changes are not seen only by a very close
observer of long practical experience. It took me a
long time. It was clothed and buried in mystery.
The first horse I ever shod was a cripple. One foot
was so bad it could not be shod; I have shod
cripples ever since, and they are all over the world, so
far as I have been. There have been hundreds of
books written on the horse, and they seem to be the
same thing continued—doctoring the effect; finding a
sore place, and making it worse.

It is not my intention in this work to travel that
old field over again, and rehearse all of the cruelty and
barbarism that I have seen practiced on the already
suffering horse, called doctoring. My intention is to
introduce something to relieve suffering. I said I use
no medicine to cure these horses. For fear you may
think I perform some surgical operation, I will state
here I do nothing of the kind. I do not draw blood
on the horse; it is hard work to do it, but it is business. It's no miracle or miraculous thing; it is science.

I use these words, founder, ambler, single-footer,
and other names, or people would not understand what
I am talking about. The fact is, it is all summed up
in these words: Horses are changed from natural in
many ways and many stages, which I will explain on
principles which will not lie.

This work will be arranged on scientific principles, with a foundation and superstructure that will stand, based, as it is, on truth, facts, and principles that men cannot supersede, if they equal. These principles you have got to know. To cure the horse, you must make him natural. I have read some books on the horse, but I could find nothing in them to clear the fog away, no system. There were receipts to cure these difficulties the horse was in, which I well knew were of no kind of use, only to make bad worse. I continued my search. It has been a hard road to travel so far. I am getting off of the subject; I do not want to write my life in this work. I will explain in this work the effect in all of the different changes, changing back to natural. I do not intend, for the sake of making a large book, to write much more than enough to convey what I want to on the horse; the simpler and less complicated, the easier learned and understood. For fear the reader might misconstrue what I have written before, I will say here I do not mean to be understood that I will make all of these lame and deformed horses natural; there are some that are past help, and this work does not take up blemished horses, such as ring-bones and spavins, curb-splints, thorough-pins. I pronounce the ring-bone incurable; it is a bone affection, and the spavin the same. Ring-bone destroys the structure of the foot; they can be relieved some by shoeing and dressing the foot, for which I may give directions in this work. When horses are blemished—the kind I have mentioned—they have lost two-thirds of their value, no matter how much they were valued, as it brings them all down on a par, save the clean-limbed, and that will be business enough. It is not the intention of this work to keep up this changing back to natural, but it will have to be done many years before the people will learn these principles, and there are millions of horses in all stages of suffering; some are there and some have just started. It will be a long time before this will be understood. It is not the intention of this work to keep up the curing stiff and lame horses; the preventive is what I want to teach and introduce; but before the owner can prevent he must know how to cure; then, in this case, he has the preventive that I will explain about in the course of this work, scientifically.

A FEW REMARKS IN DEFENSE OF THE ABUSED AND WRONGED HORSE-SHOER.—THE QUALIFICATIONS HE NEEDS TO MAKE HIM A GOOD ONE.

He should weigh about one hundred and seventy-five pounds, his working weight; five feet seven inches tall, size around under his arms forty inches, broad-shouldered, short-necked, something like a bull; muscle and strength equal to the best well-fed stallion; a large amount of courage, physical force, firmness, and resolution; an inexhaustible amount of patience, so as to enable him to come to time when he is kicked across the shop, or turned a summersault; his head should have a reasonable amount of brains; he should have a mild and passive nature, so he can stand persecution without showing any signs of anger when he is told twenty times a day, by Jones or Tom or Jim, or that old "They say," the father of all lies, that he has spoilt his horse, and he can never set another shoe for him, when the fault is more their own than the smith's, and no fault of either ofttimes, if it was understood, which I will show and explain in this work. There is no business that tries man's powers of endurance equal to that of horse-shoeing, and no class of mechanics so poorly paid, according to labor performed. He is expected to be there at his post, always pleasant, with a smile on his face when three or four wild colts arrive to be shod, or a vicious stallion, sometimes two or three, and often twenty and more; all want to get home to dinner. These colts never had a foot raised from the ground; if they have it has been with a rope tied to it, and jerked at a while; they call that breaking them for shoeing, when the fact is the owner dare not even take up a foot; yet the shoer is expected to get through this difficult task in time for dinner; during this time there are more arrivals, two or three old offenders, for the after-part of the day; a lot of old cripples, so tortured on their feet that they can hardly stand, caused by ironing their feet; and yet he is expected to cure these old de· formed horses, or he is no mechanic. They ride him part of the afternoon : the balance is filled up with the old offending kickers and strikers. They rise up on your knees, and throw nearly all of their weight on you repeatedly; and finally they smash down on your big toes, and off goes the nails; mine has been smashed off so much there is but little left. And all this is ex· pected to be endured for a miserable existence. Imagine the shoer's feelings, and this is to be endured daily until he is broken down, and crippled worse than the horse, at about forty years of age. He has put his strength against thousands of horses and mules, and it is surprising to me that shoers last as long as they do If you want your horse well shod, give your shoer plenty of time to do it, and pay him well; for no man can do a good job, at any kind of business, if he is hurried, and goes blundering along. Ironing the horse's foot is, or should be, the most scientific piece of mechanical work ever done; and yet it is but glimmeringly understood. No one is to blame; all are studying and trying their level best to find their way out of this entanglement, and I have been in that same fix for years.

Nine years previous to the date of this work I "dug out," which I will show in the course of this work. The shoer is expected to do what is impossible for him to do, and it is unjust to blame him or hold him responsible for your horse in any way, for many reasons. In the first place, he does not have your horse in his care, neither does he drive him. He shoes him and he is gone, and the owner takes no care of his feet. Perhaps he exchanges for another, or sells him—that is going on all the time, and always will be. The shoer does the best he can. The horse comes to him, his feet dry and hard-shrunken. He pares his feet and irons him. This treatment will spoil all cupping feet. In fact, there is no use trying to lay down any principles to iron the horses feet to prevent him from changing from natural, for he is traveling on unnatural feet all of the time, unless he is dead. There has been a large amount of talk about shoes, and all to no purpose. There are no curing properties in shoes. There is one principle that helps a little if proper care is

taken of the foot, and that but very few will do.
I saw at the Centennial quite a number of horses'
hoofs with printed papers on them. I read them.
This was on them all, "Caused by improper shoeing."
Same old story. I am not going to spend my time and
fill up this book with a lot of trash that has been
talked and written for hundreds of years—a large
amount of talk, but little knowledge that has been any
benefit to the suffering horse.

KINDS OF FEET.

I will make a few remarks on the horses' foot—how
to select. There are four kinds of feet on colts before they have been ironed ; then they commence to
change and assume all kinds of shapes hard to describe ; and it matters not what shape they are in,
I shall show in this work I change them back to the
natural one ; that is, put the colt's foot on the horse.
That is what I want to teach.

The foot half way between the large flat foot and
cupping foot is the best, for this reason : It expands from the weight of the horse. The cup foot contracts faster. The large flat foot expands too much
with the weight of the horse. The large peck-measure
foot is poorest of all. It has too much membrane; it
is too heavy, and changes quicker ; it is more liable to
get sore by ironing. They are all good enough for
me, as I can do what I want with them. That is what
I want to teach ; that is what all ought to know.

HOW TO RAISE UP A GOOD STRAIGHT HORSE.

This is the most important of all. The horse, while
growing up from a colt, is neglected, not intentionally.

but through ignorance in regard to his feet, and the effect it has. By this neglect his hoofs are allowed to grow in all shapes. They need trimming, and to be kept in their proper shape. A long toe does not affect the colt as much as it does the shod horse, for this reason: the structure of the foot is nearly all in harmony on the flat foot; on the cup foot it is different; the wall is thicker; it does not wear off as fast. I have seen a few, and shod them, that were stiff, that never had a shoe on. This kind should have their feet cared for, pared down heel and toe. The flat-foot seldom needs paring on the bottom, but his feet should be trimmed. Take him on the floor, hold or strap up one foot, take a chisel and mallet, trim all of his feet, rasp them true; see if he can stand with his forward feet back of straight, see if he stand well back on his hind feet, and keep him so. If you want to see if your colt is growing up straight and natural, and the structure of his feet natural, look at the top of the heel. The heel is double. If the two parts are not even, the structure is changed from natural, and should be changed back. On all, or nearly all, horse kind the outside wall grows the fastest, and is the thickest and strongest. The growth raises the outside; that throws too much weight on the inside, and warps or pushes up the inside heel. Look your horse over. You can equalize the weight by dressing the bottom. You can easily tell how this should be done if you look. This unequal weight produces the same effect on colts that it does on shod horses—the same unnatural strain on the back tendons—warping the foot or pushing up the inside heel, which turns out the toes and causes the ankles to turn in, and that makes the horse interfere. He cannot move well.

The same effect is produced from the same cause if he is run over the opposite; it turns his toes in, his ankles out. The fact is, his heels should always be kept as even at the top as possible. This keeps the foot nearly on a straight line. The point of the frog is the guide. Make a true circle from that point each way after you have got the heels even at the top. This will stop more horses from interfering than all the tinkering ever done. Of course there should be judgment used in dressing the foot. A long, pointed toe is not natural either on the horse's forward or hinder feet. Keep the feet natural as near as possible. The fact is, the colt grows up crooked for the want of proper care, the raisers being ignorant in regard to this fact, which I well know. Look at your colts, not at pictures of horses, if you want to study the horse. If you will read this book carefully, you will see these facts as plain as I do, and can talk horse as well.

I have been told that I have broken myself down bawling "horse." My lungs are the soundest part of me. I could talk this twenty times faster than I can write it. Talk comes with the knowledge; quite a number of exceptions to that rule. One thing my mouth was made for is to talk.

To return to the subject: I have straightened hundreds of colts' feet, although they had grown up deformed and crooked. The colt comes to the shoer in this condition, run over, both toes out, sometimes all, or in. On forward legs, they come with knees thrown together, ankles on hind feet run over the opposite

throwing ankles out when moving forward feet
pointing on two opposite lines, hind feet traveling
in two opposite lines, ofttimes so bad that the lines
cross each other six feet from the starting-point;
head going on straight line. The horse gets fre-
quently a jerk on the mouth for his awkwardness.
If he should happen to blunder he would be likely to
get thrashed. Then the shoer takes a scurfing for not
making that horse move well. "He is an old botch."
He tries another. He is told Wood, or Doan may be,
can shoe him so he can travel all right. The colt goes
the rounds, and the result is not good. Before I get
through this work I will clear some of that fog away.
This ends my treatise on the colt.

A FEW REMARKS ON SELECTING A GOOD HORSE FOR MYSELF.

There are many diverse tastes and different opinions and judgments in regard to the horse, so I will
select one for myself. For the road I like a rangy
horse, about ten hundred weight; foot half way between the cup and large flat foot; short from fetlock
down; large arm; heavy cords; leg tapering to the
foot; forward legs well back under; that is, points of
shoulders projecting well over; not very wide between
legs; thin withers; long, thin, arched neck, well cut
out under the throat; light, clean head; large, full
eyes; short, straightish back; broad hips; round body;
no curb joints. I never saw a horse too full at the
breast to suit me; flat leg; middling straight hind
leg, tapering to the feet; ribbed up close; full of
courage and ambition. My favorite color is dark

mahogany bay; black legs, mane, and tail. In choos-
ing a horse it depends something on what use you
want to put him to. There is a variety of horses in
shape, all good. The creator has taken as much pains
in making the horse as it has making mankind, and
there are about as many different forms and colors.
I never saw a perfect idiot, looking the whole race
over. I have seen lots of fools driving horses, and
worse than fools. I am come to their rescue. The
horse is a slave, if that word has any meaning; and I
think it has. There is no animal that is abused and
suffers equal to the noble animal, the horse. He is
tied up by his head, covered with foam and perspira-
tion, panting for breath, in cold, bleak winds, without
feed or water, while the driver is sitting by a comfortable fire. Perhaps the clothing nature provided
for him is all sheared off. Thus he is expected to
stand until his driver is ready for another ride. If he
gets in the stable during the long, cold night, he will
be lucky, and gets any water or feed. All foam and
sweat, there he shivers. In the morning you can see
him covered with frost. Such cruelty as that is hard
for me to see and not try to do all that is in my power
to relieve his suffering. Knowing as I do the pain he
has to endure, and its causes, and then sit down and
not do my level best to help him, I think it would be
wrong.

My nature is such that it causes me to suffer with
them; and I do suffer intensely, too. If I did not
know how to relieve them, perhaps I would feel different. Nearly all of my life has been spent in doing all
I could to relieve this noble animal's suffering, and

I have relieved it in a small degree. But it was only in a small field that I could work compared with this wholesale torturing that is going on.

I am fifty-five years of age; my health is giving out; I feel I am getting stiff, too. I have laid the hammer down to write this work to still keep up the battle to free the suffering horse, and to see if I can work a larger field and on a better plan to introduce this great discovery that has cost me so much mental and physical labor for forty-one years. If I fail to introduce it, and let it be buried again, I have made a failure of life after all.

The horse suffers greatly in many ways. The cause of the greatest suffering is in his feet. That I will explain and teach. I have not quit yet, nor ever will, while I am alive. I do not know as I shall after I am what they call dead. I shall be at the front under all circumstances. No matter how much the opposition, you will find me at my post. If you want to know something of the suffering of the horse, if you ever had the toothache bad, you can judge a little. That is no comparison to what the horse suffers. There is nothing it can be compared to. I will try to convey something of it, which I well know I have not the power.

To begin, the structure of the foot is changed from natural in many ways and in many different stages. Ponder, think! Can this take place without an effect? I well know it cannot. All men must see this. I appeal to all thinking naturalists and scientific men for their aid to help introduce this work. There are three Doan brothers. They have been battling for

years against a power of opposition. I assure you we
are not ignorant of our surroundings. All great
things are small at the beginning. Any great science
like this is in advance of the age. The craft is in
danger. This great discovery looms up head and
shoulders over all. I return to the suffering horse; I
cannot get away from him. I said the structure of
the foot was changed from natural. No matter how
much or how little, or in what way, or what degree,
the horse's suffering commences at the first change.
The more he is changed from natural, the more intense is his suffering, until death comes to his relief.
It will be well to mention a few cases here. While I
was looking for one of these sufferers to demonstrate
some things and relieve their suffering, I went into a
stable at Elmira. There I saw one of thousands of
cases like this, lying in a small, unventilated place, on
a pile of manure—a fine young horse, with sores on his
sides. I asked how long he had been in that condition. I think they said about three months. I asked
what ailed the horse. They said he had bruised his
feet working in the stone quarry. He was gnawing
his feet, and had holes gnawed at the top of the hoof.
There were marks of teeth all over his feet. He was
not what I was in search of. I tried to buy him.
They said he was a fine horse. It would take some
money to buy him. How much, I asked, will it take?
"One hundred and fifty dollars." That horse died;
and, worse than all, his shoes were on. He was completely paralyzed. I well knew what ailed him—cup
foot badly contracted, or, in other words, changed

from natural; his eyes looked sunken, staring, and glassy.

There are thousands in this same condition. Ponder, think, I say, again; look at your horse after you have looked this work through. That is the place to look. Study the horse as I have done; understand there are all stages of these changes, and always a beginning. There is the end above mentioned. What do you think I wanted of that horse on that pile of manure? I wanted to relieve his suffering: You say, "Why didn't you?" They would not let me. They called me a "damned old lunatic." That did not affect me any; that had become a common thing many years before. I have been told so much that I am crazy, not being a judge of lunacy. I was in Lincoln, Nebraska, some two years ago. They have a lunatic asylum there. It struck me it would be a good time to test my case. They have several hundred lunatics in that asylum. It was Sunday. It is their custom to get them, or nearly all of them, in one room, then sing. I got permission to go in. They did not act crazy; all was quiet. When singing was over, all marched out in single file. I did not learn anything satisfactory touching my case by this experiment. I am writing history of my life; I must return to the horse. As this is not intended to be a history of my life, it matters not where I sail to, neither does it matter which end I begin at, as this is not intended to be the scientific part of this work.

At sixteen years of age you can see a boy sitting on a saw-horse, about six feet from a horse. The horse interfered. His ankles were bleeding and sore. Right

there was the first scientific principle I ever studied out
on the horse. I did not get half of that. At that
time I did not know his foot was changed from natural
and run over inside, half of double heel pushed up,
causing the toe to turn out and ankle in. I saw I
could throw his ankle out by lowering the outside
heel and outside toe, and the outside heel of shoe and
toe of shoe. That throws the weight on the outside;
that will push up the outside heel; that turns the toe
in, brings the foot on a straight line. This principle,
followed up, will run the toe in or out by changing
the weight on the double heel both forward and behind. When the top of heel is even, care should be
taken to dress bottom, so as to equalize weight; give
easy toe to raise on, or he will toe in or out to relieve
the back tendons. His foot is growing all the time,
and when it gets long the strain increases. If it is
very long he will be apt to turn out his toes, the
ankles turn in. In this case he will be likely to interfere, unless the shoe is reset, the foot dressed and
made shorter. This principle will hold good to shoe
all horses that are natural, or have not been injured in
any way. If they have there is no better principle,
if it is done right. If the horse is used right, on any
decent road, and is not driven nearly to death, which
he often is. And yet other difficulties soon arise
after the horse's foot has been ironed a short time.
The cup foot suffers the most—it cannot expand.
What effect that can have I will tell you. It grows
straighter up. The sole, that is, the bottom, rises, and
most in the center; that changes the whole structure
of the foot, inside and out. That affects the coffin-

joint most. It is located nearly in the center; this change is going on to a greater or less degree all the time, if the foot is ironed. It pushes out of the cup; or, in other words, top of hoof or wall. That destroys all harmony of action, and it does not stop where the cause is located. Trace from that cause to the effect. Its effect is more than you ever thought of. It does more mischief than you are aware of; it effects the horse all over.

Now I am talking about the hind feet. They get higher, as this contraction takes place, from bottom to top. They cannot be lowered by paring as low as they should be, for this reason: you would come to the membrane at the bottom near the wall inside of shell. You must have shell for shoe to rest on, or lameness will be the result. If you do pare down, the cause is there yet. The foot is not the natural size, and this is not all. It shoves the foot forward. Of course the leg goes with it. This change is going on as the sole raises in center, where it raises fastest; I mean highest. It all goes together. After you have cupped out the foot, place a straight edge across the center; measuring down; that will tell you. Commence at side of frog, measure out to wall. That will tell you. As this change is allowed to go on in that course, the foot moves forward according to the degrees of change from natural, until the horse is nearly off his legs, and he is standing gambols out, feet huddled together, with a constant strain on the back tendons or cords; the heels closed in, structure all changed. My god, the pain and suffering this poor

horse endures! and that, too, continually until welcome death comes to his relief.

Let us continue this search. What's the matter
with this horse's back? He humps up across his
loin. Oh, I see; it's this position he is obliged to
stand in, caused by the structure of his foot being
changed from natural. Why, he has got irons on
his feet! Now I am going inside and see what I can
find in there. I see his kidneys affected, urinary
organs all affected, caused by this unnatural strain and
position which he is placed in, and obliged to stand
and travel, and draw heavy loads day after day. Of
course that effect must quite often be doctored. His
water-works are out of order by being obliged to work
and draw heavy loads when all are out of harmony.
I have changed lots of these poor horses back to natural on scientific principles, and all came right in a
little time, and no medicine used. If you follow me
you will have a wild-goose chase, for I am going to
have a horse sail. Don't back out. I will bring you
back all right. Oh, there has come a poor, suffering
horse. I must go and relieve him. I left that poor
horse in a bad fix. I did not look his fore parts over.
I will. He is braced out from the same cause. Like
causes produce like effects. I mean the horse I was
writing about. I told you how he was affected on his
hind parts, as far as I went. Let us talk about the
same horse's fore parts. Contraction changes the
structure of foot the same, and shoves the foot forward on the same principles according to the degree
of change. It changes faster on the cup foot. What
effect does that have? Strain on back tendons. That

is bad enough. His forward legs should stand back
of straight. When standing, are all of his feet in a
pile? and when moving, trotting, see what strides he
makes, and yet it would not sore him if he never had
his feet ironed. That has produced this change; and
when ironed it does not wear off. That is not all. It
is growing all of the time in some shape, and assumes
many; and with all of the experience I have had I
cannot describe these feet. Let us go up a little higher.
His chest is all fallen in. That is called chest-founder
by people that have no knowledge of the horse. Well,
what is it? changed from natural. Being changed in
this way, the head is drawn down; the shoulders drop
back, and begin to perish; he is fastened there. He
is worked in that position and wofully deformed, and
it is not seen except by a very few and never have been
seen; they are quite natural on their forward parts,
and very bad behind, and seem quite natural behind.
In some one foot is changed and its mate is quite
natural. These feet do not change in pairs. There
are all stages of it difficult to describe. My long experience and experimenting and shoeing these poor
horses enable me to see it instantly. There are other
causes that lame these horses, which I will explain.
This poor horse that I have been talking about is
changed fore and aft, but I shall have to leave him
awhile to suffer, as I have walked with tears in my
eyes away from thousands. But I will come to his
relief and get him out of his trouble before I get
through this work. He is not so bad off as he can be
made. I will come and see him again. This is the
way this work was discovered and perfected, always

on the watch, always ready to do all I could to relieve;
and I went at it where I saw I could help them. Some
I could and some I could not; but I tried and kept
trying, though not on the right principle. But I did
find out the right principle and get master of the feet
at last.

Hello, here comes Sam Grover.

"Can you set a shoe?"

"Yes; lead in. What ails that mare, Sam? she is
awful stiff."

"Yes; she has been so these two years."

"How old it she?"

"Six."

"Ever done anything for her?"

"Yes; she has been doctored; has had setons in
her shoulders; blistered. She belonged to Doc. Mede.
They think she was stiffened driving through the creek
to wash her legs off when he came home."

"I can cure that mare."

"Doc could not drive her on the road, so he let his
brother Gird have her. She has been turned out six
months."

"Did that help her any?"

"No; she sores up as quick as she is driven."

"What breed is she?"

"Kentucky hunter."

"Did they pull her shoes off when they turned her
out?"

"No."

"I've got a good young mare coming five that will
match that bay of yours. I will trade for that stiff
mare."

"I will trade. Gird told me to trade her off. How will you trade"

"Give me twenty-five dollars."

"I'll give you twenty."

"It's a bargain."

"Trust for the money?"

"No; cash down boot money on a horse trade."

"Leave the trade open till Saturday; got to go home."

"Yes; any time in a week will do."

He came in a day or two. It had frozen up rough and hard. He had to come thirteen miles over hubs.

"Well, how is horse trade?"

"All right; unhitch."

Of all stiff and sore horses I ever saw, she was the worst, and stand up. She was nearly off her legs. Her legs were all covered with scabs. That was called mud fever; all scratched with sharp currycomb and swelled. Let us get her in the barn. She is all wet with sweat. Cover up warm and feed. Another good job for to-night. Hurry to the shop. It is getting dark. Folks waiting; all in a hurry to get home. Hurry up! Shoe three or four horses; each has a little tinkering job to do, and before they are all away it is an hour after dark. Do you suppose you got a good job? I think not. Do you think the weight was equal on all of the heels of those horses? If you do it would not make it so, and if it was it would not stay so long, about which I have already written and the consequences.

By golly! in this hurry I liked to forgot that poor suffering horse I just got. I must go and see her.

On follows four or five to see too. They all want to see, and I wanted them to. I found her just as I expected to, lying down. I walked in, looked to see if she had eat her feed. It was not touched. "Did you kick her up?" I did not. "Did any one kick her?" No; if they had, they might have got it back, for self-protection is the first law of nature. This horse was down, unable to help herself; but before I can remove the cause of her suffering, I must get her up. I touched her on her hind parts; she was sore all over. I succeeded in getting her on her feet. Of all the sore horses I ever saw, all produced from a small cause, she was the cap-sheaf. Of course that called out remarks, opinions, and beliefs, and not much knowledge, but a great deal of talk.

"Doan, I guess that black man has waxed it to you this time."

Sam was black. Some one said she was chest foundered; some one thing, some another, and all disagreed. I well knew they had no knowledge where the cause was, neither did they know where the effect was. I told them I would have her out on the road in four days, and she would have as good knee action as a colt. That is rather short time. I told them what was the matter with her, as I always have; but they do not seem to see it as I do. At it I went. At that time I did not have as much knowledge of the horse as I have now.

If you will sail with me through this work, I will do all of the work. You look on; understand? I am shoeing cripples and all kinds through the day and sometimes the night, and it's night now; but this

poor horse must be helped to-night. I must have two
quarts of whisky. That is not to be had short of two
miles. I got it. I did not drive this cripple, and
told short stories. I am home now, but before I commence I will tell you where the cause of this poor
horse's suffering was located, and what the effect was,
and where and how I removed it, and that is what you
want to know and I want you to know. This is what
this long story is told for, and it is what they are all
told for. This mare had a small, round, thin-shelled,
flat foot, when natural; low heels. Let us take a peek
at those shoes. Golly! that is all wrong; that shoe is
not the shape of the foot; not wide enough across the
quarter. It is too wide at the heels. It is a long,
clevis-shape; yes; and it's too long. So is the foot;
and the toe is too peaked, and the toe-cork is too high
for the heels. "Can't you find a little more fault?"
Yes. The web is too narrow and too thick for such
feet. "Is that all?" No; let us take this shoe off
and look on the other side and see what we find there.
It's not concave; it's dishing clear around to heel—
bent instead of being hammered, and no flat rest; and
yet it sits hard on the sole. Let us examine these
feet. The toe is one inch and a quarter too long.
That should be cut off. It is nothing but useless
shell; it needs paring some. Let us look at the heels.
These heels are too low. They are all mutilated and
break down, caused by the shoe not resting on the
heel and not having a flat rest on the shoe at heel.
What else? Being too wide, it formed a lever purchase
across the quarter and warps the foot. Let us look
and see if the heels are contracted. Not much. We

will pare the foot so the shoe will rest only on shell
until we come to the heel.   Leave brace in, pare flat,
and fit all around—no springing business about it.
Well, what are you going to do with those low heels?
It is getting cold here; we can't wait for those heels
to grow.   They must be raised to-night.   Won't to-
morrow do as well?   There will be a lot more horses
to the shop to-morrow, and there will be no time.   It's
fearful cold here.   I guess you   can stand the cold.
Let us go to the shop and make a pair of shoes for
this horse.   What sort of shoe shall we make for this
horse to relieve him?   In his present condition he is
braced out; head down; chest sunken in; shoulders
dropped back: great strain on back tendons or cords;
the heels are even at top; the sole is a little raised up.
She should stand back of straight comfortable.   That
will be all we can do to-night.   We will make a shoe
with wide web, at toe quite wide; very thin at toe;
one inch thick at heel; taper from center of toe to
heel.   It should be made as light as possible; thinned
an trued so as to reduce weight; wide where the heels
rest; concave clear out to nail holes; holes in shoe
close to edge.   This concave should stop at about one
inch and a half from the heel.   The brace should be
cut away slanting toward the frog.   We want to get
the sole down by the weight of the horse.   That expands the foot.   The shoe should be made full across
the quarter; it is too narrow.   It has been cut off.
Get the colt's foot in shape—round, easy toe to rise on;
good length shoe, not stuck out at heel.   Let us go to
the barn.   I am getting somewhat tired.   It is awful
cold here, too.   These shoes were made by eye and

measuring the foot. Now this is a hard job for me and the horse. She has got to stand on one foot. It must be done. Get two nails in, and let the foot down. Back goes the foot, and the leg with it. Of course now she can stand better. The strain is off the back tendons. Now I can set the other shoe easier. Down goes the foot back of straight. Finish this job off quite easy. Now I feel better, and the horse too. It matters not what this animal is called, horse or mare. It is a mare. It is principle I am working on.

I must tell you how the nails are in this shoe; two are in the toe, six in all. None back of the widest part of the foot. No corks on this shoe. That suits me. My golly! her head and neck have gone up. Look here! that hollow is all gone in her breast, and she sticks out right plump and full. It is getting late. It It is not so cold as it was. I have removed the cause and cured "chest founder." The heart is not affected, as I have been told. She is eating hay; that's a big thing. It will be daylight soon. I must hurry up. I want some warm, soft water. We will have to go to the house, build a fire, and warm some water. Get that whisky, castile soap, and sponge, and back to the barn again. These scabs must all come off clean and lean all over.

It is a good time, while I think of it, to say that I never use a currycomb. A stiff brush is all I want, brushing always the way the hair lies. Wash off manure.

I must rub the mare dry, and wash her all over with whiskey with a sponge, and rub dry three or four

times.　Rub lightly, put on a light blanket, and make
her a good, soft, dry bed.

Gracious heavens! It is daylight, time to feed, and
I want my breakfast, too.

"Hello! Doan; sharpen these horses; have them
done in an hour?"

"Yes."

I want to say here that whiskey had nothing to do
with curing that mare's stiffness. It might have made
her feel better, and it might have helped take out the
soreness. But it was the work done on the feet that
cured her. Castile soap and water was all I needed to
cure her scabby legs. Water would have cleaned them.
I have cured hundreds since, and used no whisky; all
I use is water. It is science, principle. I wanted to
make the mare comfortable, so she could lie down and
rest and sleep. All should do the same. If the
horse could talk in a language that we could understand, you would hear louder bugling than you ever
heard from me. You would think that it was the
judgment-day, and that the supreme court of heaven
was in session.

I use the word "cure" in this book because it is in
common use, to convey what we are talking about. It
is all well enough; but I do not cure these horses—I
remove the cause and nature repairs the damages.
When I go at a horse to fix him up, I look him over
and do all I can that will make him comfortable.

The day's work is done in the shop. It has been a
hard road all day, I tell you. In all stages of suffering I have helped some, and I have made some worse,
which I well knew; but I did the best I could for

them and the owner. Their feet were in all kinds of conditions.

By George! in this hubbub I was likely to forget my mare in the barn. I said before that I had cured her, and she had not been out of the stall yet. But I have removed the cause, or part of it. I have got to polish her off yet. Let us go to the barn, move her around on the floor, and see how she acts. She must be exercised moderately at first. The change is so great she hardly knows how to use her legs. She will soon recover from that. She has been changed from natural so long, and her cords are out of harmony, she can hardly control herself; but she does not suffer. Her soreness is nearly all gone.

I will right here say to the readers of this work, in this sail working on the horse, I am alone in this barn; all are quietly sleeping. My talk is directed to you, reader, and I want you to go with me, if you will, and pay close attention. I will give you the biggest and the most instructive lesson you ever had on the horse.

Let us sponge the mare's legs, shoulders, and loins with whisky; rub dry each time; repeat this three or four times; take her out-doors; run with her awhile. Again in the barn, rub her legs and shoulders an hour or two. Let us drive her in harness. Now I can ride. Before we take this ride I will say I packed this horse's feet. These were dried up with fever, caused by unnatural strain on the cords which fasten in feet. Let us look at the bottom of the feet. The frog does not touch the ground yet. That's all right in this case. It is a little lower than the shoe-heels. When the foot is on the floor, look! she stands her fore legs back straight. Where is the weight now? It is nearly in the center of the foot. That's right. Don't be in a hurry; we will take a sail after this horse soon. We are experimenting now. There is something more, before we start, to be looked to. I told you when we dressed this foot to prepare it for the shoe we must have the brace slanting a little down toward the frog, and have a flat rest on the shoe-heel. Now the shoe rests on the shell all around, and it is up from the sole. Where is that foot-hook? Let us clean out everything under that shoe clear out to nails. Have the hook thin. The foot is middling soft. Pile in. Let us have a sail after this mare. Thunder! how cold it is. Yes, it is, but we can stand it to ride four or six miles, I guess. Golly! she moves finely. Look at that knee action. See where her head is. Whoa; let us get her in the barn; cover her up after she gets done steaming. Let us look at the bottom of the feet to see what we can find. There! that frog is down even with the heel of the shoe. Let us look at the foot at the heel, and that sits flat on the flat rest on shoe. Let us look at the bottom. This foot is not as cupping as it was. How is that? Look at heel of foot where it rests on heel of shoe. It is spread a little. What did that? Before we took this ride the sole was raised up, as I have explained before, and the structure of the foot was changed from natural. I prepared the foot and shoe for the operation. The weight of the horse is in the center of the foot. The drive settled the sole down in the cup or top of hoof, and when the sole is down in its natural place, all is in harmony of action. It should in no case go below flat. It would not kill the horse, but it would be out of harmony, for nature has formed the foot. When natural, the sole is arching and the frog intended to rest on the ground; but these changes are constantly going on in greater or less degrees. It does not affect the horse's shoulders as bad to have the sole go down below natural, that is, get rounding on the bottom. It lets up on the back tendons. It never would go down if the frog could rest on the ground. When it rises it effect is terrible. Let us examine this horse we are at work on. Now the frog is down on the ground; the sole is down or nearly so; let us try her and see how far back we can put her foot and have it sit flat down on the heel and not hurt her. See! she can put it back from the point where her foot was when we commenced on her, four feet and a half. That's boss! It's cold, and it is three o'clock. Let us go to the house. This horse wants rest. So do I. Give her good bed; build a fire. There is no use going to bed, it's so late, and there will soon be a lot of horses here to be shod; and there will be no peace. Sleep by the stove a little !·

"Hello, Doan; shoe these horses?"

"Yes, I will be there as soon as I swallow a mouthful."

"This mare is lame forward. She interferes behind; she stumbles. She never interfered, and never was lame until after that damned Bloom shod her."

Let us look her over.

"How long has she been shod."

"It is not over six months, and the shoes are all clattering now."

Well, what about this one? She is stiff. It hurts
her to go down hill, and she falls down once in a
while, and it hurts her to go up hill. And when she
first starts off she straddles out behind. Warm her
up, then she goes better, but it hurts her when she gets
up in the morning. She is awful sore then.

"Tom Jones sent me here; he said your were a
good shoer. Some think she is strained across the
loins."

"Well, it does have that appearance."

Of course I am at work at them all of the time. I
left one of that kind in this book. I shall go and see
him one of these days. Let us shoe this one we
looked over first.

"I want long corks on them; I am going to hauling
wood, and I want a good big cork on, so they will last.
Those corks that Bloom put on are all off now."

"All right." This lame foot is about one inch
longer than its mate. What is this? the hair is all off
on the back side of his leg."

"Well, I blistered his cords; they are sore."

"I see they are. Did it help him any?"

"No."

"Have you tried anything more?'

"Yes, I put on whisky, skunks' grease, and angle-
worm oil."

"No good? Why, you have been at work in the
wrong place. That is the effect. The hind feet are in the
same condition, only worse. The nails stick out and
cut like a knife, and it affects across the loins and the
kidneys. This is a flat foot, however. The sole is
down; the foot is spread out over the shoe."

These poor cripples are coming and going while I am sitting by the window over my shop writing this work, and it bothers me, but I must do it.

Well, let us fix this lame foot. Let us work on principle, and see how that will work. Let us shorten that lever purchase. How much? That foot has been shod six months; and the toe was too peaked when it was shod; and it was left about three-quarters of an inch too long then. It has been growing ever since. It takes about one year for a foot to grow from the hair down. This foot, when natural, from hair down, would be about five inches. It has grown half a year, and was about one inch too long when shod. According to this figuring, this foot is three inches and a half too long. That is a trifle too much. Let us do away with that lever purchase by shorten-ing the foot. We better raise the heels a little, for it is going to grow longer. It is growing now; but we cannot see it. Now it is shod. See where his foot is now—back of straight, weight in center. Sore some; it will be all right in ten days, I will warrant for a cent. The same all round; like causes produce like effects. We have got this foot fixed. Let us walk him around. Golly! we have lamed him on the other foot. The fact is, he was lame on both. The lever was the longest on the one we fixed first. That is, this principle effects all horses, shod or not, in a greater or less degree. This is a flat foot. I have changed him some, and that effects him. He does hardly know how to use his legs. His ankles are a little weak, caused by this sudden change. Exercise will soon bring him out all right. Yet, with all this work, he is not natural. But this is the best that can be done with him—shoeing him. Try him. Place his foot back as far as you can from point where his foot now stands, and that is back of straight. You can see he cannot get his foot down flat on heel more than two feet, and the corks are higher·than the toe cork, a little. How is this, the heels are pinched in, and the structure is changed enough to cause that, and I cannot fix it shoeing.

I have cured thousands of this kind of feet of lameness, and the owners were well pleased and talked for me; and I will thank them right here. This work is for them and all mankind and the suffering horse; and when you read this work do not take any offense, for it is not intended to ridicule. I have thought of writing this work for nine years. How to convey it in a book I could not study out, for I talked and explained continually. They did not learn much and worked. I have taken this way of explaining my methods of treatment because there is no other way of giving the information I wish to convey. It is all meant for your interest and that of your poor, suffering horses.

Well, we have not got that horse done yet. His foot is growing. He will go very well for a while, and you will hear from that lever purchase if you let it get too long. I am done with him.

Next! This horse I do not like to tackle. It is a hard job, but I can help him a little. He has got it bad, but it must be done. It will make us both sweat before we get through. This horse has a thick-shelled cup foot. He has got cold standing here. We should have shod him first while he was warm. Can't shoe

them all while they are warm; there are so many.
Some must wait. "Stand around here!" Thunder!
how he straddles!" "Back!" How he raises up his
feet! and he drags them before they leave the floor.
They do not go up very quick; if they did I should
think he had spring-halt. There is not much
"spring" motion about it. I have a mind to leave
him with the other I left in this book until I come
around again. I can't help him much. I do not
think he can stand on three legs; and, worse than all,
he has got two sets of feet on him, for they were not half
cut down when they were shod last, which was six
months ago, and they are hard as a stone. I won't
back out; that's not my name. I think we had better
shoe him on his forward feet first. He can't stand until we do, he is so changed from natural, and all is so
out of harmony.

"How old is this horse?"

"He is nineteen years old."

"How long have you owned him?"

"I raised him from a colt."

"Have you ever doctored him?"

"Oh, yes; I have tried everything most."

"His chest has fallen in some; that looks like chest
founder."

"It is not that. I have always taken care of my
horses myself, and never feed them when they are
warm; and no man drives my horses, they don't."

"Has one man shod them all of the time?"

"No, since he got stiff I have been to a good many
shoers."

"They help him any?"

"No; they say you can cure these horses by shoeing."

"I can help some of them for a while. I can help this one a little."

This horse is different from the one just shod. His feet are cup feet. His shoulders are perished some.

"Yes; some say he is sweenied."

"Ever doctor them?"

"Yes; we inflated him."

"What's that?"

"Pull the skin up like this, all loose; cut a little hole in; jerk it back and forward, and it will fill up with wind. Well, it made it look full, and plump, and soft. Before I got home it was all gone down again."

"How much did it cost you?"

"A dollar. I've paid out lots of money doctoring this horse, and he gets worse every day, and I have to doctor his water-works every little while now."

"I see his shoulders have been blistered"

"Yes; I've blistered them and his cords on the backside of his legs and across his loin."

"Ever try setons?"

"Yes, in both shoulders, and I had him roweled in the breast, and a fellow told me to cut the skin open on the shoulders and take smoked meat rinds, put them in, and sew them up, and let them rot out; that was a sure cure for sweeny."

"That help him?"

"No."

"What do you give him for his water now?"

"Turpentine."

"How much at a time?"

"Half a pint once a week, and I keep rosin in his feed-box all of the time."

"I see his legs are swelled."

"Yes."

"Do anything for that?"

"Yes. I have used gargling oil, Anderson's derm-adore, liniments, and all kinds of liniments I could hear of."

"I see he is sore under his fetlocks."

"Yes; that is scratches."

"Ever done anything for them?"

"Yes; I have tried all kinds of salves I could think of, and I bound live toads under his fetlocks; and a fellow told me to make a poultice of human dung."

"Well, how did that work?"

"It drew out the inflammation."

"Did it?"

"Yes; when I put it on every few days."

"I see some enlargements here."

"Those are wind-puffs. They don't hurt him any. Some say the cause of these legs swelling is yellow water."

"I know they do. Did you ever give him anything for that?"

"Yes, I have."

"Help him?"

"No."

"It does have that appearance, looking him over. What is this inside? He is swelled here and sore."

"I never saw that before. That is called the second stifle by some. Yes, he has strained himself probably getting up."

" What is this up here? He sinks down here over the whirl bone. Ever do anything for that?"

" Yes; I put on different kinds of liniment and heated it in with hot irons."

" Did that help him?"

" I don't know as it did."

" What are those marks on the inside of his legs?"

" I had him fired—burnt; they say that makes them stronger.

" He seems weak on his hind legs. What are these enlargements here?"

" They call them blood-spavins; some call them bog-spavins."

" What is this?"

" Well, they say them are curbs "

" What is this in here?"

" Oh, that's nothing but thoroughpin."

" Ever do anything for these difficulties?"

" Yes."

" Did it help them?"

" I can't see as it has."

" Well, we can't stand here long. We must get these horses out of here. It will soon be dark. I have got a job at the barn to-night on that Kentucky hunter mare. Well, we may as well tackle this horse. Take up! Thunder! this horse's feet are contracted. Didn't you know that?"

" They told me they were."

" Did you ever do anything for them?"

" Yes. I have used lots of foot ointment and salves to make them grow fast."

" Well, I think that did make them grow. I guess

that is a good thing. It is about eight inches from the top of the coronet to the toe on these feet all around. Did you have irons on his feet when you used this stuff?"

"Yes."

"Well, I think they grew a little too fast. Where did you put this ointment you used?"

"Well, I made a mark all around the foot just below the hair, on the hoof, and I put it below the mark."

"Did you put any on the inside?"

"Yes; on the sole."

"Did you get any on the frog?"

"No."

"Didn't you know that in putting this trash on horn or hoof that was already grown there was danger of making it grow too fast?"

"No, I did not."

"Didn't you? Didn't you know there was a receipt out to prevent it growing in case it should get to growing too fast?"

"No."

"Well, there is, and they should always accompany each other, for they are dangerous to be used separately. This is a fast age in which we live. I read a receipt the other day that would make a foot grow out from the hair down to its natural length in six weeks. The natural growth of the hoof is about one year when healthy, and no fever in it; and this is not all—with irons on it could not expand, and that would incline it to grow long and narrow. And at this rate of growth a horse could be grown up from the time it was born in twenty-four weeks to four years old. That would excel the creator."

I will show the effect of long feet before I get through this work. Let us go on with this examination of this horse.

"This horse ever been bled in plait vein?"

"Yes."

"Help him?"

"No."

"Ever been nerved?"

"Yes."

"Help him?"

"No."

"What are these scabs on here?"

"I had the wind-puffs cut open to let the wind out."

"They are sore yet?"

"Yes."

"Let us try him and see if he can stand on one forward leg while we get the shoe off the other."

It has high corks on the heel to raise it to take the strain off cords now He can't stand down on heel. It is lower with the shoe off. Well, we must work on this foot until we get it fixed or we will have him down. There will have to be some judgment used in shortening the lever purchase on this horse with all this contraction; forward legs braced out at least one and a half feet from point where they should be, and his hind feet shoved forward under his belly about the same distance and from the same cause, and run over at that; gambrels bowed out; toes in; hind feet huddled together. This horse weighs twelve hundred; weight two-thirds, thrown back on his hind legs. Now this horse has got to be balanced in some way to equalize his weight. Shorten that lever on toe, and get his weight in center of foot, on all of his feet, or nearly so, by dressing foot, or preparing shoe, or by both.

" Well, Joe, you are too tall; you will raise him too much ; it will tip him over. I will try him. This foot has got corns?"

" Yes; I had them dug out and tar burnt in."

" They are sore now ?"

" Yes."

" Ever do anything more to them ?"

" I put in spirits of salts and butter of antimony."

" Cure them ?"

" No."

" What is this hole in the toe ?"

" A veterinarian said he was foundered ; bleeding in the toe would cure him."

" How much blood did he take from him ?"

" Five quarts from each toe."

" Well, what else?"

" He corked it with tar and tow, and burnt it in with a hot iron."

" Cure him ?"

" No."

" We will never get this horse shod if we do not quit examining them. What is this hole in this foot?"

" Well, a fellow told me to bore a hole in the bottom of his foot and fill it up with turpentine. It would cure him."

" Did you ?"

" Yes."

" Cure him ?"

" No."

" Well, this shoe is on at last. The weight is in center nearly. His knee is a little weak, but I guess he is about balanced on that foot. Let us shoe the other."

" What is this cutting around the coronet or top of hoof ?"

" A veterinarian told me the coronet band was too tight. It should be cut so as to give it room to ex- pand ?"

" Did it help him?

" No."

" That operation of spreading the foot by fitting the shoe wider than the foot, so you could see the nail holes all around, commence at the toe and starting all of the nails and driving, no matter how high, by alter- nate raps so as to spread the foot where it was con- tracted ; and another process for contracting his heels to tighten up the coffin-joint when it gets too much play ; that is, when it gets to cutting through neglect to oil ; and a few other great discoveries on horses' feet, cost this government twenty-five thousand dol- lars in the time of the Rebellion."

" It's larger at the top than it is at the bottom. I guess that, let it spread."

" Did you take the shoes off when you cut the coronet band ?"

" No."

" Were the fore legs braced out ?"

" Yes."

" If he had stood up straight, as he now does, it would

spread faster, the weight being in the center, with shoe nailed on the bottom. Don't you think the bottom would have been the proper place to spread the foot?"

" Well, it does seem so."

" I have shod horses a great many years, and I have never tried to spread the foot wider at the top than it was at the bottom, but this process was recommended by Robert Bonner, and I suppose it is all right. This horse's shell is thick. If it had been thin there would have had to be some plan studied out to stop his foot from splitting open in many places. Then it would want contraction again to close the cracks. It is curious they could not see the lever; that tip-back principle is not seen by many on horses, yet it exists, which I shall show before I get through this work. I intend this work to be an eye-opener. I am writing it in the night, when all is quiet, all asleep, for I am so annoyed through the day I cannot write so well.

These poor cripples are continually coming for relief. Of course I tell them what to do. They want me to do it. I tell them I am as stiff and sore as their horses, and let them go. This book must be written.

Let us return to the horse. He is shod on the forward feet. He stands a little back of straight. Let us see how strong he is on his kness. Push him forward on his knees. He is very weak, but he is balanced about as well as he can be considering the condition his poor contracted feet are now in. His toe, that awful lever power, is growing. His knee will not go over with this job. He feels better now, but his feet ache awfully. Golly ! in all of this hubbub, folks

coming and going, horses, something the matter with
all of them ; four or five talking at one time ; all ex-
pressing their opinions and beliefs; new arrivals all
through the day, and late at night, no two affected
alike; some from one cause, some from another, all in
a hurry to get home or go to mill or some other place.
To talk with them all and balance them all up in good
shape so they will not go lame in six months, and
fail nine times out of ten, is somewhat trying.

Well, let us go on with this job. Stand out about
eight feet from this horse, take a side view of him. If
you have a good sharp eye, if you are any judge of
the horse, or even if you are half blind, you can see the
position he is obliged to stand in. I have fixed him
forward, and moved him back from the point where
they were when I commenced, at least fourteen inches,
and that is as far as I can get him without tipping him
on his knees, with his feet contracted as they are now.
Balancing deformed horses, you will find before we
get through this sail, is quite a science; and man will
have something more to do than to eat, sleep, and
wear clothes. Golly ! that makes me think it is almost
night, and I have not had my dinner.

Are you looking at that horse ? Yes. If you are
going to be my pupil you must pay close attention.
Where is the weight of that horse? See where his
hind feet stand now, and we have not even touched
them yet. They are all contracted, and eight inches
from the hair down to point of toe. These feet should
be moved back at least eighteen inches, to get the
weight in the center of the foot. Of course, we can-

not spread out his feet. We must do the best we can as he is.

Spreading the foot with nails, that is, by fitting the shoe so much wider than the foot, I do not like. I do not want to spread the foot at the toe; the heel is the place. All feet spread at the toes, on that principle, would contract the heels; they are contracted enough now. And that is not all; it would tear all the shell off; besides, when they get soaked soft, the shoe, shell and all, would go. It is curious, is it not, with all of the ailments this poor horse has, his doctors have worked at the wrong place—the effect? But I have not got through looking him over yet. He stands as we left him. What would be the effect on this horse if we should leave him, and not get his feet back, so as to have his weight on the center of his foot? There is eight hundred weight on them now. There should be more than half on the fore legs, and the horse weighs twelve hundred. That lever is rather long. In the position he is obliged to stand in his hind legs are of but little use. If we take up one of them half the weight must come on the shoer, and there will be quite a struggle before that leg can be got in a position to shoe. It has been so a long time, and the horse is sore across his kidneys. His hind parts are too low for his fore parts. Look at him; his back is humped, and there is a constant strain. All is out of harmony, both internally and externally. This horse is not as bad as he will be made yet by these effect doctors, these veterinarians, these professors of great wisdom. He will stand a little more torturing and mutilation. He is tough.

I can fix him so he can haul his half of two cords of green wood up and down heavy hills a little while yet, and suffer night and day, and I am going to do it. Come on, Oliver, let us try him. We will have a tough time. This horse is finished, and he stands well back on his hind feet, shortening that lever by dressing the foot, and raising heel of shoe a little higher than toe. Look the horse over if you must shoe, not stand and talk about shoes. This horse stands where the weight should be—in center; he is in pain, and always will be, unless his foot expands; and I well know it will not with those irons on his feet—all out of harmony, structure all changed from natural. He steps short, and every foot pains him, night and day. Still, it looks well on the outside. If you want to tell look at his movement.

Do you think these two horses were all we shod that day? No, it was not. Forty-one years wrestling with horses of all kinds—I am tired. Good-bye, poor horse, I will come and see you before I get through this work, for I am determined to find the way out of this trouble.

Supper is over. Let us go to the barn and see the Kentucky hunter. By golly! Kit, you are looking fine. Her feet have had packing in them all the time. Sponge over with whisky twice; rub dry each time. We must look this mare's hind parts over before we drive her any more, for we want all to work together "in harmony of action." That lever is too long. Weight is back of center of foot. Too much strain on back tendons. That must be fixed before the mare is driven another rod. Let us go to the shop, pare the toe and shorten. The heels are low enough. The structure is very nearly all right. Easy toe to rise on; narrow web shoe; little thicker at heel. Short corks; heel a little higher than toe. She is shod. Take a side view of her now. She stands back further on her feet."

"Is that so?"

No; her body has gone forward. Now her body has all gone forward. Her fore legs stand further back of straight. The weight is more equal on the center of foot, and she is on her foundation or base, and her head has gone up a little more. Let us go to the barn. Kit, by golly, we will make some of the great horsemen's eyes stick out on this job. Kit, we are going to take a sail now. Clean out under shoe. This frog is flattening out. That's all right. Pile in. Let us go up on the Ridge road. That is getting worn down smooth. Let us drive moderate for a while, and let her get used to the change. It is a little weakening to be changed so suddenly, and, that, too, one end at a time. She will soon recover from that. She is changed toward natural. She is even with herself instead of five or six feet behind, which I will show by cuts, and by principles that will not lie, before I get through this work. Try yourself, Kit. Golly! see how she flattens out. See where her hind feet strike, outside of her forward feet. All clear five or six feet ahead. You begin to be as your creator made you. To-morrow is the day you are to show those boys what you can do. Whoa! Into the barn; rub until dry. Pack forward feet. Good, bright, clean hay;

good, dry, soft bed.   It is two o'clock in the morning.
Let us have a little nap.

"Where is Doan?"

"He has not got up yet."

"Tell him to come out; I want to see him.   I want
these horses shod all around. I am in a hurry. Don't
you get up until this time of day? You will sleep
your intellect all away. I want them shod all around
now. I am going to drive them to Pennsylvania. I
want them sharp, long corks; I don't want to sharpen
them again this winter."

"All right."

These horses have flat feet all around.   In six
months that man came to the shop.

"Doan, I want these shoes clinched, and some nails
put in. I guess the nail iron wasn't very good."

The shoes were nearly buried inside of shell.

"Mr. Knap, we cannot always get good nail iron.
It varies so that we cannot tell until we try it. However, I will fix them up."

They came again to get shod, and settle up.   It was
just nine months. The same shoes were on. The
hoof was spread out over the shoe with the weight of
the horse. It did not kill them. See that lever at
toe. I have seen hundreds of horses of that kind settled down in front between top of coronet and point at
toe, the weight being in center of foot; the frog has no
rest, and is raised by corks from the ground. The foot
gets soft sometimes. Heel-nails always break first
from lever purchase. The horse always, when drawing raises on toe. When climbing heavy hills, the
sole settles down until it is below flat. Then it is very

weak. The coffin-joint is badly affected. The high toe-cork, drawing in this fix, weight in center, completely dislocates the coffin-joint, and in this case the horse's foot is almost useless. He rocks back on his heel; the toe turns up and has a rocking motion at every step. And yet he is expected to draw heavy loads. That lever works badly on all kinds of feet. If it has not broken down, it hurts at coronet where the ring-bone comes and strains back tendons.

This lever works both ways to a greater or less degree, and I will show what power there is in it connected with contraction.

For fear the readers may think I have butchered and mutilated these poor already tortured horses, I will say right here I never did; I have always known it to be wrong, and I never believed horses were stiffened by anything they eat or drank; and I know they are not now. I lived at Talcot's Corners when I was at work on the Kentucky hunter mare, which I have not got through with yet.

I will go back to the time I had worked at shoeing the horse nine years in the village of Northville, Cayuga Co., N. Y. Chauncey Hinman bought a pair of dapple-cream mares, very nice, black legs, mane, and tails. This place is two miles from Talcot's Corners. At that time I had a good reputation as a shoer, and did a large business in that line. I had taken my old shop down to build larger, and things were all out doors. These creams I shod the first time. They had flat feet, thin shell. I had shod them, as near as I can recollect about two years. Their owner was my regular customer; his horses needed shoeing; he

waited for me to get my shop up. He had business
about one hundred miles, and he wanted to drive it.
Having no fire, I could not shoe them. He had
waited a long time. His horse's feet had grown very
long. They must be shod. He took them to another
shop and had them shod, and went his journey and
back. I sent my apprentice to tell him I wanted him
to draw some stone for me. He came and saw me.
He said:

"I have foundered my horses."

"Perhaps that is not so; bring them over so I can
see them."

He said they were so stiff he could not get them to
the shop in a half day.

"You must," said I; "I can't go now."

It was three miles. He came. I soon saw where
the cause was. I told him I would cure them both
for four shillings.

"That is just what two other blacksmiths told me. I
had those shoes set twice while I was gone, and it did
no good. I have foundered them. I had been told
that when on the road, if you water while the horse is
warm, and then drive on and keep him moving, there
is no danger; but I stiffened my horses in this way."

They were so stiff they could hardly move. After
they had stood awhile I pointed out where the cause
was; and spent about an hour explaining. Then we
went to the shop. These horses had light limbs and
as good feet as I want on a horse, and not much
changed if they had been dressed and trimmed as
they should have been. There was three inches of
useless hoof in length on the toe. I cut it off, and

talked all the time, teaching. The shoe was a coarse botch of a thing; not concave; creased in the middle; heavy nails; long, pointed toe, with high toe-corks and high heel-corks. In fact, one of the biggest botches I ever saw. When I got these creams dressed up they had colts' feet, and their bodies came back on their base; weight in the center. They were sore in their cords. The cause was removed. I explained it all to the owner three or four times over, and told him that in a week they would be all right; if they were not I would take them and pay him what they cost him. A week afterward I was sitting on the verandah at my house, and I saw the creams coming down the road; heads up, good knee-action, feeling fine. He stopped.

"Doan, my horses are as sound as ever they were."

"Yes, that's all right." "Say, now, look here; tell me what you did to those horses. No man shall shoe these horses but you."

"Go where you please to get your shoeing done."

My God! what good did all of that talk do? I told him again, "Look out for that lever purchase."

My brother Oliver and myself had those horses and thousands of others of that kind to cure of "chest founder"—some over and over again. Talk and work and teach, and no one would learn! Horses came blistered and with setons in shoulders. The fact is, the owners looked at us and not at the horse. After you read this book, go and look at the horse.

Well, we have had a hard day putting these poor horses on their base and balance. In all stages and

degrees of changes from natural.   My head rings from
being bent over so much.

Supper is over.   Let us go and see the Kentucky
hunter.

"Kit, this is the night you were to show yourself
to those boys that examined you."

The reader must bear in mind that this mare had
not been seen by anyone but myself.

"There, Bill Jones, straddle this mare" (Bill Jones
was a boy).   "Let her sail."

She did sail better than any horse they had.   She
was a good one.   Some of the men were there who
seen her in a stiffened condition.   Do you think that
attracted their attention?   It did not, and   that
is the reason I am writing this work.   Next day
I had business at Kelloggsville to pay a stallion license.
(I have kept stallions.)   It was nineteen miles, hubby
and rough.   I was on the Moravia flats early
in the morning.   Gird Mead was leading his horses
across the road to water.   I saw him.   I knew him,
and knew where he lived, when I traded with
his hired man, Sam.   He did not know me; never
had seen me, as I knew.   It is a good time to surprise him.   He thought he had played sharp on
me.   The flats were worn quite smooth, and that was
all the smooth road I found on that trip   I let her
sail.   I saw him looking and pulled up and asked,
"How far is it to Kelloggsville?"

"About six miles."

I saw him looking at the mare's fore legs.

"Do you know her?" said I.   ·

"Well, I had a mare that would match her very

well, but she was stiff. I let her go a few days ago."

"This is the same mare. I traded with Sam Grover."

"Well, I would like to know what you have done to her."

I jumped out, explained the whole thing to him, as I always do, and sailed on. Remember that lever. The mare I was driving was worth one hundred and fifty dollars, and the one he got, seventy-five dollars. I got twenty dollars to boot. How does that loss figure? Ninety-five dollars on account of toe leverage on horses. Do not forget that that principle works bad on all horses, and worse on hind feet. I think this mare would look better with the neck strap looped over the turret to hold the collar up. I do not like that thing. She holds her head so high it feels disagreeable. Here we are at the harness-shop. "Whoa." The saddler is getting the length.

"This looks something like the mare Doc Mead had."

"This is the same mare."

"That can't be. I saw her a few days ago; she was awful stiff."

"It is the same mare."

"How did you cure her?"

I told him all about it.

"I have got a horse I just traded for," says he. "Perhaps he is the same. He is stiff. Will you go and look at him?"

"Yes, this is a different case; cause not so easily removed; cup foot; take his shoes off, cut his feet down nearly half; let him go without shoes; that will help him some."

That poor horse could hardly stand; contracted feet, leverage. I cannot do all the hard work and furnish brains, too. There are so many making more all of the time. I teach, talk early and late, night and day." Sail home; get home long before night. Thirty-eight miles' drive over hubs; stinging cold; take good care of Kit. While doing it the three or four gather around.

"Doan, where have you been all day?"

"To Kelloggsville."

"We have waited all day for you."

Horses all lame or interfering; some one thing, some another.

"Can you do it?"

"Yes, as soon as I get something to eat. I've had no dinner."

Get in shop; sleeves rolled up; at it again. Get them all pleased as well as I can. It is nine o'clock, perhaps later. Kit must be cleaned off, and made comfortable before I sleep. I will have to wait five weeks before I can finish her; but we will have lots of good sails during that time in the night. She must have exercise or I cannot cure her. This is the way I cure all cases of this kind.

Reader, do you think I sat down and waited for that time to come? If you do that would not make it so. I had lots of horses I was working on. They were not in my care, only as they came to the shop to be shod. Work and teach; give directions none followed. Day after day this work all had to be done

over and over again and no good result, some going
on from bad to worse. Do you know what I thought
sometimes? Well, I will tell you. I thought the creator had not got man finished yet. I have not changed
my mind yet on that. He needs some more work
done on him. He is not polished yet, and that is one
reason for my writing this work. Men have no knowledge of the animal, the horse. I have two brothers,
Oliver Doan and J. J. Doan. They have been ground
through this mill for years. Sometimes we were all
in one shop together, all talking about principles to
shoe the horse on to keep him from getting lame, and
how to cure. Sometimes we would agree, and at other
times we would not, and it would get middling hot;
but we still kept up the battle for the horse. We
were working for the horse, not for the man. Sometimes all scattered singly · We all carried on shops in
many places. I worked nine years in many different
shops. At the age of twenty-three I opened a shop
at the little village of Northville, in the town of
Genoa, Cayuga county, N. Y. I was a jobber and
carriage ironer, and carried on that business, connected
with horse-shoeing. Oliver commenced to work at
Talcot's Corners with Halsey W. Taylor six years
after I did. I commenced with Taylor to learn my
trade. For some reason, I know not what, Oliver left
and came where I was at work at Little Hollow for
Zenos B. Richmond, who carried on the carriage business, jobbing, and shoeing the horse. Richmond hired
him by the year. We worked a year and a half there
together—his wages thirty dollars a year and board,
he to clothe himself. He went with me to Northville.

We wrestled with the horse there several years. Then Joseph, another brother, came. He is next younger. He tried it for a while and quit. Oliver worked for me in all about eleven years. In a short time Joseph came and wanted to try it again. Then we were all in my shop together. We had lots of hard battles balancing these poor horses, all studying on some principle to shoe on to benefit the horse. Oliver had carried on business in the states of New Jersey, Pennsylvania, and New York. He soon started business for himself again. Then Joseph went with him. Thus I lost the most trusty man I ever had to work on the horse or any other kind of work. I had connected wagon-work and painting with my business. That they learned and carried on, connected with their business. Joseph changed around; sometimes he was with me and again Oliver. Then he went to work in other shops; Oliver the same the fore part of his life. Joseph carried on business in many places, and was shoer in the Rebellion for a brigade. I carried on business in ten different places. In this horse sail I came around in the same place. I always bought. Twice I bought the same property, and battled for the horse. I write this to show you how queerly this sail worked. We were learning the horse-shoeing trade, and we did learn it. We are now all together nearly in the same place. Each dropped all other mechanical work and fell in line, battling for the horse. We have made shoeing a specialty for many years, working on the horse, and intend to keep up this fight. As long as we three live single or together, we are all united.

It is perfected, as near as it can be, and iron the horse's feet.

Go with me to Auburn city. There you will see a man standing by a fine dapple-gray stallion. His eyes are sunken; he looks care-worn, and his cheeks are hollowed, battling, teaching almost night and day; J. J. Doan doing the same. This man's name is Oliver Doan. I visit them often while I am writing this work to see how the battle is going. They are curing horses without medicine. Reader, do not think this is the beginning; these boys have been master of the horse's feet about eight years; and Oliver, as I said, has been working almost night and day trying to introduce and teach this great discovery. He says he will never give it up. I looked him over the other day. I told him I thought he must give out soon unless he had rest, he was so over-taxed and broken of his rest. If we lose this soldier it will weaken our army very much. My own back is about given out, and Joe's is the same. I left them still in the field to write this book.

Let us go back to Talcot's Corners, where the Kentucky hunter mare is, and work five weeks on horses day after day and nights. I have four or five cup feet horses. I am trying to spread their feet, shoeing on the wrong principle. I tried a shoe made in this way, bevel out or incline plane, so that the foot would slide out with the weight of the horse. I worked at that for years, but I could not gain anything. I soaked the feet and drove with the same result. Sometimes the feet grew narrower instead of expanding. I made up my mind it was wrong, and for this reason: the foot

constantly sliding out and going back at every step
the horse took kept the structure of the foot in
motion, and it was badly changed from natural. It
did not remove the cause; on the contrary, it irritated
it—made bad worse. The foot was always dry and
hard. I dropped that and went back to flat rest on
heel. That worked better. I rasped the foot in front
to weaken, so the heels would spread, and put a few
nails in the toe so as not to hold the heels. Still I
could gain but little, and often lost more than I gained.
Wet and dry weather worked against me, but that
power, the lever, was the worst. For years and years
I worked to try to save horses from getting stiff, and
still they came pouring in for relief. If they had never
seen a blacksmith or shoer, they would have been all
right, or nearly so; but I did not know at that time
they were thrown in such a bad condition, as I after
many years found out by experimenting.

It is five weeks since I shod Kit; let us finish her
off. I always shoe my horses all around at one time,
unless a shoe should get torn off by accident or otherwise. This mare's foot has grown five weeks; the
lever on the toe has grown some. The heels were
too low when we shod her. Pare the toe now from
heel; make new shoes this time, the same as the first,
only with thinner heels. The heel is higher on the
foot. Look up and down the horse's leg and calculate
how the work should be done to keep the strain off the
cords; place the foot back as far as she can, and heel
sit flat down on the floor, and not hurt her. If you
get the heel too high she cannot move well, and it will
tip her on knee and ankle. This principle works the

same on all horses. This mare was contracted but very little. Now I am going to test this and see how she will stand a big drive in the month of March.

I drove here on rough roads, up and down hills, two hundred and sixty miles, at from fifty to sixty miles a day, and no founder, no soreness of cords. I had dressed up her feet for the journey. I sold her that spring to a Mr. Smith. I shod her while he owned her, which was one year. He sold her to Mr. Niles, who also owned her for a year. I continued to shoe her. She hauled wood all winter over hubs, when Niles sold her for one hundred and fifty dollars. In a short time she got in another blacksmith shop, and became "foundered" in the chest. Then there was a row. Niles came to me in a rage.

"Doan, what is there about that black mare you sold to Smith? They say you say she has been foundered. The man I sold her to wants me to take her back."

"I have said nothing of the kind. She was the stiffest horse I ever saw when I got her. I removed the cause in four days, and can do it again."

He had to take her back. I never saw her after Niles sold her. I had all the horses I could take care of. I could have bought her cheap and sold in a few days, and made some more money on toe-leverage. I could find this kind of horses any day, and all over; they were being made everywhere by the wholesale. This work is intended to be an eye-opener. It is "The Horse's Rescue," and if this does not do it, I shall go at it myself again; it is good business relieving the suffering horse.

I will bid Kit good-bye.   I told her owner that if I
saw or heard of those mutilators, blisterers, rowel-
ers, and butchers at her again, I would "go for
them."

Reader, do not think all of these sufferers are to be
cured like this mare; if you do, you will make a mistake.   No matter what "they say," give your attention and learn.   After the cause is removed on them
by working on the feet, they must have work and exercise or they cannot be changed back to natural, no
matter how long or short standing.   All must be
changed back and come in harmony of action, as their
creator made them, or no cure will be effected.   They
must be balanced on all four feet, their weight equalized on each foot and in center of each foot.   The
structure of every foot must be in its proper place and
balanced in the center.   Standing with his feet all in a
huddle under his belly, with his head down, and
asleep, you could take a natural horse by the tail and
rock him as you could a chair with rockers on it and not
move his feet or strain him or hurt him in any way on
cords or tendons.   He can rear up and stand on his
hind legs straight; kick up straight and not hurt him.
I have watched the colt stand for hours balanced
in this way asleep.   If he had not been balanced in
center, he could not stand in that position asleep.
The stiff horse can stand and sleep if his hind legs are
not shoved too far forward under his belly by lever and
contraction, and by being run over, something as a
sawhorse stands; but he has no action, and he is
obliged to stand in this way, or not stand at all.   If

he lies down, he often wants help to get up, and cannot stand then.

I had a horse I called Bill. I have seen him play
for hours in the pasture in this way; he would rear
up, walk on his hind feet, then come down on his forward feet, and kick up almost straight. I watched
him. ʹI noticed his feet all struck in one place in the
center. That horse could get his head down to eat
grass and drink water without sprawling out his legs
or falling over on his head and breaking his neck,
which I will better explain hereafter. Curious, with
all of the books we have had; they never got away
from that poor sore foot, and these wonderful shoes all
polished up. It seems to me they worked a very
small field on the horse, and it would have been better
if they had not worked that. After the horse got
so he could not get his head down nor up, they introduced feeding hay on the ground. It is curious they
always got it wrong, as I will show they have. Then,
worse than all, they want to keep it so by trying to
enact laws so that no blacksmith shall operate on a
horse's foot unless he has a diploma from some veterinary college or university, or an order from us.
"Our heads contain all of the brains and knowledge
and wisdom, and we will furnish it for you. It is inexhaustible!" My, my! do you not know a man is
known by his works? Let us take a sail, and peep
around and see what we can find.

I must pass over many years of hard knocks, working on and battling for the horse. It will not be inter-
esting, and I do not want to write it. I could not.
Let us go in the street-car shop in Elmira. Here

stands a row of horses, and it is all they can do to stand. What is the matter with them? They are all off of their base, caused by lever power in all stages and degrees of change, and all in the wrong way. "What are these holes cut in here for where the hind feet stand?" "To let the toes draw in to relieve the cords." Let us look around. Here stand some in the water—disabled—soaking their feet, which are con-contracted, and with two sets of feet, and shoes on; head down, suffering; blisters, setons, and all manner of torturing going on. On one side is the shoeing shop; on the other is a professor's or veterinarian's sign. Professor of what? Torturing the already suffering horse. And yet he gets a good salary. Look at the condition of the horses, and see if he earns it. We have professional thieves, gamblers, and liars, but their occupation is more useful than mutilating these poor helpless creatures. This work is "THE HORSE'S RESCUE." Gerard Dean is the author of it, and he does not "scare worth a cent." There are two brothers connected with this work—chips off of the old block. Let us go to Newburg, in Orange Co., and see what we can find there. We see these horses climbing up and down stairs, or inclined planes, two stories high, at nearly quarter pitch, in this deformed condition, all off base or equilibrium or balance. This is not seen, I well know. When these horses are moving on the road they are behind themselves. I can explain it in no other way better than this. It put me in mind of the puppy in pursuit of his shadow. The object always remains at the same distance. The animal is trying to get on his base or foundation. His weight is unequally adjusted.

When looking around, talking horse, a man says: "I have a fine-looking horse. He can hardly walk. Will you go and see him?" "Yes." They say he is "foundered;" flat feet all around; shoes on; weight in center; corks on shoe; frog on ground; went down through the cup; long toes; rounding on bottom; broken in front; coffin-joint injured or dislocated. I told the man to pull off the horse's shoes, cut off that lever, and put the weight on the frog. He might get well. It would help help him if he did not recover. He thought that would not do. Here is another case— cup foot. This horse is within a stone's throw of a veterinarian's office in Elmira. The owner says: "If you will cure him I will give you ten dollars." Let us examine him. One foot is not half as long as its mate, and that is contracted badly. He is only eight years old. On one he has what is called a "heart shoe," frog-bearing; not nearly as long as it might have been. Long pointed toe, and ironed solid. He was in great pain.

They were trying to shoe this horse in that way. A frog-bearing shoe should never be put on a cup foot in any case. It holds the sole up and makes bad worse for this reason: the foot cannot expand unless the sole can come down. And that is not all; if it is nailed it cannot run down unless the shoe gets loose, and then the shoer takes a scurfing. This principle is the same on all cup feet. I tried to induce him to pull all of the shoes off and dress his feet down at the toe. Cut off that lever I could not. I walked

away. Before I got through this work I will tip over
more than you are aware of with that lever.

Let us sit down on the hotel verandah and have a
rest, and see the horses pass and study them. This is
a great thoroughfare to Elmira, a continuous stream
of horses passing and repassing, nearly all lame. Some
are stiff in one way or another. It occurred to me this
is the place for me. They are in a worse condition
here than any place I ever have been in. I lived in
Tioga county, Pennsylvania. At that time I owned a
farm and was trying to work it. I always had a shop,
and was always talking horse and teaching all I could.
It soon brought a lot of cripples for relief, as it always
had. There was no place I could do it all. I might
as well sell my farm and give up trying to work at
any kind of business. I did sell it, and all of my
property except my horses and driving rigs. These I
must keep. They are all nearly new and good. I
shall need them to exercise horses if I work on them.
I had as fine a pair as any I saw in Horseheads. They
were wanted to put on the street cars. I said I would
rather see them dead than let them go there. And
they were soon dead. Before I got all of my goods
moved my Bill, that was balanced in center, had gone.
He was the first to go. I was driving the pair together. The roads were muddy. A board was buried
in the mud. He stepped on the end; it flew up, ran
into him, and killed him. You can see me in a barn.
John Saterly, born in Horseheads, examining a horse.
This horse is five years old, the very picture of my
Bill. His forward feet are soaking. I asked, "How
came the frogs all out of these feet, Mr. Saterly?"

"I think he must have cut them out on stone."

That is not it; his feet are badly contracted; the circulation is all cut off from the frog by the pressure. The sole each side of the frog. You must get him out of that."

"Will you do it for me?"

"I will."

"All right; we will have a frog in those feet in less than a year. This horse had not been used in nearly one year. He could not travel. He was a present to John from a friend. John suffered with the horse. I relieved them both. How? I will tell you. I spread his feet, and told John to drive him every day. In one year he had the colt's foot on him, and John was offered five hundred dollars for him. He would not sell him. How much did I get for him? How much did I get for that job? The price of shoeing the horse and John's friendship, and that is more than I got from thousands for the same job. I am going to send John one of these books if I live.

Where next? On the floor in David Townsend's shop, driving on shoes for two fighters; work four days at one dollar per day; have a row. I refuse to drive on shoes unless they are more properly fitted; am called a damned botch. I told them I never had slaughtered horses when I knew it, and I should not begin now. I am ordered out of the shop. I picked up my tools and told them I would have a shop of my own in this place soon. "You can't shoe all of the horses if you do," is the reply.

Where next? In a shop on the bank of the canal; wrestled with the horse early and late. There are nine shops in this place. Let us go and look Mr. Bennett's stable of horses over, and see how we find them. In a suffering condition; in all stages of suffering. I talked with Mr. Bennett. Explain, teach, all of the time. He tells me to take them and fix them up. What ails this horse in here? Sh! He is gone up; he can hardly stand. He is strained, I think, across the loin; his water-works are out of order all of the time. "That horse and his mate," says Mr. Bennett, "cost me eight hundred dollars not long ago." His mate had a flattish foot. I shod him. He was in the team at time we were talking. "What is so much straw in here for?" I asked.

"He can't stand on the ground." Let us get him out of this straw so we can see his feet. Oh, horror! this poor horse was nearly ready to fall over backward, as his eyes and general appearance showed the intense suffering he was obliged to endure, too plainly for any man that had eyes not to see. "Mr. Bennett," said I, "do you know what is the matter with that horse?"

"No."

"Well, I do. I can relieve him in a very short time, and will if you will let me. It's a hard job for him and me, too, but it must be done."

This horse had not been able to work in a long time, and had been crammed with all kinds of trash called "medicine." He had shoes on and was higher from the top of his hoof down to the point at his toe than any other horse I ever saw. His feet were quite straight up and down; his fore legs stood about perpendicular; his breast was full, his shoulders nearly all right, his hind feet weet were drawn forward under his belly by contraction and leverage, and were of but little use to him. If his fore legs had been braced forward he would have gone over backward. It would have thrown so much weight on his already overtaxed legs, they being so much off their bose. This horse was eight years old; weight about thirteen hundred. Reader, how would you like to tackle that horse alone as I did? I had a good sweat. I have thought hundreds of times in my life that the worth of a man's work is not known until he had been dead five hundred years, and not always then. I cut those feet down nearly half, balancing the horse as well as I could at that time. His feet were very sore. I put on shoes suitable for him, pared the sole so it could come down by his weight in the manner I have already described (see page 38), packed his feet with clay. Remember, no nails back of the widest part of the foot. The next morning, after shoeing this horse, he was harnessed to a one-horse wagon loaded with a small quantity of lumber, and driven at a walk by my orders. He belonged to a man that owned a mill and lumber-yard. The horse delivered lumber. I watched his feet. Do not forget to clean in the morning all cut under his shoe. If you do forget it you will fail. This horse was heavy. I balanced him with his weight in the center of foot.

Cripples come pouring in in all degrees of change from natural, interferers, and all kinds but those in a natural condition. Not one of these arrived in the lot. I fixed them all up as well as I could. One horse came that it will be particularly well to mention. He had a thin-shelled, flat foot. He was lame. His foot was large, and shod too large—up on corks; center up from ground; his foot spread too much, and was constantly springing at every step from the weight of the horse. It made him lame. I put clips on the shoe at the quarters to prevent the springing. He went off very well. I told the owner he must not leave the shoes on more than four weeks; if he did, it would play mischief with the coffin-joint; the sole would rise in center. What good did that do? In nearly six months after I saw the horse—so stiff he could hardly walk, with the same shoes on. They had not been set. I talked with the owner about it. He did not like my shoeing. He liked that lever on the toe, contraction, coffin-joint lameness, perished shoulders, and a deformed horse, better. It did not injure my business any. He had watered or fed him three or four times a day. "They say" he is foundered, and that clears up the business.

Ten days have passed since I pulled that horse out of the straw. He has worked drawing lumber every day. It was rainy during this time, which was in my favor. I did not have to pack his feet. They soaked while at work. "Hello, boy! drive up here." (It was a boy that drove him.) Let us examine this horse's feet and body. He is working back on his base fast. His hind legs stand back at least one foot farther than he did when we pulled him out of the straw. Let us look at the heels of feet all around. They are all spread a quarter of an inch over the shoe. Take him off the wagon; let us spread these shoes out even with foot, plump; this foot is flattening and lowering. The sole is coming down, and foot assuming its natural shape. The structure is gradually coming into harmony of action. He is improving internally and externally. He needs no medicine, neither does he take any. He is in my care. "Drive on, boy."

Readers, I was working a large number at the same time. Some I helped, some I made worse. Their owners all knew more than I did, or they listened to that old "they say," and went the rounds from one shop to another, until their horses were nearly ruined; then back to me again. I did not have the horses in my care, consequently I could not gain anything, continually doing the same work over again. It put me in mind of a puppy pursuing his tail, the object of pursuit ever remaining at the same distance. I assure you, reader, it is somewhat trying to a man's powers of endurances. I have a little boy, Frank. He is fourteen years old now. Since the age of six years he has stood by these poor horses for hours, sponging and working their legs with warm warter, soaking their feet, caressing, and talking to them, while I was shoeing. He was all the help I had, and see what I did to the horses. He can talk horse, and see their suffering condition nearly as quickly as I can.

Two weeks have passed. Let us look to this horse that is drawing lumber. His feet are spreading over the shoe again. We must spread his shoes again. The fever is all gone. His feet do not dry up hard now. They need no packing. He can rest nights, and can get up, and lie down. Let us spread all of his shoes out plump with his hoofs. "Drive on, boy."

I had some hard work at balancing during these intervals at Mr. Bennett's stables of horses, and hundreds of other changes in all stages and degrees.

Here come two men with a fine pair of young horses.

"They say you can stop any horse from interfering. I can sell this pair in Elmira for eight hundred dollars if I can get him stopped. I will give you twenty-five dollars if you will do it. Get in and ride. See, he creeps with his hind feet."

"I see. You would not give me that amount of money if I did stop him."

"I will!"

I had heard that kind of bugling too much to expect any twenty-five dollars, for I well knew I would not get it. I saw at a glance the cause of the horse's creeping and interfering. "Lead in."

Reader, take this lesson. This horse was run over. Too much weight on inside, which I have explained; lever on toe. He crept for this cause. He hardly dared to step. Such ignorance! Claiming to know so much, and knowing so little! The man told me they drove about six miles, and went all clear.

"I guess the old blower has stopped him," said he.

He shied around for a while, separated that team for fear it could not be done again, then tried to get him back, but could not. Did I get the twenty-five dollars? No; this is one case in thousands worse than that in forty-one years' wrestling with the horse. Let us look after this horse whose feet we spread. Try and keep track of this one we are experimenting on. It has been six weeks since he was shod. That lever has grown some. His feet are lower from top of wall to ground than it was when we first shod him. It has been growing all the time. Expanding the foot lowers it. The structure is nearly in harmony internally. He begins to play and shows some signs of action. Let us shoe him. Reader, these are facts, not lies. Dress his feet. What is this we come to cupping out his foot, not seen before? It seems to be a mass of corruption, a watery, bloody substance I cannot describe. His feet are all the same. At that time I had never seen any so bad. Let us pare and clean out. There seems to be a sole under this corruption. Shoe again, so the foot will expand by the horse's own weight. It will go easy now. This horse goes in the team again with his mate. Do not forget: Like causes produce like effects on all horses. There is no safety unless you understand the principles laid down in this work. I saw this horse three years later at work. I did not go to him. I was riding through the village of Horseheads. Good-bye, poor horse.

I improved the condition of all of Mr. Bennett's stable of horses so much that he talked continually for me. That brought all of the shoers down on me, and the doctors in their rage knew no bounds. During this battle I waked up at two o'clock in the night. Hearing a noise at the barn I went out and found it all on fire. My horse and rigs were all consumed. That day was spent in clearing up the wreck. The next day I was again in the shop battling for the horse. The cripples still came pouring in from all quarters. This shop was small. I must have more room. During this time a man was stopping at Mort

Bennett, Jr's., hotel teaching a credulous but ignorant
people how to cure stiffened and blind crippled horses.
He lectured in the streets, and was hired to cure the
stiff horses. He charged three dollars. This was
done by bleeding in the plait vein. That would cure.
It would take a few months after the operation. The
blind were cured by the same butchery; in fact, it was
all mutilation. The horses there were a bloody-look-
ing lot. This was carried on for six weeks. These
horses all came to my shop at first to be shod immedi-
ately after the bleeding. I told them they were
fooled. I balanced between contraction, run-over
feet, and leverage as well as I could. Mort Bennett,
Jr., had a very fine dapple-brown horse six years old,
the best muscled horse, I think, I ever saw; in fact,
the best I ever saw on all points. He had the best
material in his feet. That is an indication of good,
fine bone. This horse I had been shoeing. He was
badly off his base on all of his feet, and badly air-
puffed on all of his legs, caused by contraction and
leverage. His feet were walled up behind about four
inches. They had been allowed to grow at the heel
to keep him on his base and prevent the strain on his
cords—always pare the toe and never the heel. He
had gone from bad to worse until he was nearly off
his legs. I had talked with Mr. Bennett about his
horse Mike (for that was his name) which was in this
condition the first time I shod him. I told Bennett
his feet were badly contracted and he could not be
helped shoeing. He must be shod. I did the best I
could. It would not do to cut his heels down. He
would "sore" in his cords. I balanced him up as well

as possible. I well knew what would soon be the result. In a short time this poor, suffering horse fell a
victim to that wonderful professor of great wisdom.
Mike had got so bad he could hardly hobble any
longer. Something must be done. Mike was sent to
my shop with a written order from this skilful opera-
tor, giving directions how to shoe him, which I well
knew were all wrong. I told the hostler to take him
back and tell that man to send no more of his butchered horses. I would not shoe them. "Tell Mort
Bennett," said I, "that when they all get through torturing Mike I will remove the cause of his troubles
for twenty-five dollars if you do not cut his cords off."
Of course that set them all howling.

Reader, you want to know what that order was. I
will tell you. It was "pare the toes down until they
bleed; cut none from the heels; shoe thick at heels;
thin at toe; no corks." I have already written about
the condition of these feet inside caused by contraction. This order was to cut and trim the foot so it
would have the appearance of a colt's foot to look at,
although it did not say so in words. Reader, would
that work? Would it remove the cause of that poor
horse's suffering? I well knew it would not. I can
tell in advance what the result will be. Caused by
such work as that, on all contracted feet the cup foot
suffers the most. The work was done on Mike's feet
by another shoer. I saw Mike tied to a post a short
time after, head down. His hair looked dead; he was
suffering; his knees tipped and shaking. Mr. Bennett
came along. I called his attention to it. I told him
Mike would gnaw his feet in ten days. They had not

removed the cause. They had added more to it. After a few months' standing that would be harder to cure than at first. That horse was a livery horse. He soon gave out. The hostler told me he was groaning and thrashing all night and day. The hips were worn through to the bone. I called in to see him every day in hopes I might rescue him. The hostler called to me, "Doan, Mike is gnawing his foot." Previous to this I had moved up-town, got in a larger shop with three fires in it, and had lectured on the horse in front of Mr. Bennett's hotel, and exposed that butcher called "doctor;" called a crowd while I was trying to teach the people what the cause was of all their lame and crippled horses. I was dragged out of the wagon I was standing in by Robert Colwell, the boss of the town. I stood just in the same place where that slaughterer had lectured six weeks before. He took some money away with him. He heard my lecture, and sloped that night.

This book is called the "Horse's Rescue." Let us go on with this horse fight; let us look after Mike. While the hostler and I were looking at Mike's feet Mr. Bennett's came in, and I called his attention to it. Mike had gnawed his feet at the top of wall full of holes, and his feet were raked all over with his teeth. While we were talking, in came the shoer with apron on. Then there was another row. Bennett said, "Brees, what is the cause of this horse gnawing his feet?"

"It is contraction."

He was right. Mr. Brees shod this horse from instructions this butcher had given him. It was not his fault; the butcher was gone before either of them touched him. He was in the last stages. The last time I shod him I well knew it. I told Mr. Bennett I could remove the cause of all his trouble in four days, take all of the air-puffs off his forward legs, and straighten his legs. How is that to be done? Make him natural. Put the colt's foot on him. Mr. Brees says that cannot be done. It must be if he is cured. Of course there was lots of money to be bet. I was ready for that. I offered to bet one hundred to ten— five hundred to fifty dollars—I could do it. No takers. Lots of talk. No help for the poor horse. I did not get him that time. He was led back into the stable to suffer. Do you know, I could not sleep nights. I must have that horse in some way. I talked and figured in all shapes. All were fighting; called me crazy; some called me a damned fool. I well knew if I told them what I intended to do I would not get him. I passed the stable going to my shop daily. I called to see Mike; his sufferings were intense— growing worse every day. As I was passing along by the barn Mr. Bennett said:

"Doan, I guess I shall have to let you have that horse."

"All right."

"Now, if you do not cure him you will not charge me much?"

"No; I will leave that to your honor. I want him for an advertisement."

"What security am I to have if you injure the horse?"

"How much do you call him worth?"

"One hundred and fifty dollars."

"All right. I will deposit the money in the bank for you, or I will state before these witnesses, I am good for it, and will pay it if the horse dies from any cause while in my care."

"How long do you want him?"

"Four days. Mr. Bennett, this horse is to be under my control four days. If you get dissatisfied during this time you cannot take the horse. You must take one hundred and fifty dollars and the horse is mine." Witnesses were called to that bargain.

Reader, you can see a man stepping middling high and fast going to my shop leading a suffering horse. In less than five minutes his shoes were off, and his feet were in warm water soaking. I had shoers at work in the shop; horses coming all of the time, lame and stiff, to get cured. Horses were going on from bad to worse, caused by shoeing. All wanted me to shoe their horses. I told them, "When I get this horse out of his suffering I will be ready for you." Some of them coming eight or ten times a day, would not let my workmen touch their horses. I had to put up with some abuse. Let them bawl, I must cure this horse.

Reader, here is a good lesson. Let us examine these feet, the forward ones first. Let us look at the bottom. There is no hollow in this foot. It is, to all appearance, a flat foot. It has been dressed in such a way that the inexperienced could not tell where and how it was changed from natural. The fact is, his feet are filled up. They look all right. His heels are walled up four inches high from coronet down, nearly as high as the foot is long from coronet in front to

point of toe. Being dressed in this way tipped his
knees and ankles the same. His head is down; he is
thrown off his equilibrium and base forward; that is,
over on his nose, or in that direction. This is not all:
the inside of his foot or structure is all out of harmony of action; his foot is not the natural size; it
has been cut down at the toe too much, and it was
ironed solid and dead. Before we dress these feet let
them soak in warm water while we look this horse
over. Understand, this horse has air-puffs on all of
his legs half way to his knees and gambrels. Let us
see what condition his hind feet are in. They are
contracted as bad as his forward feet. His heels have
been cut down; his feet are shoved forward by this
contraction. His toe is one inch too long; the structure is changed all out of harmony. He is obliged to
stand in this position and work. How is this horse
balanced? One-half of him is one way; the other the
opposite. What must the condition of this horse be
internally, and he obliged to draw heavy loads daily?
Ponder, think! this horse was fed eighteen quarts of
oats per day, still he was thin, hair dead, no gloss on
it. He ate ravenously, and grain passed him whole.
The fact is, he swallowed his feed without masticating
it, nearly crazed with pain night and day; all out of
harmony all over—internally and externally. I was
obliged to keep heating water all of the time. I
heated it on my forge. This poor horse would fall
asleep and partly fall, and tip the tub over and spill
the water. I had business enough, yet I was abused,
while I was at this work, by many different ones for
neglecting my business. They all had cripples they

wanted cured. My men I paid $2 per day. Customers
would not let them shoe their horses. They said they
could get their horses spoilt anywhere. No argument
could convince them I could not cure all of their
horses shoeing. Some I could cure, and had cured
They all wanted it done, and wanted me to do it. My
God! what a load on my poor back and head—nearly
all cripples. They were increasing on me. I discharged my help to save money. They were of no
use to me. I did not want to earn all of the money
to pay them to sit and look at me work. The fact is,
I was obliged to lock my shop and put curtains up at
the windows in order to go on with my work. They
kept up such a confusion I could not work. And yet
there was not much to be learned. It was their opinions and beliefs and abuse.

Let us see if we can go on with this work now.
This poor horse continues to fall asleep. We can't
pare his feet yet, he has had no rest. Some of the
pain has gone. We will have to let him soak and
sleep a while; we can't work on him yet. Some one
pounding on the door every half hour for admittance.
No admittance! I was alone in the shop. After I
had been annoyed awhile I paid no more attention to
it. That set them howling. All I could do that day
was to wash Mike in warm water, keep his feet in the
tub, and let him sleep. A good night's rest will help
us both. In the shop again in the morning, Frank
can keep Mike's feet in the tub, while I shoe and fix
up other cripples. I must have money to keep the
wolf from the door. Let us pare and cup out his
foot. Let us cut the heels down half. They are

that much too high at least. Pare none from toe; cup it out; it is filled up; it is hard as a stone. That will do, now. Soak him more; when it gets soft we will cup it more. The doors are open now. Mr. Brees comes in, apron on, to see and talk. His shop is nearly opposite from mine. All in a bluster, he said: "That is not doctoring horses; that is nursing." "Yes, this horse needed some of that." This uproar was kept up by many in the shop and all over the town. Being in the business of tracing cause to effect and effect to cause, I well knew what ailed them. Beat and excel them was what I wanted to do, and relieve the suffering horse. That is what I went there for. They were all strangers to me. Let them fight while we look at this horse. If you wish to learn a lesson, look at the horse we are working on. Now he stands braced out forward; now his knees are tipped, yet his cords hurt him. He can scarcely stand. How is that? We cut his heels down; that is the cause. Where is the weight of that horse now, or what is the effect of cutting his heels down? Before we did that I told you how his weight was divided, and the effect of it. This operation throws him off his base with two-thirds of his weight on his hind legs, which were also badly off their base before we cut his heels down. He should be balanced or poised in the center, and his equilibrium restored, that is, equalize his weight on the center of each foot, and balance him between the four. This looks like a rather hard job, yet it can be done. It will take a little brain-work withal. We must get rid of some hallooing around this shop; no one can do anything this way.

Lock the shop again! Let us finish cupping out his feet. It will not do to cut away much near the wall at toe; it is thin there now. Pare down next to the point of frog until you can spring the sole a little with a pair of shoeing pincers all around the frog. Pare the brace very slanting toward the frog. Care should be taken to cut the sole even. Feel with pincers. There, these feet are dressed for shoeing. Keep them in warm water. They have been days all of the time. In comes Mr. Bennett. He says he is losing two dollars per day by the horse lying still.

"Mr. Bennett," says I, "my time is not up yet. This horse's feet are badly contracted. I cannot fix him unless I have time."

Now we will make a pair of shoes, narrow web, for this horse has a very thick shell; six nails on each side. Nail clear around to heel—light nails. I am going to spread these feet. It will be necessary to turn the shoe-heels down a little to hold against the brace, so as to spread at the heel and take the strain off the nails and the shell. Nail solid, and clinch. The shoe should rest only on the shell all around; the foot should represent an inclined plain clear to the very edge of the wall, and be left so when ironed. All should slant toward the center of foot. The doors are open. It is nearly dark. Mr. Brees came in in a bluster when I was at work on the last foot, drawing the shoe down solid, he looking on. When done, I dropped the foot down, and said: "There, Mike, I guess I have got you fixed at last." I had been some time getting these shoes on to suit me. They did suit me, for the operation called out the remark I made.

Said Mr. Brees : "I think you have fixed him." He starts for the hotel, and tells Bennett I am spoiling his horse so I can buy him cheaper. That starts another uproar. I was in some fear they would get the horse away from me. Yet I did not fear them. I held the horse. Let us look at these feet again. Readers, you remember how they were when we first examined them. Now look in the bottom of these feet. There is a deep hole in this foot. It is cupped out deep, and yet it is not cut through in any place ; no blood drawn. His foot is narrow, and the shoe follows the shell around clear to the heel even. The foot has an elongated appearance, and it is so. The horse stands braced out, chest sunken in, shoulders dropped back, head down. He does not gnaw his feet. He soon quit that habit when I got him in my care, and yet he can hardly walk. "Mike, to morrow is the last day I can hold you on the contract. We must fix you for the night. You can lie down. That will save your cords. Your poor feet ache yet, and they are feverish. To prevent their drying up too much we will pack your feet with sponge, filled with water, and tie cloths on them. It will not do to tie them tight; that would give you pain. We will gather the cloth above the hoof, and sew it so that it will not hurt or stop the circulation of the blood. You must have a good soft bed. It is late at night. I will let you out of some of your trouble before the sun goes down another day." This horse is not in my barn, but in Mr. Bennett's, which is open to all. This work, when I am gone, must be inspected by all to see what I have done. Mr. Brees saw his heels cut down, saw him thrown back in this position. All talk. And I let them. I had to.

Mr. Brees's nephew had a good eight-year-old horse, which I wanted to get to cure. I told him I would do the job for ten dollars, as it would be an easy one. When I first talked with him I could not persuade him to let me have the horse, and I dropped down on the price. It was of no use. I was obliged to give it up. His horse's heels were walled up very high, tipped on knee; lame in one foot—lame in both, but he could not see it. I told the owner that if he was mine I would cut the heels down, and straighten the horse out very quick. He looked at me when I was talking. I walked away in search of another sufferer, which I should soon have room for.

Let us go and see how Mike is getting along. It is morning, and not light yet. All is quiet, all sleeping. We will have to go to the shop, heat some water, take the tub to the barn, and soak his feet while he eats his breakfast. Then we will take him to the shop.

It may be necessary to state the plan I intended to follow out in experimenting to prevent inflammation taking place by expanding Mike's feet so much at one time. I well understood this contraction and expanding principle that was constantly at work, caused by wet and dry weather, and tight and loose shoes. It did not kill all its victims, but a great many it did. I had now to spread the foot and flatten it out at once. If I did not do it, there would be no cure. The plan was to have the foot as soft and pliable as I could make it, so as not to hurt the horse. Then I must watch his feet by feeling to see that no unnatural heat

should get the start of me, and I prevented it by soaking and packing with sponge, as I have previously described, after I had spread his feet. I think this
horse's feet are soft enough to spread, and I am going
to try to spread them. The shop is locked; curtains
up at the windows. I am alone. I cannot hold his
feet and spread them; my arms are not strong enough
to do it in this position. I can make a screw, but that
will take me nearly all day, and my time is growing
short. This horse is expected to be on the road to-
morrow. It will be of no use to ask these fighters to
help me, and I have other reasons for not wanting
their assistance, which I will explain hereafter. I will
take Mike to my barn, and get my wife to hold up
his feet. The reader can see a frail woman holding
up the foot of a horse that weighs about twelve hundred, thrown off his base by contraction and leverage,
struggling to stand on one foot, which he takes away
many times; it hurts him so to stand. Do you know
she was in great danger of getting hurt? She weighs
about one hundred pounds. We were alone in this
barn, but we accomplished this difficult task. It is
two good men's work. We flattened his feet out by
spreading about three-fourths of an inch. Look at the
bottom now. It has the same appearance to look at
that it did when we commenced work on it, but the
cup is all gone, and the foot is flat. Who can tell how
this is done unless he sees the operation? No man.
This horse's heels are low now. I had cut them down
half or more, and expanding lowered them still further.
The horse's heels are wide; his foot is nearly round;
he has got the colt's foot on, and the structure of his

foot is all in harmony inside and out. His body goes forward on its base with weight in center of the foot.

It will be well to more minutely explain this process of preparing feet of this kind for operation. This horse's feet were badly rolled up in at the base of heels. Expanding raises the heels until the wall gets perpendicular. When it passes the line it lowers. In order to have it come in perfect harmony when expanding, you must use all the judgment you can command. If you leave the heels too high you will tip his knee; if too low, it will strain the cords, and either will throw the horse off his base to a greater or less degree. He will not move well, though it will not kill him. After the foot has been expanded, the shoe should not be taken off again in any case until the hoof has had time to grow and settle. Then it may be removed. If you should take the shoe off before, the foot would go back, which would create great heat, and cause great suffering to the horse; to get him out of which the same work would have to be done over again.

But we will finish this horse. As I said, he has got to go on the road to-morrow. Spreading this horse's feet did not seem to effect him much at first. He tried them by stepping first upon one, then the other. For a while I watched him. His head went up. I moved him moderately around the barn floor. At first he did not seem to have full control of his legs. I was in danger of being hit with his feet, and yet it was no fault of his, the change being so great. Let us give him a chance to recover; he is changed in many ways. Let us take him outdoors and lead him around. In no case at first get on the horse; he has all he can do, if he is changed on all of his feet at one time, to hold his own weight, until he has time to recover his equilibrium and balance. It gives him a sick and weakening sensation; all is changed so suddenly internally and externally. I led him on the back streets. He soon wanted to trot, and I ran with him, my hand holding his halter at the head. After running some time with him, his legs flying in all shapes, he seemed to go faster. We started through the business part of the town, which I was obliged to do to get to my shop. Mike swung me and carried me clear from the ground many times with his head. I could not help it. He was a powerful horse in all ways. He was coming to himself. I got him in the shop as quick as I could, locked the doors, got his feet in some hot water, rubbed and washed his legs, and rubbed all of the air-puffs off. The air-puff is caused by the skin being loosened by unnatural action of the feet and legs, which forms a vacuum, which fills with air. It in no case should be opened. The cause is removed. Let us rub the air out through the skin while Mike's feet feet are soaking in warm water. They will stay out as long as we can keep him natural. Nearly all horses are badly changed from nature when air-puffs appear in many ways and stages. Of course that sail through the town attracted the attention of many. Some said I was crazy; some called me a "damned old fool." I understood all of that blowing too well to let it effect me. I got in the shop and let them pound the door. I kept on a straight line and on my base, which they did not at all times. Let me paint a picture, while Mike's feet are soaking, of what I saw pass this shop one day. This is only one of thousands, which can be seen almost any day, and many times some days, if you have eyes. The railroad crossing was close to my shop. They had raised and graded so it made a little rise. I saw a horse and wagon coming, the horse thin in flesh. The wagon had two seats; three persons were on each seat, and there were some bags in the hind part of the wagon. A man on the front seat, with a hickory club as large as a broom-handle, five feet long, was pounding the horse, which could hardly move. The man was badly off his balance. I cast my eyes to the horse's feet. They were very long; his hind ones so long that he could not rise over the lever without breaking his legs. I stepped out into the road and stooped down to see what shape he put his feet in to get up that slight grade. No two feet were traveling on the same line. He was wringing and twisting to draw that load, and that club was playing on him constantly. He turned his toes some in, some out. He could not rise over that lever. Do you know what I thought at that time? Can it be possible the creator has made such a botch making mankind? This has the appearance of a perfect botch. It has occurred to me many times since that man was not in any wise perfected yet. He has still something to learn, and I continue to hold the same opinion. Let us look this wagon over. It comes in all right, as this work is called "The Horse's Rescue." This wagon is heavy enough for two horses; in fact, it is a two horse wagon. Every wheel makes a separate track, something as a snake would crawl; wheels grinding on the shoulders of the axle, which has not been oiled in

three months; so much gather that they are constantly
sliding on the ground, trying to keep on a straight
line. If they could move the way they are set they
would travel on lines that would cross each other sixty
rods ahead of the point where the wagon stood. The
driver being badly off his base, and out of harmony,
and the wagon running on the wrong principle, added
greatly to the horse's suffering. The poor h rse, also
off his base, trying to draw that heavy load up an inclined plain rising over a long lever, has rather hard
work; and yet he had to endure it, and it is no fault
of his. Look out for that lever! There is a power
in lever principle.

After this poor horse has dragged that load up hills
many miles, for his reward he is stabled in some old
rookery you could throw a cat through; cold, bleak
wind and snow howling through; some old rotten
clover-stack hay for his rations; the place where he is
tied and obliged to stand has not been cleaned out in
three months, and ofttimes more; his hind parts elevated according to the size of the pile.

Reader, the horse has four legs. It makes a vast
difference to him how he stands; give him his head,
he will tell you whether the position he is obliged
to stand is not right. How is he going to rest lying
in this position—hind parts elevated in this way?
Some morning he is found cast. Then club and boots
are used to help him up; if this does not raise him, a
chain is put around him, and he is drawn out of his
uncomfortable position. He cannot rise. The hard
treatment, that lever, the abuse he has been obliged to
endure, have exhausted all of his power of endurance.

And this is no uncommon thing; it is a very usual thing. Take a peek around. I have been peeking around many years. I went into a shop in Auburn city, and I saw two men turning horse shoes. I looked at them a few minutes, then walked away. In a short time I met one of these men on the street. He said to me:

"Were you in my shop peeking around to-day?"

"Yes," said I; "I was in your shop."

"I can beat any man in the state turning shoes," he rejoined; "I can turn one hundred shoes in just forty minutes!" All talking about the number of shoes made, and none about the principle the work should be done on. This man was badly off his balance. There is great danger of shipwrecks and collisions when driver, horse, and wagon are all out of harmony. But let us not forget Mike. The plan must be carried out to prevent inflammation taking place in Mike's feet. I was with him, taking his feet out of warm water for a time to see if I could feel, by placing my hand on his hoofs, any change of heat arising. I did not perceive any change. I thought my plan was going to work. Of course there was no sleep for me that night. This horse was out of my control in the morning. He would be put on the road the next day. There was no use in protesting; they all knew everything that was worth knowing, and what they did not know was of no use to any one. I had to take all of the chances and do the hard work. When daylight came you might have seen a tired man standing by this thankful horse soaking his feet in warm water, and washing his cords, helping them to change back to their natural place to give him as little suffering as possible. That plan holds good yet. It does help and relieve the suffering sooner than if it was not done. There is one thing yet to be explained, that is, how that process of spreading Mike's feet worked. When the foot contracts the sole rises in the center. That pushes the structure of the foot up in the center and raises it out of the cup or coronet at the top. Expanding lets it down. These wonderfully wise people could not see how this was done. The hostler swung his hat. "Doan has cured Mike. I don't know how, but he has done it." The shoes had to be looked at and patterned after. They are just the thing. Of course they must steal the secret; it is a big thing. Those lips on the shoes at the heel are not of much use. He has cut the heel down. Mr Brees and his relative (the one who had the stiff horse I tried to get) are going to cure their horse I saw in the shop. I could sit in my shop and look in theirs. This horse being buckskin in color, we will call him Buckskin. Before we commence on this horse we must see Mike off on the road. He was to let out. I was at the barn and watched him. He was whipped up when he turned around the corner and fell on his knees. He was not yet used to the change. But he was driven and hurried off his legs, which I told them over and over again, they must not do. I thought to myself, "What is the use of trying to do anything with such a pack of damned fools?" I am not yet done with poor Mike. We will let him sail a while. He is still in very bad shape.

Let us see what they are doing for poor Buckskin.

We can see from my shop. This is a good time to
trace cause to effect. They are cutting his heels down.
That is right so far, but they have left the toe at least
one inch too long. They have got his shoes patterned
after Mike's as near as they can. He is coming out
of the shop. He has to be pulled out, for he can
hardly move. What is his condition now? He is
thrown back off his base the furthest I ever saw. Let
them work; it's no use to say anything to them; it
would only set them to bawling. The crowd gathers
around this horse. All talk; no one knows what ails
this poor horse. The owner looks rather worried.
His horse is in a worse condition now than ever, he is
braced out so bad that his back sinks down. If you
should get on him he could not hold your weight. He
can hardly move This horse stand now on the opposite side of the street from Mr. Brees's shop. It is no
use to talk to them. They all fight me. Let us walk
away. We will watch that horse and see where his
suffering ends. I have many horses to look to. They
need my care. I can't relieve them all, but I will do
all I can. I work for the horse, not the man. I
nearly always had from one to four horses in my barn.
Some my own; some belonging to others; and which
I was caring for in different stables, and my shop was
to be kept up. I had almost a night and day business
to watch the changes and effects in all stages I was
determined to get master of this complicated business.
I was sure there was a way out, and I would find it,
let it cost what it might. It is morning again. While
going to my shop I passed the place where we left the
buckskin horse. He was about two rods from where

we left him the night before. His owner was with him, and looked worried. He had a keg with a swab in it, and was daubing his feet. I walked in. I felt sorry for him and his horse. Said I, "What is that stuff you are putting on?"

"It is tar, kerosene, and soft-soap."

"Mr. Brees, it is of no use. You had better give me eight dollars. Your uncle cannot steal this great discovery. (I know not whether he was his uncle or not, but their names were Brees.) The principle is what I want to lay down correct in this work. They had disabled this horse completely by throwing him off his base, cutting his heels down. They had lengthened the lever so much it had sprung his back down and thrown nearly all of his weight back of center. There he was fastened, and was obliged to stay. They knew no way out of this serious trouble. I would have helped them out, but they would not take any lessons. This was early in the fall. The horse was missing, and I lost track of him for a long time. I think it was in the month of March following that I saw Mr. Brees doing his chores at his barn. I went in. There lay this Buckskin horse. I asked, "Has this horse been lying in this condition all of this time?"

"Yes."

"Does he stand up?"

"He can, but lies down nearly all of the time."

"Are those the shoes you had put on last fall?"

"Yes."

"Have they ever been reset since?"

"No."

"Mr. Brees, it would be my advice to pull those shoes off, cut off his toes some, pare the toes down well; cut no more from the heels; give him room to travel around, and put no more shoes on him for six months. That will help him some. It will not cure him by any means."

He did so. I saw him driving Buckskin many months afterward, and he was quite a horse. His knees were tipped yet, but if they had done what I did to Mike's feet after cutting his heels down, and shortened his toes a little more, he would have gone back on his base or nearly so; instead, it threw him further off. It would have straightened his legs at the same time. Mike is in trouble again, but it does not surprise me. I have got used to this business. It has become a common thing; I well knew he would be. He was in a very bad shape when he started from the barn. He has been on the road about two weeks. Mr. Bennett said:

"Doan, there is something wrong about Mike's hind parts."

"Yes; there always has been since I knew him."

"Can you fix him behind?"

"Yes, if I can have him in my care and control four days. Nobody must use or exercise him but myself during this time."

"All right," says Bennett, "go ahead."

It is a hard job to get this horse's hind feet in the soaking tub and keep them in. My little boy Frank cannot do it; that's a man's business. I shall have to neglect my shoeing for a while almost entirely to attend to this horse and those I have in the barn. Mike was

was divided against himself. His forward parts were changed so as to let his weight go back on the base, which it did when he stood still. But his hind parts were constantly pulling his fore parts off the base—always on a strain—when he was on his feet (which I have explained). When traveling he had to draw his hind parts with his forward parts over that lever, caused by contraction, drawing his hind feet forward under his belly. It hurt him so that it caused him to amble. I saw when he left the barn what position he was thrown in. But what could I do? They were all so smart, and they were losing so much money by their horses lying still. Some people are always stopping spile holes and leaving the bung out. The fact is, Mike was divided against himself. How are we going to put him in harmony of action, balance him in the center, and take those large air-puffs off? The principle we applied on his forward feet will work behind more than it did forward to change him. It seems to effect all horses more on their hind legs changing them back to natural, and it affects them behind more to change from natural to unnatural. I soaked Mike's feet, spread them, and carried out my plan as nearly as I could under the circumstances and the surroundings I had to contend with. The sole is the guide in spreading all feet. Some require more, some less, according to the degrees of change. No rule can be laid down. If the foot is skilfully dressed and prepared, you can spread until the sole comes down nearly flat. You must look when you are spreading to see if you can see it come down. It must spread at the same time clear to the top of the wall. If you do not see it flatten after you have spread a little, you must stop and walk the horse around or run with him. Spread in pairs so as to drive the sole down. Look and see how much it has come down. Soak in warm water, spread again; continue to move him around until the sole is down flat. Some horses are so bad their feet are pushed clear out of the cup at the top and pinched in at the bottom. If great care is not taken in preparing the foot for this operation, the foot will get pinched at the top of the wall, the bone not having room to go down between the cup at the top. It would not kill the horse, but it would cause him suffering for a few hours, then it would matterate and cause a flaw in the hoof. It should be spread enough to give it room to go down before he is driven much. These are cases of long standing, as a general rule, but there are many exceptions to that. If you do not cut the heels well down you will be likely to get him pinched, for this reason : it would spring the foot out at the bottom, which would throw it together at the top. You must see it go together both top and bottom.

Let us look at Mike after spreading his hind feet, and see where he has gone to, caused by spreading the foot half an inch. His body has all gone forward on the base; his back has lowered across his loin; his forward parts are relieved of their constant strain. He is united again; that is, the cause is removed. Some hard work will have to be done yet to make him comfortable. The air-puffs have all gone around on the front side of his legs. It hurts him. He stands up on his toes. He won't put his heels down to a flat rest. He must be got down on his feet one at a time, stand him in a tub of warm water, while those air-puffs are rubbed out through the skin. This shop is locked, curtains up. I am alone. This is a heavy and power- ful horse. There is no other way to get him out of this fix except to compel him to stand on one foot, which must be done by raising the others. It is "business" to hold up the hind parts of that heavy horse, he standing up on his toe, and keep him in the tub and rub his legs at the same time, and change around and keep it up for three or four hours. Walk him around the shop. Soak and rub. Hold him up while doing it; get him nearly down on his heels; air-puffs are nearly all gone. Open the doors; out we go. Run with him awhile; tie to tree, take up one leg, rub the other, the horse straddling and throwing two-thirds of his weight on me all of the time. Change legs five or six times, then run with him again ten minutes; tie to the fence the same. Up with a leg by main strength; rub and change. Keep this up. Run and tie for two hours or more. Then run with him to the shop; get both of his feet in the tub of warm water. He stands down on his heels flat rest. The air-puffs are nearly all gone, and some hair is rubbed off in spots. That will soon come in again. His trouble is over for a while. I had no time during the operation to listen to bawlers. I could hear them any time, and not go out of my way. It affects the air-puffed horses on their hind legs all in this way, and they have got to go through this or no cure. It is business, but it brings them out all right in a short time if it is done as it should be. Mike is changed, or the cause is removed. He should have a chance to recover from the effect of this great change.

His hind feet were not so hard, and it did not take so long to soften his feet. After this hard day's work for me and Mike, I got him in his stable and made him as comfortable as I could by packing his feet with clay (other packing would do as well, the object being to keep his feet moist). Thus I left him and went to my barn, where I had business for more than half of the night exercising, caring for, and watching the effect of changes on horses, and the time it took to recover from the change. These horses were different from Mike, which I will explain by and by. It is morning. I must go and see Mike. I was at the barn before there was much stir in town. I found Mike in a bad fix. The hostler was there. How is this? Some one has been driving this horse, and has nearly driven him off his legs. He stood up on his toes, and could hardly stand on his hind legs. The hostler told me Mike was out all night. Of course there was some loud bugling. It could be heard ten rods at least. This hard work is to be done all over again to get him down on his heels. It will take me all day, and it did; besides, it has caused Mike unnecessary suffering. I pulled him out of the barn. I had got in the middle of the street. Mike was hobbling upon his toes. Mr. Bennett, hearing the uproar, came to the front door of the barn.

"Doan, what is the matter with that horse?"

"It is the change."

"I don't like that kind of change."

"I will have him all right by night. If you want

one hundred and fifty dollars come and get it, and let me have the horse"

He walked away. The same process—soak, rub, run, and tie to go through with again, all caused by their not doing as they agreed. How do you like, reader, the business I am at work at? Let us stick. Never give up the ship. I got Mike in the barn at dark that night. He was down flat rest on his heels, and his ankles were weak. I bandaged his ankles, packed his feet, and left him again, and told them he must have rest or they would have him down. The next day I soaked his forward feet and spread them a little. They had grown some. It had been nearly three weeks, the foot flaring from top of wall down to tread. If it was not ironed. I would be wider and not wear off, which it could not for this reason: the wear was on the shoe and not the hoof, and it was ironed so it could not expand. What would be the result if I did not spread his feet a little? The sole would raise, he would be thrown off his base again, according to the degree of change of which I have already written. He has six nails on each side of these shoes, put there on purpose for this operation. Let us draw out two of these heel nails on both sides. We have spread his feet and given them liberty. They will spread with his weight if they are kept soft. Do not get discouraged. With all of the hard work we have done, he is not right yet. His toes on his forward feet have more lever. They have grown since his shoes were set three weeks ago. Spreading his feet at the heel will help him some, but that does not shorten the lever by any means. To have him right he should have had all his feet fixed at the same time. I cannot do away with that lever. If I could it would be one of the biggest things man ever invented. I can see no way except to kill the horse; then it would cease to grow. Putting on trash to stop a foot from growing too fast, or to make it grow faster and ironing, causing great fever and heat, and preventing nature from having its course at the same time, is rather antagonistic and claiming a little too much power. Horses must, if ironed, travel on unnatural feet all of the time, with the lever at a greater or less degree of length. Before I get through this work I shall tip over more than you dream of with that lever power. I started to go to the end of the whole business. We will put Mike in his stable again, pack his feet, all four. The ignorant never have seen anything wrong about the horse's hind feet, which should have equal care. His hind feet and legs are necessary to him. He sends himself off with his hind legs, and draws more with them if he is as the creator made him—which a very few are that have been shod—he does not stay so but a short time. We will have to let Mike sail on the road three or four weeks and watch him. Take care of his feet; no one else will. Neither will they pay for doing it. They had rather sit with their feet on the back of chair tops and smoke. Doan will shoe, balance all the cripples, and cure them and keep them cured. He is willing to do it, and we are willing he should. We can drive the horses off their legs, and then go to him. It is not necessary for us to be broken of our rest, neither is it any use for us to know how he does it.

Reader, this has been going on in this way for many years. I will say right here that I never received but five dollars in forty-one years aside from the price of shoeing, except what I made by buying and trading for these cripples, curing them and letting them go again. That five dollars was paid to me by Mr. Hatch, of Auburn city. I gave half of it to my brother, J. J. Doan, who did nearly all of the work. Mr. Hatch gave me all I charged, and would have given me more, but that was not my object. I wanted to introduce this great discovery, and relieve the suffering horse; and that is what I am writing this work for. I have put thousands of dollars in the pockets of others, and will continue to do so if they will read this work, and study the horse. It is no trouble to look at a horse. They are before you nearly all the time. Let us look at a pair that are passing now. These horses are in Horseheads, the place I am at work in now, and shall be for some time to come yet.

This pair of horses are about six years old—a matched pair of browns. They are valued at one thousand dollars. I have looked them over in the stable many times. Let us take a side-view of them in harness. In order to see these horses as you should, you must see two pairs at the same time; and yet there is but one. You should see this pair first, as the creator made them, before man tried to improve on them. They stand with their forward legs back of straight; heads up, neck arched, head in, with mouth closed; weight equalized on center of all four feet; balanced in center; no strain unnatural in any way; their head pointing on a straight line, and feet all pointing on a straight line, providing they have had their liberty to exercise and wear off their feet as fast as they grew, and been trimmed and cared for. They stand the perfect natural horses, as their creator made and intended them to be. Now we will look at them and see man's improvements, trying to make horses over, or, in other words, excell the creator.

I had looked at this pair of horses almost daily for over a year, passing and repassing. They are fitting these horses for market for coach horses; it will not do to say anything to them; neither it will it do to point out any defect in them, or tell them how to improve their movement; it would set them bawling. Readers, let me tell you their suffering condition, then you can step out and see thousands all around you; and, travel where you will, you cannot miss seeing them if you have eyes and use them. I will try to describe the suffering condition these horses are thrown in. The causes are many, and hard to describe. As this work is tracing cause to effect and effect to cause, we will begin at the first cause. That is, the fallible being, man, is ignorant of natural laws and the suffering produced by abusing them. These laws are the creator, and I recognize no other. The horse is the innocent and helpless sufferer, and is part of the creator's works. Through ignorance he has been made a great sufferer—the greatest of all the creator's works; and I send this work on its mission for the purpose of rescuing them from their deplorable condition; and I appeal to the supreme court of heaven to back me up. Man's courts would be of but little use to me; no justice can be had in them. Let us return to this pair of horses. They are all thrown off their base in many ways, which I have explained. Like causes produce like effect. This is a pair of matched horses. This is to show you how well they work and come together, and shows their action and movement together, and what a hard time a man has that has no knowledge of the horse, and the cause and effect he is obliged to contend with, and does not know it. The nigh horse is badly off his base on his forward legs, and a greater degree on his hind legs. Two-thirds of his weight is on his hind legs. His feet are all different lengths, and all run over; some traveling the same line, some not, and none on straight line. He wrings his feet at every step, and ambles on his hind feet. This movement is caused by contraction, leverage, and run-over feet, produced by ironing and not balancing him and equalizing his weight; and that is not all. Contraction has lengthened the lever on his toe to a far greater length than you are aware of. You cannot see it beyond the toe of his foot, and yet it is. This horse is nearly always lagging behind his mate, unless he is constantly urged up with the whip. Let us look over his mate; he is the same, only not quite so bad off. On his hind legs the lever is not quite as long; he single foots. They are both thrown back off their base badly, and are obliged to stay so, for all the great wisdom their owners have contained in their heads. Let us look at the gaggers and see if they help the action and movement of these poor tortured creatures. Readers, remember these horses are drawn down by contraction and leverage, braced out and fastened there.

Now they are trying to make them carry high heads by over-draws and checks. What is the effect of this? It adds greatly to the suffering of these horses. It throws them off their base further than they would otherwise be. Their necks sink down, their noses stick straight out, and they have the appearance of camels; the lines are so arranged they turn their heads out nearly one-quarter around, when they should point on a straight line when the horses are traveling on a straight line. And that is not all. They have been kept in the stable not very light. They are brought out in the sunlight gagged up, and obliged to have the sunlight pouring in their eyes, while the driver must have a shade over his tender eyes and head. This is a rather hard picture, but these are facts.

Let us look at the driver; he sits on the front edge of the seat; he appears as though he was sitting on a jug. He wants to go faster, his hands extending out toward the horse's loin. With each hand he has the appearance of pushing on the lines. He does not like the movements of his horses, but is ignorant of the cause. It does not take a very clear observer of human nature to see the unrest and worry he is obliged to endure, caused by the awkward movements of his horses. Let us watch him circle them. He will be obliged to make a large circle, or they will be likely to fall. See, he is turning them to the left. The near horse's head is drawn by the lines the course he wants him to take. His mate's head is drawn the opposite. Reader, is it not curious that these horses cannot move together? Let us look and see how they handle their feet. They have but little knee action. They drag one foot over the other. If they are hurried, they will be likely to tread on their own feet, and on each other's. The near horse sags back on making this circle; the off horse swings his hind parts out against the trace.

There are all degrees of this awkwardness, according to the change. This pair are not very bad yet. They were sold, I heard, for one thousand dollars, to a gentleman in Bath, Steuben county, N. Y., though the story is not to be relied on; but it can be done any day, and is every day, all over the world. Horses are sold and bought, and large prices paid for them, in all stages of change from natural, and ofttimes they are in the last stages. It does not seem to affect the sale or price, for this reason: the people are ignorant of the horse, and the position he is in. I could have balanced them better than they were if I could have shod them in my shop, by dressing their feet, making the levers on the toes of equal length, shoeing them all around at the same time, having the hind feet in pairs, and the fore feet the same, and work to one-sixteenth of an inch both on shoe and foot, eye always on run-over feet. I could keep them from showing their defects by limping, for they limped equally on all their feet. I have balanced thousands of these **poor horses** between contraction and leverage and run-over feet in forty-one years, and while I am experimenting nights I am doing all I can at this hard business daily to get money to keep my horses, which I have no use for only to see if I can find out what ails all of these poor cripples. My close and careful work

on the horse's foot gave me a good run of business;
more than I wanted. Many thought I could cure
their horses by shoeing, for this reason—they did not
limp. That was all they knew, or could be taught
about it. They would come pouring in from a distance, sometimes thirty miles, and ofttimes more.
Some I could help, some were out of my reach, and
I could not help them by shoeing; but I could get
them out of their trouble, if I could have them in my
care a short time.

"What will you charge me," they would ask, "to
cure my horse?"

"Well, it is worth from ten to fifty dollars to do it.
It depends something on what ails the horse, and what
condition he is in when I commence on him." About
nine out of ten would rail out on me in this way:

"When you get ten dollars out of me for shoeing a
horse you can consider yourself damned smart;" or,
"When you fool me you will have to be smarter than
I take you to be."

That kind of talk I have heard daily, and many
times a day, in the past ten years. Before I get
through this work I will show you these smart men
could be fooled badly. I experimented on the horses
a little, just to see if I could fool them. I did not
take any of their money.

Mike has come around again to be shod. He has
done some traveling. His shoes are nearly all worn
off his feet. These shoes were flat all around, and
were nearly worn in two at the toe. Their wearing
off saved Mike's cords some. His forward shoes has
been on seven weeks, his hind shoes four weeks. He

looks fine; his hair begins to look bright and glossy, and yet he has been traveling out of harmony some, for this reason, that the lever on his fore feet has been the longest. If it had been the longest on his hind feet the effect would have been more serious, which I well knew when I set him sailing. Mike always had a good friend peeking around, watching and caring for his feet, to see they did not dry up hard. Mike, we will put the polish on you this time.

Reader, I have laid down the principles for expanding the foot by shoeing a little on the Kentucky hunter mare. That principle is right, and all there is, except to spread it out at once. We will make the lever on all of Mike's feet equal length. The colt's foot he must have. All is nearly in harmony of action; structure is nearly right. We will shorten the lever a little shorter than natural; his feet are growing all the time. It will wear the toe of shoes off some if we do not put on corks, which we will not do. In this way we can fix him so he can go six weeks very well, with good care taken of his feet. Then he will want to be changed back again.

Reader, how would you like to follow this business for forty-one years? I will tell you about the pay before I get through this sail. Perhaps you will like it better. That is what all seem to be after. I have an iron-gray in my barn. I always, or nearly always, had from one to four, seldom more than four, at one time. This gray is five years old. It was stiff when I took it to cure. It is not mine. I have forgotten the owner's name. It is no loss to me, however. I took his horse to cure. The bargain was this way: I

was to cure his horse for ten dollars. He was to pay
me for the feed while I had the horse in my care, or
furnish the feed, and he chose to furnish the feed. He
owned three farms. He told me if he continued to
have as good luck as he had had he would soon own
more. He came with the feed. It was a small jag of
wet wheat straw taken out of a stack half rotten—not
fit to bed a horse for me. I said nothing. This horse
was thin in flesh. I fed her well with good feed of
my own. She was so badly thrown off her base that
she could hardly move or turn around on her forward
feet. She was quite natural on her hind feet. I told
him it was something of a task to get her back on her
base; it would take me about two weeks before he
could take her home. This is in the winter. I shod
horses in my shop days, and had these cripples in the
shop, soaking and preparing them for spreading their
feet. Nights I was in the barn or exercising these
horses. While changing them it affects them. It
would set them howling worse to see these horses
while going through this change. It would put me in
danger of being mobbed; if they did not do that it
would bother me some about my work. I could do
better when they were all asleep. I had all I could
handle without being bothered. Night after night you
see a man in a barn with an overcoat on—cold winter
nights—heating water in the house, washing and rubbing these horses' legs; sometimes in the street running with them; sometimes driving; sometimes riding
them. When you commence to change them there is
no stopping. Then you must go through. I had no
help; I had to do it all. I stood alone, nearly all on

my track. During this horse fight a Cornell student
arrived in town, a graduate under Prof. Law. He put
up at Bennett's hotel. He had a large stock of knives
and instruments. They were polished nicely. What
use he made of them I know not. I have no use for
such. He had a lot of bones of horses' legs that had
been spavined and ringboned. He told me they were
all curable but one; the pastern joint where the ring-
bone is located had grown solid together. That, he
said, was incurable. I told him cases where the bone
was so badly affected as they were it was out of the
power for any man to cure, for this reason: he could
not remove the cause. The bone is full of holes; the
enamel is all off; the bone is ragged and rough. You
cannot make it natural and smooth again. Of course
that set him to howling. He was an effect doctor. I
a ked him if he ever saw a horse's foot expand or
spread at the heels at once three-quarters of an inch.
No; it could not be done. They say it would spo l
the horse. You would be arrested for cruelty to animals. "Look here, professor, are you personally acquainted with that personage, 'They Say?' I have
heard so much about him I would like te see him and
have an introduction. He seems to be very wise.
Nearly all appeal to him and quote him. If I could
get acquainted with him I might get him to help me
cure horses. I am spreading horses' feet and curing
them every day, and nights too, and no one is smart
enough to tell how it is done. I can't see any danger
from They Say. This new-born babe on the horse had
just started out after graduating at Cornell University. He will learn, like all others, by experience. It

takes time and practical work, like all other great things.

Reader, let us go on with our work. This iron-gray had been shod before she had grown up to her natural size. Her feet were not their full size, when first ironed, and were held by the shoe from growing natural; the sole raised. It served her as it does all others; threw her back off her base, and held her there, and she partly grew up in this condition. It is a hard job to get such cases back on their base. In about ten days I did accomplish this hard task. She had good knee action. During these ten days I had some cold rides in the night when all were asleep. Her shoulders did not come back as easy as some. They must be worked back by drawing loads after you remove the cause, and you must keep it removed; that is, keep the structure of the foot natural, and watch that lever at the toe. This mare's head is up; she moves very fine; not many move better. I will drive through the town and see what the effect will be taking this sail. They all seem to look at me. I do not see one looking at this mare. The fact is they do not know her. The horse led through the town ten days ago was foundered; that is incurable. It is the same color. No argument could be produced or used to convince them it was the same horse. The good care and good feed with it had changed her wonderfully. I drove past my old friend the blacksmith and shoer. The better success I had the more his wrath increased. There were several men with him standing in his shop door. He commenced as I was passing to rail at me so I could hear it. I drove on. The thought came to me, "This is rather hard after ten nights with but little sleep, and days the same." I had others I was working on in different stages of change toward natural to care for, and they were not all in my barn. It was the last straw that broke the camel's back. This man had dogged me nearly one year, and had no cause for doing so. I had had as much patience as any man in that town, but it was exhausted. At last I must shake that man off. I have carried him long enough. He is no good to me in this work, and a damage to himself. It will be better for us both. So I turned and drove back and pulled up in front of his shop. The parties were all there.

Reader, I assure you this was what I did not like to do. I had tried to be friendly with Mr. Brees, and was then, but he did not seem to look at it in that light. I did not want to shoe horses. I wanted to cure stiff and crippled ones if I could get enough to live out of it. I could not cure all of these horses shoeing; that was what made the most of them stiff, with the bad treatment they are are obliged to endure. I asked Mr. Brees if he had plenty of business.

"Yes; what of it?"

"I think it would be better for you to attend to it then. Mine is no part of yours. If you meddle any more with my business I will tell the people you are slaughtering more horses than any man in the Chemung valley. They will believe me as quick as they will you. I want you to shoe. The more you shoe the better my business will be. You slaughter and I will cure and keep still. We will build up a big trade.

Try that. Do not set any more troublesome fellows on me." That stopped that racket.

But let us dispose of this iron-gray. I kept this gray two weeks. The owner took her home. She had her spreaders on. I told him he must put her in the team and work her; it would help her shoulders by drawing to come back to their place. She was nearly all right. I saw him drawing coal with her. She was traveling fine, and on her base; good action. I charged him to not take her shoes off. I would do that when it was time. I told him to drive around so I could see her when he came to town. He lived about three miles away. He did not pay me for keeping, shoeing, or curing when he took her away, but I was safe enough. He owned three farms. I was very busy. I thought he would come around. I had no time to run after him. He was to come to me. Time passed, and I did not see or hear from him. He was almost a stranger to me when I took his horse to cure. In about six months this man drove up to my shop with this same mare, the stiffest I ever saw. If one can be much stiffer than another, she had the extra touch. She was thrown back further off her base than she was when I first commenced on her. I was surprised to see him and her too. I asked him what he had been doing. He told me Dave Townsend told him to pull those spreading shoes off. They were pulled off in his shop soon after she went out of my control. This was the reason I did not see him around. Mr. Townsend ran a shop in Horseheads. He tried hard to make the people believe I was crazy. I was very much in his way. He worked a very small field on the horse. He might run a peanut stand. He did for a short time. The poor horses would not have suffered quite as much if he had kept at that business. He caused this poor horse suffering that I cannot describe, and this man came back to me to have me get her out of it again. He said he would try me once more. If I did not do it this time he would give me up.

"How did she act after you pulled her shoes off?"

"I thought she would die. I had to stand her in cow manure all of the time."

"It would have been better for her if she had died, then she would not suffer. She is not much use to any one as she is. Dave Townsend can get her out all straight. He does it with angle-worm oil."

I did not touch her, neither did I get anything for what I had done. This man I will have to let go free. I think it is wrong to abuse a perfect fool.

Reader, we have another case to dispose of. Here stands Mike at the same post where he stood nine weeks previous. Let us look him over. No man could tell by looking at him if he had not known him and seen this change take place by degrees. He has been almost daily on the road and improved all the time. His feed, when I commenced, was eighteen quarts of oats per day. It was reduced to twelve in a short time, for this reason: Mr. Bennett had a partner in his business. He started to go to Elmira, his wife with him. He went part way and came back, drove up to the barn, ordered the feed taken off of Mike, ordered another horse. He told them in the hotel, "I was not afraid of him; my wife was."

I was always peeking around.   In the evening I
walked into the hotel.   There were several around the
bar.   Mr. Bennett had a number of new bits.   They
were counseling about the best bits to hold Mike to
keep him from running away.   I told them Mike was
coming to life; he wasn't running away.   I would
drive him on a slack rein, and there would be no danger in doing so.   There was no reply.   I walked away
and let them fight.   They will be scared worse when
I get this horse balanced in the center.   At that time
I had not fixed his hind feet.   Let us look at Mike
after he is balanced standing at this post.   I shall
never forget that horse.   While looking him over in
all points I pronounced him the best horse I ever saw
at that time.   I have not seen his mate since.   There
is a great change in him.   I stood up by the side of
him.   I am five feet seven inches tall.   I put up my
hand, and could just reach to the top of his ears.   He
stood natural and easy; his hair was sleek and glossy,
and as handsome dapple-brown as I ever saw.   "Mike,
you are as near as the creator made you as I can make
you; and yet with all the hard work I have done on
you nights and days, your owner is as ignorant as ever
he was.   He does not seem to realize this wonderful
change in you.   He cannot see you gnawing your feet,
suffering night and day; shrunken and shriveled up;
all air-puffs; stiff and sore; hair dead, and you nearly
so, but he tells the people there was nothing the matter with you, only a little road sore.   I wanted to cure
you for an advertisement, Mike.   I am well paid now
if you would only stay so; but I well know you will
not; that lever will grow, contraction will take place,

and you have the ignorance of your owner and many others to contend with. I will care for you all I can when I can get a chance. No medicine has been used on you internally ; no butchering. The cause of all your trouble has been removed by expanding your feet and dressing them, and making them as your creator had made them before they were slaughtered by ironing them. Hiram McConnell, the veterinarian of this town, tells me that that butcher I drove out of this town cured you. I suppose he had reference to those shoes he ordered Mr. Brees to put on, that caused you to gnaw your feet. Now I would like to know, in the name of reason and common sense, how McConnell came in possession of so much wisdom about this complicated matter." He was an agent for the railroad company, and was obliged to be at the depot all or nearly all of his time. He kept his medicine to cure horses there. I cured without it. He did not cure these stiff horses with all of his trash.

The fact is, some wanted to drive me out. I had good friends before I left that town. Their craft was in danger. I think I will drop in there soon again, and try them another battle on the horse ; I have not quit yet. I must clear away some of this rubbish before I can go on with my work.

Mr. Bennett and I had a few words about shoeing a horse ; I shod his horses. He had traded and got one. It was a strange horse to me. I shod it, and it interfered afterward. He wanted me to try him again. I did, and charged him for setting them over. He found fault. I told him I was tired working for him for no pay and no credit. If he had given me credit for curing Mike I would not have said a word.

"I paid you for shoeing."

"Yes."

"Then you have no honor."

So much for that hard job. Let us go on with this horse fight. It is paying business.

There was another racket around Bennett's hotel. Mike ran away. Mr. Bennett was in the pump business. A party of three went out in the country to set a pump. Some pumps made up the load. Mike was the propelling power. Jack Racker was the agent and boss. He was a reporter for the papers in this town, and was a clever fellow. He was quite a bugler—a good match for me on that. I was sorry to see Jack hurt, for he did get hurt; his face was badly bruised, and shoulder injured. There was no use of my telling them anything before or after the shipwreck. I was in the last stages of lunacy. They knew it all, and I let them have their own way, and kept on a straight line. Mike spread them all out along the road, pumps and tools, and made a bad shipwreck.

While all this racket is going on I must go and see Mike. I am quite a hand to talk with horses. I enjoy talking with horses better than I do with some men.

"Mike, how did you come to shipwreck those fellows so?"

"I did not have room enough for my hind legs to have full swing."

"I see the skin and hair are all off your cords, above your hocks; that must have hurt you?"

"It did; the cross-bar of the fills was chawing my legs at every step. You see, since you made me as my creator made me, I need at least eighteen inches more room to clear my hind legs. I can make long strides now, and I like to do it; it scares them some, but if they will give me room I will scare them worse, if my feet are kept as they are now."

The fact is just as it is stated above, and that was the cause of the wreck. As this work is called "The Horse's Rescue, and Cause and Effect Book," this comes in all right. Such ignorance adds to the suffering of the horse.

The old, nearly worn out spreading shoes that I pulled off of Mike were ordered to be carried to the hotel, where they were looked at and commented on. "These are the shoes," they say, "that cured Mike." These shoes had no curing properties in them; it was the principles I worked on—removing the cause; nature did the curing.

Mike was a natural trotter, and if he had been in good hands would have been hard to beat. He was ambitious, and had great powers of endurance; for strength and muscle I never saw his equal. There is no use setting any price on him. The price of horses is governed and regulated in many ways—sometimes by fear, by fancy, by the size of a man's pile, and how he obtained it, and the owner's circumstances and surroundings. This horse Mike was soon missing from his stall. I missed him, for I had visited Mike's stall daily for nearly three months, though I did not always find him there. Where he went I know not. I never saw him after the wreck but once, that I can remem-

ber. Fear was the cause of Mike's changing hands.
He might get stiff and lame again; he might shipwreck some one again. And ignorance was the cause
of all.

There is not much use trying to teach a man when
he thinks he has all of the knowledge. Such a man's
atttention can be attracted with children's toys quite
easy. I have seen children wearing men's clothes. It
is no indication of wisdom. A man's grandfather may
give him three thousand dollars, but that does not add
to his knowledge. It does have an effect sometimes
in this way; it will cause a man of small intellect to
wear a pair of boots three inches longer than his feet,
soles about one inch thick, causing him to toe out and
interfere, knocking his heels at every step; his head
thrown back of a perpendicular line, with a segar in
his mouth lacking only a few degrees of sticking
straight up; hands in both pockets nearly to elbow.
He can bend a little every five minutes to look at a
fob chain, but he could not bend enough to see the
lever on the toe of a horse's foot. It might strain him
across the loin, being thrown back off his base in a
small degree, on the same principle that his horses
are.

I do not want you to think a man's foot is any comparison to a horse's foot. I speak of this to show the
difference. Ignorant people are always making these
comparisons. Mankind nearly always take their boots
or shoes off nights, and sometimes days if they hurt
their feet. I have worn mine a good many nights, and
clothes too, while working on these suffering horses'
feet. The horse is obliged to wear his shoes day and

night if they do hurt. For many reasons the owner
does not want to pay for moving the shoes, and he
does not feel the pain the poor horse endures. I wish
they all could for twenty-four hours; that would be
long enough; you would hear the loudest bawling you
ever heard. Man's feet do not grow in length; his toe-
nails grow; if he does not cut them off he will be
likely to have his attention called to the end of his
toes if he wears boots; and this is not all; his foot
has joints, and his foot has no shell; it turns up at the
toes when he walks, if the soles are not too thick and
are made of leather, if they are three inches longer
than the foot; but it is rather torturesome to break
such boots in in any weather. When they do not get
soaked with water it hurts at the top of the instep—
where the ringbone is located on the horse. They will
slip up and down at the heel, which wears the skin off
the heels, but that will grow on again if you can stand
the torture a few hours each day. It will be necessary for you to have rest from this suffering quite
often. If you can stand it until these boots assume
the shape of sleigh-runners, it will be more easy to
raise over that lever. I notice they do not all accomplish this difficult task, and they toe out, which runs
over their boots. Then they interfere and are constantly wiping the mud off of their boots on their
trousers at the ankles at every step. But this is no
comparison to the horses' feet. Take all into consideration. The shell of the horse's foot does not bend
as the lever lengthens, if it is not ironed, without producing injury in some way. If it is allowed to get too
long it may cause it to sink down in front, or it may

turn up a little. If it does it must split at the toe or break nown. I have seen colts' feet split from point of toe to top of wall on both forward feet from this cause that never had a shoe on, and have drawn them together with nails. That is the best way I ever tried. It stops the cracks from springing apart at the top. If you can do that on any plan the new hoof will grow out sound. If you cannot do that, it will crack as fast as it grows. There is no bending that lever on the horse's foot, no matter how long it is made by ironing, or allowed to grow, without producing injury in many ways. It has joints and bones, but they are clothed with a shell, and when out of harmony of action the result is fearful.

The horse's foot cannot be compared to man's, and yet this is not all. He has four feet and legs to be balanced on, which I have already remarked.

Men ask sometimes if horses take cold from pulling off their shoes! There is as much reason in asking this question as there would be in asking if there was danger of horses taking cold sleeping in the barn-yard with the gate open. It all goes to show the ignorance of men concerning the horse. Their feet do get cold, and the horses get cold all over and shiver and suffer; they are as sensitive to pain as mankind; and irons nailed on their feet, with a row of nails driven inside of the shell half way to the hair, does make their feet cold in frosty weather. The frost will follow the nails, which are very close to the membrane. Nearly all shoers fit the shoe so narrow the nails start inside of the shell. The feet being bound up, and the structure all changed from natural, causes heat. That will warm the foot some, but does not relieve the suffering.

Here came Mr. Bennett again with another stiff and lame horse—a light-limbed young horse.

"Doan, what is the matter with this horse?"

"I should think you might see."

"He wants his feet soaked, don't he? How far have you driven him?"

"About eight miles. It is all 'sposh.' I should think if that was all he needed he would be cured now."

"His feet must be well soaked. The best way to soak horses' feet is to drive them in mud and water. Your horse's feet are badly contracted, and that is not all."

I walked away. This horse was badly contracted, and he had two sets of feet on him, a very long lever, and a heavy, bungling set of shoes, entirely too large in every way, if his feet had been properly dressed. I did not touch that horse. It looked to me as though Mr. Bennett had gone to buying stiff horses for me to cure for nothing. That would have been all right if I had chosen to do so. It is good business to have others work for you for no pay, and grow poor all of the time yourself. Some get very wealthy that way, and sometimes you can hear them brag about their wealth. Some folks may think it is the part of a man. It may be in some cases; in this case it was a total failure. I will have to let this case go in with some other rubbish I have just cleared away, and pass on.

It is uphill business here all alone; no backing out. When I first came in this town I was very cautious.

My experience had taught me it was rather dangerous to tell a man his horse was stiff. It would hurt the sale of him, and yet they were nearly all of them stiff that had been shod—lame in a greater or less degree, and they were in a worse condition in the Chemung valley than in any place that I ever had been in at that time; and I heard as much horse talk as in any place. They all claimed much knowledge of that noble animal. My! is it not queer? It is so all over. I have taken the pains to demonstrate that.

Soon after I came in this town I was looking over the stables. There I can be found as quick as in any place. You can see me in a horse doctor's stable, or veterinarian, as they are sometimes called. His name was Hiram McConnell. It was Sunday. Hiram had a little time that day He was caring for a horse while his feet were soaking. He seemed like a clever fellow. I talked with him some about his horse, which was a trotter. He was called Billy Crawford. This horse, I heard, cost Hiram eight hundred dollars. That may be the truth, or it may not; folks can lie. That matters not, for it will not cure these horses. I could see Hiram had some unrest about his horse. I ventured a few remarks. I told him he could not cure him soaking his feet; he was not working on the right plan.

Hiram, being rather a quiet fellow, took it all quietly and kept on at his work. I looked over his stables (he had the best in town) and walked away. This horse had contracted feet. He had shoes on. His feet needed cutting down at least one-third. It would have helped very much. At the time I first looked at

Billy he could have been cured very easily. I tried to
get this horse. Some weeks after I had a little talk
with Hiram. He said he would give one hundred dollars to have him cured. I told him I would cure him
for that. I thought at that time I would be able to
get him soon. I was very anxious. He was going on
from bad to worse, which I well knew. I visited him
often; it worried me very much. I did all that was in
my power to get this horse to cure. I finally gave
it up. I watched Billy the same as I had others I
was at work on—one belonging to a lady. She was
an agent for sewing machines, and traveled on the
road. A Mr. Wright took care of her horse, which
was a six-year-old roan pony. He had got to
be such a cripple on his forward feet he could hardly
hobble. With all the wisdom Horseheads contained,
they could not tell what ailed the horse, neither could
they get him out of his trouble; but they could call
me a brag and a damned old fool. It does not take a
very smart man to do that, and I got lots of that kind
of music. They could do that easier than they could
cure horses. All that ailed this horse was that his feet
were all cut off; that is, the shell was nearly all cut
off. His feet were not of the natural size. He was
on his base. His feet were not contracted. He was
ironed down solid, and was very sore, caused by this
botch-work. I soon got him out of his trouble by
giving his feet room and packing them. In a short
time he had his natural feet, and sailed all right. I
told Mr. Wright he must keep his feet soft. I did not
mean soak his feet all of the time when he was in the
stable. All at once this horse became dead lame

about three miles away, and could hardly be got
home. Wright brought him to the shop to find out
the cause.

"Mr. Wright, what have you been doing? You
have soaked this horse's feet too much."

"It was some trouble to soak this horse's feet. I
have got a ground floor in my barn I dug a hole in
the ground and filled it with water, and tied him so
he would be obliged to stand in it."

This horse had flat feet. After his feet got to be
their natural size the fever was gone, and they needed
but very little soaking. He had corks on his shoes,
and the frog did not touch the ground. The weight
is in the center of the foot. Driving on dry roads his
weight drove the sole down; or, in other words, he
went down through the cup or top of the wall. His foot
was rounding on the bottom, which affected the coffin
joint badly and threw all out of harmony of action.
If it had been muddy it would not have been as
likely to go down. The frog would have had a rest.
This often happens on all flat feet where the frog has
no rest. It is easy enough to get it back, dishing the
shoe, as ignorant people do, to get it off the sole,
that only makes bad worse. Most people, in cases like
this, will run from one shop to another until their
horse is nearly ruined. To pull off the shoes is all that
is necessary. The weight of the horse on the frog
will push it back to its place. I told Mr. Wright not
to soak the horse's feet. "Put him to night on the
floor. In the morning he will be all right. He will
lie down; his feet will dry; his weight will be off
them, and as they dry the sole will rise up."

In the morning Mr Wright said the horse was as well as ever it was. Five years afterward I saw this same horse and the lady that owned it driving it forty miles from Horseheads, where I was at work. I talked with her about her horse. She said he had been all right ever since I got him out of his trouble, and yet if I tell any one what I can do, and do it, they do not all see me do it, and there is always plenty to fight and bleat, calling you a brag. It is almost as dangerous to find out anything new as it was two thousand years ago.

We will go on with this horse fight in this town. They begin to worry some about my spending my money, and yet not a man has paid me a cent for curing his horses. I shall have to stop spending my money soon, curing their horses for nothing, or some of them will hang themselves. Then I shall be blamed for that. They do worry so there is danger. We will try it a little longer, and run the risk.

Here comes Jack Bennett with the American Star stallion. Jack is a wide-awake fellow; got lots of cash and horses. He likes horses, and has lots of time to play with them. His star horse is a natural trotter, and is the nearest natural of any horse I have seen in or around this town yet, or was before he was slaughtered in his feet. Jack sent his horse to school at Corning to teach him to trot. He went to Corning to to see how Star was learning. He soon saw that something was wrong. He could not trot as well as he could when he left home; and that was not all. There was danger of his being spoilt. Star had white legs nearly to his gambrels: the blood was running down

on the inside of his legs, and there was danger of
cutting his legs off. Jack brought his horse home.

"I can beat those fellows myself," said he. "This
is the last time I send Star to school. Doan, what is
the matter with this horse? He never cut his legs before in his life. There must be some cause. He is
not right in some way. I can tell when my horse is
right by driving him five rods. I want you to fix
him."

"All right."

When Jack was around talking horse I had to stop.
I could not get a word in. He could talk louder and
faster than I about what was the cause of this horse's
trouble. They had shod him in this way on his forward feet with flat shoes. The shape was well enough.
The shoes were concave, but there was too much flat
rest on the shoes. The surface for the shell to rest
on was five-eighths of an inch. The shell is three-
eighths in this case. The way the foot was dressed;
one-quarter inch rest was off the shell and on the sensitive part of his foot. It made his feet sore. They
were ironed down solid and dead ; not a particle of
give. The concussion soon caused soreness. Let us
fix his hind feet. The cause of his legs being cut
was they had been shod so they both toed in ; the
weight was unequal on his heels. They had run over a
little—enough to cause him to hit his legs on the outside heels of his forward shoes. He did not spread
his hind legs enough to pass clear. He was out of
harmony of action all around, and that was the cause
of all. After I had shod him, Jack said :

"I will try him. I can tell in driving him ten rods if he sails all right."

Jack came back.

"Doan, he is all right."

This great science of working on the horse is called bragging by men that have no knowledge of the horse.

To-day while stopping to rest a little I was called a brag. "They will not place much confidence in your book, you are such a brag." ·He quoted that old fool "They," as all ignorant people do. A man might think, to hear such men talk, that *they* or *they say* was the highest authority that could be appealed to—equal to the creator. The man that perfected this work never paid any attention to what They Say says; if he had, it would never have been perfected. I would like to have some of these wonderfully smart teachers tell me how to introduce any new discovery without writing or talking about it. You cannot put any machine in practical operation without talk to introduce it; and of all the machines I ever saw, the horse is the greatest. When he is as the creator made him, he is the most complicated. Men have tried to improve this machine, and have spoilt nearly all they have worked on, sooner or later, by ironing their feet. No proof is needed; neither will it admit of denial, for it stands in bold relief all over the land, go where you will.

Let us go to the fair at Elmira and see the show of horses while there. It will be best to keep quiet. Some big guns on the horse will be there, and we can learn more to get in some quiet place and look on. It will be no use to talk horse here; you will set them on you, and that will bother you in your lesson. The only way for the inexperienced to learn these great truths is to watch these horses when they are in motion. They cannot tell by seeing them standing. The natural horse will stand sometimes, if he is all right, with his legs sprawled in many ways, and yet be all right, or nearly so; and he can be made by dressing his feet and shoeing, to all appearance, while standing, to look and seem natural to some. When put in motion, he will show his deformed and suffering condition in many ways. This panorama of horses that is passing is hard to describe. They have all been brought here to be looked at, and to look at them is what I have come for. The more the horse is deformed and changed from natural, the worse he is used. If he is stiff and sore, he must be driven around the track and scored, to warm him up preparatory to trotting. He must be jerked, whipped, and sawed, swung nearly off his feet, being all out of harmony of action, which causes him to cut his heels, and pound his own legs to pieces. These horses are nearly all thrown back off their base, or tied up in some way or degree on their feet. They do the best they can. See how that lever they are obliged to rise over throws them up. They go into the air, tangled all up; break, trot forward, run or trot behind, some on one foot, some on both; some lame on all four feet; and yet it is not seen by these great horsemen, which I shall show if they are honest by the premiums when they are declared off. Some horses burst their feet in many places at top of wall, caused by contracted feet. Then they pull off and quit. Such horses cannot trot fast. They foot short and rapidly. They are all tied up on their feet and out of harmony. Their feet pain them night and day; they cannot rest day or night. The driver does not feel the pain these poor horses are obliged to endure, but that does not prove this suffering does not exist, neither does it remove the cause, which cause is ignorance. They are all trying to make fast horses, and this process ruins nearly all and makes them slower. The next object is money, and ten lose that while one makes; the country is no better off for all this wholesale slaughter of these horses.

If the people understood the horse, and would take good care of him and keep him natural, or nearly so, it would be a pleasure to ride after him. The horse likes to sail when he is all in harmony of action. I like to drive a good, sound horse; and if you will take good care of him, he will sail you as far in a day as you want to ride. In this race after money the horse is the greatest loser of all. He loses his sleep, caused by pain; he loses the use of his feet and legs; his life is shortened, and he finally loses that before he is in his prime.

I cannot go on and describe all of these cripples. I have written enough to show you where to study the horse. Every foot on one horse may vary in degrees of change, and it throws him out of balance on each foot and leg according to the degree of change.

Billy Crawford is here, and is showing himself; he was quite a trotter once. He is young yet, but is lame on one forward foot, that is, he is limping. He seems stiff all over. He ambles and straddles. The lever is too long. He cannot get there; he is a long way behind. It is the best he can do If he was untied he would show them some good stepping. It is no use trying as I am now. These are facts, and can be seen at any fair in the United States.

There is a cause for this condition of the horse, and it cannot be removed by bawling at me. You will not learn these great truths that way, nor will you any other great science. The horse is a machine, and so is man. The horse is a horizontal machine, and more complicated than man; for this reason: he has four legs and four feet to balance his weight on, and he must be balanced in the center at the same time, and the structure of all four feet must all be in harmony of action when he is put in motion, or you will see a bad movement, and the motion will cause heat and soreness.

You let him stand still. When in this condition he suffers greatly. The soreness will disappear some when he is still. As soon as you put him in motion it increases. The more you run him the more he is obliged to suffer, while in this condition. And that is not all; he is divided against himself in many ways, and on no two feet alike. There are hardly two horses to be found that are out of harmony alike, and and in the same degree of change.

A man (that is, he thinks he is a man; he is large enough in bulk), knowing I was writing this book, told me he would give a dollar to read it.

"But I don't care anything about your book," said he.

If it was a child five years old talking like that, we ought to, and would, make some allowance, but when men thirty or forty years old talk like that, there is not much hope of their improvement. As though a man could read any book without first caring for it. That is what causes all improvements and progression.

This man told me, a few days previous to this conversation, that he had set seventy horse shoes in a day in winter, and the first horse did not get in the shop until ten o'clock, and it was dark at about four o'clock. If he went without his dinner it would give him six hours to do this work. I have no doubt that he did the work; it is too often done. Notwithstanding all this boasting, owners of horses, when you hear a man telling about setting seventy shoes in six hours, if you get in his shop you will be likely to take your horse home with two sets of feet on him, and in a worse condition, or soon to be, than if he had not touched him.

I must brag a little. I can outbrag them all; that is what ails them. If they could beat me bragging they would be all on an equal footing; but they can't —I never met a man that could. But no man ever heard me brag about the number of shoes I set in one day, for I knew that the people were not all fools, and that they could and do see something.

There is no use talking; it will only end in confusion. I have no recollection of setting over forty shoes in a day, and that was spun out to twelve hours; but it was fairly done—nothing extra. The pay was small, and I was obliged to do more than I ought, in order to keep the business up. I have spent one whole day—and faithfully to—shoeing one horse that was going to make a trot, to please the owner, and charged no extra pay; but I followed the horse to watch his movement and action; and many are the horses I have shod in forty-one years, and followed in this way.

This show of horses is not all over here yet at this fair. I am here following Jack Bennett's star stallion. He will not show himself until these amblers and shufflers and single-footers get through. Here comes one down the track. My golly! How he does amble and single-foot.

This is Hiram McConnell's champion stallion. He is not old. He was once called a trotter. He belongs to a horse doctor, and his home is in the same stable with Billy Crawford. He is a long distance behind in this great horse show. This horse I have looked over many times before he came to this horse show of speed. There is a cause for this slow, stiff, straddling, single-footing, ambling motion, and I well know what it is; but there is no use talking when you are all alone in the fight for the horse. Their time is more taken up in trying to make themselves and others believe I am crazy. This was red-hot in this town. The more big things I did on the horse, the crazier I got. My, my!

This stallion was changed from natural in many ways, and in many degrees of change, and every foot was changed different from the others, and different degrees of change; and he was so sore he could hardly straddle around the track. Sometimes, when looking at the deplorable scene, I feel bad, and think there is no use. They brag and call these horses all sound, or nearly so; there is nothing the matter with them.

Reader, I have gone off by myself and rolled and laughed about these horse shows at many fairs, and you can do the same when you study the horse. After you read this work you can see it as quick as I do, if you will give your attention to it. If you do not you must suffer loss, and your horse will suffer. No man on this earth, that has got any fine feelings, would allow his horse to suffer if he could help him out of it, and knew how to do it. You must learn as I did. It need not cost you forty-one long years of experimenting, and the hardest practical mental and physical labor that a man ever did, and a power of opposition. My God! it makes the tears come in my eyes and my head ache, and back, shoulders, and hips too, to write about it. You need not go through all of this. Tears are no proof that a man is a baby. Before I get through this work you can tell better. I have to laugh sometimes at these horse shows. I cannot help it. I would not if it made the horse suffer. I do not laugh at the movement of the horses. It does me good to laugh. It is no use to tell you what I laugh about. I suppose these great horsemen have seen me off by myself laughing, and that is one reason why they called me crazy. What did I care what they called me, as I well knew they did not have any knowledge of the deformed condition of these poor horses. They were nearly all that had been shod in this condition. In some degree you can see this any time where these poor horses are put in motion.

Here comes Jack Bennett with a double team. This

is the first time I have seen Jack to-day. He has got
his sorrel trotter and American Star stallion together.
Star takes the outside track; the mare is a good trotter, see them sail. The mare is running nearly her
best, and Star trots. Not a break, no whipping, no
jerking around; they go several times, Jack swinging
his hat over his head. Star is the most natural horse
I have seen in the Chemung valley, and Jack knows
how to keep him so. He does not drive him to death.

Jack stopped at the stand and blew his bugle and
laughed at them some and drove off. He does not
trot his horses for money, and does not keep his horses'
shoes on. This horse I shod for this surprise for
Jack, a few days before this great horse show; and as
soon as the horse got home I went, or Jack came and
got me, and off came Star's shoes. He stood on the
ground floor.

Jack was a great talker, and I tried to beat him talking. When we got together you could hear some of
the loudest horse talk you ever heard, because we
tried to talk each other down; and each had to raise
his voice a little at every word, and it would get to a
yell. Jack could beat me talking. Jack told me all
the objection he had to me was, I talked too much;
and that was all of the fault with him, but I could
beat him balancing horses.

Let us look at this tirade of cripples going home
from the fair. Tirade is a proper word to use, for some
of these horses were tied up on their feet, and in many
ways caused by bad shoeing and ironing their feet, and
some had two sets of hoofs in growth. Of all the
sights a man ever saw this capped the climax. I have

told you of their movement on the track. I cannot
describe this scene; they are deformed in so many
ways and degrees, straddling, stiff, poking along,
nearly all got cards on their bridles. They took premiums according to their class and degrees of worth,
and yet not one of these horses was entered as a cripple; neither did the judges know they were cripples.
If they did they were not honest. Reader, what
chance do you think a man would have with such
judges if he was to be tried for lunacy for talking
horse? I had to look sharp and keep watch of my
surroundings in this town. I have not yet got done in
Horseheads bawling horse and experimenting on the
horse to know the cause of all of these horses' troubles,
and they are many. I must buy and work on many
to prove and test their ailments, each separately, in
order to know if this principle of working on the feet
would remove the cause of this trouble and suffering
condition of these horses. This is no easy task, but
it must be done in order to know. Opinions and beliefs are not knowledge. These things must be proved
by experimenting. It occurred to me after I had
worked on these horses some time, that it ought not
to cause any inflammation by changing these horses
back to natural by this process—spreading the feet—
if it was done right, and if I did not go beyond natural, that is, spread too much. It is rather hard business to work on these horses almost night and day to
prevent inflammation taking place after spreading. I
must test this thing. I must have another horse. If
it kills him it will be my loss, and no one will know
what did kill him.

This horse I prepared in the most skilful and care-ful manner, to test this operation. I made the foot very soft by soaking in warm water—water is all I ever use—that is natural; that is needed, and is the best; it leaves the foot all right. I want no trash on horses' feet for me. Just at night I spread these feet, that is, the two forward feet, and let the sole down flat or nearly so, and exercised him some; put him in the barn, fed him, and thought I would sleep to-night. I did not go to the barn until morning. I lay on the lounge—not any sleep that night. It was not the loss of the horse that kept me awake. I never stop for money when I want to test anything. I went to the barn, the horse was eating hay; he had not got over the change yet. I well knew he would not without more exercise. I felt of his feet; they were cool; no heat unnatural in them. That's a big thing to know; that will save me lots of work, and that is not all; it proves that in changing the horse toward natural, if done right, no heat and fever or inflammation is produced by the operation; if he is put in motion when in harmony of action none is produced. After this operation the cause is removed, the unnatural heat is gone, and the foot does not dry up as long as it is kept so. This old shell on some of these horses of long standing is hard and dried up, caused by great internal heat that closes the pores in the shell; it seems dead, and there is not much life in it, and it does help to soak and keep this old shell soft. This old dry shell cannot be all cut off at once, and if you do not keep the bottom spread it holds the new from growing natural. There have been **sets of feet grown and cut off, of long-standing cases.**

When this old dried shell is removed, and new growth of hoof takes place, the old shell kept spreading at the bottom so as to allow the new to grow natural, you will find, if you try it, if you keep the structure of the foot in harmony of action, you have removed the cause of more suffering than you ever thought of There are some cases I have seen that are incurable; some of long standing are quite easily cured; some of short standing are hard to cure; all, or nearly all, are caused by ironing their feet, and ignorance is is the great cause of all this suffering the poor horse has to endure.

Reader, I do not want you to understand by this experiment that there is no use in washing these horses' legs with warm water and packing their feet while they are going through this change. I have already written that this treatment holds good, and always will, and you must always take care of their feet. After the fever is gone they do not want much packing, neither do they want much soaking. After they have got back on their base they want work in mud, snow, water; that's what they want. Standing in the barn will spoil the best horse ever was, and driving him when he is out of harmony of action will do the same.

Here is another experiment. I prepared one of these contracted feet and let the sole down to its natural place. It required five-eighths of an inch to do this on this foot. I at first measured all of the feet before I spread. I do not now, unless I want to know how much I have spread the foot, or to show others; the sole is the guide in raising and lowering if it is

prepared right for the operation. The colt's foot in
shape is the object structure of the foot—all in harmony of action—when done on all feet of horses and
mules this is the point to aim at. After spreading
the foot, as I have above written, I waited six hours;
the horse was not lame. I had spread both of his feet
the same; he was doing well: no heat in his feet unnatural. I closed or contracted his foot one-eighth of
an inch by measure by pressing the shoe and foot together to see if there would be any heat caused by
this operation unnatural; and how long it would be
before it would take place, and what degree of heat
would take place by this sudden change toward the
unnatural. The horse pointed his foot out instantly,
and was lame. I was shut up alone in my shop. I
put my hand on his foot; I could feel the heat arise;
the horse's suffering seemed to increase with the heat,
and did. I left him in this condition about fifteen
minutes; I had learned all I wanted to on that change
toward the unnatural. This was a sudden change the
wrong way. Unwilling to see the horse suffer any
longer, I put it back to its original place, one-eighth of
an inch, put his foot in the tub of warm water a short
time, then moved him around the shop; in less than
fifteen minutes the heat was all gone, the horse stood
up straight with his weight on the center of his foot.
The man that allowed Dave Townsend to fool him by
letting him pull the spreading shoes off from that iron-
gray got in this hot business; if they had been long
enough on to get settled and grow more they could
have been taken off and no trouble would have arisen
from so doing. He drove her home over the hubs,

about four miles. It was winter, and that helped to set this heat a-going, and it increased according to the degrees of contraction, and she went off her base according to the degrees of change from natural; and she went fast, too, and he lost money fast, and she continued to suffer, all caused by Dave Townsend and the owner of the horse's ignorance. This principle of heating horses' feet holds good; expanding too much will cause heat according to the degree of change from natural. So much for Dave Townsend's skill on the horse.

Here is another experiment in this town. George Woodrough is a horse trainer by profession. George was my true friend, and so was his father, Dr. Woodrough. George's stable was close to mine. I let him in my stable after I had been working on these horses, and he knew what I did on their feet. He had a very fine mare, valued at five hundred dollars; he told me she hopped behind; she was not trotting well; she would go level at a moderate gait, but when he wanted her to sail she would tangle up and hop on one foot; he could not keep her level; he said she had a record and she was going back; I told him it was a limp; he wanted me to look her over; at that time I had not seen her move; I told him if I could not tell which foot it was she hopped on I could not do anything for her. I must see it in the foot.

"George, if I tell you which foot she hops on without seeing her move you will think I know what ails her, won't you?"

" Yes."

" It is the nigh foot; that is the foot."

" What do you see there ?"

" Look in front of these two feet, they are not mates ; this lame foot is contracted ; look at the heels : this lame foot is not as wide at the heel as its mate by half an inch, the sole is raised, the lever is longer, structure out of harmony, there is more strain on the tendons, it hurts to raise over that lever which is not seen at the toe ; it tossed her up on that side and throws her off her balance."

" Can you level her ?"

" Yes, if you will let me."

George had not seen these horses at that time go through this change. I told him I was afraid he would be scared. This is a valuable mare. He said he would not. This was about ten days previous to the fair. He wanted to show her at the fair ; he had a mate to drive with her ; he wanted her level. I told him I must spread her foot. I told him how she would be in a short time, and he must follow the directions, and pay no attention to the bawling, for there would be lots of it. " We must exercise her," said I, and you must do it. I have all of the horses I can handle now. If you get her ready for the fair I will operate on her, and you must do the rest of the work. I will tell you how." I thought I would come out in daylight on this job ; George was not as much of a night bird as I was. We got her in the shop and went at it. I prepared her foot and spread it ; it took George two days to soak her foot to get it soft.

I took this mare right through the business part of this town, limping and standing upon her toe. A crowd soon gathered around to know the cause of the

trouble she was in. In order to keep clear of this
rabble I was forced to battle with them nearly all of
the time, so I might be able to go on with my work.
I was obliged to tell them a lie. I told them it was a
very bad ankle sprain, and kept on moving her around,
going through the same process in getting her down
on her heel to flat rest. This process they all have to
go through; some it affects more than others. It did
not last long with this mare. I took her in the shop,
closed the doors, and worked on her there. I soon
got her down all right, no limping. Out I came in the
street again. This is quite a business town. I led her
all over the town; the crowd gathered in many places
to learn how I cured her so quick. I told them I had
a way that belongs to me. George and I took a sail
after her around the town and out in the country to
see if she was level. She went all level, no hopping.
This foot was spread half an inch. Of course it must
have time to get strength after this change, and settle
and grow before it could get strong. After this hard
day's work with this horse and others I thought I
would walk down town and see what kind of a racket
I had made.

I walked in the Riant House. I got it slap in the
face. "You're a dam purty man, you are. You have
spoilt George Woodrough's five hundred dollar mare."
"You publish this in the papers; you can spread it
faster and it will be less trouble." This man ran a
cooper shop on the bank of the canal. He came to
me after this to get an old cripple cured, not worth
curing. He bragged on her very much. He said she
came from Orange county; she was a fast sailer. I

did shoe her, but she was so much out of harmony
she was not worth curing. If I had tried he would
have fought me, so I could not do it. Such fools as
these I heeded not. This mare went to the fair, and
I followed her to superintend and see that her foot
was not allowed to get dry. She had not had time
enough. The drying up of the foot would raise the
sole up. If it was but a small degree it would affect
her action at that time. She showed all level. In six
months after this fair two men came to this place and
bought this mare and paid a big price. They came
from Williamsport, Pa. George was to deliver her at
that time; my time was all taken up experimenting.
I did not shoe any horses. In the morning George
was going to start with this mare. I went in the
stable. It was hubby. He said he was going to ride
her. It is a long journey. He had her shod for this
journey. I cast my eyes down to this mare's foot.
"George, this mare will be very lame before you get
through. Why, look at them levers on the toes. She
never can stand that." It is no use describing this
botch job.

"I have got my pay and pay for taking her through,"
said George.

The men that did this skilful work on this horse's feet
were my warm friends. This valuable horse was
slaughtered the first time she got in the shop after all
my hard work, and yet I charged nothing for my
extra work. They got pay for spoiling her, and they
would like by their actions no better fun than to see
me crucified or got rid of in some way. That I was
not ignorant of. Stay I would as long as I wanted to,

and did, and worked on those lame and crippled horses of all kinds.

George returned. I asked him how he got through. He told the man the cause, and they removed it by removing the shoes, and that is the way to cure thousands of lame and crippled horses, and never nail or have nailed on any shoes unless it could be done by men that have more and better brains than these men seem to have. A man's work corresponds with the caliber of his brain, quantity and quality and degrees of development, and when this is understood a man will not be in so much danger of being killed for curing stiff and lame horses as I was in Horseheads. It was a hard job for me to cure, and keep cured, so many horses where there was so much slaughtering. They could slaughter twenty times faster than I could cure. One man could do that, and there were hundreds at it, and those that I had cured they would slaughter over again if they could get them, and yet I tried to keep up with them. If they had thought of that they might have got me in the asylum. I was experimenting, and they were ignorant of this fact, and had but very little knowledge of the horse or any right or wrong principle to iron a horse's foot. Still they had some power to control others to fight me, and did, and yet after they got through they were as big fools as they were two years before. As for knowledge of the horse, I never learned in that way, and I never saw any one that did. I sometimes fight with my mouth to clear away the rubbish, and have to yet. If I paid attention to all who advised me, I could never get through. They seemed to differ so on all points, and make none. It would drive a man like me crazy. My mind is so weak, and I have been told so very often I can hardly tell myself. If I am not crazy now there will be no danger.

Let us go on with this horse fight. It is time to go and see Billy Crawford. Poor Billy, I can't get him. He has got to die by inches. He stands in a box stall. He is not seen out on the road lately. I must see if I can find the cause. I well knew he would go on from bad to worse. Poor horse, if I could only get you how quick I could relieve you of some of that suffering. I can come close to you; your owner I cannot reach. He did talk with me about you once, and I thought I was going to get you to cure, but that was all wind, and that will not cure suffering horses. There are lots of that kind of horse doctors all over the land, and yet these poor horses like you are owned by them. They cannot cure them, neither will they let any one else. I have performed some cures in this place. I should think he might let me have you; you are of no use to him now that you are past work. I suppose he is afraid you will take cold if you do not have shoes on. My God! what is the use of this poor, dying horse having shoes on, standing in the stall month after month? If some good and wise man can tell me I would like to know. These shoes holding the foot from growing natural, and two sets of feet in growth on at that. This work is to expose all such ignorance as that. Look at this horse; eyes sunken and staring, and glossy hair all dying. He is very nervous, eats ravenously, pot-bellied; he stands with his back humped across the line; head drawn down,

and is so stiff and sore he can hardly move. If
he does it hurts him fearfully, and yet the owner of
this horse is a horse doctor. There is a boy sixteen
years old that takes care of this stable of horses. He
was blamed for this horse's stiffness, which I well knew
he was not to blame for, and I am going to rescue him
before I get through this work. I talked with this boy,
and told him the cause of his favorite horse's trouble,
and told him he would go on from bad to worse unless
it was removed. Then I walked away. I had given
up all hopes of getting him. It was not the pay that
I was after. I would give ten dollars to get him, but
I well knew I could not get him if I had offered to
do it in this way. Hundreds of such men have
talked with me for hours at a time about their
stiff and crippled horses, and told me they would give
me big money if I would cure them, but it was all
dead wind. It would have been just as well if it had
never been blown. The horse remained a cripple the
same. I have cured, or nearly so, hundreds of these
horses; so much so, they called them cured, and they
thought they were at least. They talked so, when I
well knew they were not. I did relieve their suffering some for the time. With all of my hard work, I
could get but little credit in this town.

While working in my shop some months after this
talk with this boy about Billy Crawford, he came to
my shop. He had never been in my shop that I knew
of at that time. In a pitiful way he approached me.
"Mr. Doan, will you cure Billy for me? I will pay
you. I have money of my own,"

"It will hardly do for me to go to work on him

without your father's consent, will it? I have never
had any of your father's horses in my shop."

"I get all of the horses shod and take care of them.
He will not know anything about it. It will not do
for me to put spreaders on his feet. That will be
rather too high-handed without his consent."

"My dear boy," said I, "I can help your horse
very much without spreaders if you will not let any
one know I am at work on him. Should your father
find I was working on Billy he might make trouble
for me and you too. If you will follow directions—
my directions, not others'—I will put Billy sailing on
the road in two days."

"I will do just as you tell me," said the boy. ' This
is to be kept a secret, and we two must keep it."

"Yes; all right. Fetch up Billy."

This horse was brought into the shop. I had not
seen Billy in a long time. He had been growing
worse daily, and the boy knew it, and that was the
cause of his coming to me. The horse had shoes on
all of his feet, which had grown very high and long,
and were badly contracted. In one of his forward
feet he was very lame. It was contracted more than
the other. He had been lame in that foot ever since
I knew him. It was pinched badly   "If I dared put
a spreader on this foot," thought I, " how easy I could
get him out of that, but it will not do. I must do the
best I can in the old way. That way is slow, and this
foot is so full of heat it will be a hard job to keep it
soft."

It will help him wonderfully to cut his feet down,

and it would be better if he could go without shoes unless the work is done better than this seems to be.

Let us move this horse around, and see how much he is out of harmony of action, before I commence work on him, and we will watch the result. After you read this, look around, and you may see some cases as bad as this. There are not many put in motion that are as bad as this horse had got to be. They are so out of harmony they cannot be put in motion and run in any way. The whole business is completely tied up and clogged internally and externally, cords all out of place; structure of feet all out of harmony of action, and no two feet alike, consequently no two of the cords of the legs are alike. This horse's shoulders were not mates. One foot had been worse than the other for some time, and was yet. Certainly it will require some brain work to get this horse sailing on the road in two days. I told the boy that if he would take good care of Billy I would not charge him except for shoeing the horse; and he did take good care of him, "Stand around, Billy." Heavens! I cannot describe this horse so you can tell how badly off he was from so small cause, and that is ignorance, blind and wilfully so. But I have started and I must go through. When this horse was made to move he straddled his hind legs the widest of any horse I ever saw of his size, and raised them the highest. It was done with a stiff and slow motion. He was very nervous, and seemed to tremble when I made him move. I backed him, and he dragged his feet and his hind legs; he seemed to have but little control of them. Some would call this spring-halt. It was not that, for

he had got past all spring motion. His movements
were slow and stiff. He would not move at all unless
he was forced to it. It hurt him in many ways. He
was very sore across the loin and kidneys. In fact,
he was sore all over. This soreness and stiffness cannot be removed in two days. It will take time for
that to disappear after the cause is removed, and that
cannot be done by the process I am obliged to work
on , but I can change.him back toward natural many
degrees in this way, and his suffering will disappear .
according to the degrees of change toward natural,
and if I can relieve part of his suffering I shall be well
paid. We will fix him behind first. It will be necessary to cut away all useless hoof, and shoe on the same
principle I have shod all others for expanding the foot
by the horse's weight—his forward feet the same.
This is all I can do. .One of the forward feet is rolled
under at the heels. The structure of this foot is more
out of harmony than the other three. If I could have
this horse to do as I wished, I would soon put his feet
in shape. By spreading, I could put his foot in or
out of harmony. Cutting away the useless hoof and
shoeing this horse on scientific principles—thin, flat
shoes—helped his movement at once, and this same
treatment will help all horses that are in this deformed
condition, and there are countless numbers all over
the world, and countless numbers of people that are
ignorant of this plain fact, as the owner of this poor,
suffering horse was.

"Bub," said I, "take this horse to his stable; soak
his feet well in warm water all around, then pack
them all with cow manure; that is the cheapest and

best, and can be got with little trouble. It will draw out the soreness, keep the foot moist, and stay in better, and there is no stone or gravel in it, as there might be in clay, for the sole to settle on between the sole and shoe. I want the sole to settle. After you have softened his feet, drive him, moderately at first, on smooth roads. After a few days you can let him sail. Pack all of his feet when standing in the stable nights. Never neglect it; and keep the feet moist while going through this change and afterward unless you want to drive a cripple. Before you drive clear all out under the shoe." I have already written enough about that. This is a lesson to this boy. I called him "Bub." I never learned his given name. I write as I talk. Men use different words to convey the same ideas, and I may use some that others would not. It is principles on the horse which I want to convey, on relieving the suffering horse scientifically without medicine.

I watched the change and action of this horse. He was driving by my shop daily, and many times a day. In ten days the spring-halt was all gone; he settled down across the loin; he changed back wonderfully in that short time. This "spring-halt" business is called by great horsemen "string-halt." With all of my experience I have never seen any strings about it. Some say it is caused by horses sweating too much in the flank. What is the use of talking such baby talk as that? After they have removed the cause of this difficulty on scientific principles they will know. Until they do, or see it done, they must remain in ignorance of these demonstrated facts.

I superintended, shod, and cared for this horse's feet, with this boy's help, for several months, and we had the satisfaction of seeing Billy quite a trotter again. He got to looking well, the hair brightened up and lay sleek; his body rounded up; he could rest nights. If he was not in harmony of action on his forward feet he was so much so that it would not be seen by such judges as awarded him a premium at Elmira six months before. He could have been put in harmony of action if I could have been allowed to do it by his owner.

They called all of these stiff horses in this place "foundered," and classed them in four kinds. After I had cured them it was something else—"road-sore" or "rheumatism," or they would get stiff again. I had worked almost night and day in this town, and had spent hundreds of dollars besides what I earned shoeing, a great deal of which was paid me in promises that were never fulfilled. I saw that my money was going fast. I must change my course or there would be danger of shipwreck. I used no medicine, consequently I could not get any pay for my skill.

A thought occurred to me to experiment on the human family. I always have been experimenting and watching the result. I picked up two castaway beer bottles, went to the brick-yard, put some brick-dust in them, and filled them with water. Then I got some of the ingredients from a hen-roost to make up this composition, and locked it up in my desk. They would have it I used medicine in some way. I thought, as I could not have my way, I would let them have their way, and see what the result would be. Soon there came a man with a lame horse. This was a common thing at all hours of the day at my shop. Some came thirty miles and farther. All came to get cured for the price of shoeing the horse. My fame had spread far and wide. This horse had been lame about two years. His shoulders had been blistered, and his cords, too, until the hair was all off. He, too, was sent to me. He wanted me to tell him what ailed his horse. Tired nearly to death, talking with so many from morning until night, and working at the same time, I told him it was coffin-joint difficulty, as it was. But that was not all of his trouble; he wanted to know if I could cure it.

"Yes," I replied, "I can, but it will require some powerful medicine to reach that."

I heated up my water, prepared the foot, put it to soak in the tub, went to the desk, which I unlocked, and took these two bottles of medicine out. I poured some of the contents of each in the water. Then I put the bottles in the desk again and locked it. After this horse's foot had soaked a short time I dressed and shod it. All that ailed this horse, or rather the cause of his lameness, was having irons put on his feet by some one that knew but very little about the horse. Some smith had cut off the sides of his foot, set the shoe too narrow, and run it out at the toe. The lever would have made him lame if nothing more had taken place. The coffin-joint was out of harmony. I told the owner he would go better by degrees; in ten days he would be well. At the end of that time he came to my shop and told me it turned out as I said it would. I did not practice this new process of curing horses long, neither did I charge any extra aside from shoeing. I soon saw they could be humbugged by me, and easily too. But this was not what I was aiming at. There were too many at work at that now for the pay. I did not cause the horse suffering, and they did. My health from this laborious work was likely to give out. I decided to make a bold stand right in the hottest of this battle for the horse. I would find an old horse that was well known by many and was stiff and lame, and what they called " foundered " of long standing. I searched around for a long time to find the one I wanted. I could hardly go amiss of stiff and lame horses, and they were all for sale, but were not what I wanted. At last one came to me. I saw standing tied in the street an old-looking, stiff, white mare, poor in flesh. She seemed shriveled and dried up around her shoulders; her neck dropped down from withers; eyes sunken. She stood braced out, with her feet huddled together. I looked her legs over. She was of Messenger stock; her limbs were as smooth and clean as a deer's. The hind feet and legs were quite natural, and she stood well on them. I looked in her mouth, and saw that she was old. She had a parrot mouth—that is, the upper teeth shut over the under ones. I knew she could eat, for that kind of a mouth will allow the grinders to come together when old. While I was looking the horse over, a man came who was her owner. That was what I was waiting for. I had made up my mind to have this mare providing I could trace her past life, if I had to pay twenty times as much as she was was worth. Her stiffness was of long standing; that

I knew, and her worth to me was not ten cents except for experiment. I did not tell him what I wanted her for.

"Will you sell this mare?" I inquired.

He said she was a pet in the family; "the old women could drive her." They can drive all such cripples as this, but not far in a day (I did not tell him that).

"Whom did you get her of?"

"Marshal. He keeps this crockery store right here. His father raised her. Let us go in and talk with Marshal."

"Mr. Marshal, can you tell me this mare's life from a colt?"

"I can, nearly so. She was owned by Yankee Weston. At three years old my father bought her. She had always been in the family until I sold her to this man."

"How old is she now?"

"Twenty-three."

"How long has she been stiff?"

"She was foundered when she was eight years old."

"According to that, she has been stiff fifteen years."

"Yes."

"How was it done?"

"Father let the hired man have her to drive, and he nearly drove her to death. She has been stiff ever since."

"Did you ever try to do anything for her?"

"Yes; we did everything we could. She has been

blistered, seatoned, and roweled, and she ran out two
years. It did not seem to help her."

"Cap.," said I, "what will you take for this mare?"

"Had I better sell her, Marshal?" said he.

"Let him have her if he wants her," replied Marshal.

"You may have her," said the owner to me, "for
fifty dollars."

"Here are four ten-dollar bills," said I. "I will
give them to you for her."

"If you will let me keep her one week—that will
finish up my fall's work—I will do it. I will bring her
down."

He came as he agreed. That was the biggest horse
sale that had been made in that town, and it would
have gone hard with me if they had hauled me up for
lunacy. Paying so much for such a horse as that, in
the fall, did show some symptoms of insanity; but,
said I, I will risk it. I will kick up a bigger racket if
they do not take better care of their horses. After
clearing my shop of some work I had on hand, I led
this old mare into the most public places, and commenced talking horse in order to attract attention.
After the crowd had gathered I told them the object
I had in doing this was to get their opinion on this
horse. ' Many of you," I told them, "know her. I
want you to say, in your judgment, if you call this
horse foundered of long standing. Marshal says she
was stiffened fifteen years ago." They stared at me,
and looked at each other. Finally I got some of
them to pronounce her foundered of long standing. I
told them they had better put some private mark on

her or brand her. I was going to try to cure this
horse without medicine, and in six months they
would not know her. Then I went to another part of
the town. As I marched away I heard muttering like
this, "The damned old fool is crazy." That I knew
would come, and worse, before I started out. I got
another crowd in another place, and told the same
story over. This I followed up for several hours, then
led the horse up Main street. She hobbled along,
stepping about eight inches, one foot over the other;
head down; lame on both feet, and lamer on one than
the other. On my route home I was in the center
of the street. People were passing and repassing on
all sides of me. I had got to be quite well known at
that time. I took it on all sides, but all they could
get out of me was, "My money paid for this horse."
I led her in the yard at my house. My wife looked
at her. She did not say much, but I could see she
did not fancy my purchase. I put the horse in the
barn. Next morning she had to be led through Main
street to get to my shop. I took the center of the
street. This street parade got up more opposition.
The old women took it up, and they went to talking
horse. When I had attracted their attention I thought
there would be hopes that some of them might want
to know what all of this racket was about. In that
case there would be a good chance to teach them.
But these rackets would rise and fall, and no one
seemed to learn anything about the horse. By their
talk I judged they knew it all, and for this reason they
could not learn. When a man arrives at this stage of
progression, there is not much hope. When a man

is satisfied with what he has got, he is not prepared for anything higher. I was not satisfied, with all my experience and experimenting. I wanted to try and see what effect it would have on this old, chronic, long-standing case, to please myself, and as long as I paid my way, and was burdensome to no man, and the money I used was the proceeds of my own labor, it was the business of no man to interfere with my business until I wrong or injure some one, then, of course, I should have been amenable to the law.

This old mare I took into my shop, pulled off her shoes, and dressed her feet. They were so rolled up by contraction on the bottom that they had but very little frog They had the appearance of a grain of coffee on the seam side, and they were very hard. I well knew this was a long and hard job, and what the result would be I knew not. I had taken a bold stand. If I failed whose business is it? Where is there a man that has not made some failures in life? But in this town I was in the way of some, and they had their dupes to help them do their dirty work, and they had lots of it to do in many ways. I put my spreading shoes on. After soaking very soft and spreading her feet the first time one-quarter of an inch, it affected her very much. She could not control her legs. I moved her around the shop, soaked her feet, and washed her legs and shoulders with warm water. While she stood with her feet in the tub, I held my leg in front of hers hours at a time, and tapped her on her hind parts to get her on her base. If the time had been kept, it would have amounted to a month that I spent night and day on this mare.

When I was in my shop shoeing this mare was there. My little boy helped me. He could wash her legs and move her around. I had other horses to take care of at this time. I worked on her in the stable cold winter nights, and exercised her nights for six months when all were asleep. After I had spread her feet the first time she was so bad I did not show her. She could not stand on three feet while I packed the other one, but would come down on her knees. I kept her feet soft. In a few days she could stand up quite well, though one foot kept lame about ten days. The shoulders were so deformed, and had been so so long, that it seemed impossible for them ever to come back to their natural place. This was the cause of my having so much work to do to get her there, but she could not stay. I pulled her neck on top, rubbed and pulled the skim on her shoulders, and washed them in warm water; the fact is, I was in the barn nights with this horse and others, or on the road driving them more than half of the time that winter. My wife told me one night that I was a fool. I did not quarrel with her, for I had had some serious thoughts on the subject myself. I was losing many nights' rest, and obtaining no reward. I was buying feed to keep other people's horses, and curing them for nothing. When looking at it in this light, it did not look very promising. They could not read my thoughts. I was determined to excel as a worker on the horse's feet, and fit myself for a teacher; and before I can instruct, said I to myself, I must know something to teach.

This old mare was to be my last experiment. I **could not expand her feet** enough at **one time to let**

the sole down to its natural place. It had to be done
by degrees and without taking off the shoes. At the
second change I spread her feet three-eights of an inch.
This did not effect her as much as the first. It made
her lame on the same foot as it had at the former
change, but in about ten days she recovered from that,
and begun to have knee action and stay on her base
better. This was encouraging. This was a light
mare; her weight did not seem to hold the sole down:
it was inclined to go back. It had been that way so
long that a little raise would effect her. If she could
have been put to drawing loads it would have helped
to draw her shoulders back to their natural place and
kept the sole down, and she would have got out of her
trouble in half of the time. That I knew, but I had
no such work for her to do. This horse must have
good care, and if I did it myself I would know it was
done. I fed her fine middlings. She was old, and in
order to cure she must thrive and grow fat. The skin
around her shoulders must be got loose and filled up
underneath with fat. Withal, it is some work to limber up such cases as this.

While I was working on this horse's shoulders
George Woodrough came up. He says:

"Doan, why don't you use some liniments on her
shoulders? It might help you."

"Yes," I replied, "it might, but I would not put
any on her for twenty-five dollars. If I should I would
only have to go through all of this work again. I am
experimenting on this thing to see if this trash has
any curing properties in it. I am well convinced it
has not, and have been for many years; and I am go-

ing to know, by reducing this whole complicated business to demonstrated fact for myself, then I shall know when this is done. If it proves as I think it will, I will sait that down as knowlege. There is no knowledge in opinions and beliefs for me, especially what others believe."

After working on this mare about four weeks I took off her shoes and cupped the feet out and pared them down some. They were then narrower than the shoe. I closed the shoe, and nailed it on. This mare's feet were kept soft all of the time—spread next time half an inch; that let the sole down, or I thought it ought to, nearly flat. It did not come down to suit me. This was in the day-time. The horse must be moved around; this sole must be got down in some way, soon after spreading, or it will play mischief. It must all work together in harmony. I led her out of the business part of the town. Her movement was bad. After I got well out of the business part of the town I got on her to ride, not for pleasure, but to add weight, so as to settle the sole down. After riding in this way for some time, I would get off and look to see how this plan was working. It was going down all right. It was rather hard work for me, worse, I thought, than riding on a rail. I hurried her up, but she could neither trot nor run, and did not seem to have any gait, but all kinds of gaits tangled up together. While going through this exercise I passed some laborers that worked in the brick-yard, some white men, some black. They were loading a boat with brick. They hooted at me, and swung their hats, which did not affect me any. I knew as well as

they did what kind of an appearance I made. I knew
what I was trying to do, and they did not. I well
knew what they would be, some of them, after pay
day. They could wheel brick after others had made
them by having a man to superintend the work.

This mare for four months after this was not much
seen in the streets in the day time, not that I cared for
what I was surrounded with, but I had to work in my
shop during the day to get money to live on, and work
on the horse nights. I do not wish you to understand
I did not sleep any. My rest was not long at one
time. My mind was so fixed on this job I could not
sleep much. All hands were watching this old mare,
and I could not tell how it was coming out myself.
This last spread let up on the mare, and she stood her
fore legs back of straight. She was lame on one foot
the same, and about the same length of time. After
having got this mare on her base, reader, it will be well
to look her over and see the condition her shoulders
are in. They look enlarged around and at the point of
the shoulder, caused by the shoulders being shrunken
above. Let us look and see if her shoulders are alike.
The side that she was lame on when I bought her, and
lame every time I spread her foot, is many degrees the
worst. She is crooked.

Reader, do you want me to tell you my thoughts
when I first saw this? I had not seen it before, as the
deformity did not show until I got her well back on
her base. I knew her shoulders were deformed, but I
did not think one side was so much worse than the
other. I said to myself—for I was alone—"The cake
is all dough ; these shoulders will never be mates, that

is certain. If this old mare was back in some swamp dead I would give twenty-five dollars. I guess I have come out of my hole too far this time. They have got the whip row on me now, certainly. Well, the world is as big as it ever was, and I have got lots of time yet, and if I fail I can move to another place. If the mare is crooked, she is not lame; and she stands up good on her legs and has got good knee action. I will spend five months on her yet. If she never gets well and straight, the principle is right. Reader, there are all degrees of deformed shoulders, and they are not always deformed in pairs. It is seen only by men of practical and experimental knowledge unless they become very bad. They are all caused, or nearly so, by ironing the feet. These degrees of deformity of the shoulders are regulated by the degrees of contraction of the feet. Expansion, that is, settling down below flat, does not effect much. If the horse is balanced up between contraction and leverage the shoulder is affected. If his feet are not contracted alike, his shoulders are not affected alike. You cannot iron a cup-foot horse and nail on his shoes as it is usually done without these changes taking place.

In the fore part of this work I left two horses. The first was badly thrown off his base by contraction on all his legs. When, as a boy, I first commenced working on the horse, for several years I did not know that cutting the heels too low and leaving the toe too long would throw the horse off his base as this horse is if no contraction had taken place. I was not alone in this ignorance in that day, and as far as I can see, nearly all are as ignorant now of this simple fact

as they were thirty-five years ago. I just saw one
pass, with a man on his back, so stiff from this cause
that he could hardly go; completely off his base; back
settled down, and in no shape to hold up weight. I
should think this man, by his looks, would weigh
about two hundred pounds. His knowledge of the
horse must be very slight. Horses thrown off their
base in this way, and worked for many years, or even
if they are not worked, get in the same fix as this old
white mare I am working on now, and from the same
cause, contraction and leverage, which become chronic
and seated, and the longer standing the harder to
change back.

Let us look at the hind legs of this horse. It has
been a long time since I have seen him. He was
young when I left him, and is well along in years now.
He has two spavins. They are called by the veterinarians and professors of great wisdom of the horse,
"blood" or "bog" spavins. These doctors tell about
curing these spavins. They burn, blister, and daub
on all kinds of trash, and charge for doing it, and yet
the horse is lame and so stiff I can hardly raise his
feet from the floor to shoe him, it hurts him so. He
cannot bend his leg, and I have many times been
obliged to raise the whole hind parts of these cured
spavined horses clear from the floor before they could
stand, and yet they were all cured. They did not
limp because they were stiff and lame in both legs.
Let us see if we can trace from cause to effect and see
what we can find. All horsemen and thinking men
will and do allow that what is called spavin is caused
by a strain or sprain in some way, and that is what I

think myself. A horse may slip and injure himself running or playing, and there are many that do. I will say right here that there are more horses sprained by contraction and leverage than all other causes put together. When horses are thrown off their base, as this horse is, by contraction, it lengthens the lever very long. When a horse has to rise over that lever, draw a load, and hold up two-thirds of his weight all of the time, and when standing or drawing, he is in no position to hold up this weight. I should think there was danger of straining the gambrel joints. Horses in this condition you cannot go amiss of if you will look at them. They are in all degrees of change from natural. What is the condition of these horses, if they lie down, when they want to rise? The horse always rises up on his forward legs first. Then he comes up on his hind legs with a spring-like motion. The more these horses are thrown off their base, no matter from what cause, the more the strain on the gambrel joints in rising. It is in many ways a strain on these horses to rise. The kidneys are strained; in fact, it strains the horse all over.

Now, quacks, come on with your firing, blistering trash and cure these spavined horses, or any other, without removing the cause, if you can, with two-thirds of his weight on these crippled legs. All you can do, or ever have done in this line, is to torture the already suffering horse, and there has been a great amount of that done all over the land, and no good result derived from it for either the horse or its owner. This I have known for many years.

Let us look the ringbone over a little. I have seen

one colt in my life, I think, that was foaled with what is called ringbone. I did not see this colt until he was about four months old. The mother had ringbone on both forward feet. I was looking at this colt. I thought I could see a little enlargement around the top of the wall. It did not look quite right to me. I watched him. At about eight months he began to show signs of trouble in his forward feet. When he traveled over frozen ground I could see it hurt him. At one year old he was lame in one foot. With all of my study of the horse this is the only case of this kind I ever saw. I think nine-tenths of the ringbones are the result of irritation caused by contraction and leverage. To raise over the lever irritates badly where the ringbone has its rise. I have experimented on these in this way by shortening the lever and giving easy toe to raise on. They would go better as long as the cause of the irritation was kept removed. I never meddled with their feet spreading. I never have seen one cured. I have seen lots of men torturing them and watching the result, and have had as good opportunities as any man. I have lived with horses all of my life, and been straddle of their legs, or had their feet on me in some way (and sometimes they were on my head), and their teeth, too. I have had these ring-bone curers come into my shop to heat up their irons. They would have several kinds, which they would heat red-hot; kept some in the fire heating all of the time, so as to keep this red-hot business of torturing the horse a-going fast. I have seen this done on ring-bone horses, when the cause of their worst trouble was that the toe of the foot was one inch too long, and had shoes on at that. These horses can never recover from their lameness with this lever on the toe, and growing longer all the time, and the foot made still sorer by the most barbarous treatment a man ever witnessed—that of burning. Horses treated in this way would be disabled for six months at least. I have watched the result of this butchery, and have seen no cure and no relief. Reader, do you want to know how I look on these burners of horses? They put me in mind, when I see them at work on the horse, of the wild and uncivilized savages tattooing themselves and each other by burning and disfiguring their own bodies; and yet these fine-feeling men have threatened me and my brothers, J. J. and Oliver Doan, with prosecution for cruelty to animals. What innocent and sympathetic barbarians these men are!

This horse I have been writing about in the fore part of this work is not yet as bad as he can be made. I may get around and see him again. I have many horses to watch, many miles apart, and some hundreds of miles This watching has been kept up all my life. Let us go back and look at this second horse, which I left in this work—the one I had such a hard time balancing up between contraction and leverage. It has been some time since I have seen him. His knees and ankles were straight when I shod him. He is now tipped on knee and ankle on both his forward legs; both ankles behind are crooked. His head is down; ankles swollen all around; cords seem to be thickened up; he looks bad. Poor horse, they have got you in a bad fix. I suppose the reader will want me to tell the cause of this horse's trouble, and the way out of

it. That I can do. I understand this whole business.
As complicated as it may appear to you, it is as easy
for me now to tell you the cause that threw this horse
in this position, and the principle to work on to get him
out of this fix, as it is for you to pick up a basket of
chips; but to get him out of it is quite another thing.
It is a hard job, and yet it can be done. I have
learned something since I balanced this horse. That
was the best I could do with the cup foot at that time
on him and all others. I have now got to be master
of the horse's foot. I can do as I like with it. I can
expand the foot on the right principle. Contraction
is the great cause of this horse's first trouble. Then
to divide between contraction and leverage, the best
that could be done at the time when I shod him last.
He has been shod many times since, and they have
left him too high on the heels by not dressing his feet
properly, or the fault is in the shoe partly; in both
perhaps. They have thrown him forward off his base
by this work, and he has been so so long it will be a
hard job to change him back. I have tackled horses
that are harder to cure than this. This horse's shoulders are not half as bad as they would have been if
he had not been balanced up in this way. His shoulders are badly out of harmony. He will not be
as bad to get on his base. The way to go to work is
at the feet. This cannot be done at once; it will take
time. It will have to be done by degrees, the same
way I am working on this old gray mare; but he is
different. She is thrown back off her base; he is
thrown forward. He has more ailments than she.
His knees and ankles have all gone forward, and yet

with all he has had done to him, the first cause has not
been removed. This horse is the one that had so much
experimenting done on him, and still he is alive; and
to the first cause there have been several more added.
The structure of the feet have been out of harmony
all this time. This horse's feet and legs are nearly
paralyzed, and he has been a constant sufferer all this
time. After long-standing cases like this there is
some work to be done to let this horse down at the
heels, change the structure of the foot back, and put
it internally in harmony of action; relax the cords on
all four legs, and equalize his weight on the center of
each foot, and balance him on an equilibrium in the
center, and equalize the lever in length on all four feet,
and equalize the weight on the eight separate heels so
as to cause him to travel on a straight line; and yet
this can be done, so much so, that it would be hard
for the closest observers to tell where the defect is if
there is any. There are many cases that are past cure.
They can all, or nearly all, be helped. Old horses are
not worth curing. They are never as good as they
would have been if they had not been in this condition. Young horses are easier to change back, and are
as good as ever. This poor horse is the final result of
thousands and millions on the globe. There is no use
describing the process of curing him. The same
method by which I cured the dapple-brown called
Mike cures all the troubles they are thrown in that I
have laid down in this book. I never tried to cure
bog or blood spavin by throwing the unequal weight
off their legs or removing the unnatural strain to see
what the effect would be. I considered them incur-

able, and do yet. I will leave that for some more scientific man than I am to test. I shall spend my time in introducing what I know. The horse cannot be cured or the cause of this trouble removed while he is standing in the stable. After the change he must draw loads, and that will draw him back on his base by degrees. The first change will effect him very much, and he should be helped by washing and rubbing his legs in water as warm as he can bear, and keep it up. Do not get tired; if you do, you will never cure any stiff horses. This is the only way they can be cured. The effect doctors can sometimes find the effect when it gets very bad. That is a little of the effect to tinker at. They have a good long list of names for the effects, many of which have no meaning, or, if they have, it does not remove the cause that produces the effect. I have had many of these fellows gather around me, trying to put me through an examination, asking me what I was going to do in cases of ossified cartilage and navicular disease. Poor fools! what can they do? They have dissected some dead horse's feet, and found that this or that had taken place; and this trouble had shortened the horse's life, and in many cases caused his death by the suffering he was obliged to endure from being out of harmony in many ways internally and externally. I would ask these wonderful talkers, What help is it to the live horse in this same suffering condition that you are able to tell what ailed these dead horses? They can see no farther inside these horses' feet than I can to tell what condition it is in. All they can do is to open them after the horse is dead. I can make them as

they were when they were colt's feet. If they have
been contracted very bad, so as to cause ossification,
expanding lets the body come back on the base and
helps in many ways that they have never seen, and
which I think some never will see. They have so
much talking to do they can spend no time to learn
this great science, and that is not all; they will have
to take as much as two lessons before they will be
able to teach. I use no medicine, and work on the
feet, the cause of all this trouble, and cure ; they work
all over the horse, and use all kinds of liniments, blistering, and butchering, and the horse goes on from
bad to worse, and no cure is effected.

After I get the colt's foot on in shape, and all in
harmony of action, and keep it so or nearly so, and
nature does not repair the damages caused by contraction, then I think there is some trouble inside that nature cannot help. I never applied this principle on
any horse that I did not help, and wonderfully, too.
When I quit one of these horses the effect doctors
need not take the job of curing. Their medicine is
useless trash, and their butchery is worse. If I can
do this as I state, that is proof enough.

I read a small piece in a paper about ten years since,
written many years ago by Dr. Gangees, on the horse's
feet. They had been held, he said, from growing natural by ironing. That was all he could say about it.
He knew nothing of the effect it produced. They had
been elongated. He was an Englishman. Here are
some sayings of a horse-shoer, also an Englishman,
who wrote a book in 1700. His name was William
Osmer. He was a practical horse-shoer. They had

stiff and lame horses in his day. They called stiff
horses "shook in the shoulders." He said in his writ-
ings that the people were "shook in the head," and I
think he was right; and that saying holds good yet.
He said, too, that the cause was in the feet, but he
could not get them out of their trouble. The English
have spent as much money experimenting on horses'
feet as any nation on the globe, without doubt.
There are many things to look to at the same time;
and in changing these horses all must work in harmony. The cause of failures in the spreading of
horses' feet is due to the fact that the men who have
attempted to do the work could see but one thing at
one time, and that one thing they did not see as they
should. It is very simple when understood.

My experience and trying to introduce this science
convinces me that Robert G. Ingersoll's lecture on the
"Skulls" is the soundest lecture I ever read or heard.
Bob did not mean to say that the skulls had any knowledge in them; he meant that the brains· that were inside of the skulls were what did the business. He
said in this lecture, at the first start, "Man advances
just in the proportion that he mingles his thoughts
with his labor." There is more sense conveyed in
these few words than whole volumes written by some
that are dogging on his track.

That is the way this work was perfected—mingling
thoughts with labor for forty-one years; and I have
had lots of dogs at my heels, but I never felt I was in
danger. It is queer; some folks will not no anything
themselves nor let anyone else if they can prevent it.
What a lot of trouble they do have!

I had to tack ship sometimes in this horse sail.
Those that were with me sometimes, blowing their
bugles for me, would change their tunes and blow the
other way. Then I would be obliged to tack ship. It
is queer, when you think this matter over, how quick
a man can change a tune on his bugle after he gets
used to blowing it. In order to understand these sudden changes on these bugles you must trace from the
change to the cause of the change. These changes
are constantly taking place in all things.

About the first stable of horses I tackled was Mot
Bennett's, in Horseheads—not the hotel keeper, but
his uncle. He was carrying on a heavy business at
that time in many ways. He was building railroads;
he was opening an avenue six miles long to connect
two towns; he kept a large lumber yard and sawmill;
he had all kinds of machinery connected with this to
get out brackets, cornices for buildings; in fact, entirely too much for any man to carry. He had lots for
sale on this avenue. He gave employment to a large
number of men that wanted work. But times changed
on Mot. He bucked at it hard to keep it going, but it
was no go; it balanced over the wrong way for him.
Men that he had paid thousands of dollars would not
take his promises to pay written on paper any more.
I shod Mot's horses through these trying time. It was
all charged on the book, and the amount was about
forty dollars. I well knew I would stand no chance
to get my pay. The big fish always eat up the little
ones. I took my pay in an old wagon at about three
prices, and let it go at that. Poor Mot, I liked him.
He was a whole-souled fellow, but he was carrying too

heavy a load. He came home from his hard day's
work over taxed, and sat down in his chair, his speech
lost. In a few days Mot passed away. Some time before this I was talking horse in the streets. Mot said
to me, "You had better go to work." This remark,
coming from him, rather shocked me. I thought of
his horses that I had been caring for, and the one that
I pulled out of the straw—that four hundred dollar
horse; besides, at that time I was doing more hard
work and working more hours than any two men in
that town. Eighteen hours a day and night were put
in; the fact is, I was nearly used up. The cripples
kept increasing on me. I was over-worked, and I was
obliged to send some away, and I dropped Mot's horses.
Money I must have to live on, and to buy feed for
these horses that I was experimenting on, or I should
fail. This caused his bugle to change, but the blast
did not blow me off my base. I was likely to lose all
of my friends in this town. Some fought me for curing and some for not curing their horses and keeping
them cured. The whole business seemed likely to
turn against me. I made up my mind I would switch
off awhile and rest up. I was about whipped in this
horse fight. I went to my shop, threw both doors
open, got a shoe-keg and set it near the door, took some
papers and books and commenced to read. I did not
read much; I did not get a chance. New customers
kept coming all of the time to crowd out the old ones.
I could not do all of this hard work. They would
come an go. None of these men stayed with me all
of the time They did not come to my shop except
occasionally. There was not one man in the lot that

knew how much work I was doing, and I came to this
conclusion : It was none of their business if I take a
rest. I made up my mind to clear away some of this
racket. The horses commenced to come. I sent them
all away. I was asked :

"Are you not going to shoe any more horses?"

"Not at present."

Some would ask : "How are you going to live?
You live, don't you?"

"Yes; I can live anywhere you can. There are
plenty of shops in this town where you can get your
shoeing done."

I sat on that keg every week-day for two weeks and
sent all away. That seemed to quiet the noise for a
time. Then I resumed my work. The horses came,
all I wanted to wrestle with. I had bought a house
and six village lots in this town. The street-cars ran
past my place. They run from Horseheads to Elmira.
The distance is six miles, and that was the main wagon
road. At the time I lived in this town it was a great
thoroughfare. Here I saw some of the worst cruelty
I ever witnessed dealt out to these poor, stiff horses.
It was all I could do to keep cool. This was going on
daily, and Sundays it was worse. It was brutality run
mad, made so by rum.

When I commenced this work it was to be confined
to the horse's feet, tracing cause to effect and effect to
cause. This book was not named until I had made
quite a start in the work, and as it is called "The
Horse's Rescue," I shall have to meddle a little with
the rum question. I never have talked much on that
subject, but I cannot see any way to steer on my course

without coming in contact with it. I have heard lots
of men lecture on this subject, and talk about the
effect of rum on the human family, and I have seen
the effect punished while the cause remained undis-
turbed.   In all of these lectures I ever heard or read
I never heard one word said in defense of the long-
suffering and abused horse ; and as I am come to their
rescue, I shall work all the field I can to accomplish it.
This lecture on rum is to show that it affects the
horse in many ways, and badly, too, all over the United
States, and I have been over some of it.   It is the
same in all places, some worse than others.   I will
give you a little sketch of this wholesale abuse caused
by rum in this God-serving town where I am battling
for the horse.   These are facts. . They are no third
hand business.   It was a common thing on Sunday for
me to see three and four wagons pass my house at one
time, going from Horseheads to Elmira, four in the
wagon, one horse drawing the load, and he stiff and so
sore on his feet—caused by ironing his feet by such as
are whipping and pounding him—that he could hardly
keep on his balance ; all swinging their hats over their
heads ; one plying the whip, sometimes a club ; crossing and recrossing this street-car track every ten or
fifteen rods   Some of these beings called human were
so badly off their base they could not sit up straight
if they tried.   They would balance over in all shapes,
some forward, some backward.   Some would hang
over sideways, and they were constantly changing, all
the time yelling and whooping ; horses going as fast as
they could be made to go in their deformed condition.   This could be seen, passing and repassing all

days. Sundays with me part of the day was spent fixing up my patients, the horses, making them as comfortable as I could. The shop I did not work in in this place; they would not bring any work on that day, so I got a little rest working in my garden, which is no labor to me; it is enjoyment. I could enjoy myself hoeing and weeding in my garden on this day as well as anything I could do, if it had not been for this panorama that was constantly passing; that destroyed all. It was very annoying to me. Of all the damned sights I ever saw, these are the worst to me. I use the word "damned" because it suits me the best to convey my feelings. Damned means condemned, and, if somebody does not get damned for abusing these horses, neither of these two words has any meaning at all. I think the damning should rest on the cause.

What kind of compositions these poor, duped specimens of humanity had been taking into their stomachs I know not; they did not seem to know what they were doing, neither did they seem to see where they were steering to. These are fit subjects to have the horse! If these horses were balanced in the center and limber there would be some brains spilt. One cripple sailed past my house, after crossing and recrossing this track. He was quite a sailer, for a three-legged horse, for one was not of much use except to keep him from tipping over. I told my wife, "There will be a shipwreck soon; that craft cannot sail long in this course without one." In a few days, not far from my house, this wreck took place. The driver had been helped into his wagon; up-town he went, steam all up, and no regulator. This two-legged, perpendicular

machine in the wagon was so badly off his balance
that it fell over the horizontal machine—the propelling power. The center or vital part was all in middling order, so much so that it was dangerous to set it
in motion without a governor. Somebody started it,
and down it came. It ran wild. Out went the man
headfirst, struck his head against a stone, and knocked
his brains out. This horizontal machine kept on going, and if there had been three or four more in this
wagon in the same fix the first was in, this machine
would have run the same until it smashed up some
more. The horse smashed up at his stable. This
kind of steam all adds greatly to the suffering of the
horse.

One Sunday, while working in my garden, there had
been more than usual of this kind of business going
on, which seemed to come from up-town. There
must be a fountain, it occurred to me, up there where
all this corruption has its rise. It all seems to come
from one source. But I have got all I can attend to
working and experimenting, and if they will let me
alone I will them. I can only fight on the defensive.
There are too many balanced over the wrong way for
me here. I shall, in order to carry out my plans, keep
as quiet as possible. It seems to be going rather
smooth now. I think they have made up their minds
to let me go on in peace.

After hoeing in my garden all day Sunday (I
thought it was Sunday, and others told me it was), I
asked several through the course of the day, and my
wife said it was. From what I could see going on all
around me I could not tell. To look at the day it

seemed like all others to me; and I am so forgetful that if there had not been somebody to ask I should have lost track of this day. The canal was close to my house, and the boats and street cars were running. This was a great place for cars in this valley. I could hear the locomotives blowing their bugles, and the music came from all directions. I could hear them many miles away, talking with each other, at all times of day and night. I could hear and see this without stopping my work.

I had my sleeves rolled up, vest and coat off. It was a warm day. My garden was quite large. There was six large village lots all in one garden. It lay close to this great thoroughfare. The Sunday did seem to me to be the most business day I had seen in a long time. All seemed to be in motion—all life and action. I did stop and rest on my hoe and take a telescopic view of what was passing. The streets were full of horses, some running, some trotting, or trying to; some limping at one end and some at both; some stiff; in fact, they were in all stages of deformity. I could see I attracted quite a little attention. They stared at me; that is, some did, such as had sense enough left to do this. They could not stare long at a time. If they did they would be in danger of a smash-up. There were lots of machines running on this street without governors, and they did not always run on a straight line. When a man got on this road, if he did not attend strictly to business, there was danger of shipwreck. Milk wagons were running morning and evening; some selling it by the quart and half pint, some taking it to the creamery, some to the cheese factory, and selling it. The birds were singing, the street cars were making extra trips. They left Horseheads every fifteen minutes for Elmira; the same coming to Horseheads. It was a sorry day for these poor, crippled, and deformed horses. Street cars off the track; men jerking the horses on the mouth, jamming them back, yelling, "Whoa, damn you!" every half-minute, the horses at the time standing as still as they could. Some had all they could do to stand, and were almost ready to fall over backward. Some, unable to stand, did fall, and yet they were obliged to do extra labor on this day called Sunday. It did seem to me they were all let loose on these poor horses this day. Some of them were run from morning until morning again.

There was all kinds of music, pianos, organs, violins, and I actually heard roosters crow, on this day, on the backside of my lot. I saw the water run in the creek. I did not see it stop and pile up in heaps. There were fish in this water, and they were constantly in motion.

Reader, when I bought this place I intended to ornament up this ground and fix up a pleasant home. There was a large, lively stream of living, sparkling water on the backside. When I bought this property I thought it was in a sightly place. In this I was not disappointed. I could see too much, and the sights did not suit me. I saw too much cruelty and abuse practiced on the helpless horse, and it made a hell for me. I gave up fixing up the place, and this was the cause of my moving.

On the day following this red-hot day of abusing

these deformed horses I was on my way to my shop.
Reader, I was loaded to the muzzle. It would not
take much to touch me off. I was the horse's sworn
friend, and always had been through life. Right in
front of Bob Colwell's place of business, the boss of
this town at that time, I met Jack Racker, the cat's-
paw general of all the dirty work that was to be done.
He said to me, "Doan, they are going for you."

"What have I been doing now, and who is 'they'
this time?"

"The authorities of the town."

"Bob Colwell, what is the charges?"

"Well, I sat up-stairs in my house writing for the
paper, and I could see you hoeing in your garden all
day. They are going to arrest you for violating the
Sunday laws."

"My, my! did you write about me?"

"No."

"You should have done so; it would help fill up
the paper."

"I told them you would be the first man up here
Monday morning after working all day Sunday in
your garden."

"You told a lie; there were lots of folks here when
I came. Jack, what do you think it will cost me?"

"I can't tell you."

"Tell that great business personage 'They,' you
quote so much, that I will pay all the fine they can
get against me, and I will double it if they will let me
lay it out."

"What would you do with it?"

"I would give it to some poor widow woman that

was trying to support herself and her children. Not
one cent will I ever pay to any authority in this town
or in any other for the use of this day you call Sunday, for this personage you call 'They' to convert to
his or their own use; but I do intend to have a lot in-
dicted before the grand jury for violating the license
law on all days, at the next court, if they do not stop
drugging these poor fools, causing them to kill themselves and others, and misuse and kill and cause to
be killed their helpless horses, and endanger innocent
parties, and place the lives of children and all living
things in jeopardy. And this is not all; it is very annoying to me when I am at work on Sunday. If it is
not stopped soon I shall appeal to the courts."

This lecture was delivered in front of the office of
the boss of the town. Let us go on to the shop.
There will be a lot of cripples waiting. That racket
is stopped. I wonder what will come next.

Reader, I suppose you want to know how the old
white mare gets along. It has been four weeks since
she had her feet spread. The same shoes have been
on all that time. She has been driven every night in
some by-road. She is not lame, and is growing fat—
improving slowly. She must have her feet dressed
and spread again. Her feet do not dry up now, and
there is not much fever in them. I cupped out her
feet and pared the shell properly for this spreading
operation. It is the same proces . It is by degrees I
am doing this. It could not be done on this mare all
at once, she was so badly rolled up. I closed up the
shoes, nailed them on, soaked the feet soft, and spread
them one-quarter of an inch again. That let the sole

down as far as I wanted it. In all I have spread this mare's feet one inch and three-eighths at different times, and yet it is not more than five-eighths of an inch wider than it was before I spread it at all. Every time I spread this old mare's feet it threw her off of her base on both feet and lamed her on this same foot that she was lamest on when I bought her. She was lame on both, and had been for many years. This time she was not so lame on this foot, and recovered sooner from the effects of the change. As she progressed toward natural by degrees she was easier to get on her base ; the time lessened, and the effects lessened by degrees the nearer she approached natural. This is encouraging, certainly. She does improve slowly ; her shoulders are not mates ; she is very crooked yet, and both badly deformed. She does not look like the same horse now I have changed her ; this is certain, and the cause is removed. This long-standing effect around these shoulders is stubborn and tough. I know the bones are not broken ; all else will yield by degrees, but it must be slow. It has yielded a little now ; and if it has yielded a little it will yield a little more. This is the way I reasoned with myself in the cold barn many cold winter nights while others were sleeping or sitting by comfortable fires. Days I was in my shop doing all I could to relieve the suffering of horses for the same men that were fighting me their level best in many ways. Some of them were poor dupes, which I well knew, set on and made so by a jealous, ignorant set of pretenders of great knowledge of the horse. I well knew I could out general them working on the horse. A man did

not have to know much about the horse in this town
to do that. In this town, where they worried so much
about my spending my money and so much time, I
was obliged to sue two men after waiting one year for
my pay for shoeing their horses. One of these men
lived in a house that cost forty-five thousand dollars.
Bragging all the time about their wealth; I never
heard them brag about their knowledge. The fact is,
they did not have much of that. That was a scarce
article on the horse in this town. I want to ask these
men who this time belongs to, and how much money
they have got invested in time. Some folks talk and
act as though time belonged to them, and they wanted
to monopolize it and convert it all to their own use,
as they have many things. I have used as much
time, probably, as any man of my age, and others
have used it, and yet there seems to be lots of it left.
Some use time in one way, some in another. It is used
in many ways. Some use it fighting against their own
interest and others' at the same time, and do not know
it; and that was what the ignorant part of this community was doing in this town for two years fighting
me. I suppose they will fight this work if they ever
see it. Then they will be fighting against their interest. It will not hurt the sale of this work; it will
help it to sell. It will call the peoples' attention to
see what all this racket is about. That was what I
got up so much racket in your town for, to get the
people's attention attracted to me. I wanted to teach
them something about the horse. I well knew they
did not know but little about this great science of
working on the horse. After this science is under-

stood, the long lists of names laid down in books for effect will be buried with many other dead and useless names and things of the past. There will be no effect to name. Men lose money and their horses too. If there is a way to prevent it, and they know it to be a fact, they will grasp it very quickly. All they want is to know that this is a success (and it is, and all of the howling and bawling of these effect doctors will not make it otherwise).

After working in this town, with no one to help me but my little boy and my wife, I thought I would teach a young man. He had worked at blacksmith-ing a short time, and was trying to learn how to shoe and work on the horse. This horse business requires two good, able-bodied men at least part of the time— one to hold up the feet while the other spreads them. Sometimes he is obliged to hold up more than half of the horse's weight. It takes some strength and cour-age to tackle all kinds of horses in this way, and yet it must be done if these horses that are in this fix are ever to get out of it. This young man saw me do this and helped me some, and yet he did not have confi-dence enough in himself to do it. He could not stand the opposition we were surrounded with. It did not take much to cram him down. I soon saw he would not make a good soldier in this horse fight. He dared not come right out and talk. He was shy. He dared not get up a racket. He could not stand that. I soon saw he would be of little use to me. I wanted fear-less men to introduce this science; no coward could do it. The horse he must not fear; he must drive and handle him in many ways, and all strange horses. All of the time he was too weak on his knees. I dropped him. In about one year I went in his shop. He was shoeing horses. The work he was doing looked rather ragged. He told me, "This is the way I am doing it now."

He was driving in old stubs in the old holes, with the lever all left on the toe, and growing longer all of the time. I said to him:

"This is not right; the horse is the sufferer. Your customers will go back on you."

"They do not know the difference," said he.

In that he was partly right. Some do know when they have got a job that looks well. This ironing a horse's foot is quite a different thing, if botched, from other mechanical work. It causes the horse to suffer. A man can botch a job on a wagon, and yet the wagon does not suffer. I have seen and heard some groan as if they feel pain. The cause was a botch job, and it caused the horses to suffer that was drawing these wagons. To set the tire too tight on the lumber wagon dishes the wheels one inch each too much. What effect can that have on these deformed horses? Put on forty hundred weight on rutty roads, then you can tell. If the wheel runs in the rut at all it con-stantly crowds and grinds against the shoulder of the axle This causes the horse to suffer. I have had many of these new-born babes on the horse try to talk and lie me down to build themselves up.

I shall state here I know the horse's condition has grown worse for the last twenty-five years, and for several reasons. Since shoes for the horse, and nails to nail them on, have been made by machinery, the

shoer, as soon as he can learn to weld on a cork on the
toe in a bungling way, buys some stock and sets up
the business of slaughtering the horse. He works on
no principle, either right or wrong. He brags, and his
friends brag for him, and· they know less, if it is possible, than horses. He is safe enough if they all get
crippled on his hands. The creator has made such a
botch of making the horse, he can't eat or drink water.
All kinds of grain will make him stiff or lame in all
degrees, some on one foot, some on two, some on all,
in all degrees, and yet he must eat or he will die. In
some places they are nailing on cast shoes. In this
case the foot must be cut to fit the shoe.

Of all the damned fools that I ever heard talk, the
biggest is men that claim that horses are stiffened by
what they eat or drink. There are so many degrees
on the same horses, and on the same horse; and these
men gather around me in herds almost daily, teaching
me these wonderful truths they claim to know, and all
driving stiff and lame horses in some degree. If
what they say is true, they are a careless, ignorant lot
of fools, and their talk bears witness against themselves, and it needs no other proof, for their horses are
enough to condemn them. They are nearly all crippled in a greater or less degree. That needs no proof.
It crops out all over the land in bold relief; and if
these horses are stiffened by grain and water, why do
they scurf the shoer so much for spoiling their horses
and run to him to get them cured—the same place
where they get them spoilt? It is curious how many
tunes can be played on one of these lying bugles when
some men get to blowing them.

There are many animals that eat grain, but none are stiff and lame like the horse and mule. All animals drink water, and it does not affect any but these two species in this way. How is this, you wonderfully knowing men? I should think you would appeal to the creator to have an improvement made on these two species of animals. According to your reasoning, there is something wrong in their construction, or you should use more reason and judgment about feeding grain and giving them water, knowing, as you claim, so much about the cause of all this. Suppose you experiment a little and stop giving your horses grain and water, or a very little, and keep their feet ironed, and that by a botch; you can tell soon where the cause is. They feed all kinds of cattle, young and old, the strongest kind, and they are tied up and have but little exercise; yet they do not get stiff by anything they eat and drink. The ox is kept shod in many places the whole year round, and fed grain, and heavy too, and I have seen them when warm drink a half-barrel of water at once, and have shoes on at the same time, and not get stiff. My father lived among the rough hills of the state of Pennsylvania. He kept them, shod and fed them, and yet I never saw him have a stiff or sprained ox. He worked these oxen. The ox's foot is split; the shoe is in two parts, and there is no contraction. The lever does get long. It does not effect the ox as it does the horse. The lever on the ox's foot does not extend beyond the useless growth of the hoof. On the horse it is very different.

After I get this work from the press I am ready to

go to school to these great teachers to see what great
discoveries they have made on the horse Some have
never been out of the town in which they were born.
If they can tell me how and on what theory or plan
they obtained so much knowledge of the horse's foot
and the cause that threw him in this deformed condition, without any experience or experimenting, they
will confer on me a great favor. They can make their
independent fortune out of that. It will do away
with experimenting on all things, and save a vast
amount of useless labor. This is the way all great
things have been perfected. It will save mental taxa-
tion. I wish I had known this new theory forty-one
years ago; my back and hips and shoulders would not
ache so while I am writing this work. I have heard
in my life folks talk about using common sense. How
plenty that article is I know not. There is not much
used for the benefit of the horse, that I know. The
article of reason, talking, and working on the horse is
almost out of use. Judgment, there is lots of that of
all kinds. There is all degrees of it. They all differ
using judgment. There is good and poor judgment
used on the horse. Of that article ninety per cent
used is very poor. Useless opinions and beliefs are
used by the wholesale. Still the horse suffers. Ignorant men have the impudence to tell me I cannot cure
these horses, and never did. Any one would think, to
hear them talk, they knew all things, and were in all
places at the same time. Now I want these poor fools
to tell me how they know I cannot cure these horses.
They are in one place drawing manure, which they
can do after somebody has made the wagon to draw it

on ; that they could not make. I am hundreds of
miles away curing these horses. I could do this in a
small village and they be ignorant of the fact. It
might be put in print in the daily papers, and such
ignoramuses as these never know it. They seldom, if
ever, read ; and yet I have had nearly all of my abuse
from this source. To get drunk on what they call
whisky is the hight of their ambition. The next is to
abuse and misuse these helpless horses in many ways.
Reader, if you ever try to introduce this science, my
experience has taught me from such to turn away.
They cannot take in this great science ; they only
fight ; you cannot teach them. The higher always
teach the lower. You cannot get teachers from the
lower to teach the higher ; that would be too much
like spreading the horse's foot at the toe or at the top.
You must select naturalists and scientific men—men
of brains, men whose word is good, not liars. I have
studied man some in the same time I have been study-
the horse. There are men that can and do lie, and it
is wonderful how they will multiply. Liars are very
prolific. If one big liar should tell lies out of whole
cloth before six or eight bearers of lies, it is surprising what a crop you will have in a short time, and
how they will multiply, and what a field they will
spread over. They are borne in papers, on the telegraph, and telephone, in the mail, and across the ocean
and under it. I speak of this for this reason, to post
you up. All this I have had to contend with in trying to perfect this work and trying to introduce it.
Before I get through I will show you where I experimented a little on this lying business. The lying fruit

some are very fond of. They can masticate and swallow and digest this easy. They seem to relish it, too. No matter how large this fruit is, they can swallow it, and some have swallowed so much of it that it is almost impossible to get them to taste the truth. It is surprising how full some folks will allow themselves to be stuffed with lies. Why do you not investigate for yourselves, and go for facts and see them demonstrated? and then you will know these lies are only told to deceive you by men that want to keep up this torturing business on your poor, suffering horses, and put down this great science. They are badly scared; their craft is in danger of being wrecked, and they do not like to be made out worse than fools. When this science is introduced they will feel exceedingly small. This is certain; it is and has been almost a daily occurrence for many years to hav a lot of teachers gather around me, all talking horse, all talking at the same time, all directing their lesson to me.

Since I have commenced writing this work several have told me they were going to write a book on the horse. I told them if they wanted to I had no objections. "That is all right," said I. "You may know many things about the horse that I do not. Your book would perhaps sell as well as mine. You have as good a right to make books and sell them as any man." But they would have to write different from what they talk in order for the reader to understand what they wanted to convey. If these books ever do come out I will compile them. Then you will have the best guide to cure these lame and deformed horses that ever came from a press. I have tried to learn these lessons so I could talk them. I may give a short lecture that I have learned from these teachers after I get this work out. I can talk it better than I can write it. It is very complicated. It requires quite an expert to talk eight or nine men's lessons and carry them all along at the same time, and all disagreeing on all points, opinions, and beliefs. The more a man believes the less he knows. The more he knows the less he believes. A man that is satisfied with what he has got of knowledge is never prepared for any more.

I have no power to convey with my pen these horse lessons that I have had. I think after taking five or six hundred more I will be able to talk it. I am going to try to learn them. If I can learn to talk nine men's talk at one time on the horse, that will be a big thing.

It has been now one month since you have heard from the old white mare. It has been all of this long month the same thing—continued talking, shoeing, and working on all kinds of lame and crippled horses, early and late, sometimes all night. These few horses that I write about are only now and then one of thousands I have worked on in forty-one years. This fight for the horse has been a long one, and it is not over yet. We are just getting in the hottest of it now, but the hotter the battle the more glorious the victory —for that we are going to have. It has got started, and it cannot be stopped. Too many have seen this work done—scientific men, which I shall refer to before I get through this work.

This old mare is doing finely. She must have her feet dressed as before and spread a little. I did not measure her shoe to see how much I did spread it. It needed but **very** little. The sole is the guide on all feet. I cannot furnish any reason, sense, or judgment in this work. I want all I have got for my own use. You must use your own on this work—all you can command—and use it all of the time in all cases. They all vary in many ways, as I have already written many times.

I spread after this operation a little every ten or twelve or fifteen days, according to my best judgment. The object in doing this was to keep the structure of the foot always in harmony of action, and this coffin-joint and all others as near their natural place as possible all the time. So as to have her improve, I did not leave anything undone for one hour that I could do to forward this work I was trying so hard to do. I had got this mare's feet flattened out, and the growth not wearing off. The shoe nailed on to hold it spread would also hold it from spreading; at the same time, if the foot was allowed to grow on the course it is inclined to grow and not spread, the sole would raise up in degrees according to the time it was held at the bottom. This would affect the coffin-joint and throw her off her base and affect her all over according to the degree of change from natural. I kept this mare and changed her shoes several times to keep the lever on the toe as short as I could, and spread her feet many times a little. You ought to see what I was spreading her feet for by small degrees. I kept up rubbing her shoulders often, and nights many hours at a time. I drove her nights. There was no let-up on this job for six months. Reader, imagine, if you can, my feelings,

which I well know you cannot, after all this hard work
and no reward to perfect this work, to have a lot of
ignorant men insult you daily and hourly. I can tell
you how I feel sometimes, just like taking my flat
hand and mutilating their bugle. They are not of
much account. They will have to pass off of this
earth as many have, and not take much with them.
Knowledge is all they can take, and of that they will
be a little short. What a man knows is all that makes
him anything. What another knows does not help all
others only such little as he can teach them; and
where there is no material to work on it is up-hill business. To make something out of nothing is a very
difficult task. When talking horse and that kind of
talk, which can be heard coming from me all days and
in all places, I have been called drunk by the ignorant.
I never had any abuse from the enlightened part of the
community. If they did not help me they did not insult me. I am about as fearless as the most of men,
and yet I do have fear. I do not drink alcoholic
drink of any kind for many reasons; one I will mention is this: I am afraid I will get killed by drugs of
some kind. I am not afraid to die, but I do not want
to fail to introduce this great science on the horse that
I have worked so many years to perfect.

The last resort of the ignorant, if they cannot keep
pace with others in this race of progression, is slan-
der. Read the history of the past, imperfect as it is,
and it will give you a little light—enough to open your
eyes a little and put you on the right track. You can
never learn this science or any other by fighting, lying, and slandering others. You may go well dressed,

and yet it does not add to your knowledge. When I
work on horses my clothes do not please some, and yet
I wear them all days. These horse needed my care.
All days and nights I wore a strong pair of pants, a
heavy woolen shirt. Suspenders I never could get to
hold a horse; pants with patches on the legs, three or
four on top of each other, and if some were leather it
is all the better; then a stout leather apron over all.
It does save your knees and legs some. And yet with
all this protection I have had all stripped off clear to
the floor, and some skin with it; cords laid bare on my
legs; suspenders broken; buttons nearly off, and pants
too. In a shipwreck like this I usually used to use
horse nails for suspender buttons. Sometimes I used
them, for weeks; they would hold better. When I
wanted some stock, or five cent's worth of tobacco, I
did not take these nails out or change my clothes, or
wash. I walked in all places of business through the
day, and night too. My business was working on the
horse all hours, and I must be harnessed for it, and it
has been so for forty-one years. I was slovenly and
smelt bad, the result of wiping manure off of others'
horses on myself and clothes daily that they should
have cleaned off themselves. I have cleaned hundreds and thousands of horses in this way before I got
them shod, and when the horse left the shop he would
be cleaner than he would be again from that time until he came to be shod again. Sometimes I would
clean eight or ten in one day, and have the most of
this filth and stench on myself or clothes, and be
obliged to breathe and smell it all of the time. My
God! it is a great wonder I have not been stunk to

death and rotted down by my blood getting bad by
breathing this filth, all caused by people not keeping
their horses and stables clean.   Breathing this foul air
in stables will make the blood of the horse impure
faster than anything else can ; cattle the same.   We
all are judges, and all constantly judging each other.
Some judge one way, some other ways, and there are
all degrees of judgment on all things.   Others can
judge as they like.   I do.   But I never judge a man's
worth by the money or the wealth he has, neither by
his wearing apparel.   He might sit on a throne of
solid, pure gold, with a crown on his head that out-
dazzled the brightness of the sun, and be clothed in
royal robes that were decorated with costly diamonds
that hung in festoons, with the costliest plumage, with
a trail twenty feet long in the rear trimmed the same.
All this would not have any effect on me in judging
his worth.   It would not add any to his worth or
knowledge or goodness.   A fool can be dressed in this
way, and many have been.   Such men as these can
never cure these suffering horses.   They like pomp
and show too well, and what they call ease.   I would
rather be in some cold barn relieving the suffering of
one horse than see all the pomp and show on the globe.
Working men are what is required to cure and introduce this work.   To pomp and show I never bow and
scrape.   Neither do I worship any man.   A dead man
would be of as much use to me to introduce this science
as a sit-still.   A king on a throne is about as useless
as a dead man can be.   Work and business is the plan
of operation in this world.   Live men are what make
things move, and sometimes they move things some

do not want moved; and this work on the horse, if I mistake not, will remove some deep-rooted errors of longer standing than any stiff horse living at this day. The horse has suffered hundreds of years on this globe, all caused by error and ignorance, and many times dishonesty in many ways. I hear many times when I am talking for the horse, "He is a big blower." If I could not talk more sense than some of these blowers talk on the horse I would never open my mouth again. They know but little or nothing about the condition the horse is in. This I well know, and I will give my reasons for knowing. But very few ever have worked on the horse's feet, and those that have did not do it right; and all of these men that are bawling around me never worked on the horse's feet. How can they know anything about it with their horses all stiff? How can you know so much? It took me forty-one years almost, days and parts of nights, and many nights all night. Many and many are the nights I have lain in bed studying on this work until light, and not slept one wink Days and nights I have experimented. This work cost money, and I earned it all. It cost me forty-one years of the hardest mental, physical, and practical labor a man ever endured, and lots of persecution and abuse by jealous fools.

I will say right here that when I get stuck on this horse business I will send for some of these great teachers that have been trying to teach me so much. I will let them know when I want them. With all this hard labor I have stuff enough left in me now to face a regiment of such bawling fools. They are of

no use to me; neither are they in the way of introducing this science, only one gets tired hearing their
bawling. I have no trouble only with this class. This
is the class all scientific men have more or less trouble
with. Ignorance is the cause of all. There are millions of men on this globe that never invented anything, and never had one original thought; if they did,
they did not have courage enough to talk or write it,
and if all men had been as big cowards as they there
would not have been any improvements or discoveries
or progression made; and yet they will talk and brag
of their knowledge, and it is all borrowed. It had its
origin in other men's brains. They can commit to
memory some of these great principles after others
have discovered and perfected them by applying themselves, and that seems a hard task. This horse science
is different from many other sciences. It requires
something besides brains, and yet brains are the first
qualification. Without them there cannot be any
horses cured. It requires great strength and courage,
resolution and firmness. A man that is constantly
twirling a handkerchief around a stove-pipe hat, and
keeps one or two women constantly washing and ironing to keep him starched and clean, and who finds
fault with their work, and does none himself, would
be of no use to any one in this horse science. Removing the cause of these suffering horses is harder
work than it is to make them so; that is, shoeing
them, which is what makes them so. There are a few
exceptions. I can iron a pair of horse's feet, and drive
them a thousand miles, and they would perform the
journey better by doing so, and they would suffer

from the effect but very little, if any, in the time I was driving them this journey. It would not be done in the way it usually is done and ordered to be done. To begin this job I should want the horse's feet all natural as the creator made them or intended them to be; that is, the structure of the foot internally in harmony of action. I would cut away all useless growth of hoof and true up the feet. This dressing the bottom of a horse's feet, heel and toe, if it is nearly natural, is or should be the finest piece of mechanical work ever done on any machine. The horse is a machine. If this dressing is not done nearly right you will spoil this machine, and not know how you did it. If you cut the heel too low, and leave the toe too high, if only one-eighth of an inch each, it will make the heel one-quarter too low, and leave the toe a quarter of an inch too long. Shoe all around in this way with bungling, heavy shoes; start on your journey with little changed off their base, your horses will tell you of it in this way; if you will notice them, by showing soreness, if they are not very stiff and lame. This is not a very botched job compared with some. This same principle doubled will slaughter the best pair of horses, if the shoes are allowed to remain on two months, that ever lived, if they are driven on hard roads. I do not mean it would kill them; it would make them stiff and sore until the cause was removed. It serves all the same, according to the degrees of botching, on all feet, singly or collectively.

Now, reader, whoever you may be that is interested in this work on the horse enough to give your attention, I will try, as near as I can in this work, to tell

you how I would shoe a pair of horses to perform a
journey of a thousand miles, and what I would do
after the journey.   I cannot tell you as well as I could
if you and I were standing by and looking on this pair
of horses.   They need a little dressing on all of their
feet, some in one way, some in another, and they all
vary in some way and in many degrees; and all horses
do more or less.   True up; do not forget this heel and
toe business and lever on the toe; it is growing all the
time; it is not going to wear off much.   It will take
about a month, we will say, to make this journey.   I
am going to shoe these horses and drive and take care
of them myself.   (I would trust them in no man's
hands.)   Then I would know they were cared for.
The colt's foot on the horses you are shoeing in shape
is one thing to look to.   Shoe thin and light.   After
trueing up the feet let the shoes follow the shell clear
around the heel; shoe only a little longer at heel than
the foot.   Flat rest on shoe at the heel; dress foot to
fit and fit it.   No spring in any way.   Make the toe a
little shorter than natural, for this reason, it is growing all of the time, and this will save the cords.   Not
a cork on these shoes, the roads are dry and hard.
Nail with very small nails; nail in toe; no nails back
of the widest part of the foot; the heel should have
liberty, as all of the foot should, but it cannot if it is
ironed.   Every night, after driving all day on hard
roads, the horse's feet will have unnatural heat.   Do
not forget your horses have got feet on their hind
legs.   But few have noticed this.   They get hot too.
They travel the same distance that his forward feet
do, and the concussion is about the same.   I carry a

foot hook, and clean out all dirt and gravel under the shoes, if there is any. I look to see, then I will know; pack all feet with cow manure; this takes out the unnatural heat. If I did not do this when the horses lie down after driving all day, this heat would dry up the foot or cause it to dry up. In this case, the weight being off the center, the sole would rise up. If it is only a little degree, it effects when the horses rise on their feet. The weight will settle the sole again. It causes irritation. If they are packed this will not take place. In wet and muddy roads this would not be necessary. There would not be the concussion. The water and mud would take out the heat. This is the way some horses get very badly stiffened right after feeding and watering, by not taking care of their feet after hard drives. And if they did do all this, if they were botched ironing their feet, no packing or soaking would prevent until the cause was removed and kept removed.

At the end of this journey I find my horses, with this care, as limber as they were when I first started. The shoes are about worn off their feet, and all nearly worn in two at the toe; and some of the hoof at the toe is worn off. This is all right for me and the horses too. I wanted it to wear off; the lever has been growing all the time, and wearing off has shortened it. This takes the strain off the back tendons, and, with other care I take of them, keeps my horses from getting foundered.

Remember, I told you before I shod these horse they were nearly natural. In this case the frog before shoeing on all of their feet rested on the ground. I put on the shoes thin for several reasons; one is this: I want the frog to rest on the ground. After I get these horses shod the same as before I nailed the shoes on. If I raise the center of the foot up from the ground the weight of the horse is in the center of each foot. Then drive on hard, dry road. I could not drive five miles before the coffin joint would be badly affected on all their feet all out of harmony of action. Put in motion in this condition causes unnatural heat. They would settle down through the cup at the top until the frog comes to a rest on the ground in the center. At the first start on this journey I would be all out of harmony. I do not want these horses to change any, either way, if I can prevent it. This is the reason I dress the heel of the foot flat and give the shoe flat rest at the heel. I do not want any springing and changing internally on any of these eight feet on this pair of horses. The heel has some liberty as the feet grow. Shod in this way they will spread out, if proper care is taken of them, by small degrees, in driving them. If the frog does rest on the ground I am not smart enough to cure and keep cured stiff horses, they standing in the barn week after week. I drive horses to cure them and have them improve all of the time, and if they are natural I do my work to keep them natural. Another reason for not having corks on these shoes: they are of no use on dry roads. I do not want my horses up on stilts at any time. Another reason for having the shoes light: the horses will not raise their feet so high, the concussion on their feet is not so great, and the greatest reason of all is, it will not shipwreck me on the road and at home.

I told you I would tell you what I would do at the end of this journey with these horses, and here she goes. If I did not know more than some folks do about a horse I would pull off their shoes, if they did take cold, and never nail or allow any one else to, an iron on their feet. Then you would not stiffen so many, giving them something to eat and drink, and you would not cause your horses to suffer so much, and you would enjoy your ride after them better.

Reader, it is impossible for me to tell all the fault I have had found with me and my work on one thing, that is, the toe-corks would wear off on horseshoes. They wanted big corks, and they wanted them to stay big. They wanted them sharp, and to always stay sharp. With all of my skill this I could not do. If I could have done this it would have been a big thing. I could give better satisfaction. I could have made horses stiffer, and they would get stiff faster, if I could stop the wear on the toe of the shoes. They tried hard to get me to do it. I have sent lots away on this account. It is curious how hard folks will try to get you to spoil their horses. Then after you have done it they will tell far and near that you did it. Some they will tell they are foundered. They ate some oats or drank water. What do all these contradictory stories amount to? Simply nothing. If they came from a lunatic, or some one that had lost his reason, a little consistency might appear, and some allowance be made. The fact is, the condition these poor horses are thrown in, caused by ironing their feet and other abuse, is so complicated it is hard to convey with a pen or in any other way, and I get very tired. Some are changed very suddenly, some are years changing. These slow changes I cannot describe, except in this way: You cannot see them change; it is like the hill of corn. It grows and yet you cannot see it grow. The change on thousands of these horses is so slow you do not notice the effect until they get very bad, and yet they have been changing for many years. The degrees are very small on some, and the degrees of change vary on the same foot. These variations depend on the treatment the foot or feet have had. They will vary on every foot on the same horse. This is the way some change from natural. Some will change in a large degree in twenty-four hours, from many causes.

This old white mare is one of these cases. The first cause was ignorance. The driver did not know much about a horse; if he had he would not have abused her by driving her off her legs on hard roads. The concussion on her feet caused heat. The structure of the foot at the start was out of harmony in some degree, as all are that have been shod for several years, as she had been. The lever at the toe was some degree of length, as all are, out of harmony; then kept in motion up and down hills, on dry, hard roads, for twenty-four hours, and drawing a load. This will cause some heat internally in the foot, a strain on the cords or back tendons. This mare was used badly. The owner well knew this. She must have rest. She is tied in the barn, no care taken of her feet, for this reason: he did not know it was necessary. This mystery he had not solved. She is sore and stiff. She must not be moved until she gets better. The consequence is, when she lies down the weight off the center of foot, with all this heat in her feet, the foot dries very fast. When it starts on this course the sole rises; the heat increases the more the foot contracts, and in a very short time the horse is completely thrown off his base and balance and equilibrium, and fastened there, and there he will stay until the cause is removed. This is a large degree of change, and rather sudden for the comfort of the horse and his owner. I have seen hundreds of horses made very stiff in driving twenty miles on hard roads with a botched job on the end of the foot called the toe. Do not get too wise. You may learn something. All horses are in great danger of being served in this way, and many times worse, by ironing their feet, all superintending and bossing this great science and none knowing but very little or nothing about it. The horse is the sufferer, and the owner suffers too. If he does not suffer with pain he suffers loss in many ways. He pays his money to have his horses spoiled. He loses money in this way. It takes more feed to keep a horse that is a constant sufferer night and day. They cannot perform as much labor in any way, and it shortens their lives. If you start on a journey it will take you longer. You are liable to get shipwrecked at any time by not understanding this science. If you change or trade while on the road, or at home, this will not help you out. You will be liable to get wrecked from the same cause in a short time. I have helped thousands out of this trouble in my life. For many reasons I know this is not understood. The only way out of this trouble is to learn these truths, every man for himself; then you will know this is the only safety. You cannot learn much from " They Say." He does not know much about the horse.

I must tell you how I got the worst wrecked on the road I ever was in my life in many ways. Some was due to listening to " They Say," some to a sneak thief, some to not using reason and judgment after my judgment told me better. I was twenty-eight years old at that time. I carried on the wagon trade connected with shoeing the horse. My market for some of these wagons was in Tioga county, Pennsylvania. The distance from my place, where I carried on this business at that time, was about one hundred miles. It was up and down heavy hills nearly all the way. I knew the road well. I had taken wagons over this road and driven horses. This is the way I nearly always went for many years before and after this trip on this business and other. I have business there now, and have had every year since I was twenty-one years old, sometimes twice a year, seldom driving the same horse or horses. When I would get home I would sail after these horses about three hundred miles or more, and not be missed at home except by a few, and sail in all right, no wreck on the horse. The horses were fitted for this journey in many ways. The last thing I did was to prepare their feet, and that was the last thing I did to them every night, to see that they were all right, while I was making up this train to go over this road. There were ten in all. I had ironed a heavy wagon for one of my neighbors. The wheels were in the shop. This man came in. He had a kettle in his hand and a lot of rosin. "They say," said he, "that this is good to prevent the spokes from working. Melt it and pour it in hot, and roll the wheel around. It will run up in the spokes and coat the hub over on the inside. That will keep the grease from going up into the spokes, causing the spokes to work."

He fixed his in this way. I, fool-like, without even thinking, fixed all of my wagons the same. These wagons were made up in two trains. My team was at that time a small pony team, a stallion and a mare. I drove them together. They were hardy, well fed, and had had plenty of exercise. They were good ones, tough and young. On the rear of these trains must be a sulky and second-hand wagon to return in. There was a man who wanted to go with his team for the pay and to see the country. He never had been over this road. I told him it was a hard trip. "I think your team," said I, "taken up out of the pasture, will give out. They are old, too, and it is hot weather in July."

He said they could stand it. I yielded, and told him he must have his horses' feet dressed up for this trip. This I did for him. The wagons were all wooden axled, and must all be greased. When I commenced to do this I soon began to do some big thinking. The rosin had got on the boxes, and when I put on the wheel and turned it, it would powder up, no matter how small the quantity. It would set the wheel! I scraped and dug all off that I could, but I could not get it off. "I shall have trouble from this rosin business," thought I. "It will crumble off and wreck this train, just as sure as it moves." I greased

up, and hung a big pail of grease on the hind end of
the wagon.   The last job I did preparatory to this
sail was to shoe and dress up my horses' feet the day
before starting, put them in their stable, and gave
them a good, soft bed.   I had a young man at work
for me in the shop; the two first letters of his name
were Clark Cheeny.   In the morning, while I was
harnessing my horses, this young man came to the
barn with the shoeing tools.   I had not looked at my
horses' feet.   I had just shod them, and I did not
know they had been out of the stable.   What's up?
I drove the mare a little ways last night and she tore
off a shoe.   This was something she had never done
before.   The shoe was nailed, and the nails put in the
same holes.   I stood all this and more.   If ever a
man deserved damning and kicking he was one.
After I returned from this trip I tracked up this sneak
to see how far he drove the mare that night.   I tracked
him thirty miles.   How much farther he lamed her
that night I know not.   So much for a sneak thief.   I
started on this hard trip, not in the best of humor,
on account of my mare having been driven all night,
and I being oblige to drive her all day.

I had sailed only a few miles before I heard some
of the biggest bugling I ever heard from wagons;
nearly all were playing, and all playing different
tunes—all caused by listening to what "They Say,"
says without thinking.   The horses had all they could
do to draw the wagons on level roads.   Going on in
this way for a short time, some of the wheels refused
to turn, and slid on the ground.   This will not do; it
will kill the horses and spoil the wagons.   This is a

nice shipwreck, and only three miles sail. Well, there is no other way except rig up and remove all the cause I can and sail on. It is no small job to take off forty wheels and clean off all this grease and rosin on the arms and in the hubs, and yet it is the only way out of this trouble. I suppose I shall have to learn by experience like all other heedless fools. I think when I put any more rosin in wagon hubs "They Say" will know it. This is the way I reasoned with myself. It was too late to use judgment and sense on this job. The wreck had already happened.

After greasing up, I set sail again. It was down hill for a few miles, to Lake Cayuga. I crossed this lake on a ferry-boat. It was small, and we had to make two trips to get all over. It had rained hard all the night before, and the roads were somewhat muddy and slippery. There was no way out of this small town except to climb a long, steep, muddy clay hill, but it must be done.

After the wagons had stood a while it was almost impossible for the horses to start them. The rosin had crumbled off and ground up with the grease, and I must say it is the poorest axle grease I ever had on a wagon. I took the lead with my train and succeeded in getting it about a mile up this hill. After waiting a long time I saw the other train coming with only one wagon.

"Beach," said I, "What's the racket now?"

"The horses could not draw all of the train. I commenced to drop off some and this is all I could get up with. That rosin has set the wheels on some. They are scattered all along down the hill."

"Leave your team," said I. "I will take mine and we will repair and make up that train again."

After greasing and cleaning off rosin, I sailed them up to the other train. We were not to the summit yet; that was two miles farther. After rigging up we set sail again. These wagons soon commenced to yell again. The grease was all gone and there was no place near to get any.

"Well, Beach, they will have to yell until we get where we can get some grease; this darn rosin business is the biggest eye-opener I have had in some time."

We doubled teams and drew them up hills, then each would take his train. The horses could draw them down hill unless his train had too many wheels get set at one time.

"It is hot, Beach; these horses must rest, and these wagons must all be rosined off again and greased. I am going to try the farmers and see if I can get some lard and a little flour to put with it. They may not want to spare as much as I want; it will take quite a lot, Beach, to grease all of these wagons, and we want some left in case some wheels should get set again. We must stop pulling these horses so or we will kill them all this hot weather. I see my mare favors one of her forward legs or feet. She must have hurt her shoulder pulling up that first hill. I can't tell."

We had anchored on level ground; the mud was about two inches deep here, sticky clay. The wheels were all loaded. I went to a farmer's house and asked them to sell me some lard and flour.

"How much lard do you want?"

" I would like twenty or twenty-five pounds."

" Oh, we can hardly spare as much as that."

I told the lady my story about the wreck.

" I will pay you double price if you have got it."

I got the lard and repaired up again. After a few hours' wallowing around in mud, grease, and rosin, these wagons were getting play very fast by friction. That helped the horses some. The wagons did not receive much benefit. They ran better after this last treatment, as the yelling gradually subsided.

There was another storm gradually arising. I had been watching that. If it kept on increasing it would completely shipwreck this train. This is the propelling power. In many ways the mare was getting lamer by degrees. I could not see the cause in the foot; the shoulder did not swell; that looked all right.

" Beach," I said, " We must anchor. These poor horses look tired."

" It is not night yet."

" No matter, they must have rest."

I did not rest much myself; I could see danger ahead. It was not on account of loss or lack of money to see me through; I had about five hundred dollars in my pocket. This article I have found, when travelling, to be the best friend I ever had, and I never intended to get out of it if I could possibly help it. That would be the worst wreck I could make. What worried me was, I did not want to wreck this train, of which I was conductor. After stabling the horses, this rosin business had to be looked to on forty wheels. The yelling had quieted down. They had worn and cut so they would not get set; but there was great danger of their cutting and wearing al lout before I got them to market, caused by this rosin crumbling off and grinding up and setting some of the wheels to cutting. At any time and all of the time, if I could have got that old liar "They Say" by the nape of the neck I would have made him yell for a while, louder than these wagons did.

Beach fed the horses. I heard a racket in the barn, and I went to see what was up. I found Beach there, one of his horses, the oldest, choking, reeling, and about to fall. She was so old she could not masticate oats. She had been trying to swallow them without chewing, and had got choked. She succeeded in throwing them out of her throat and recovered. I did not know she was so old that she could not eat oats, until then.

"There is another danger to be looked to, Beach; that mare ought to be fed ground feed. This feed does not do her any good."

"Oh, she will go it. I have seen her in that fix often."

In the morning we started this train on a new plan. This was, to move slow. Motion creates heat. All is out of harmony. The propelling power is not fit to run. When any of these wheels get to yelling we must stop and rosin and grease them. If this is not done some of these wagons will be spoiled. The skeins and boxes will be cut all out.

In making up this train the stallion came out head up, full of life, ready for business; the mare was lame. Beach's team looked shrunken; heads down. We moved on slowly, stopping often through the day.

When any of the wheels set up their yell we removed the cause. The lameness increased in my mare a little through the day. I could not see the cause. I well knew it was no nails that held the shoe on. She was young. She had a colt's foot on her, and a good one.

"Beach, here is a hotel," said I. "The sun is two hour's high. We must stop here for the night. Switch off beside the road. We will drop these trains. These horses are all very tired, and we will not kill them, if it takes all summer to get this train through."

"Doan," replied Beach, "I don't like the looks of things here. Why, look at the sign; it is all daubed and smeared over with something. Look over the door; that is all daubed."

"Never mind that," I rejoined. "I am going to anchor here for the night. It is a half day's drive to the next port for our horses with this train. It would be likely to kill some of the horses to make it to-night. Unhook; let us get the horses in the barn and have a rest."

All seemed very quiet around the barn and house. The landlord was asleep on a lounge, but he roused up and showed us where to put our horses. After this was done I saw him get a heavy log chain and pad-lock and go out to the wagons. He locked two wagons together on one of these trains. I asked him what he did it for. He said: "To keep folks from stealing them."

"I think there is not much danger of that," said I. "They can get all the wagons they want now. There are some that are not locked. They can take them.

Beach, this man is a trifle too honest. I think it will be well enough to watch him."

We cared for the horses, making them as comfortable as our surroundings and circumstances would let us. This landlord watched for an opportunity to draw out Beach. He had noticed I was conductor of this train by hearing us talk. He inquired about my circumstances financially in a round-about way. After conversing a short time he asked Beach if I carried much money with me. Beach told him: "Enough to defray expenses." This was an eye-opener for Beach. He did not sleep any that night. He said to me: "There is something rotten here, Doan." Beach was a man not easily discouraged and no coward, but he did not like the surroundings.

Night came, and we went to bed; that is, we pretended to. There was no sleep. Beach's head was out of the window all night. The racket commenced about eleven o'clock, by the barking of dogs, five or six at one time. This was kept up all night, caused by comers and goers. They seemed to be on horseback. The landlord was up prowling around, and the visitors had business in and out of the barn all night. Beach was on the watch. He was where he could see them come and go from the barn. He yelled at some of them during the night. This hotel, I may say here, was not in a village. It was in a country place.

In the morning we found our traps all in their places. Beach asked the landlord what the racket meant that we had heard all night?

"Oh, there was a fellow who came to borrow a saddle."

Beach did not swallow that. Later on he inquired about this house, and learned from some that it was a hotel for horse-thieves. The horses seemed to feel middling well in the morning, after their long rest—all but my lame mare. She was getting very lame.

We moved on slowly. In the course of the day we passed through a toll-gate on an old worn plank-road full of broken planks and holes. I stopped, not wanting to get up any row on the road with any one. I told him this train all belonged to me to pay toll on, which I well knew he had no right to take. I handed him a bill. He took out what he pleased. I did not look to see how much he did take. I put the change in my pocket and moved on, the train all following. After going about two miles I heard a man yelling; I looked around; I saw it was the gate-tender. It was hot; he was a short fat man; he had heated himself up bad. His face was very red. He was wiping off the sweat. He yelled at me, and said I did not pay toll, only half.

"If you don't pay the balance, and me for coming after you I will have you arrested for running the gate."

"I did not run the gate," I replied. "I don't know how much you did take. How much do you want now?"

"I want one dollar."

"I am going to stop at this hotel to feed. There we can arrange this matter. There is no hurry. It is not necessary for you to run yourself to death. In the first place I have not driven on these planks. My teams could not draw these wagons over these holes.

How much will it cost me for running the gate, if I do
not pay you the dollar?"

"Twenty-five dollars."

"I think I will not give you any more money. I
shall be back over this road in a few weeks. Then I
shall want to drive on a trot. If you do not have this
rubbish cleared out of the road I will have the stock-
holders arrested for obstructing the highway. It is
dangerous as it is."

After feeding and taking a rest we moved on, the
mare growing lamer all the time. After standing, it
hurt her badly to start. We went three miles farther.
Here was a hotel kept by a fat, red-faced, burly-look-
ing fellow. We were tired. Beach says:

"If I had a drink of good whisky I would like it."

This was the first time we had called for anything
of the kind.

Said Beach: "Cap, have you got some good
whisky?"

"Yes, sir; I have." He slammed a decanter down
hard enough to break a common glass bottle all to
pieces. "There is some that does not stink of turpentine."

We turned out a little and smelt of it. Turpentine
was all it did stink of. We smelled light of that and
moved on. After traveling many miles, stopping
often to let the horses rest and stop the yelling caused
by rosin, we came to the foot of Addison Hill. This
is a long heavy hill. It is about three miles from
base to summit.

"Beach," I remarked, "this is a settler; it is so
hot. The road winds through the woods; not a

breath of air. When we stop going up this hill we will have to block all of the hind wheels on all of these wagons, or the pressure above will back the light wagons over the blockings. The horses can't hold them and rest. This will be lively work after you sing out 'whoa.' This is the way I have always had to do. A prop dragging does more hurt than good. It will turn light wagons over. The weight settling back will raise up the light wagons and throw them all around in many ways. We must not pull these horses more than a rod at one time. In this way we must climb this hill, if we get up it."

After working up this hill about half way I saw that one of Beach's horses was not right. It was not the one that got choked. This horse had stood it well up to this time. It was hot; he was overdone; he had, what is called by some, the thumps. It is the palpitation of the heart.

"Beach, we must get these wagons out of the road and anchor here. That horse must not be drawn any more now. He would drop dead on this hill."

We blocked up, took off the horses, got in the woods in the shade, and stayed there until it got cooler. After resting a few hours the sun got lower, and we tried it again. This horse had got over thumping, or his heart had. We slowly worked up to the summit; then it went better. After about four or five miles we came to the river and pulled in at a hotel. There we were within fourteen miles of the port I was sailing for with one very lame mare. We put up for the night. In the morning I soon saw one train wrecked. My mare's leg was badly swelled from hoof to top of shoulder. She stood with her weight forward all on one foot. I moved her around. She went on three legs.

"Beach, this looks like a shipwreck. Well, we can sail some yet. You can draw your train eight miles. It will be level that distance along the river. Then it will be six miles over heavy hills. Your team cannot draw the load up them. I will make a single harness out of my double harness and hitch the stallion single, and lead the mare behind, and leave the balance of my train. This is the best I can do."

After rosining and greasing, we set sail again. Beach ahead now, I in the rear, the mare with a long rope tied to her head, so as to give her plenty of room she hobbling along on three legs. The mud was deep along the river. It had rained nearly every day since we started; showers many times a day; then it would come off hot. We moved slowly, stopping often. In time we sailed eight miles. Then we must take leave of the river and climb hills. This cannot be done with any propelling power we have got."

"Beach, drop off here all of the wagons but one, and we will sail on. I think we can get through with two wagons. I wish to make the port I started for with some of this train, if it is wrecked, as it will be, and badly, too. There we can repair up. It is at my father's farm. We can turn out some of these horses and they can rest up, that will help them."

Readers, you can see us winding our way up and down the heavy hills of the state of Pennsylvania with a small part of this wreck. I am going to tell you the cause as soon as I find it. A little before night we arrived at my father's house. This is where I always found welcome. Welcome was always around there to his children, of which he had not a few. There were eleven boys and two girls, scattered all over the country. These arrivals were no surprise to him. It was a common thing for some of them to sail into this port days and all times of the night. Sometimes four and five would be in this port at one time, to rest up and repair up wrecks, and it was all free. Reader, I assure you it took some hard knocks and some hard work to keep this free port open. I have sailed into this port to repair up many wrecks, sailing over these hills with wagons and horses. They would happen in some way with all I could do to prevent. When we arrived this time he soon saw there was another wreck. He was out flying around (he was no sit-still), stripping the harness off the horses.

"Gerard has got his thumb in his mouth. That is a sure sign things are not going to suit him."

"Father, this pony has come this long journey, and drawn heavy loads. She is growing worse all the time, and I have not been able to find the cause; it commenced the first day. If I had some shoeing tools I would take off her shoe and give her foot a thorough examination."

"Those can be had."

Frank was started for the tools on a run. Beach's horses were cleaned and turned out in a shady pasture. Frank soon came with the tools. I removed the shoe, and commenced this search by paring thin shavings off the sole of the foot. I soon saw the cause of all this trouble. There was a row of nearly square spots. These formed a circle the shape of the shoe, and the spots were the same distance apart that the holes in the shoe were. I took my knife and cut in a little, and the matter spurted out three feet. I cut the other three open in the same way. They all discharged in about the same way. These spots, or places where these nails went in her feet, were under the shoe when it was on.

"It was a wonder she did not die with lock-jaw. If I had a pint of tar I could soon make her quite easy from pain."

Frank was started on a three-mile sail, on a run. He soon came back with the tar. While he was gone I made a boot for her foot. It had a sole on it, and laced up. I put in plenty of tar, put on this boot, laced it up, secured well, and turned her out in the pasture. One of my brothers took his team and we pulled in, the first wrecked train. The other train I pulled in two at a trip, with the stallion. These wagons all had to be washed. They were all one complete daub of mud. They had worn all of the play they would need. Rosin is the poorest axle tree grease in the world; that I know. I have had a trial of it. I never tried the best. I have seen it advertised. Beach spent ten days viewing the country while waiting for his poor old horses to rest and recover what they had lost from many causes, preparatory to sailing this road over again. One he hitched to the sulky, led the oldest behind, and sailed out on Addison Hill; at the very spot where the one he was then driving gave out with the palpitation of the heart, the one that he led dropped dead in the road the first day. Another wreck. She was removed out of the highway and we sailed on. In a short time the other's heart began to thump, and he had to stop then. In this way, after many days, he arrived home. This horse, before we started, was quite a good farm horse. He can never endure any more hard work. Beach went with me on another trip a few years after, over this same road. We got through better; we had learned by experience. I was obliged, with my small pony stallion, to draw all of these wagons around over heavy hills to market them. They were a hard-looking lot to sell. I was obliged to trade and traffic some for cattle and then sell them—horses the same; no rest for me. They did not shine quite so much as they did when I started. A little varnish makes a vast difference, in some folks' judgment, in many ways and about many things. They will bite a shiny bait very quick. It will attract their attention. My wagons looked like second-hand. Well, they were, and I knew it; but I had as good a right to sell second-hand wagons as others for all I could get, and at it I went. After six weeks hard work they were disposed of in many ways.

This mare's foot must be looked to to see what condition it is in. The boot is on and has been for six weeks. She has been over her lameness for a long time. She has run in the pasture. The first treatment, when I put this boot on, is all she ever had to her, and it has been six weeks. I am going to sail this road over again. The last thing to be done, always, with me, preparatory to a sail on land with horses, is to prepare their feet all at one time; no botching and hurting about this business on the horse's foot-at any time on my horses or on any man's horse. This is a rule I always have adhered to. The best I can do, it will be bad enough for the horse in a short time. I removed the boot; the foot had grown, that is, the hoof had. There had not been any wear on the hoof on this foot on account of the boot, and it had useless hoof on. That did not effect her much in pasture. I pulled all of this mare's shoes off when I turned her out. This is the way to do with all horses. Examining this mare's foot, the old sole was all loose, or nearly so. I took it all off. Underneath there was a new sole grown. At this time and stage of growth it was white and soft and very tender. There was no contraction. The foot had not had iron nailed on it. It had its liberty.

I must get back to my shop and see to business there. This foot must be fixed and this tender sole and growth must be protected. If this is mutilated now and she gets fever in her hoof it will ruin her. She must have something to protect the sole for this drive—a wide web, and a very thin, light shoe. It is something of a chore to fix this foot up, to keep all protected, and keep the mare sailing on the road and not spoil her; and yet it can be done, and this is the way to do it: The dirt and sand must all be kept out of the foot. It will be necessary to have a piece of calf-skin large enough to cover over the bottom of the foot and come up above the ankle, so as to form a boot leg. For fear this might wear through on the bottom and let in dirt and gravel, there must be another thicker piece, the size of the foot, put over that, and the shoe nailed over all It requires some patience and skill to nail this shoe on the foot and get it all in good shape, and not prick the foot with nails, with only one-quarter of an inch shell to drive nails in, and that all covered up out of sight with leather; and yet this was done. I have bent over thousands of horses' feet, fixing them in this way and many other ways, until I almost see stars. After getting this shoe on nicely there must be some tar warmed, not hot; I do not want to spoil the new growth on this tender foot by burning in any way. This damned burning busi ness I am down on, on horses and on everything else. That belongs back in the dark ages. I poured a little tar in at the heel, pulled up the calf-skin around the ankle, laid it in plaits, and sewed it No tying to shut off the circulation. It took me some time to fix this foot. There are many things to look to working on horses' feet. The foot was not contracted.

This job suits me. The frog has a rest in the center on the ground. I am ready to sail again. This treat-ment on the foot where nails have been driven in the foot by accident or any other way is good. I always made a success in this way. Care must be taken of the foot or it will contract. That will spoil the foot and horse at the same time. I have seen lots of horses spoiled in this way by not taking proper care of the foot. If it should contract, spread it, and hold it out. It is easy to do this.

I sailed home; no wreck on the way; not a limp on that booted foot, and I left it on until the boot wore through. By that time the foot had got quite hard. I kept it protected for some time. I am going to tell

you the cause of nearly all this trouble and shipwreck.
Part was my fault. That rosin business was my fault.
I listened to that old liar, "They Say." I did not use
reason until it was too late. I think Beach's horses
would have made that trip if it had not been for rosin.
They were lugged to death. There was no let-up on
them. They had to draw up and down grade nearly
all the route, and no help for it. They were not fed
up for such a trip, and were old; and yet we could
have favored them and would, and we did all we could.
Rosin would block the wheels, and blocked the game.
Part of this wreck was caused by a sneak thief, taking
my mare out of my stable in the night, lambing her
around all night, tearing off or twisting around her
shoe, and causing her to drive four nails into the bottom of her foot. That was the biggest eye-opener I
ever had at that time. I had had some before, one
about nine months previous to this. That caused me
to stare, but as it is on another subject I will save that
for another book, which I intend to write. These eye-
openers caused me to begin to think more and use more
reason and all the good judgment and good sense I
could command about all things. I am using more of
these articles now than I ever used in all my life, and
yet I make some mistakes. These wrecks and mistakes have all been lessons to me. It has been so all
through life—wreck, repair, and sail What is the use
of getting scared ?

Let us go on with this horse sail. You cannot expect to own and drive horses without having some
lame in some way and in many ways. The only thing

we can do is to remove all the cause we can, and keep it removed.

It has been some time since you have heard from the old white mare. She is doing finely. She is improving all the time. Her shoulders are nearly alike. When she trots fast she seems a little stiff. I am not going to move out of this town, on account of this old mare. She is far better off now than I expected her to become when I commenced on her. I am well paid for my labor if she never improves any more. I have worked on this mare five months. It is March now. I shall soon want to sell her. She is of no use to me any more. It will be a rather hard job to sell her, for she is very old. I must let her go if I give her away. They will not know this mare in this town. She has not been seen in a long time. She does not look like that old mare I had towing around the streets last fall, and no argument can be used to convince them, and I shall not try. I want her off my hands. I am going to start this science in another place, if I can. This has been a tough town to work on the horse. It has about killed me. I have taught all of the time, and no one seems to be interested in my science, that is, to learn it. I cannot get their attention except when I am bugling in the streets, and that has become a common thing with them. They do not seem to understand what I am trying to do. They stare a little and go about their business, unless I set up a yell. Then they go for me:

"Say, Doan, what do you do for a horse that has got a sore neck?"

"Where is your horse?"

"In the barn over here a little way."

"I cannot tell until I see the horse."

"Come, go over and see him."

"I will go with you."

After travelling about half a mile—"It's that big gray; his neck is awful sore, and has been a long time. I have used lots of stuff on it. I can't heal it up."

"It is chawed up; that is certain."

"Now what would you do for that?"

"I would remove the cause very quickly if he was my horse, and you can do that as well as I."

"What would you do?"

"I would take off that collar and haims, the weight off his neck; wash his neck clean with castile soap, grease it with butter or lard, castor oil, or sweet oil, any of these things will make it feel better. It would get well without anything after the cause is removed."

The fact is, ignorance is the greatest drawback a man ever had. This team of horses was not very well matched. As for size, one was a small, low pony, the other was a tall, rangy horse. The tongue of the wagon was heavy enough for an ox-cart; the yoke was very heavy; the breast-straps were buckled up short on the tall horse in such a way that he had to hold at least two-thirds of this weight on his neck. The collar was a small, nearly worn out thing, cut apart at the top and let down, with no pad. The collar lacked five inches of reaching to the top of the neck; the hames were drawn tight together with a hard strap, and that was twisted at that. I told him to remove all of this

rubbish, and keep it off, and his horse's neck would
get well in a very short time; then put something on
him fit for a horse to work in, and if you must use
that cart-tongue and ox-yoke, there are plenty of
hickory saplings; cut one, run it under the forward
axle, bend it down and strap it to the tongue. That
will take two-thirds of the weight off these poor
horses' necks. What is the use of these horses standing tied all day to posts with this weight on their
necks? It gets painful. I always keep all the weight
off my horses' necks that I can. It is not much
trouble, and if it is it will pay you, and save your
horses suffering more than you are aware of. They
will endure more: their necks will keep their shape,
and will not get sore if they have a good collar well
fitted, and hames to fit them. You cannot have nice
horses and have them all chawed up with rubbish for
harness.

"Say, Doan," says another, "my mare is getting
wind-puffs on. What do you do for them?"

"Keep the horse natural; that is the way I do it."

"You're a good talker."

The fact was I was getting very tired talking, and
keeping so many horses all sailing, doing all of the
work, but very little pay. I begun to get a little sour.
I could not help it. They did not use and take care
of their horses as well as I did, and they could spoil
them faster than I could cure. I am not going to
give up this horse fight yet. I am going to come out
with this old white mare. I will give them one good
surprise before I leave this town. These are facts I
am writing. They are no dreams or fictitious tales.

I dressed up this old mare a little for this surprise. She was fat and clean ; not a stain on her. I kept her so all of the time. She did not stand in the stable to do this . she had been driven nights, not to death, then half starved. She had the best of care all of this time in all ways. I had been in this barn with her nights for nearly six months, more than half of my time. Of course I was not always to work on her. Looking at her I cannot tell why I did this, only I was pleased with the result. It was a big thing. She looked young around her head. Her eyes are large, bright, and full now. The skin is filled out plump with flesh. She shows no wrinkles around the nose ; she never did much, like some horses. She is full of life ; she looks a little wild out of her eyes. I cleaned and combed her tail. She had a long tail that almost touched the floor. Her mane had grown, though it looked a little ragged where the collar had chawed it before I got her. I drove her in breast collar. I wanted to give her neck a chance to fill up. I was doing my best on this old mare to please myself, and at my own expense, and it was no business of any man. I combed and parted her foretop, braided it to keep it out of her eyes, and braided ribbons in so as to make tassels. This I always do on my horses in hot weather. I do not want my hair hanging in and over my eyes. I cannot see as well. Besides, it will annoy a horse, and cause him to toss his head when he gets sweaty. I put on a new harness, hitched to a light buggy, and sailed out. After driving a while on the ourskirts of the town I sailed down Main street. It so happened there was a band of musicians blowing their bugles. This mare liked music; it waked her up some. She put on more style on that account, and yet I did not attract much attention; neither did the horse. After driving around this town a few hours I did not seem to surprise any one; then I began to get surprised myself. I talked with some; they did not know this mare. There was only four in this town that knew this mare, and no argument could convince them that it was the same old mare I led around that town six months previous, and talked in many places and told them I was going to try to cure her without medicine or mutilating her in any way. I told them they would not know her, and they did not. Doctor Woodrough's residence and mine joined. George, his son, was a horse-trainer by profession. His brother was around the stables. These three men knew what I was doing, and trying to do. Our barns joined. I made the fourth man that knew this mare in this town. They had seen her often, and watched the change. While driving around this town I passed a grocery. There were several standing around. The Woodrough boys were there. They saw me pass. Says George: "There goes Doan with that old mare he had towing around here last fall."

I overheard them talking, but I did not stop. It was no use. I sailed on. George and his brother got up quite a racket about it. They told me these men said this mare I was driving was a colt. I had let that old mare go long ago. They would bet twenty-five dollars it was not the same old mare. The boys were ready to bet with them, but it turned out all wind, as it usually did. I always had money to

back up this great science, and have got some now.
There is no danger of losing on my side. That I well
know. After all this hard winter's work only a few
have learnt anything, for this reason, they cannot see
as I have done anything on that old mare I had last
fall. She is changed so her identity is forever lost to
them. They can see nothing but that old mare I
was towing around last fall, and they cannot see her.
I can see them both at the same time. With science
I can change young horses in a very few days so
much their owners would not know them if I did not
tell them anything about it. They dare not swear
it was their horse, for this reason. I have been called
a dangerous and bad man; some have told me they
would not dare take their horses in my shop. Such
cowards must drive stiff horses. I have had horses so
lame and stiff they could hardly move; if they did it
hurt them very bad—brought to me to cure. Before
I was allowed to commence on them I must give security three and four times the horse's worth, for fear
I might spoil them. I would like some of these
afraid and cowardly men to tell me how it would be
possible to spoil one of these horses. They are already
spoilt, and some have been for many years. They can
be made worse by these effect doctors in many ways,
and are, and they are paid well for doing it. I never
heard of one case in my life where they were asked to
give security if they killed these horses burning and
mutilating them. Some died with the lockjaw, caused
by seatons being put in their shoulders. Some do get
killed by these effect doctors; some stand the torture

well. It is surprising how much they can stand of
this treatment and live and work, their feet murdered
to death at the same time. My God! they must be
tough.

Poor old gray, we must soon part,
To do this, it will almost break my heart ;
We have roamed together almost night and day,
From the mill I have carried middlings and given you good hay.
This is hard for both you and me ;
To help other poor horses there is no other way that I can see.
This great discovery I must introduce ;
There are thousands like you suffering the same abuse.
I have changed you back as your creator intended you to be ;
If there is any defect in this job they cannot see.
No mercy to you they will show,
Through deep mud and snow you will have to go ;
It will not be long, this abuse you will have to endure,
You're getting old ; your time is most out, that is sure.
They are such poor judges of species of your kind,
They cannot tell if you are old, stiff, lame, or blind.
On the road they will pound you through
Night and day, with or without a shoe ;
If any shoes they do put on,
They're often a thousand times worse than none.
Poor old mare, after you I have sold,
On you I can not have any more control.
You will have to take your chances as all others do ;
I may never hav you again to shoe.
Up and down hills you will have to go,
With all lengths of levers on your toe.
This pain and suffering your driver cannot feel ;
Its effect extends from top of shoulder to the heel.
If you could talk and tell them where the cause all laid,
Then to part with you I would not be so much afraid ;
But as this complicated matter now stands,
There is no safety in any man's hands.
The trouble with your feet will not be all you will have to endure,
You will have to sleep on piles of stinking, rotten manure.

How all this trouble and suffering can be overcome
Is more than I can tell, your drivers are so dumb.
Nearly all of your fellow-creatures are in the same plight,
The same as you, they are obliged to suffer day and night.
With sore cords, pains, and aches in their feet,
Some are so bad they cannot stand long enough to eat.
I would like to relieve the suffering of all of your kind;
How to do it I cannot tell, they all seem so blind.
This is the reason why I put you away,
Is to see if I can introduce this some other way.
On all of the centers I have equalized your weight,
Taken off the toe-lever, and made your feet mates;
And put the structure of your foot all in harmony of action,
And it would stay so if it weren't for run-over feet, leverage, and con-
    traction.
By ironing the feet this cannot be prevented
With any steel or iron shoe that man has ever invented.
The dangers that you are surrounded with are many;
I do not know as I can help you to steer clear of any.
That old ditch called the canal is close by;
That is where old horses like you are taken to die.
When horses like you have been crippled and old,
To go on the canal then they are sold.
To last one trip is sometimes all they care,
In doing this they are stripped of flesh, hide, and hair.
I have seen them in herds plodding their way
Toward this ditch, there to end up their day.
When you were young and limber you had better homes,
Now you are stiff, you must have all the flesh chawed off your bones.
This is the best place for that that can be found,
Search where you will, the world all round.
It serves all the same, young, limber, stiff, or blind;
A worse place for a horse or a mule you cannot find.
It galls and chafes them both fore and aft,
All caused by so much side draft.
Horses on this ditch can never travel and draw on a straight line.
If men had this work to do it would be tedious they would find.
This side draft can never be overcome, this is sure—
Remove the cause, no medicine is required to perform the cure.
Water to walk on by man or beast the creator never made,

In that we have to swim, drown, or wade.
In order to do away with this side draft that galls them so
In the center of this ditch and water they would have to go;
If the water was shallow so they could wade and not be drowned,
Then in this case they would always be aground;
If the water was deep enough for the craft to float,
These poor horses could not swim and draw a loaded boat.

I cannot see any argument in favor of this ditch use;
It always has been a great place poor horses and mules to abuse.
Their suffering with pen and ink I cannot portray;
I think this old ditch ought to be done away,
For many other reasons besides the horse's abuse.
It's had its day and outlived its use.
It always was a center for corruption and crime;
It's outlived its day and had its time.
It always has been a slow-poke of a way to travel at best.
In my boyhood days I took it in my head to go West.
On this stinking ditch four hundred miles I traveled;
It was lock up hill, lock down, in no place level.
All this long sail my fare I paid,
And yet more than half of it on foot I made.
Sometimes I would be many miles ahead
Viewing the country, sitting on verandahs in the shade.
You may call it what you will, good or bad luck,
Every few days all these crafts in the mud are stuck.
The cause of all this shipwreck was many miles away;
No one could tell how long in this stinking mud they would have to
    stay.
Of all the nuisances that ever were on the face of this earth
This old stinking ditch called the canal is the worst.
All must wait for the breach to be repaired;
These poor horses and mules, O my God! how they fared!
In mud, cold, and sleet, necks girdled clear around,
Obliged to stand up and sleep, no place fit to lie down.
In its day it might have been of use if they could have used other
    power;
As it has been and now is, on them is only slaughter and devour,
To navigate this old ditch with this power or any other
It always would be crowded with wrecks and bother.

My object in going West was the country to view;
Of course I wanted to see all that I traveled through.
I was green, of course, as all new-beginners must be,
But experience soon taught me down in this ditch I could not see.
Down in this small, stinking cabin I cannot stay,   -
If I do all of my money and time will be thrown away.
The next course for me, I think, to pursue
Will be to go on deck, there I can have a better view.
There in the scorching sun I seated myself on a box;
In a very short time my head received an awful knock.
After my brains were nearly knocked out,
"A bridge ahead!" I heard four or five shout.
These arches are quite thick across this old stinking pool,
A man will soon get his eyes open unless he is a fool.
Before he has traveled on this ditch very far
He will soon learn these bridges to beware.
All was new to me, I was always gaping around,
"Lay down there, unless you want your bones ground,"
As quick as thought I ducked my head down;
This was a narrow escape from being killed or drowned.
I do not want to be drowned in stinking water like this;
It's unsafe, I know, but I will run a little more risk.
I have paid my fare through on this boat,
And I am going to keep track as long as there is a plank to float.
This is rather tough to sit here in the hot sun and heat,
And see sore horses whipped, pounded, and beat.
This craft, too, moves at such a very slow rate,
If I was in a hurry it would be tedious to wait.

While seated on the stern of the boat, looking about,
I heard another yell, "Bridge ahead! look out!"
Nearly all of the boat under the bridge had passed,
As quick as thought, my safety was the bridge to grasp.
This I very quickly saw, to save my life, must be done.
The craft moved on; over the center of this ditch I hung.
In those days I was young, resolute, strong, and spry.
If I lose my hold it will be wade, swim, or die.
Over the bridge-rail. heels over head, I went.
By this time I had thought my money was foolishly spent.
If I do not keep my eyes open, and a better look-out,   .

I shall get killed or drowned before I get to the end of this route.
On the sea of life we must all sail:
  t is no kind of use to bawl, weep, or wail.
I am going to try the tow-path awhile and see how that will go;
It is hard to pay my fare on this craft and go afoot, I know.
It's not much fun to sit on that boat and watch bridges ahead,
And run the risk of having your brains knocked out of your head.
The poorest investment in my life that I ever made
It was when my fare on this old craft I paid.
It was on a pleasure trip when I set sail that I was bound;
Dead in this old stinking ditch I did not want to be found.
I have shipped aboard, I won't back out,
I am going to see this craft through to the end of the route.
It won't do for me to get very far ahead:
I may lose track—their horses, too, are liable to drop dead.
Horses on the canal never get tired on their legs,
They are in such a hurry they must eat, while they work, out of
        bags.
When it came night, in this craft to sleep I would go;
And that could not be done, the musketoes speared me so.
The bullfrogs would all begin their bugles to blow;
It seemed to me they all tried each other to outdo,
All seemed to be blowing their biggest blast,
And all trying each other to outlast.
This bugling was kept up during the nights;
To make matters worse, on the tow-path there would be fights.
This craft they tried night and day to run,
And that was out of the question, impossible to be done.
Every few days this old ditch out this slime would spew,
Then all would be wrecked—boat, passengers, horses, and crew.
This was so this whole route, along the whole line
There was a racket about something nearly all of the time.
At that time when all was in repair and new
There was a large amount of produce crowded through.
In the summer to this old ditch it would center;
Not a pound could they carry through the cold long winter.
In the summer many times they would wait and tarry,
All for the want of more freight to carry.
In long summer days could be seen idle crew
In the fall they would all have more than they could do.

The cause of all this and all other fluctuations
Is the want of system and better regulations.
In the fall, when the most work was to be done,
This old ditch was crowded full and overrun.
Right in the worst time you could have this work to do,
It's froze up solid ; there is no such thing as getting through.
We have got business, resolute men of this make,
This ice for many miles they will pound and break.
In order their freight to market to get
They will work night and day in cold and wet,
In this last fluctuation in the fall.
With many it's make or break, perhaps lose all.
After all these poor men and horses have done,
It's full of loaded boats unable to run.
With any power this old ditch to navigate,
It always would have to be done at this slow rate.
In its day it was the best they could do,
It was all well enough, it was all they know.
Better power has now taken its place.
To lay out money on this ditch is only waste ;
To keep it up in repair, I mean.
If men think and have eyes it can be seen
With railroads and steam it never can compete ;
Nearly always wrecked, and that, too, in fleets.
If you try to sail it is only half the year round,
And then in fleets you're frozen in or on the ground ;
Then the produce you are trying to market take,
The people would all starve before the port you could make ;
And that is not all; you cannot get the work to do.
They will not wait for this old ditch to crowd it through,
To conduct the produce of a country through such a place
Must always be attended with shipwreck, trouble, and waste.
This is the way it always has and will have to be done,
These troubles never will nor never can be overcome.
There is nothing in favor of this stinking ditch can be said ;
A man might use a little argument in its favor if he was out of his
　　　head.
You cannot carry perishable produce at any time of the year ;
It will not be long, if you get any to carry it will be queer,
They cannot carry hogs, cattle, neither alive nor dead,

They would all die, s.ink, and carrion before the port was made.
This ditch, there is no safety shipping anything on it;
It is liable to get sick itself any time, and vomit.
There can be hundreds and thousands of things said
To prove this old stinking ditch called the canal is dead.
What surprises me the most is it lived as long as it did,
Take in consideration the filth and corruption it has been fed.
The railroad now must take the lead,
On corruption and carrion it does not feed.
And furthermore, it's got more sea to sail,
And with it carries the United States mail.
All over this republic its centers are made,
All systematized, and has got the balance of trade.
The producer his products to market can get this way;
It can be marketed and get return the same day.
This system causes produce more evenly to run,
This is the way fluctuation in trade away must be done.
With railroads all systematized and running on this plan,
It's folly any longer through this ditch produce to try to cram,
For many years it has gradually been falling to decay,
It's became a nuisance now, and should be out of the way.
It to rise again it never can, that is plain to see,
The produce of the country from it seems to flee.
I cannot see where any longer it's of any kind of use,
Only make slaves to pay taxes, and stiff, lame, blind horses to abuse.
We cannot help what has already been done,
But we can prevent any more suffering and crime from this source to
    come,
In this way—clear away this rubbish, it's no longer of any use,
It will do away with lots of crime, suffering, and abuse.
Clear away old rubbish and make room for new,
This is what all mankind on this globe have always had to do;
This is so all over this world, sail the globe around,
Through this purifying mill we all have to be ground.
This old stinking ditch has a long time been dead,
And yet with corruption, filth, and carrion of all kinds it's fed.
With disease it is constantly inoculating along the whole route,
By puking, vomiting, and spewing this carrion out.
As it now is and always has been, empty or full,
Do all you can, and yet it's a stinking old cesspool.

It will get sick, and out this slime and corruption will run,
Nearly always, when this takes place, great damage is done
Abandon now this old nuisance, this has got to be ;
The inhabitants of course from it cannot very well flee.
All full of pools of dead, inanimate corruptions it lies,
This is the cause of sickness, disease ; in this it has its rise.
There is only one way left now that I can see,
As the people do not want to leave their farms and houses and flee,
Is to bury this center of filth and corruption under ground,
With other dead things of the past, so deep it cannot be found.
T.is should many years ago been done,
Instead of squandering the people's money trying to make a dead thing
         run.
There should many years ago appropriation have been made,
And men set to work with scraper, plow, pick, shovel, and spade.
With some good live men this job to superintend,
This would not be a great task , it would soon come to an end.
This work for our country's sake should now begin ;
It would save a multitude of suffering, crime and sin.

    Fine palaces to build, to make tyrannical laws,
To punish the effect, will not remove the cause.
If with tramps you do not want to be overrun,
Something besides making tyrannical laws must be done.
There never has been a law that the people could not break,
And they always have and always will for liberty's sake.
That tramp law smells to hell of tyranny and oppression:
It's a disgrace to a school district, town, country, state, or nation.
Do not be in a hurry your neighbor and brother man to pursue,
Look around ; there may be some one in pursuit of you.
With such corrupt legislation as we now have got
All are liable to stink carrion and rot.
A worse law in legislative halls you could not make,
It caused all paupers and tramps a different course to take—
" As we can no longer for help with safety to the people appeal,
It's safer now, when our money is all gone, to steal."
That damned tramp law is got up on such a wise plan
It's bound to take our liberty away, do the best we can.
These smart and good and wise men to the center of each state we
         have sent

To ruin us legislating for themselves, they seem hell bent
If they do not change the course that they now pursue
They will financially wreck the ship of state, passengers and crew.
They are fast sapping the people's hard-earned money away
To build costly palaces for themselves in to stay.
We do not any longer want our money to pay
Tyrannical men our liberty to legislate away.
For many years it has been going on from bad to worse;
Many laws you have made for us are only a curse:
And the course you are steering now and want to take
Is to make yourselves rich and of us paupers make.
Heavy taxes to pay, and that used for pomp and show,
Will soon shipwreck us all, that we well know.
We will all have to drop in line if this course you sail,
We will all be made paupers, of this there will be no fail.
Spend the people's money in doing so, of them make paupers and
     poor,
Then tax them to build reformatories, prison pens, in them to secure.
The blackest laws of these or of any other times
Is to legislate, make laws, to make paupers, then make poverty a
     crime.
If we do not have wiser, honester, better men at the helm of the ship
     of state
To hell and destruction we will all go in this wake.
Of all the damned, unmerciful tyrants a man can ever see
Are men that will legislate to take other's liberty away, and themselves
     go free.
And this, too, for the awful crime of not having a cent.
How do you know, if these men ever had any money, how it was
     spent?
Do not be in a hurry your fellow-man's liberty away to take,
He may have something new that cost his all to make.
To all mankind, rich or poor, to them mercy show,
You do not always know the cause that made them so.
Sit down with them; have a little chat; your time may be well spent,
He may have a new discovery that cost a large fortune to invent.
There are many ways that a pauper can be made,
And if we do not wiser men select we will all be paupers, I am afraid.
By legislation legalized robbers all over the land are found,
In rings and monopolies they all seem to be bound.

In our legislative halls this corruption seems to center,
Raise their own salaries, make tyrannical laws for others; in this way
    they winter.
In this course you are sailing : look ahead; there are breakers, can't
    you see ?
Of all the damned mean robbers is a man that will sell himself for a
    fee;
All for a few dollars for himself to try to make,
He will place the lives and property of a nation at stake.
Poor, blind fools, do you think you know what you are about?
The first thing you know you will be all turned inside out
If you should make a law to confine me even to a stake,
That would be the first thing with me that law to break.
With knapsack on my back, through mud and snow, without a cent,
Night and day I would travel to break that law i would be hell
    bent
This would be just the way our liberty and freedom was bought;
For seven long years the soldiers suffered, died, and fought.
Tyrants, do you think you can our liberty legislate away?
If you do, try it; you will find some of the same mettle they had in
    that day.
It does seem to me the first principles of this government you have
    lost;
The way you legislate, act, talk, you seem to think yourselves boss.
We do not intend to pay you much longer to rob us, we will have you
    know :
The first thing you know, out of our legislative halls you will go.
Legalized thieves and robbers of yourselves you have made,
And at that damned business you have carried on heavy trade,
To rob us and build up powers of your own :
These facts to us have a long time been known.
Steal our hard-earned money, to buy yourselves a position,
Then legislate to make ten times worse our condition ;
Enact laws to prevent us from so to do,
Then sell us and yourselves to this damned robbing crew.
This is what you have been doing for many long years;
Weep for your crimes now with scalding, bitter tears.
You have been now in the balances weighed,
No more confidence to do our business in you can be paid.
Our great ship of state you have wrecked and stranded,

Quarreling and fighting for yourselvs a position it to man.
You have scuttled this ship and deserted it, too,
This is just the way all robbers and pirates do.
There is no use of denying this, it is all true,
And worse, you have done, you have murdered some of the crew.
Poor Garfield you shot down without any cause;
He has been these many years battling against tyrannical laws.
My God! what do you think is going to become of this nation?
Rob us in many ways, fight, murder—all for a position.
All the legislation for many years for yourselves that you have done,
It has made your own condition worse, no good to us by it can come.
All over our great republic this legalized robbing we have had:
They have shipwrecked the whole fleet, and now they are playing
    grab.
For little or no service big bills are poured in, just take note—
My good God! no wonder this fleet no longer could float,
With such men as we have had to steer this fleet of our nation.
If they are allowed to go on they will sail us to hell and damnation.
If we follow them any longer the course they are pursuing
You will get all the hell you want; it's already brewing.
In the case of Guiteau, look at the useless expense of his trial;
He committed the act; that was seen; it will admit of no denial.
Poor, unhappy, unfortunate man he must be.
And his case could have been disposed of without so many robbers to
    fee.
In either case, insane or of sound mind,
A verdict against him they would have to find.
About this poor, unfortunate man I shall have no more to say;
I do not believe in hanging or killing my fellow-man in any way.
As things look now, something will soon have to be done;
In this corruption the fleet of the United States cannot run.
The only way now that I can see to pursue
Is to clear away this damned rubbish and begin new.
For condemned they are by the overruling power;
If they are allowed to go on, themselves and all others they will de-
    vour.
They seem no longer able to keep this ship afloat,
They might possibly run an old, stinking canal boat.
If that they should wreck there would not be so much loss,
Such a craft as that they might possibly get to boss.

Their works are enough to condemn them, no more evidence is
    needed;
Their power in thousands of ways they have exceeded.
Our servants to represent us we have sent to the center of our nation.
They have been duped—bought to make unwise legislation.
Some men have such an awful greed for the glitter of gold,
They will sacrifice the lives and property of a nation and let it be sold.
And that is the power now with it this nation they are trying to run,
To rob us of that first that had to be done;
They all seem trying to see which can get the biggest pile.
In doing so they have got into a devil of a rile
The flag of seventeen hundred and seventy-six will not fade,
The stripes for tyrants and traitors, thieves, robbers, they were made.
Some seem trying their level best to pull it down;
On their wise and honest, faithful heads put a crown.
This government on the opposite principle was built to run
To put crowns on our hired help; I think it will be hardly done
For many years, now we have lived under monarchical reign,
And now it has become despotic.   Some are being slain.
Robberies and riots all over our country we have had,
Now it looks as though corruption and misrule had run mad.
There is no use trying to cover it up: it stares you square in the face.
The way our government for many years has been run is a disgrace.
It would be tedious for a man to write where this corruption all had
    its rise,
If he knew, and had the time, and was ever so wise.
Just to open your eyes I will give you a little history of a few.
In the first place, we are sold to this damned robbing crew;
We are taxed and robbed in thousands of ways;
Without representation they have made us underlings and slaves.
They are usurpers of power which to them does not belong:
They raised their own salaries themselves, and that was wrong.
The people never authorized them this mean business to do;
It was all planned by that robbing, sneaking, treacherous crew,
That was done in the beginning of that great General Grant reign,
Right in the very time when all around was to be slain.
Our country was in danger; the rebels in destruction it had laid;
To render us a little assistance fifty thousand dollars a year to him
    must be paid
And that must be secured a term eight years long!

Fellow-citizens, if you do not clear yourselves of these sappers you are
    gone.

In this salary grab, of course, they all had to take a hand:

Like all other corruptions, it is contagious; it spread all over the land.

To double like this is easy for you, we all very well know,

But we have to work for very small pay, and that comes slow.

You doubled our taxes on that damned robbing raid,

And now you put on pomp and show, and say these taxes must be
    paid,

And if you do not pay it we will sell you out of house and home,

And as paupers and thieves over the country you shall roam.

It seems to me for servants you are putting on considerable style :

The first you know, out of our legislative halls you will go in a pile ;

This damned tyrannical yoke we do not much longer intend to wear .

We have stood now about all we can possibly bear.

For frauds, robberies, and corruptions all other nations you have out-
    done,

If that is what you are trying to do, you excel. I will not except
    one.

Even old ancient Rome you outdo in your blind race for gold—

For that their happiness, country, honor, and lives were sold.

As for you, General Grant, something more must be done;

Such services for your country and great laurels you have won ;

A crown should be put on your head, you should have another fee,

Of this whole band of robbers you should be king bee.

This honor you certainly have won, it is plain to be seen.

To see this the people do not have to be very keen.

It is widespread and well known over the land,

That robber chief you have become of this entire robbing band.

Now, sir, I do not see as we can honors any more on you bestow;

We are getting very poor; you hav squandered our money and robbed
    us so.

Raising the salaries all over our whole entire nation.

It affected all, rich and poor, all in the same relation.

It caused men who had the poor laborers in their employ

To close up. " We cannot run, these heavy taxes do us so annoy."

Some would try a little longer to run by cutting wages down,

This has caused thousands, what are now called tramps, to run around

To see if they could get some work, employment find;

And now for doing so they have made laws to make it a crime.

Mr. Grant, do you not know to prison for begging we have to go,
All caused by you and your damned rotten, robbing crew?
You have robbed us and on us heavy taxes laid,
And criminals and slaves and paupers, too, of us you have made.
When you pilot of our nation eight years were made,
Four hundred thousand dollars to you was paid.
And extras that all cost us money were thrown in,
And now you are around begging for help again.
What you did with all that money of course we do not know,
Unless you spent it sailing around, setting yourself up for a monkey
    show.
If now a beggar and pauper you have got to be
After all we have done to help you, it is of no use any longer that I
    can see.
You will have to take your chances as all beggars and paupers do.
Your money has been spent without doubt for pomp and show ;
Of ours we have been robbed by heavy taxes to pay you
And your damned, corrupted, thieving, robbing crew.
We do not intend any longer by you robbers and tyrants to be run ;
To work and slave night and day for small pay is no fun,
And give it to you to squander and sow broadcast,
And be shipwrecked, made paupers, and in prisons at last.
Of all the damned robbers that I ever heard of, of this or of any other
    time,
You are the biggest, the meanest of this or any other, for crimes.
You have got so you are so bold you do it in the broad daylight,
Then try to cram it down us, and make us believe it is right.
On scientific principles by honest men this government was made to
    run,
And now by legalized robbers and thieves corruption it is overdone.
No matter what business you are doing, on a large or small scale,
When you are overrun with sit-stills and sappers it must fail.
The idea of taking the hard-earned money of thousands of men,
And giving it to a lot of blockheads, robbers, and thieves to spend !
These pills are a little to big now ; they will not go down ;
You have made them too big of late ; it has caused the people to look
    around.
You have rung in taxes in all conceivable ways you can,
And down in your own pockets the most of it you cram.

You have made a great mistake; you have got the whole business
    wrong end too;
It's bad, I know, but it is so, we are the government in place of you.
Of course we understand the principles of this government and plan.
And you have as much to say about how it shall be run as any other
    man.
Until you are chosen by the people them to represent,
And to all of the great centers of our great nation are sent.
Then in relation to this government you are changed clear around,
Then you are our servants, then by honor, fidelity, you are sworn and
    bound.
We have trusted this great fleet of our nation in your care,
You have betrayed your official trust, embezzled, robbed, plundered
    beware!
Some men seem to think and talk, as it is now it must go on,
To rescue this nation from your grasp it cannot be done.
When we look over this great fleet of our nation and take a view,
Then say this all must be eternally run by this damned robber crew,
I do not wish any man on this round globe any harm,
But the way we are sailing now, there is great reason for alarm.
If we do not tack ship and steer a different course soon
To hell and destruction together we will all go in this vortex and mael-
    strom,
When men come clamoring around the great center of our nation
Pleading for aid to keep them from poverty and starvation.
After we to them have hundreds of thousands of dollars paid.
To do this it has by law paupers, beggars, criminals of us made.
Sappers and leeches, do you always think, with your blind greed,
You can always grind us down to the earth and on us feed?
The principle that you are working on now, if you could carry it out,
Will ruin you as it has us, of that there can be no doubt.
On labor the support of this nation depends and has its rise,
And if we cannot clear ourselves of these leeches she dies.
What a damned lazy, burdensome set they seem to be,
They are no earthly use to this government, and nowhere that I can
    see.
These robbers are fast sapping out the heart's blood of our nation
And covering our land with prisons, poorhouses, and desolation.
We have for many long years these robbers and spendthrifts tried to
    keep up,

But we see it's of no kind of use, they only grow more corrupt.
Before you get us all in the poorhouse and prison pens,
You will have to some of that money you stole from us spend.
When a nation gets corrupted and rotten a the core.
The people have no confidence, no safety any more.
If you steer this fleet of our nation and keep it secure,
You must keep all of the centers of this great republic pure,
Then we can battle with outside corruption and keep it at bay;
No stream can be kept pure when the fountain is corrupt; it must be
    cleared away.
You have inoculated your poisonous venom all over our land,
And now you hang around the center to be fed in bands.
I see, now, business seems to take a little different course,
But it is no better; it's going on from bad to worse.
It has the appearance as though they were going to disband now,
As all robbers do when they get in a row.
They are going to divide up; of course they begin with the biggest
    thief,
That is General Grant; he is now their great robber chief.
Thirteen thousand dollars, five hundred a year, he wants us bound;
That won't do; that's too much; there won't be enough to go
    around.
If you have started out on another damned robbing raid,
Do not be such a hog; there will be thousands of others to be paid.
Mr. Grant, we will have you and your robbing band to know
On us you cannot rivet chains that gall and chafe us so.
This is just the way that damned salary grab was played,
And all over our land beggars, paupers, and thieves it made.
If this great nation you are going to ruin and the spoils divide,
That is to be seen yet, you can tell better after you have tried.
It looks now as though that is what you are trying to do—
You and your damned selfish, thieving, robbing crew
If it is a division of all now that you are trying to make
A share of that we all have, and that we intend to take,
The principle of this government is equal rights to all mankind,
And in that, too, we intend to have a share, you will find.
As for being made paupers and slaves by such as you,
That you and your damned robbing crew can never do.
On scientific principles by this government you was educated to fight,
And you have turned robber-chief, doing it in broad daylight.

At fighting you may be good—you ought to be; it is all you know.
For the course you are taking now with this nation will show
The principles of this government you do not understand;
If you do, so much the worse for you, you ought to be damned
If fight is all you know, and that is what you want to do,
We will give you all you want before we get through.
These sappers and leeches and robbers at the heart of our nation
Are driving the supporters of it to despair and desperation.
Nearly all of the blood on this green earth that has been shed,
Has been caused by tyrannical laws that tyrants have made.
Poor, blind, ignorant, selfish men you must be to think
You can grind us down with taxes, and yourselves not sink.
In order with success to run this fleet of our nation
The laborers and producers must be in a prosperous condition.
When hoggish, selfish, bad-principled men get the balance of power
Through ignorance, tyrannical laws they will make, themselves to
     devour.
For all crimes committed on this earth retribution must be made,
Either before you leave this earth or after you are dead.
This is the decree and law the creator has made for all;
On your own merits you must sink, rise, or fall.
No other provision the creator for us has ever made;
All sins committed by ourselves, by us they must be paid.
All nations, when they get corrupted by their blind greed for gold,
For this, sooner or later, to destruction they are sold.
Now this is just what all of this trouble in our nation is about;
We will go the way all others have gone if it is not purged out.
Like causes produce like effects; search the world around,
No argument can be used; to destruction they seem bound.
All can see plain enough after it is too late;
It will be no time then to grieve and mourn your sad fate.
This will be the sad result, and that, too, very soon;
This is the way of all nations—when corrupted, this is their doom.
All men seem to have their sphere and bounds to fill,
And all should in harmony live and show each other good will.
But when selfish men make tyrannical laws, on us encroachments
     make,
It causes all mankind then a different course to take.
To live in shanties and hovels, and at last be crowded in prison
     pens,

It causes men to rise up and try themselves to defend.
Whether they can or cannot, they always have and always will try;
It seems to be their nature; for liberty they will fight until they die
Now these encroachments are talked and felt all over our nation,
And if there is not a change soon, it will be laid waste in desolation
Capital to do business we must have, that we all well know;
But it is a curse to this nation to spend it in pomp and show.
From all business of this kind no returns can be had.
It is only squandering the producers' money; no dividends can be
made.
I suppose some think they are doing big things at the center of our
nation,
Squandering our money building palaces all over God's creation.
Of course in this robbing raid they must all have a share.
Producers and laborers, you are the treasury; take care, take care!
Some are trying to save all they possibly can in this way,
By converting all they have in bonds, then they will have no taxes to
pay.
This throws the whole burden on those that are the least able it to
bear.
Remember the principle of this country is equal rights; beware, be-
ware!
No laws that you have made do we recognize when your powers you
exceed,
No privileged ones in this government on us much longer can feed.
Laws that you have made, no matter when or by whom they were
made,
The most of the burden on the laborer and producer is laid.
My God! the most pitiful sight that a man ever can behold
Is to look over this nation and see men robbing themselves for gold.
In the course you are pursuing now, you will soon have to know
You have been robbing yourselves; you had better go slow.
When the time comes, with your plunder, where you can steer;
That is a mystery to me that I cannot see clear.
When this robbing that you have begun all over our land breaks out,
Then you will see the cause when it is too late, without doubt.
It does not seem as though people would be such selfish blind, fools,
By legislation to rob themselves and sail right into a whirlpool.
In order for this fleet of our nation to successfully be run,
Capital and labor must be balanced as near as it can be done.

As it is now them that is the best able have no taxes to pay ;
In this way the whole fleet of our nation is balanced the wrong way.
With interest on bonds, and idle capital in vaults doubling on us,
With this, and many other robberies, will cause the boilers to burst.
This great fleet of our nation out of balance cannot sail ;
Do all you can to prevent, unless you change, it will fail.
If out of balance you sail, it is easy enough to see
In favor of the laborer and producer it should be.
As it is now, you are killing the goose that lays the golden egg,
Filling the prisons, poorhouses, insane asylums, causing them to beg.
Now you seem to be bewildered in a fog, and failed ;
You act as though your compass you had lost, rudder and sail.
You have been drifting out of your course for a long time ;
You cannot sail this great fleet in corruption and crime.
Equal rights to all mankind in this government it was to be,
And in safety no other way it can be run, you will soon see.
You will have all the business you want, the best you can do,
If all are honest—pilot, mate, passengers, and crew.
When robbers and traitors to the helm of the fleet of our nation turn,
There will be trouble enough ; these facts you will soon learn.
Unless the people all change their course, and right-about face,
We will all sink together with this fleet in everlasting disgrace,
For by trickery, bribery, and rascality the business is nearly all done ;
Some damned scoundrels started it, and in this channel they run,
In order to keep pace in this blind race and keep up.
To hell and destruction we are sailing and growing more corrupt,
If in filth, carrion, crime, and corruption you try this fleet to wallow
    through,
And all out of balance the wrong way, that you can never do.
If you want again to get this fleet of our nation afloat
You must elect honest men when you come to vote.
That will balance it up on the original plan,
And that is equal rights to all, every man.
Clear away the leeches and robbers so many to fee,
Then you can get this great fleet of our nation at sea.
How can anyone do anything with so many prowling around ?
It would be a blessing to this nation if some would get drowned.
The first thing to be done is our expenses to curtail ;
There is no use trying to run so, if you do you will fail.
Knock the wages down more than one-half on the whole crew.

If you ever sail this fleet this is what you will have to do,
And throw out no more such attractive bait as that salary grab,
That caused the people with corruption almost to go mad
Next to be done will be to tax all property on the equalization plan;
Make all bear their part of the burden, both woman and man.
Next, there should be only a small appropriation made,
To set idle men to work with pick, shovel, and spade,
To bury this old canal; it stinks; it has a long time been dead.
There is no use of its having any more carrion to it fed.

Now I will bid you all a hearty adieu,
The whole entire, dishonest, robbing crew;
But I intend to keep watch to see the progression
You make sailing this great fleet of our nation.

I have sailed myself out of my course;
I must tack ship and go to work on the horse,
To follow you any longer, that I cannot safely do;
It would shipwreck and ruin me, as it has you.

When a nation gets so selfish, so ignorant, and blind,
As to rob themselves, there is no safety I find.
When on themselves they make robbing raids,
There is danger ahead, I am afraid.

There does not seem to be any way to make them see—
To be robbers of themselves they are bound to be,
In rings and monopolies all over our land,
To ruin themselves they are bound, if they can.

When on you this great destruction and calamity comes,
Do tell, what will with your plunders be done;
When all are trying each other to devour,
Who will stay the hand, then, of this unruly power?

When at the center of our great nation it is begun,
What then, do you think, to save this great fleet can be done?
When the people have no standard or center to rally round,
When the old flag of seventy-six you have pulled down?

When thieves and robbers are at work at our nation's heart,
Lookout, take care, beware; that is the vital part.

You will have to stop that soon, without doubt,
Or you will cause this nation's blood to all run out.

For the love of money, selfish, avaricious greed
Has caused other nations to suffer and to bleed;
And some themselves to death they have bled,
And have become extinct, and now are dead.

Unless you are more honest and liberal, you will see,
The same as it has been with others, with you it will be.
If you are not more harmoniously united, every man,
For a house divided against itself cannot stand.

You will bring destruction down on your own heads;
In rapine, slaughter, and blood you will make your beds.
It is liable at any time now to break out,
And when it comes it will be like an avalanche, no doubt.

No one can foretell in advance what will take place,
It is easy to see; it now stares you in the face.
I mean just when the great crisis will come,
That will be soon if there is nothing to prevent its being done.

This avalanche, if they would, could be turned a different course.
I must quit now and go to work on the horse,
Poor old gray, a customer for you I have found;
He cannot tell that you were ever lame or unsound.

All I want for you is just what I paid last fall;
The feed and work that I have done, you are welcome to it all;
And I will take you to the shop and shoe you all around new;
This will probably be the last for you I shall have a chance to do.

For all this long winter's work on you I am well paid;
The lesson I have learned is enough, now I am not afraid.
All stiff horses on this principle can be cured, I find;
The older they are, and of long standing the longer the time.

Now I have got you shod all around, nice and new,
I will bid you good-bye; it may not be a final adieu.
You look fine now; good-bye, good-bye, poor old mare,
I may come around again to see how you are.

After working almost night and day through this long, cold winter to demonstrate and satisfy myself what could be done for old stiff horses of long standing, I found myself more than paid. I found in this search that this science, if followed up, would perform wonderful cures on all. This was to put the cap-sheaf on all of my experimenting. It went beyond all my expectation. I was surprised myself. "Now," thought I, "I can tackle almost everything in the line of stiff and lame horses, and this I am determined to do. This science I am going to introduce." This is the way I reasoned with myself: I have got the biggest thing on this globe—and I have not changed my mind yet on that, neither can I. After all the searches of others, for no one knows how long, this complicated and difficult mystery they have not solved and cannot. This job on this old mare has completely cleared the fog away. No matter what the people say to the contrary, I am going to start out and try to introduce it in some new places. I know what I will have to contend with. It will be the same old music that I have heard so long. The first thing to be done will be to close up my shop and business in this place; the next will be to have a fat pocketbook, for nothing can be done without that toward introducing this great science; that I have demonstrated to my satisfaction.

Reader, you may wonder where I got all my money at that time aside from what I earned in my shop. It was instalments and interest from a farm that I sold that I was using to rescue the suffering horse. After receiving my annual instalment, the next thing to be done was to get some bills printed to advertise this great discovery and science and announce my coming. This bill was drawn up in this way:

"PROF. GERARD DOAN,

THE CHAMPION HORSE-SHOER OF AMERICA,

Having made horse-shoeing a business for many years, and study-

ing the natural horse and all of the changes from the

natural to the unnatural, its effect in all

of the different changes, has

made the great

dis-

covery how to cure

foundered horses of long stand-

ing—water, chest, and grain founder; perished

shoulders; remove all air-puffs, corns, coffin-joint lameness,

hoolers, shufflers, single-footers, and horses that hop behind in speed-

ing. All these cures I will perform without medicine.

I will deliver lectures free. All owners

of horses and mules will do

well to attend.

I will be at your place, etc.

I did not advertise on this bill all I could do with-out medicine. I well know this was more than they could stand. I put on "professor" because I thought it would help me. They like the sound of these big-sounding titles. I have seen as big fools with "professor" attached to their names as I ever did without; and my attaching it to my name did not help me any, as experience proved. After this bill was drawn up,

I sailed for the city of Elmira to get it printed.   The
printer read it over.   I said to him : " It's a big thing;
don't you think it is ?"

"Yes; but I do not believe it."

"You will print the bills, I suppose, if I will pay
you ?"

" Yes."

After arranging this bill with a cut of two fast-
sailing trotters at the head, I closed a bargain with
him to strike me off sixteen dollars' worth.   After
this job was completed I sailed for Horseheads.   After
my arrival I stood with my bundle of bills under my
arm on the walk.   A man drove up.   He says to me:

" Professor, one of my horses is lame; the other is
getting wind-puffs on him."

While I was talking with him there was a stranger
to me standing by.   He heard our conversation.   After our talk was ended I turned to walk away.   He
said to me, " Are you a veterinarian ?"

"No; I am not.   I work on horses' feet.   I have
done that for many years, and I have made some
quite big discoveries recently.   I have been getting
some bills printed preparatory to traveling and lecturing, and getting up schools to try and see if I can introduce it."

"Come to our place first.   I am a veterinarian.   I
will help you.   I would like to travel with you.   I
can cure spavins, ringbones, pole-evil, and thistloes.
I can work on the outside and pick up some money
that way.   I will do all of the posting bills and secure
the halls to lecture in.   If you will come to our place
I will take some of your bills now and put them up

if you will just fix the day and evening on them that you will be there."

" Where do you live ?"

" It is in the state of Pennsylvania."

" How far is it ?"

" Sixty miles."

" Is it a large place ?"

" Oh, yes; it is a large, thriving business town, and lots of stiff and lame horses."

" When I start this science in a place I have to stay some time to introduce it. I want a big field to work. There is no use stopping in a small place. This is a rather hard science to introduce. It is in advance of the age to cure horses without medicine. I will come to your place first. I will fix the time on some bills. You put these bills up in all of the public places, and secure a hall for the evening. I will be on the ground."

After arranging matters at home by dividing my money with my wife, closing my house, she and my boy Frank left this town to visit their relatives and friends in Auburn city and other places, I was prepared for a long campaign battling for the horse. With my shoeing tools and bills in a heavy satchel, when the day came I set sail. I arrived in this town about noon. I must say I was never more disappointed in my life. I do not remember the place's name, neither do I remember this veterinarian's name. It was a little huddle down in a sunken place surrounded with high mountain peaks. There was no way I could see out without looking nearly straight up. One old run-down, dilapidated hotel. About the first object I saw in the form of a human being was one man who had another poor, drunken man by the nape of the neck, kicking him almost to death. There were two or three old stores. The first thing I did was to look and see where all of those bills were put up. I looked this town all over, and no bills could I find. I walked in the hotel, and inquired for and about my veterinary friend. They told me where he lived. I, with satchel in hand, walked up to his house. He sat on the verandah, tipped back in a chair, reading the news of the day. He seemed surprised to see me. I accosted him in this way: "The bills are not up, I see. How is this?"

"Well, I showed them some. They did not believe anything in it. They said it was a damn humbug."

"Then you hav not secured any hall to lecture in?"

"No."

"Did you think they would believe it could be done? This is just what our business is to teach them these principles, truths, and facts."

I soon saw this man was of no use to me. He was entirely too weak in the knees and garret. Golly! this is a hard battle to fight alone. I am not going to leave this town without giving them a brush. I am going to lecture in this town on the horse if there is not one man to listen. I am going to look this town over. I will get up some kind of a racket.

I walked up to what they called a livery stable. There sat the proprietor on some rubbish. Pieces of old wagons, harness, and old boards were all over the floor. He sat with both elbows on his knees, his chin resting on both hands to hold his head up. I approached him, as cautiously as I knew how to, on the horse. I saw the condition of his row of fine horses at a glance when I first stepped in. It would not take a very close observer to see they were in a very bad condition. The whole row stood on piles of manure that elevated them behind at least a foot too high. Some were ankle-cocked; some off their base badly; in fact, they were a hard-looking sight. In a roundabout way I commenced to talk horse. I carefully closed upon him at last. I told him they could be cured without medicine. Then he exploded. He railed at me:

"Do you think we are all damned fools here? Do you think you can humbug us?"

There was no use in talking with him any more. There would be danger of getting some of that rubbish over my head. Next I walked into a blacksmith shop. I glanced around. I saw things were all kept in good order. The work all looked mechanic-like. There was some good work finished and partly finished. Only one man was in this shop. I asked him if he was the proprietor. He said he was, and worked alone. I saw he had quite a head on him, though his body was very inferior. He was deformed, small, hump-shouldered. He did not look as though he was able to shoe horses. But he did, I saw, and his work looked well. I soon saw I could talk with him on the principles of working on the feet of horses. I had my pasteboard foot to show him the principles to work on. He soon saw the whole business. I spent about an hour with him. He was the most i

looking man I saw in that town, and the best mechanic. I visited two other shops and had a chat
with the owners. They stared at me when I told
them I could perform these cures without medicine on
principles of science. They looked at me as though
they thought I was insane. Night came. A few collected in this little huddle. To leave this town without delivering a lecture on the horse I was determined not to do. I saw some boxes on the steps of a
store. I asked permission to take one. I rolled it
across the walk in the street. I quietly got myself on
this base to attract their attention. I commenced by
a few introductory preliminaries, stating my business
in their place; my disappointment on account of the
bills not being posted and no hall secured, and the
field was too small to try to introduce this great
science; but if you will listen I will give you a short
lecture here. This bugling attracted a few. I sailed
out at the same time. I kept watch of the crowd. It
was not a large one, not more than five or six at one
time. They would come and go. This changing was
constantly going on; it was rather discouraging to try
to teach science in this way. I saw they stared at
me a little while, then moved away. Others would
do the same. There was one fine-looking man I saw
staid at his post from the first. I saw he was interested, and that induced me to go on. If it had not
been for him I might just as well have been in the
woods on a stump talking to trees. After this lecture
was over I rolled the box back, and walked back to
the hotel. I remained in this place part of the next
day. While sitting in the hotel this listener to my

lecture came in, seated himself, and commenced to draw me out in conversation on the horse. Said he: "You are all right, stranger, but I do not believe you can introduce it. What will you take to teach me what you know about the horse? I am in earnest."

"I do not know as I could teach you all I know on the horse," I replied. "It has been a life-long study with me. If I was going to remain in this place I could and would teach you some very valuable lessons."

The remark I made to this man when he told me he did not think I could introduce this science was, "I will or burst; that is, I will sink every dollar I have got, then earn more, and go at it again."

After this noble-minded and gentlemanly man passed out. I inquired who he was. They said he was the physician of their place. At that time I commenced to reason with myself in this way: It took me a long time to learn how to introduce it. I can see now that I sailed out before I was full rigged. I have got no books with these principles and rules laid down. They cannot remember all that I say to them if they listen. I must write a book. Here is the sticker—for me to convey all this in a book, and if I do, that will not sell as this matter now stands. They would call that a damned humbug, as they do me. That will not do yet. It must be introduced first by doing the work in order to get good, reliable, substantial, noted scientific men for reference to put in the book. I am going to leave this town and sail to Auburn city. I have a brother there, a horse-shoer, and another twenty miles from there. They are both

good workers on the horse's feet. I am going to enlist them in this horse fight. That will be easy
enough to do, for they have been and are now trying
to solve this mystery. I sailed for Auburn. On my
way I stopped at my brother Oliver's place of business. He was located in a small inland town at that
time surrounded with a beautiful country and well-to-
do farmers. I walked into his shop. He was seated
on a saw-horse. I shall never forget how he looked.
tired and sick, thin in flesh, cheeks sunken, eyes the
same. "What's the matter, Ob?" said I.

"Well, the fact is," said he, "I am about used up.
I am nearly ridden to death with so many crippled
and stiff horses. They come pouring in on me from
many miles away. They keep me nearly all of my
time holding them up. I can fix them up, and do,
some that are very bad, but it is killing business for
me, and small pay. I can hardly live out of it."

I said: "I have got something I want to show you.
I have come on purpose to do this. It solves the
whole mystery we have so long been trying to find
out. I can tell you how you can cure all of these
stiff horses."

I took out of my satchel my pasteboard hoof, and
explained the principles it was done on. He saw
it all at a glance.

"That will do it, I know," said he.

In a few words it was all made clear to him. He
could do it as well as I could. His long experience
and the progression he had made enabled him to grasp
this new discovery instantly. It was what he had
been many years reaching after.

"Oliver," said I, "I am going to Auburn to see Joseph. I want you and him to help me introduce this science."

"You will meet with a power of opposition in many ways," said he.

"That I care nothing about," I replied. "I have been pulverized through that mill. I want to beat them if I can. I am ahead here. If you will take hold of this they never can excel you; equal is all they can do."

After staying over night, the time all spent talking horse, I sailed for Auburn city. I found Joseph in his shop wrestling with all kind of cripples. I soon found a way to let my business be known.

"Jo," said I, "when you have leisure I have got a big thing on the horse I want to show you."

"I thought you had got something," he replied, "or you would not be around. If you have got any-thing new on the horse I want to learn it. I will be one of your scholars."

After explaining what I could do with a horse's foot, he said:

"If you can do that, and not produce any inflamma-tion, that is all I want to know; that will do the whole business. I want to see that done."

"We must have a horse."

"I will find a horse. There are stiff horses enough; you can hardly find one but what is stiff."

"We want one that is bad."

"I know of one that we can get. She is six years old. She is so stiff that after driving her, when she comes in the stable, she is so sore that she will lie down nearly all the time."

" You will find it will bother us some to get these horses to work on.   Their owners are afraid we will spoil them."

" We can buy them."

" We do not want the horses.   The best way I have found is to hold ourselves responsible for the horse. There is no risk to run caused by the work we will do on them   This saves their lives many times."

" All right; that we will do.   I will have a horse before night."

Business was hurried up in the shop.   We got the six-year-old mare.   She was owned by Mr. Westlake. By holding ourselves responsible for one hundred and fifty dollars if she did not come out all right, we got full control of her.   She was fed and kept in Joe's barn.

The next day after my arrival we were at work on a horse.   Only one bill was put up, and that was in Joe's shop.   This work was commenced in Auburn city over eight years previous to the date of this book. This mare was badly off her base on all of her feet. On her hind legs above her ankles were large air-puffs. The work on this mare was done all at one time; that is, her feet were all prepared and expanded at one time. She was changed back to natural at once; that is, the cause was removed.   Mr. Westlake was to see this work done.   I well knew it would not do to let him see it.   It would have brought the whole town down on us.   After the feet were prepared they were all made soft.

"All ready," Joseph said; "we must have West-lake here now to see this work done."

"No," said I; "that will not do. We must put the harness on her first, and have the wagon in readiness at the door to hitch her on as quick as her feet are spread. If we do not we will have her down. We must put her in motion, then she will soon recover from the change."

The spreading was all done as quick as it could be, with care and by measure. There is no kind of use to write any more about how much these horses' feet are spread, they vary so, and on the same horse.

After this work was done we hitched her to the wagon and sailed out of the city a few miles and back into town. Joseph got out to go in a store on business and left me sitting in the wagon. After a short time this mare began to balance over back and forward, and acted as though she was about to fall. She did not have the control of herself yet enough to keep on her equilibrium. This is the way they all will be more or less, according to the degree of change. While sitting in the wagon the people gathered around. They asked me what ailed my horse. I replied, "I guess she is all well enough." "That mare is sick;" "she ought to be taken out of the harness;" "she is dying now;" "she ought not to be driven any more."

While this was going on around me, Joseph came, jumped into the wagon, and we sailed out of that crowd of bewildered people to the barn, put the mare up for the night, and cared for her the same as I have done for all others.　When it came time to retire, I said to Joseph: "I am going to bed.　I am tired."

"Are you not going to do anything to that mare's feet to-night?"

"No; she is all right."

"Her feet will be turned all wrong side out before morning."

"You can tell better in the morning.　I will pay for her if they are."

When I got up Joseph was in the barn caring for his horses.

"Jo, how are the mare's feet?"

"They are cold; there is no heat in them."

"That is boss; that settles the whole thing.　The air-puffs are all gone; she begins to show her deformity; it will take time to bring that back.　Work and exercise will bring that all right after the cause is removed on all horses; but remember it must be kept removed.　We will let her rest awhile.　We went to the shop.　Joseph had hands at work for him.　When we got there the shop was full of horses.　There was a long row there waiting to have their feet ironed. Joseph, with hat in his hand, walked up and down this row of horses, looking them over, I suppose, to see what condition they were in.　After he had looked them all over, he swung his hat around over his head and said, "I can cure every horse in this shop without a particle of medicine."

There were several standing around.

"Hold on, Jo," said I.　"They will call you crazy, as they have me; you will get in the lunatic asylum the first you know."

My advice did not stop his bugle. He kept it going. That helped me. Mine could rest a little. This is making a little start in this place, sure. Said Jo: "I have got a six-year-old mare; her legs stock up behind; one is swollen very bad. I have used lots of liniments. I cannot take it out. She interferes badly, too. I have shod her heavy and light, in all ways I can think of, but it has all done no good."

"Put a pair of spreaders on her, Joe; put the structure of her feet in harmony of action, and the swelling will leave so quick the skin will be all loose on her legs. It will stop her cutting her legs off at the same time."

She was soon in the shop. Joe did this work himself. We spread her feet, and hitched her to the wagon. It threw her on her base, and she traveled at once about eight inches apart. The swelling did go out, and left the skin loose. So much money thrown away for liniments. This will work the same on a large per cent of all the horses on this globe. This fever has its rise from internal heat in the foot, caused by being out of harmony of action. It is not necessary any longer to write all the particulars about how I worked on the different horses in this city. The principles are already laid down in this work; that is, as far as I had got at that time. I made some new discoveries after I left this city.

For six weeks brother Joseph and myself battled for the horse early and late. During this time we operated on quite a number of horses. It did not seem to get advertised, and this was the reason the people would get their horses cured and say nothing about it

They thought it would injure the sale of them if the people knew they had ever been stiff; or if they did sell them and they ever got stiff again, no matter what the cause was that made them so, they would be likely to get into a lawsuit; and that is the case many times, and this is caused by ignorance. If this science was understood it would save a vast amount of trouble from that source and many others.

"Joseph," said I, one day, "I am going to leave this place now. I will leave the unfinished jobs in your care to finish up."

I made no charges; presented no bill to any man. This is the place where I received five dollars from Mr. Hatch for curing his horse. He insisted on my taking it, and would willingly give me four times as much more. He knew me, and had for many years. He told me, "Take my horse, cure him, and I will pay you your own price." Joe did the work on this horse. I shared equally with him. That left me two and a half dollars, which is all the reward I have ever received from any man for work done for them aside from shoeing in my long life of forty-one years battling for the horse

I must tell you a little story about Mr. Hatch's horse, then I will leave Auburn city. Mr. Hatch, hearing I was in the city at work on horses, looked me up. Said he: "I have a horse; he is a good seven-year-old horse; he is stiff, unable to work. He was so when I got him. I traded for him. I want you to go and look at him."

"I will do so."

This horse was turned out in a low, wet pasture.

We found him standing in this position : hind parts at least eighteen inches higher than his forward parts, with his forward feet in the mud and water. He had placed himself in this position to save the strain on the back tendons. He could stand more comfortable in this way. The mud and water helped keep the fever and heat out of his feet at the same time. In fact, he could hardly move around. We pulled him out of the mud, and got him on hard ground. He was a large, noble, fine-looking young horse, with flat-tish, good feet. I took out my foot hook to clean out his feet. He had shoes on. While cleaning out his feet I came to some tow or cotton packed under the shoe at the toe. I commenced to dig it out. I knew it was of no use, no matter what it was.

"What is this, Mr. Hatch?"

"Well, a veterinarian that has charge of the street-car horses told me he could cure him by bleeding him in the toe, then turn him out; so I had that done."

"How much blood did he take out?"

"About ten quarts; five quarts to each foot."

"And here he is in this mud hole yet?"

"Yes; and I want him to work."

"What do you want to do with him?"

"I want to draw hay."

"You can have him to-morrow."

Reader, such ignorance as this ought to be exposed. Men calling themselves veterinarians, who do not know anything only to make bad worse and torture horses in this way and many others.

I told Mr. Hatch what ailed his horse. I towed him to the shop, and now I will tell you his feet were con-

tracted some, as almost all horses are that have had
their feet ironed. This was not the worst trouble
with this horse. He was badly thrown off his base by
cutting his heels too low and not cutting the toe down,
leaving the toe at least one inch and a half too long.
This was a short job to remove the cause of all of this
poor horse's trouble. His feet were soft; he had
soaked them himself. I did the work on this horse.
This wonderful wise veterinarian had commenced at
the toe of this horse's foot; cut back towards the point
of frog crossways at least two inches deeper as he
went back; he had cut a large hole through in this
useless hoof in order to reach the sensitive part of the
membrane, as it is called by some. This had been
done long enough so nature had in a measure repaired
the damage. The first thing we did for this horse was
to pare these feet well down at the toe until this hole
was all gone, cutting but little from the heel, just
enough to true and level his feet up; cupped them
out preparatory to spreading his feet and letting the
sole down to its proper place. We spread this horse's
feet five-eighths of an inch, and shod him on his hind
feet. Toward night I led him home, standing on his
toes. He balanced back and forward a little. I explained that to Mr. Hatch; told him he would be over
that in the morning. He could put him to work. It
would be better to do so. He pulled out his money to
pay me.

"You had better wait and see how you like the
job," said I. "I will come and see how he gets along
in a few days."

I did so. He was drawing hay. This horse was on

his base, head up, limber, about half a neck ahead of
his mate, and was the limberest of the two. Mr.
Hatch pulled out his money to pay me. I charged
him five dollars. It was not the money I wanted; it
was to introduce this science. Some may call this
bragging. I will say right here that when all such
men as they get this great science learned, after some
one else has studied it out and perfected it, they will
have more to brag about than they have now. It is
not my intention to write the experience of my brothers working on the horse. They enlisted in this horse
fight, and have been at it ever since, and show no
signs of giving it up. I have got it started in two
places, by two practical men of long experience,
working on the horse.

Now I will sail back to the old battle ground in
Horseheads. When I started out on this campaign I
sold out all of my interest in my shop. I soon secured
another, a good, new shop, rigged up; all stocked up
new. "I must have money," said I, "or I shall be
shipwrecked soon in this way." I did not put up any
sign. I never had a sign on my place of business, but
one, in all of the places I have done business in.
I soon found a way to call trade. When I saw a lame,
crippled horse I went for him. It soon spread, and in
a short time I was overrun again with horses. This is
the way I always advertise when I commence in a new
place; but this was no new place; this was the place
where I got jerked out of a wagon head-first for talking for the horse. It is not necessary to write all the
particulars about this second attack on this town,
battling for the horse, only enough to lay down some

principles that will be of use to the horse and his owner. My life I never intended to write, and I well know no one else can. Neither do I care to spend my time in that way. So I will hasten along with this work. While battling in this town a man came to my shop to get a horse shod. His name was Wix. He was a teamster. His was a large, middle-aged horse, thin in flesh. He was badly off. It was all he could do to stand; he was thrown back off his base on all of his legs; his hind feet were thrown forward so much by this same cause I have written of that he appeared about to go over backwards.

"Mr. Wix," said I, "that horse is so far gone I do not think I can balance him by shoeing; and I do not think he can stand on the other leg if I was strong enough to hold him up. He will break down on one leg. He cannot stand, that I know; but I will try him."

After balancing him on his forward feet first, which helped him some, I tried him on one hind foot. After lifting and tugging a long time, with a large proportion of this heavy horse's weight thrown on me, Mr. Wix on the opposite side trying to hold him up, that is, from going over sidewise, I finally, by main strength, raised his foot. The other leg gave out, being able to hold but very little weight. The lever tipped him over, and down he went flat on the floor. Mr. Wix pounded him, and after struggling a while he managed to get on his feet again. This was in the heat of the summer, and a very hot day.

"Mr. Wix," said I, "this horse will not be of use to you if we do shoe him; he cannot be balanced by

shoeing so he can work or stand long. I do not think
he can stand on one leg long enough to shoe."

Mr. Wix said he could hold him up. He must have
him shod, so at it he went. After struggling a long
time he managed to raise a foot. Down went the
horse broadside ; then he must be pounded up again.
Wix tried it again with like result. I did not like to
give this job up, so I tried a new plan. The horse had
shoes on, and his feet were quite long. I cut the hoof
off at the toe and around; cut the nails out in this
way. We got the shoes off, then cut the hoof away
on the under side at the toe. That helped him some ;
it let him go forward on his base a little. Then I tried
him again. After a hard struggle for me and him,
Wix holding him all he could to keep him from falling over, I succeeded in getting his foot up without
his falling. I worked as fast as I could, cutting the
hoof away at the toe, holding his weight at the same
time ; holding his foot up only a short time and
changing legs often. In this way I let his body go
back on his base by degrees. After a long, hard struggle I got him shod. In this way I shortened his toes
and pared them down at heel and toe, the toe the
most ; gave him a long shoe at the heel ; corking the
shoes the highest at the heel. This was the best I
could do, shoeing this poor horse, and as well as any
man can do for a horse in like condition without expanding the foot and putting the structure of the foot
in harmony of action, which his was fearfully out of
order.

Reader, you may ask, "Why did not you do that?"
You ought to know by this time. How can a man do

anything when others will not let him?—when they will only gather around him and fight, and blart a lot of nonsense?

After a few days Mr. Wix came into the shop.

"Doan, that horse is dead."

"How is that?"

"I found him down this morning, out doors on the manure pile, unable to rise. I took the axe and knocked him in the head, and took him to the bone-yard."

"How did he get outdoors?"

"The door of the stable was behind his stall. He broke his halter and knocked the stable door off the hinges."

The fact is, he was tipped over backwards with contraction and leverage, as thousands are. This lever works both ways, and there is a power in it. It has tipped this horse over; and the discovery of this will tip over and shove from the base some institutions, so that no power can put them back, built as they are on false teachings and no principles or foundations, only tinkering at the effect.

There are two levers that tip horses over backwards. They both work in harmony of action; they are both caused by contraction; the fulcrum of both is at the center of the foot, above the coffin-joint. One runs up the leg; the other runs out at the toe, beyond the point of hoof. That is not seen, and yet it is equal in length to the other. When any degree of contraction takes place, the levers both start at the same time. They are connected at the center; they are not independent of each other when contraction takes place. The useless growth of hoof on the toe, if there is no contraction, is the end of the lever. How can these poor horses stand, thrown in this position? Feet moved forward, or body back—have it either way if you please, it is all the same—this lever running up the hind leg to the extreme point of the horse, with two-thirds of his weight at the end of the lever, and with his feet thrown forward, caused by contraction. Follow that lever down to the fulcrum; look the horse over; look at that lever-purchase breaking him down; then look at the one on the toe of equal length working in harmony with it, one lifting, the other pulling down. There is some power, I want you to know and see. These principles will not lie, nor can they be ruled out. Contraction works the same on all of the feet on all horses expanding too much. I have explained that the length of these levers vary on the same horse. The length they can get is according to the size of the horse and the degrees of contraction. When the horse gets as bad as Wix's was, the lever is farther away from the fulcrum, as long as the horse's leg is, and to the extreme point behind, I mean as far as the horse's body extends. Of course there could not be any lever beyond where there is weight. On this horse science, when a horse is thrown in this way, there is no power that can raise him except his foot is expanded, or it can expand itself as his creator intended it should. Reader, I want you to understand that these poor horses endure some suffering before this takes place. This is called by the ignorant, strained across the loin. About that they are right. The horse is strained across the loin, and badly too; but the cause they know nothing of. A horse thrown in this way will struggle hard to retain his feet, and many times he is crammed with all kinds of trash, bled and blistered, when the cause all lies in his feet.

In the fore part of this work I left a horse that had not been balanced up. He was badly off his base. He had become spavined. He went over backwards, and horses would go more off their base were they not divided against themselves. Being on their base forward saves them somewhat. Sometimes it will not do that. When they get very bad behind they must go down. Being on a constant strain all of the time, and drawing loads, or traveling in any way, and rising over that lever, all out of harmony, they are soon ruined in a greater or less degree. To balance them up only adds more effects in number. By splitting it up it only makes this entanglement more complicated. Not a cause is removed. It prolongs their sufferings. Sometimes, and many times, it causes their death by suffering. I have seen lots of this kind.

After battling alone in this town, working on all kinds of cripples, from far and near, ten months, not one soldier could I enlist to take hold of this science. My health was fast giving out, and money too. I decided to sell my property and try a new field. I soon did this. When I wanted to sell I always put on a selling price. It always went. I collected all I could by asking for it. Some I took in promises that have never been fulfilled. The old gray mare I sold on one year's time; that is due now. I must collect that. I want to see her, and see how she fares, and see if she s limber yet. She is four miles away, if the maon wns her yet that I sold her to. I had not seen this mare from the time I sold her, nor her owner. I went on foot. I found all at home. The man paid me. I told him I wanted to see her. We went to the barn. She stood there with a row of horses, with a rack of black, moldy hay before her, and with plenty manure enough to lie on; very poor and dirty; no one could have sworn for certain she was the same mare I sold to him one year previous.

I did not let him know what I wanted to see this mare for. There was a boy stood by. I told him I would like to see her move off a little. She had shoes on. This boy was soon on her back, sailing her up and down the road. I saw at a glance she was limber, and more so about the shoulders than she was when I sold her. That was what I went four miles on foot through deep mud to see if working another year after the cause was removed would make any more improvement. It did. She was as limber as any horse, and had as good knee action as she ever had. In that all horses vary some. I asked him if she ever had been lame in any way since he owned her. He said she had not.

Reader, this man never knew this mare had ever been stiff or lame before he bought her, and he does not know what mare it is; neither does any that once knew her, except the Woodrough brothers. I found out what I went for, and sailed home.

Next thing was to look up a new field. I set sail. I made up my mind to start somewhere in the lake country. I stuck my stake at Lake Ridge, six miles from where I commenced to learn the trade of horse-shoeing, and four miles from the place I first started business for myself. Lake Ridge is situated on the east bank of that beautiful sheet of water Lake Cayuga, with as beautiful surrounding country as a man ever looked at. In a very short time I had a new shop erected in a cheap, rough manner. All I wanted was to work on the horse. That was to be my business in this place, and I wanted no other. I put up one bill in this shop, and went for the first cripple I could get. I was soon overrun with all kinds. I did not say much about spreading horses' feet for several months. I well knew that would scare them away; stopping them from interfering, balancing, equalizing their weight on their feet; straightening run-over feet, and many other troubles the horse is suffering with, caused by shoeing, was what I did and talked about. I will give you a few lessons. While I was in this place a stranger led in a pair of horses. He wanted a shoe set. I saw one was lame and stiff on his forward feet. While setting the shoe on the other I learned they were young and twins. They were a good pair. I said to him :

"Would you like to have that other horse cured?"

· "Yes."

"How long has he been stiff and lame?"

"It is about two years."

"I will cure him for the price of shoeing."

"You may shoe him."

All that ailed this horse was run-over feet. In ten days he was nearly well, and soon recovered entirely. This man told me after his horse got well about taking him to Prof. Law, of Cornell University, to have him examined. This horse had a very small enlargement on the inside of his leg. The professor told him that was the cause of his lameness, charged him twelve shillings, and wrote a prescription to get filled that cost ten shillings. The horse must not be worked while under treatment. The man could not get along with his work at that time without using this horse, so the medicine was never used. I shod that horse over three years. He was all right as far as the most of people can see. He was not lame. So much for professors.

This is only one case of hundreds of this kind that I balanced up while I staid in that place. After getting a good run of business and well established I thought I would venture a little further. It would not kill my business dead. If it did scare some away, there had got to be more cripples than I wanted.

Mr. Jefferson lived near this place. He was the owner of a stallion. I had seen him several times. He was badly off his base on his forward legs; his knees were badly tipped, weak, and shook; cords seemed thick; legs swelled. This horse was well along in years, and had been in this condition a long time. I said to Mr. Jefferson :

" Would you like to have that horse's legs straightened and all the swelling taken out so you could see the cords and tendons clear down to his feet?"

" Well, yes, I would if it could be done."

" Well, sir, it can be done. He can be made as natural as he ever was."

I told him all about how I would do it, and how he

would be afflicted. For a short time he would be affected more on one leg than the other. That would
cause him to limp. It would last only a short time on
this horse.

I did not put on spreaders. This horse I could fix
without. He was a heavy horse. His weight was
over the center of his foot. His heels were too high,
contracted some. The principles are already laid down
in this work that I do this work on. There are only
a very few horses that can be cured in this way. This
was one of that kind. I mean expanding by their
own weight.

To cut this story short, I gave him directions what
treatment to give the horse: Soak and wash the cords
in warm water; drive. In a short time all would
come right. Away he went for home. I well knew
I had started a racket, but there is nothing like being
prepared for it. In a day or two I saw Mr. Jefferson
drive past my shop. His horse was lame. He stopped
at the hotel across the way from my shop. He sat on
the verandah, looking over toward my shop. I was
in my shop at work, at the same time watching his
movements. I wanted to have a talk with him. He
showed no signs of coming to the shop. I left my
work, walked over and sat down on the verandah. I
saw he looked rather sober. Said I:

"Mr. Jefferson, how is the horse?"

"He is awful lame. I wanted to go about three
miles further, but I think I had better go home. It
will not do to drive him. If I get home with him I
will do well."

"You know, Mr. Jefferson, I told you in advance how this would all be."

"Yes; I know you did."

"If you will do as I told you, you will come out all right, and your horse the same. Drive your horse where you want to go. Before you get back he will be nearly over his lameness, and will gradually get strong and better all of the time until he is entirely well."

He started out. His horse was quite lame. After he had gone, there was a man who told me what Jefferson said before I came over from the shop. He did not tell me anything new. I had been through the mill. He said, "I guess I have let that old fool spoil my horse." This is not all the place he told it. I knew he would before I commenced to work on his horse. I cared nothing for that. They nearly all do the same. I well knew he would be my friend in the end, and he was, and is now, as far as working on the horse is concerned.

In a short time Jefferson drove in the place. He said he had been where he wanted to go, and had come out of his way to tell me that before he got three miles his horse was entirely over his lameness.

"He has got over the change now," said I. "You will have no more trouble."

His tune was changed in my favor.

Now this horse's head had began to come up. In a short time he had as clean, straight, tapering legs as any colt. Mr. Jefferson said it added seventy five dollars to his value at once. This job did some advertising, but that was not all I wanted. I wanted them to learn and know how this was done.

When I first commenced in this place, the landlord bought a good four-year-old horse. I stood near when they was looking this horse over. I saw he was off his base. Of course it is no business of mine. They are nearly all so in some degree, greater or less. I did not have anything to say. I saw he had a hard, horn-like foot, and he would be likely to have me shoe him. He would be kept up in the stable; he would grow worse and get stiff, in spite of all I could do, in a short time; and he did gradually grow worse. The winter before he was sick; in the spring he would get down, or cast, and had to be helped up, caused by contraction throwing him off his base or balance, and fastening him there. This winter he stood in the stable nearly all of the time. His owner did not have much for his horses to do. He did not get out much himself, his health not being very good. Time slipped away unperceived, and this horse stood with his shoes on all winter, without being reset or having his feet cut down. His feet had grown high and long in this condition, all out of harmony of action. They gave him a thirty-two mile drive after a load, up and down heavy hills, which about floored him. He was so sore and stiff he could hardly move. He would not move unless he was made to. Of course I was always around when these wrecks took place. I knew about what time they would take place. I told Mr. Ives, for that was his name, what ailed his horse, and I thought I could cure him. "I can remove the cause of all of his trouble. It will be a hard job; his feet are in

about the worst condition of any I ever worked on."
After making a conditional bargain with him, I went
to work on this horse. Reader, here is a lesson. I
dread to tackle this horse again. His feet were very
high. About half-way from the top of his foot to the
bottom, they were pinched in all around. He had to
be changed by degrees. This shell could not be all
cut away at once. I cut his feet down as far as I
could, and spread them. They were as hard as they
could be; it took a long time to get them soft enough
to operate on with safety. At this time I did not have
control of this horse. I exercised him myself. This
was a tough job. I wanted this horse used every day.
In about four weeks I took off his shoes, cut his feet
down, spread again, and so on every four weeks. I
wanted to do, but I could not have him in my control
to do as I liked ; so I quit and let him go. I kept
watch of him. His shoes were allowed to remain on
three months. His toes got long; the structure of his
foot was nowhere in harmony of action when I quit
him. He was not driven on the road. At that time
of the year he was working on the farm, plowing, and
putting in crops in the spring. It did not hurt him to
rise over that lever on soft ground as bad as it did
when he was sailed on the hard road. He took one of
these sails; it wrecked him at once. Of course I was
around again. This poor horse was in a terrible suffering condition. I told Mr. Ives what ailed his horse.
He thought the trouble all lay in his shoulder. He
did not have much shoulder; he was deformed so.
This time he was so stiff he had to be pulled along.
Mr. Ives I saw was getting discouraged about his horse

He was not such a horse as he wanted. He made him
so much trouble that he began to talk of taking him
off to have his shoulders doctored, or dispose of him
in some way. I made up my mind, while I was
around looking at this poor horse, to rescue him, let it
cost what it would. I said to Mr. Ives:

"What will you take for this horse?"

"You dare not make me an offer."

"Oh, yes, I dare. I will give you fifty dollars."

"He is yours."

I pulled him across the road to my barn. Now I
have got this horse in my control. Whether I can
cure this horse or not, I can help him wonderfully in
about one hour by dressing his feet down. There was
no time lost until this job was completed. I put on a
pair of spreaders, cutting his feet, and letting him go
back on his base some. I soon had both of his feet
in warm water, soaking, washing his legs and cords.
I soaked his feet the remainder of that day, and packed
them at night. The next day I drove him eight
miles and back, up and down heavy hills single, and
he drew a heavy load of stock for my shop. He
sailed very comfortably, no limping, and yet all the
cause I had removed then was what I cut off his toes;
that shortened the lever some. After making his feet
as soft as I could, I spread them about three-eighths of
an inch. Of course it affected him badly at first.
The shell and sole of his feet were just like horn, and
did not seem to have any life in them. The shell was
completely dead and shrinking all around the sensitive
part of his feet. When I spread his foot I did not see
the shell come down. He was on his base; his weight

was nearly over the center of his feet, and yet it did not press the sole down. This was a hard-meated, strong, ambitious horse. This sole must be got down according to the degree I have spread his foot, or there will be trouble. To do this I led him out of the shop. He was badly off his base, caused by my spreading his feet. His feet internally were very sore; any change either way would affect him badly. A number were standing around. I put a boy on the horse and told him to run him a hundred rods and back. The road was dry and hard. After he returned I looked to see if the sole had come down. I cleaned the dirt all out under the shoe. It was not down as far as it ought to come by spreading his feet three-eighths of an inch. "Give him another sail." I looked to see what effect that had. The sole was nearly down flat on the shoe. "That will do." It made him step short. His feet must be put in warm water a short time. Next, pack his feet, give him a good, dry, soft bed, so he can lie down and rest and sleep.

Of course while this running business was going on in the streets, it called out remarks. Some said they would not have a stiff horse used that way. All this bugling I cared nothing about. I knew what I was doing and they did not. I was the owner of the horse and could control him. It took this horse ten or twelve days to recover every time I expanded his feet, and that I did once a month for a long time. Sometimes I would be sailing all right, or nearly so; once a month I would be partly wrecked. Every time this took place, I could hear this: "That horse is worse; I guess you will **never do much for that horse.**

After working on him many months to get rid of that old, dead, lifeless shell, his foot was smaller than it was when I first commenced. How is this? I had got up to the small place in his foot. Now I can go ahead. Now I have got where I can flatten out his foot and it begins to show more life. Remember, this horse did all of my work, long and short drives, and was driven on purpose to give him work, and I had all the exercise I wanted in the shop at the same time, balancing cripples; in fact, it was getting red-hot for me. So I made up my mind to have a little rest after getting up my crippled horse in good shape. To leave for a while, I sailed out. I had business in New York, Washington, and Chicago, tracking up a shipwreck somebody had made of one of my inventions. To please myself I wanted to find the cause of it—that is, where it was located. It had made quite a racket for many years. I hauled in at the center of this, our great republic. I always had time to spend looking after the interest of the horse.

You can see me standing in the streets of New York city for hours looking at the condition of horses as they passed. The flat feet seem to stand it the best on all horses. All cupping feet that I saw were in a very bad condition, and the horses that had that kind were badly out of harmony of action, off their base and balance in many ways, which I have already described and explained. My time was mostly spent while in this city looking at horses. I next sailed to Washington. While standing on the verandah of the hotel I saw coming down a beautiful, smooth driveway toward this hotel a very nice single turnout. I saw the horse was a prompt driver. He was quiet lame in one forward foot. The rig pulled up at a post. There was only one man in it. He jumped out, tied his horse, and went into the hotel. I looked his horse over. He was a fine, beautiful young horse, His hair looked as though somebody had tried to take good care of him; but he was a cripple on all of his legs. One of his knees was badly tipped forward; on this leg was a badly contracted foot and high heel; the mate was a little better; the hair was nearly all burned off his legs all around his feet. They looked as though turpentine had been burnt on them. This gentleman did not stay long in the hotel. He soon was sailing again after this cripple. I did not intend to stop long, so I thought it would be of no use to get up any racket here on the horse. While this gentleman is sailing around I will give you a little description of him. He had on his head a very shiny stove-pipe hat; white vest; pants the same, and white gloves; he is sailing around here again. He jumped this time clear from his wagon on the top steps; he has a cane under his arm about the size of a pipe-stem, with a ribbon tied to it. Well, I suppose he carries that because he wants to. He went in the hotel again. When he comes out I am going to try and see how close I can get to him talking horse, and not shock him away from me. This kind of men are very sensitive. I find my long experience has taught me that one of the most skilful things a man ever tried to do is to approach some men and begin to talk about the defects of their horse, and not shock them away from you; and yet these horses are all, or nearly

all, cripples that have been shod in some way. I am
going to try this man when he comes out. I can stand
as big a shock as he can. I never have been shocked
off my base yet, and I have had lots of shocks from
many directions at the same time. I placed myself by
his horse on the side the crooked leg was on. The plan
was with me to be looking at his horse's forward feet.
He came out and commenced untying his horse.

"I see you have a fine-looking horse here," said I.

" Yes, he is a good one."

"I see he favors one foot a very little."

" Yes, he has been foundered twice. I have just
been having him fired."

" What does that cost? "

" Five dollars each time. I have had him fired
twice now."

" Don't you know what makes your horse lame; look
at his feet ; can't you see this foot he is lame in is not
like the other in any way? It is contracted feet that
ails your horse. That burning will do him no good ;
it will make him worse."

I shocked him in his wagon telling him the truth.
He said the horse was good enough for him, and away
he sailed. The last of him that I saw was the top of
his hat. My God! is there any hope of cases like
this? I meet thousands of such, and have for many
years. Of course it is impossible to write in detail all
that has come under my observation, looking over
this field of cruelty to the horse. I stopped on my return trip a while in Baltimore. There seems to be a
transfer through that city by horses. All of the cars
have to be drawn through. The horse has very heavy

loads to draw. It is one continual whip and slash
during the whole time. If these poor horses were
in shape to draw, it would not be quite so bad. As it
is, it is fearful on them.

While I was in New York city on my return, I met
my old friend, Hiram McConnell. I told him I was in
the old business yet, battling for the horse. No im-
pression on him could be made yet, I saw. I sailed for
Lake Ridge. I stopped for the night within sixteen
miles of home, at a hotel. Morning came. While sitting in the bar-room, one of my neighbors came in.
He seemed to be surprised to see me.

"Why, here is Doan. Your family will be awful
glad to see you. It is talked all over the country you
have gone off crazy, never more to return.

This was nothing new to me. This man was badly
off his base. He asked me to lend him a dollar. I
refused to let him have it, and told him his family
would be glad to see him at home. I left him and
sailed home. Of course I was crazy. I had got to
running around, and the meanest of all was I did not
tell everybody when I was going, and what my business was. In a few days I sailed west, to Chicago,
looking horses over in different states and in Canada.
These fields I have looked over many times in my
life. Canada is the worst for botch-work on the
horse's foot of all the country I have sailed over. I
soon sailed in home again.

Previous to this sail I closed my shop, packed my
shoeing tools, and went to Philadelphia to try to introduce the science. It was in the hight of the Centennial, and but little attention could be attracted. I had

a long talk with Howell Gerard in that city, the cele-
brated horse-shoer. I think he could have been
enlisted. He had a stable of horses of sixty, with
shoeing-shop connected. It was all rush headlong.
At that time their attention could not be attracted.
My time was mostly spent looking over this great field
of slaughtering horses, and here they were, in the
wholesale business at that. They were killing them
so fast they had to have men employed to clear them
away as fast as they killed them. It is a sickening
sight to see two deformed horses suffering every step
they take, before a long, heavy car, full, inside and
out, of people, the whip playing on them nearly all the
time. Some, perhaps, are only going sixty rods; and
what all this hurry and rush is for—what they are in
pursuit of that causes them to hurry so—I cannot
understand, unless they see a cent ahead. I suppose
they are afraid somebody will have a bigger pile when
they come to die than they. I can see no other excuse
they can give. It is a want of feeling, I suppose, for
the poor, suffering horse, or they could not do it.

I returned to Lake Ridge again and opened my shop.
I have not quit in this place yet. While working in
my shop a man from Ithaca drove up. He said he
had two valuable horses; they were both stiff; one he
had with him. They were valued by him at about
seven hundred dollars. I think his name was How-
land. No matter. He asked me if I could cure them.
"Yes, I can if I can have them; this one I can, I
know." He told me if I would come up to his place
and look at his horse he would pay my fare and give
me my dinner. "I think that would hardly pay," said

I; "I can make a few dollars here at home." Then he made another offer. "If you will come to Ithaca I will build you a shop."

"I have a shop and house of my own here."

"You could get more work up there."

"I have enough to kill four men here. I do not do half the work that comes here. I can't stand so much hard work. I am getting old and stiff myself."

"Well, I am going to bring my horses here for you to shoe."

"That you had not better do. It is a long way to come. I am full nearly all of the time. It might not be so I could shoe them. I cannot cure your horses by shoeing them."

Another offer: "If you will cure this horse I will make you a present."

"I do not work for presents."

"Well, I will give you ten dollars."

"I would not do it for ten dollars. It is worth more than that to cure any stiff horse."

"Will you shoe her?"

"Yes."

She interferes behind badly; heels low, toes long, contracted badly, and off her base on her forward feet She had flat shoes on her forward feet. I commenced to work; he commenced to give orders how it should be done. Those shoes were all right to go on again; no new shoes must be used. I soon saw there was no use trying to teach him anything. When a man has got that far advanced he knows all there is—about as far as a man can get—it is dangerous to try to get any farther. He might supersede the great Jehovah. I saw I could do nothing for him. I shod his horse the best I could. Then he began to talk cure horses again. I told him, "If you will bring your horses here, pay the keeping, and let me have full control of them, I will take care of them, and cure the two for fifty dollars." He drove off. That was the last I saw of that generous, noble-minded man.

While I was operating in this place, brother Oliver stuck his stake in a new place about twelve miles from me, at Groton, there to try and start curing stiff horses without medicine. I saw and talked with him many times to learn how the battle was going. He said it was red-hot. He got horses and cured them for all that. Some came from many miles away. While I was operating at Lake Ridge something took place that caused quite a racket. It was this: The boys, I call them, but they were as big as they ever would be, asked me to lecture. "What subject do you want me to lecture on?" "Oh, choose your own."

Whether they were in fun or not I did not know. I rather thought they were. They said they would furnish house, light it, and put up bills. I should be at no expense or trouble.

Notice was given out before the bills were up. I saw they were not going to get the bills up, so I saw to getting them printed, paid for them, and sent some to different places, putting them up myself over the country. The time came. I had quite a full house. I lectured in an old deserted Baptist church. I told them I was going to try and see how big a field I could work and experiment on, talking or lecturing on scientific principles, taking the whole Bible for the text or

center, then sail around and work up the outside. I
told them before I started it was only an experiment.
I made it go so well it shocked them, and it was felt
for many miles away. I told them I would try it
again the next Saturday night. When the time came
I was there at my post. The house was closed ; no
getting in. There was no one around only the neighbors, with one exception, and that man was John Cor-
win. I had shocked them all away but him. He told
me the people thought I was crazy. I told him that
was nothing. They would soon recover from that.
They were only shocked a little. On this experiment
I came near sailing into the lunatic asylum. Some
thought I ought to be taken care of, and yet I had
harmed no man. Well, it was only a lot of bigots and
peaked heads. I think there is not much danger yet.
It spread over quite a large field that I was crazy.
There was one that took great pains to tell this all
over. He had kept it up for more than a year, so I
thought I would try another experiment. This is
where I experimented on lying, to see how fast it
would multiply, and how far they would sail. This
man's name was Mr. Vorhees. I had done his shoeing for many years. I liked him, and do now, and he
liked my work. I went to my shop. There were
several there sitting around. I told them I had bad
news to tell them. " What's up now ?"

" Mr. Vorhees is crazy !"

Some made one remark, some another. All told
what the cause must be of his losing his reason. In a
few hours it was many miles away, multiplying, spreading. It had started, and there was no stopping it. It

was news for three months to some, and I do not know but it is going yet. It is about me

Since I have commenced to write this book I have had letters from parties threatening to put me in the asylum, there to remain the remainder of my days, and during the same time I have been obliged to write twenty-six pages answering letters. I commenced and numbered the pages so they could make a book to sell. It would save them the trouble of writing one. One of these men was a purple-nosed lawyer. How much it cost to color his nose I do not know. It did not cost him much. He was one of the kind that sells us out. I think I am in my right mind yet, allowing me to be the judge. I have stood it remarkably well considering the surroundings. I will have you know it takes quite a good head, and he needs to be a good financier, to sail clear of the asylum and not get crazy; to work on horses, cure them without medicine with so much opposition. But I am going to try a little longer. This horse that I am at work on now, his name is Prince. The soreness has nearly all gone out of his feet, and yet his shoulders seem somewhat stiff. I tracked this horse back to a colt. I found he had been kept up in the stable nearly all of his life on account of his being unruly and shod very young; before he had got his growth. He had grown up a deformed horse; he could not bear to have a toe cork on his shoes. It would sore him on his cords on hard roads. If his feet were allowed to get half an inch long it would affect him the same. I kept this horse nearly two years. He gradually grew better. I never put any corks on his shoes. In the winter I put in what are called frost nails. The heads stuck up along the shoe on the sides; none in the toe. When they wore off I drew them and put in more; beveled the toe of shoe off to save the leverage. In this way I could sail him sixty miles in ten hours, and he would be no worse for doing it. I mean after I had spread his feet, got the structure of his feet all in harmony and kept them so. He was a good horse and a hard one to follow. He was a nice-coated dapple-brown, in fine condition when I let him go to rescue another that was about dead, caused by abuse, night and day drives, and poor care. I must give you a description of this animal as she stood tied to a post. I looked her over, that is, her bones, for I could see some of them in many places. As for flesh, she had none on, and the hide was off and worn through to the bones with the harness. Her hair was faded and dead; the hide on her ribs was set; no stirring that; blood, scabs, and sores on every ankle. She stood with her head down. She was sick. She rattled badly in her throat at every breath. I saw she had a fine, clean, cordy deer leg, and points about her, if she had good care, that would make a good sailer. I made up my mind to rescue her. She was only six years old. While I was looking this mare over the owner came out of the hotel. I asked him if he ever traded horses.

"Yes."

"I have a horse that I will trade for that mare."

After looking mine over he said he would trade even. I told him all right. We changed horses in front of the hotel. There were quite a number standing around. I took my frame over near my shop and let her pick some grass. When she put her head down to eat she discharged badly at the nose and rattled in her throat. She was very cross. If I rubbed her on the ribs she would try to bite and kick me at the same time She appeared savage, and was when I first got her and put feed into her. If I attempted to go toward her she would jump at me, mouth open, and kicking with both feet at the same time. Poor horse! she was so near starved to death she was afraid she would lose some of her feed. She ate ravenously, and as fast as she could, and kept watch at the same time.

Now for a man to make a horse trade like this is evidence enough that reason is dethroned. No matter; I am going to loosen the hide on this mare and use no medicine; cure that rattling in her throat and heal every sore on her by removing the cause. The place to begin is at the feet. There is the place I always begin, after giving the horse water and a good square meal. She is rather dangerous to handle, she is so sore. The danger will disappear gradually as the sores do, and she will quit kicking and biting at me after she gets over being afraid of starving to death. Her feet were badly out of order in many ways. After straightening them up, I washed her sore ankles off clean with soft, warm water, and took her to the barn. I had a small piece of corn just beginning to harden up. I cut it, corn and stalks, and threw it in to her. She would stamp her feet, kick, eat, bite, and jump at me if I came near her when she was eating. She was in constant motion all of the time. I think I never saw a horse in my life so nervous as this one, all caused by suffering, starvation, and abuse. She looked wild out of her eyes. She had a large, wild-looking eye. Some told me I would get killed with some of these horses yet.

At this time I had rented out my shop. I did not work for others on horses, for this reason, I had been badly injured in the shop working on a horse. From that injury I have never recovered. I was hardly able to take care of my own horses for two years. I had to change my course then. In order to live and provide for my family I went to trafficking, that is, buying at wholesale what I thought I could market and make a little on. This business I followed. That was the business I was doing when I rescued this mare. It was sailing on the road, sometimes long drives. I put this mare the next day after I got her on the road; fed her well. She was soon all clear of her cold, no rattling in her throat. Her hide, as she put on flesh, began to loosen; holes in her skin where the bones had worn it through, slowly filled out. My little boy, twelve years of age, took care of these horses. As she gained in flesh she became less nervous by degrees. Stamping, kicking, and biting nearly all disappeared. A truer and kinder horse and better sailer on the road or on a load I never wish to sit behind. I have given you only a little sketch of the hard wrestles I had in this place. I stopped five years here. My health gave out. I could not stand sailing on the road nor wrestle with hores any more as I was then; that I could not do. I thought perhaps I might go West, keep cattle, and make a living that way. I soon found a customer for my place, and made a sale. This mare brought ninety-six dollars. She had a very bad name as being ugly and cross or she would have brought one hundred and fifty dollars. When she was led out to sell I think I never saw a finer picture of the horse kind. This mare never had a particle of medicine, either internal or external, while I owned her, although some said I doctored her up. It was all done by kind treatment, good care, and feed, and worked nearly all of the time; nicely haired over in a little over a year. Look at her sores and scabs! I did not cure this mare, I only removed the cause, and I did that when I rescued her.

In three months after I let Prince go I saw him. He was so sore he could hardly go. They had shod him and slaughtered him the first time. He had the damnedest botch job done on him I ever saw; toggled up on corks at least an inch long, and nothing right about the whole job. He soon changed hands. Next he was ten miles away in a team drawing heavy loads, going good; and I saw him since I have been writing this book pass drawing a heavy express, going well. I saw him only a few days ago standing before a buggy in this place. I looked him all over. He looked well; his feet looked well; he stood well on his legs; did not appear to be sore; it is about six years since I first spread his feet. There are only a few as hard cases as Prince was to get on his base. I never had as hard a case in all of my work on the horse.

I am going to sail out of this place west of the Missouri River on the plains. I stopped in Lincoln, Nebraska, awhile. Of course my time was all spent

looking over the sale stables. There were lots of
horses changing hands in this place, some very good
horses. The most of them were in some degree stiff.
They poured in from nearly all the states and from
Canada, but I saw that very few sound ones had shoes
on. I saw a very fine looking pair. They were some
along in years. I saw their feet were badly contracted. I took up their feet to look at them. Their
frogs were all gone; their feet had some trash in them
that looked like verdigris. Horses in this country, if
they iron their feet, get stiff very quick for this reason :
they do not have much rain ; the feet contract very
fast. I selected me a farm on the winding trail called
the old Santa Fe route. This was a great thoroughfare. Horses and mules were constantly passing in
droves.

I had a good chance to look them over as they
passed, all more or less stiff or off their base. I built
what is called a house. While I was at that there
were almost daily horses driven up around my shanty.
Some days several teams, all stiff ; some so sore they
would be covered with sweat; some lame. They
were all horses brought in from other states. They
all wanted to sell me a team. I was not ready to buy
yet. It was rather laughable to hear them brag of
their poor cripples, and warrant them sound ; and some
old horses had got to be quite young again. I did not
stay long on the plains. I found it wanted a tougher
man than I was then to care for a herd of cattle; and
that was not all. There was more wind than I wanted
to sail in at the time. I sailed east this time. Brother
Oliver was moving to Auburn city to try and see

what luck he would have in that place introducing curing horses there without medicine in brother Joseph's shop; back in the rear of Joseph's hack, livery, and boarding stable he commenced this business, Joseph doing all he could to help him. It went slow; no money to fall back on. He was soon starved out, and was obliged to go to work by the day for others in order to live, and that was what I found him doing when I sailed into this city from the west. This is the third time I have lived in Auburn. After getting settled I went to his place of business to have a talk with him. He was at work for another man, and at the same time curing stiff horses. He had some on his hands all of the time caring for. He continued on in this way. I was sick and unable to do work of that kind. I did but very little work for six months. After resting up for six months I began to feel better. I decided to tackle the horse again. I well knew I could not hold out long, for this is hard business and poor pay, not enough to live. The first thing to be done is to curtail expenses. I started out to find a place. I found a small, new shop, with rooms over the shop. It was deserted, empty, five miles south of Auburn. I found this was for sale. I bought it for four hundred dollars, and I rigged up new again to try and introduce this great science. This is where this work is written, over my shop with a checker-board for my writing-desk, with a *Scientific American* spread over it. The first thing when I came in this place was to commence to talk this science. How could I introduce it unless I did? No one knew anything about it but me, and they never would un-

less I talked and tried to teach it. The first thing was
to tackle the first cripple I could get. This was the
second time I had been in this place. Through the
influence of some of my friends, after a long time, I
got a cripple to work on. In a short time I found
myself obliged, in my old age, to work for less pay
than I ever had in my life, and nothing but cripples
to work on. Of these I had more than I wanted
The price of shoeing was dropped down as soon as I
opened my shop. Of course I must do it the same,
or have no work, and my work was all stiff, lame
cripples, four times as much work to do it. My
health was not good enough to do this; it wasn't what
I opened this shop for. I had made up my mind to
cure no more horses by expanding their feet for no
pay and make others rich and grow poor myself, and
they not learn or even try to learn this great science.
I will bury. As for killing myself, and all for no purpose, only being in hell red-hot all the time, that business is about played out.

Reader, this is the way I began to reason with myself. I found my brothers began to feel the same.
They had done thousands of dollars' worth of work
to try to introduce this work, and yet no help came.
That is what we wanted. We wanted the people to
give their attention and see and learn this science. I
have had men in my shop getting their horses shod,
who, when I tried to tell them what made their horses
stiff, would say: "I don't want to hear anything
about it. I am in a hurry; I never had a stiff horse
in my life." These same men's horses were so stiff
they could not back without dragging every foot. The

cause of their talking so was they had become so accustomed to driving and using stiff horses they did not know when they were stiff. While I was in this place battling for the horse, brother Oliver got back in his old place in the rear of Joseph's hack stable, there to try it again. We met often and talked the matter over, and to compare notes, so as to see how the battle was going. We thought we were gaining slowly. Of course all of the shoers were on our backs, and veterinarians the same. The last time I saw Oliver we were riding after a horse that had been laid up for six months unable to work. He had had this horse only a few days. He was now able to sail and keep doing it, and grow better for it. He told me he was able to cure these horses yet, and carry twelve men on his back, if they did not drag their feet on the ground too much. After I had been at Fleming Hill six months I saw a very fine young dapple gray stallion pass my place of business. I saw he was badly off on his forward feet.

I soon learned he was owned by a man in Auburn. He was kept near me during the summer. I saw him many times. I saw he was getting worse all the time. I did not mention this to any one. It was no use. I would not be allowed to touch him; besides, I did not want to get my old wounds torn open anew; but I watched the horse. In the fall he was so crippled he could hardly get along. I learned he was formerly owned by D. M. Osborn & Co , and had become almost useless. They must get rid of this horse in some way. He is of no kind of use to us. Orin H. Burdick, of the firm, bought him. What he paid for him

I know not. In the fall Mr. Burdick brought this horse to J. J. Doan's stable to have him kept for a while. Joseph saw the condition this poor horse was in at a glance. He told Mr. Burdick his horse could be cured for fifteen dollars, no medicine used, and a cure warranted or no pay. I have no time to do it. I can bring a man that will do it. Oliver soon came around. They told him all about the operation. Mr. Burdick soon saw the principle was all right. He left the horse in their care completely, and never got weak in the knees or head since he first enlisted in this army battling for the horse, which I shall show before I get through this work. Oliver had made quite a start previous to this; he had cured several horses for different parties, and Dr. Quigly was one. He proved to be a good soldier. He is a scientific man. He soon saw the principle was all right. I saw that with such men as these to help we could make it go now. They were not afraid to talk and tell the truth. We have got in the hands of men of science, men that can see the change in their horses at once and how it is done.

I was soon in Auburn. I found Oliver in a box stall with this gray stallion. "Now," said he, "we have got a good horse and a good man. This horse is well known to be a cripple; he is a fine one, and a horse that will attract attention, and I am going to cure him. I have got this business in the firm where I have been trying a long time, and on this horse hangs the whole business. If this job does not wake up the people I am going to bury the whole science." While we were talking Mr. Burdick came in. I told him what we had been trying to do for ten years, and we wanted him to help by talking, if this job pleased him. He told Oliver he should have all the horses he wanted, and at it he went. He was quite a horse lecturer in that town. When such mechanics as Burdick indorse this great science small heads have to stand back, and they did. It has been quite calm since, as far as fighting against us has been concerned. It had effect five miles away at least in this direction; it calmed the racket around me and infused new life in me. I told Oliver: "Now is the time to write this work. It will sell now. I will go home and commence. You keep at work. I went to Auburn quite often. I walked in the stable to find Oliver; there I always went first to find him. He had a fine saddle horse to work on that belonged to D. M. Osborn, straightening his legs, taking air-puffs off, balancing at the same time. There were seven or eight of the most scientific men in Auburn city taking lessons on the horse. One was Cyrenus Wheeler, the patentee of the Cayuga Chief harvesting machine. Burdick had waked them up. He was there, and Dr. Quigly and several others. I saw it was a go this time. After they left I swung my hat over my head. I could not help it. I told the boys:

"It's a go this time!"

So much for a good, honest, live man to help. When we can get such men as these enlisted it will go. "They are known all over the word, nearly, and it has gone ever since, and it cannot be stopped now. It has taken a heavy load off three men's shoulders that was hard to carry. We had carried it for many years. Mr. Wheeler has had a horse fixed, John Os-

born two, Mr. Burdick three, all of this firm and many
others of this city. There is no discount on this
science. Oliver was up here a few days ago. While
he was here the man that keeps Mr. Burdick's stallion
drove into town. The stallion is kept near me. We
looked him over. He is as limber and sound as any
colt, and stands his forward legs back of straight,
head up, and needs no gagging to make him do it;
he is one of the best stallions now in the country that
I know of for raising stock for many reasons: he is
the best dispositioned stallion I ever saw; he is pow-
erfully built, well proportioned, good at both ends,
just the right size, a beautiful dapple gray. Six months
ago this poor horse was a worthless, suffering cripple.
He has been out of his suffering many long months.
That was done by this science of spreading feet. This
horse's feet were spread an inch and a half in a very
short time. With all this staring you in the face
what is the use fighting any longer? Why not look
into this and see for yourselves? Blowing and blart-
ing will do you no good.

With a few more such men as Dr. Quigly and Burdick to work it will not be long before the poor suffering horses' condition will be bettered in many ways.
All it wants is some live and honest, fearless men of
brains to do this. When it gets started it will spread
fast. It is only one process that does the whole business. It is not such a wonderful thing, after all, when
it is understood.

The next day after Oliver was up looking at Mr.
Burdick's stallion I went to Auburn. I have traveled
over this road on foot many times on this horse busi-

ness in one year and a half. I wanted to see Mr. Burdick to get the privilege of using his name in this scientific work on the horse. He was gone away. I waited for him to return home; he said he had been up to look at his stallions. "Mr. Burdick," said I, "I have got along with my book now where it comes to you. Can I use your name in this science?"

"You can use my name in any way you please and I will add a little myself; you can say the work done on my stallion has added to his worth five hundred dollars. I would not have him put back where he was last fall for that; and that is not all; my brown horse that I have just had fixed can out-trot his mate, which he could not do before I had him fixed; he sailed out at once; it let him loose, untied him. The mist is clearing away."

This was the last he said to me. I walked away. This is encouraging, and this work is still going on and spreading, and it will continue to do so for this reason : it is right, based on principles that will stand, and all trash and rubbish it will clear away and shove from their base, just as these poor horses are.

There is one more mare I want to mention. It is the Westlake mare of Auburn city. It is nearly nine years since I changed her back to natural and put her in harmony of action. She never changed hands; he owns her yet. I have seen her nearly every year since and looked her over as she was passing and re passing. She was on her base and limber, looking fine. She was a good animal and is yet. When I changed her back she was badly deformed and showed it. Working on this mare I learned a lesson. I did not spread her forward feet quite enough to let her down between the cup at the top. She was badly contracted; she was completely raised out of the cup and shut out by the wall closing up below. By driving. it drove the sole down, not being room at the top of the wall for the bone to go down. She got pinched or wedged in the cup. After driving awhile I saw she was not going well. I soon saw the cause. Her feet began to bulge out at the top and both sides It was too late then to help that; it made her sore only a few days, then all was right; if the feet had been spread one quarter or over an eighth of an inch more she would have sailed all right. This was the first and last time I ever got pinched in that way. I explained the whole thing to Mr. Westlake and have talked with him since; his mare was cured for all that; it only set her back a little. All horses that I worked on were in Auburn city at that time, but that mare I have lost track of. I offer fifty thousand dollars to any man that will bring me a man that never made a mistake in life. I want to see him; it would be a big sight to me.

I will pass on now. I could write about thousands of horses that I have worked on. It's of no kind of use. All are cured by the principles that are laid down in this work. That is what I claim; and more, it will almost raise a horse that is nearly dead, and this is a fact, as strange as it may appear to some. This great science is classed with the highest; it is one of the great sciences of the sciences. It cannot be grasped at once by men of small caliber of brain, but they can

learn it by degrees, as all other great things are
learned, if they will apply themselves, which they
will have to do or suffer loss. And Mr. Kirby, the
well-known inventor of the Kirby harvester, has been
taking lessons. He saw this work done and measured
the feet before spreading, and stood and saw the feet
spread, then measured them after this was done and
watched the result. He wanted to know for himself,
and that is the way. I never had any trouble from
such men as these, and this kind of men will be the
men to help introduce this science or it never can be
done. My long experience working at mechanical
work has taught me this—the higher must teach the
lower; the lower cannot rise all at once. How can
they? And all men that fight this work with all
this evidence before them, coming as it does from men
well advanced and developed in science, men of char-
acter, of good standing, and they have earned it and
they are not going to indorse a science unless it is all
right and then have to fight against such men and evidence as this, any longer will only expose your
ignorance. Here will be the great center of action to
set it sailing, for sail it will, and no power on earth can
stop it. Now, what is the use trying to throw blocks
under the wheels of progression? They always have
had to move out of the way and always will. There
are lots more of things to learn yet. I have got
another bigger thing than this horse science, which I
have been working on about twenty-five years to perfect. I shall if I live bring that forward when I get
it so I can handle it as well as I can this horse business. On that I challenge all the wisdom, knowledge,

and brains concentrated on the globe to excel. Millions may equal; excel they cannot. It makes the horse as the Creator made him, and that is as far as man can go on that case. The created, I think, will hardly excel the Creator. In experimenting and studying this horse business I have undermined some foundations that have been reared on false teachings, and they will tip over, and they ought to, and it will be a godsend to the suffering mule and horse when they are scattered to the four winds or buried with all other false teachings of the dead past. This is what I have been trying to do for many years. In place of this entanglement of nonsense I will leave you some principles that will take you safe through all of this trash and rubbish and let the light of day in on you. This foundation that I have built in this work, and the superstructure reared thereon, will stand. Ages and ages can roll on eternally, and it will be there. It is founded on truth and principles of science, and after I am dead I want no man to worship me or erect a monument to my memory. All I ask is: Take care of your horse! All the headstone I want is a natural horse and carved on his side "Gerard Doan, author of 'THE HORSE'S RESCUE.'"

THE HORSE'S APPEAL FOR MERCY.

Do on me some feeling, judgment, and mercy show,
I cannot travel with these long levers on my toes.
Just look at my feet, you can see very plain,
Every step I take on my cords there is an awful strain.
To rise over these long and peaked toes,
It me all out of action and balance throws.
And that is not all, I have no use of my feet.
All contracted, sore, full of unnatural heat,
The structure of my feet are all out of condition to run;
To travel in this way, and not hurt, it cannot be done.
Look at my heels, all pinched up, you can easily see;
They are not as my creator intended them to be.
I am worse off than you think I am. I know
They ache and hurt me so I can hardly go.
I wish you would take me and have my feet spread;
I cannot stand this long, I shall soon be dead.
Iti s cruel to pound me around in this way,
When all of my trouble can be removed in a day.
Unless this is done, I never can any better be;
I am growing worse every day, you can plainly see.
I shall soon be of no kind of use to you;
You will only have me to feed; no work can I do.
When I am completely thrown back off my base,
What condition am I to put in a race?
I will only be laughed at; they will of me make fun;
The condition I am now in, I cannot trot or run.
To whip and jerk me, it will only make matters worse;
To get there in this condition I cannot first.
With all lengths of levers on the ends of my toes,
If you hurry me in this condition, out of balance all goes.

When this takes place, I have all I can do to stand on my feet;
And contracted feet is the cause of my losing the heat.
To pound me around on this hard track in this way,
I am always ten times worse for it the next day.
If you could only see the inside of my poor feet,
You could soon see the cause of my losing the heat.
They may look to you all right on the outside,
And yet for all that good horses as I have suffered and died
From this cause that I am now telling you about;
And if you keep on, I will go the same way, no doubt.
I cannot last long pounded around this track every day,
To have my feet contracted and bound up in this way,
My suffering is very great; the cause is all in my feet;
They pain me so day and night I cannot rest or sleep.
Sore, and stiff, and sick, and lame you pound me through;
I assure you it is worse than death; it may be fun for you.
If you would cut my throat, let the blood out of my veiins,
I would to you thankful be; it would end all my pains.
O my God! is there never any relief or help to come?
Have I always got to suffer in this way—every day be run?
Creator of me and all that is great, wise, and good,
Is there no way that my suffering can be understood?
O my God! in some way do to me send relief!
I appeal to you now; to my groans my driver seems deaf;
For there must be a great first cause of all that is created,
And to that, like all others, I must be related.
I well know on me in creating you have made no such mistake;
That I cannot eat or drink, and from that cause no comfort take.
I know myself where all of the cause is well enough,
But I cannot talk and tell, and I assure you it is tough.
It is not caused by anything that I have drank or eat;
It is nearly all caused by botch-work done on my feet.
It is caused sometimes by leaving my heels too low.
That throws me back off my base so I cannot go.
If you leave my heels too high, it is no better, you can see,
That will throw me off my base, cock ankle, and tip my knee.
If you dress my hoof, and get it all right to a fraction,
To look at may yet be out of harmony of action.
Internally the structure may badly changed be;

Put me in motion; if you have got eyes you can see
I will have to step short and have a crippled, hobbling gait;
When my feet are in this condition, my God! how they ache.
That causes great internal, unnatural fever and heat;
That causes my ankles to swell; it has its rise from my feet.
Tinker and toggle me up the very best way you can,
No relief to me can come until you my feet expand,
For the sole is raised up; all is out of harmony of action.
I cannot move well; this is nearly all caused by contraction;
There is other causes connected with this complicated matter,
But, with all, it relieves the most to make my feet flatter;
That lets my weight go back on my base a great degree,
And liberates the coffin-joint, and lets all go free.
Then if you will just look at the tops of my double heels behind,
And you find them even, you are all right so far you find.
Do not forget I have four feet that are of use to me;
They are, or can be, all affected the same, you can see.
If the heels are not even at the top, they are not right you will find,
That turns the toe in or out, I cannot travel in a straight line.
If my ankles are thrown in from this cause, to travel it would be
　　　　queer,
And not sore my cord badly, and not cause me to interfere.
You must look my feet all over singly in order to see,
They may all be nearly right but one, and that badly be;
And they may all be steering in opposite directions, so
I cannot trot, run, walk, it sores and hurts me, you ought to know.
Do, for my sake, look at my feet, crooked, many ways overrun,
All caused by shoeing and the awful botch work on me done.
There is a right way and wrong to do this, you ought to know;
It must be done so all will work in harmony, or I cannot go.
To have my feet in pairs, traveling on opposite lines,
My weight all thrown off of balance, it is hard, I find.
My good God, creator of all that we can see and of me;
I never can tell all of my suffering and how to get free.
You have power to all I see and behold to create;
And now is there not some way better care of me to take?
This contraction throws two-thirds of my weight on my legs behind;
And this is not all, it spavins me and strains me across the loin,
And that throws all internally out of order, too.

When this takes place no one seems to know what to do;
Then there will always be a lot of quacks gather around,
To kill me with blisters, and cramming me with trash they seem
    bound;
To balance me up by allowing my heels to grow and not my toes;
That, too, is no better; in a short time over the other way I will go.
It is plain enough, all might see, it's as plain as a be;
Then, with all this, have my shoulders blistered, it's hard for me.
Then to be all out of harmony in many degrees and ways;
With all this, have to draw loads, great mischief with me it plays.
O my God! I wish I never had created been.
To live a long life of suffering in this condition I am in.
I cannot hardly get my head down to drink or eat;
I am thrown in such shape caused by ironing my feet;
Neither can I get up my head any better than down;
In fact, it throws me in such shape I can't turn around.
Clear past the center two-thirds of my weight is thrown back;
Sometimes this is done slow; it is according as my feet contract;
It all depends on the care and treatment my feet has had.
I am in all stages and degrees of suffering; sometimes very bad;
I wish you could see the fearful condition it throws me and holds me
    so;
You would have the cause removed, and more mercy on me show.
Oh, dear! with shoes on me, and on me two sets of contracted feet,
Can't you see where I have gnawed them? On this manure heap,
All paralyzed, unable to rise or stand for the want of care,
There I am obliged to lie month after month and breathe foul air,
Although I am down now, and unable to rise, walk, or stand.
With all this, if you would cut my feet down and them expand,
I would soon recover, and grow strong, healthy, and spry;
And if that is not done, for there is no other way, I must die.
This is the last stages, and there are thousands like me all over the
    land.
This is the final result, paralyzed, unable longer to stand.
When I get this way, O my God! look inside of my feet,
They have become inflamed; now something more than a little heat;
All life and action completely destroyed for want of circulation;
And this, too, is all located in my feet—my foundation.
When my base or foundation you destroy and undermine me,

I am not of much use; I will have to come down you will find.
To be down in this way, sick, fearful pains to endure,
And breathe this stench; no bed, only stinking manure.
O my creator, God! this stench and carrion are enough to kill me;
If there was no other cause, this heat is taking my hair off, don't you
    see ?
O my creator and father God! this I do not comprehend,
That we have such a life of pain and suffering to spend.
Sure you could not, creating us, made such a mistake
That we cannot eat, drink, walk, stand ; no comfort take.
We can neither go up hill without hurting ; the same down.
It hurts us very bad to rise on our feet; the same to turn around.
It hurts me so it causes me to raise my hind legs high,
And I cannot help it, my forward legs I can't bend if I try.
I am all pinched, bound, and murdered with contraction,
And I have no control of myself, and I suffer ; I have no action;
I cannot back without almost killing me dead,
And it hurts me the same, from the same cause to go ahead.
Sometimes I am divided against myself, you can easy see ;
If I am all right on my forward feet, divided I shall be
Unless my hind feet are all in harmony at the same time.
All true should be toes, of equal length, and all travel on a straight
    line.
How can I travel divided against myself, all out of harmony, too?
You can see, reverse it, it is all the same, no good can it do ;
To fix me all right, my feet at the same time must be in harmony of
    action,
And to do this you must remove all leverage, run-over feet, and con-
    traction.
That will let my weight all go back on its base you will find ;
That will equalize my weight, balance me at the same time:
Poise me on my equilibrium in the center ; I mean to be understood.
Unless you understand this, to work on me you are no good;
You will be throwing me off my base in many different ways,
And in this suffering condition I shall have to be all of my days.
No more blisters, seatons, rowels, burning, liniment do I want around
    me,
The whole trouble is removed by working on my feet ; you can see
My suffering is great, and I am deformed enough already now,

Without burning and mutilating, to cure me you know not how.
If you can find a place around me that is the least bit sore,
The first thing will be to go at that, and sometimes make more.
Almost any fool the effect can nearly always find,
Unless he is a perfect blockhead and nearly blind.
If you can find all of the effects; you have only half, you can see,
Burning, blistering, mutilating them will never cure me.
The suffering from this treatment has been hard to endure;
Added to all others, the cause you must remove in order to cure.
O my creator God! how I have had to be tortured and suffer;
It has been a good thing for us all that we were not tougher.
How is such treatment as that going to put me on my base?
If you will and do it, I will take the back seat and give you the race;
You never have cured or helped one horse treating them in this way
Either in ancient or modern times, or in any other day.
And if that is all you can do is to mutilate the effect,
I am better off without you, if my feet do contract.
I can get around a little if I am stiff, lame, and sore;
When you get at me I am always a wreck six months or more.
To work on you have no theory, principle, plan, or foundation;
It is doctor the effect, when you can't find it, and all is mutilation.
You have been all over me, mutilating in many different ways,
And all is wrong; not once have you seen where the cause all lies
All you have done has been very great damage to me;
Spreading my feet at the top is all wrong, you can see.
I have been worked on on the great Dunbar plan,
That was recommended by that great joining of fallible being—man.
A great fulcrum of principles and science must then be made.
When to him for nothing twenty-five thousand dollars was paid,
For there is not one thing laid down in that work to me of use;
It is all torture to me; no help; only mutilation and abuse.
Spreading my feet at the toe, that is wrong, you ought to know.
That will throw my heels together; in doing so
That will cause the sole to raise; that throws me back still more
Off of my base again. My cords, O my God! how sore,
And this is done so as to give the coffin-joint a little more play.
Then it must be contracted again for fear it should get too much
　　　and run away.
And the toe must be kept as short as it can possibly be.

To keep and prevent the coffin-joint from separation, you see,
There is no use saying any more; it is like this all the way through.
To spend my time with this baby trash I can't, I have other work
to do.
Poor, deformed, and suffering, tortured horse of hundreds of years,
For many long years I have heard your cries and shed tears;
And now I have got this work nearly completed and done,
And when it is finished, to your rescue I shall come.
No man on this green earth can intimidate me so,
That for your relief I dare not the same old bugle blow;
For I shall be in the center and in the hottest of the fight,
No matter where or when nor what time, day or night.
No quarters will I give until I do away with some of the poor
horses' abuse.
There never was an effect without cause, of that you may be sure;
And the cause is removed with this science and that in the cure.
And now I am going to tell you what this science will do:
It will cure nearly all cripples, I will except only a few.
Of course there are cripples that the cause is not in their feet;
They can be crippled in many ways; I will assure you it is not
what they eat.
You may ask, What is the reason this has not been done years
ago?
I cannot tell you, sir, for the reason I do not know.
But there is one thing that I do know. of that I am very sure,
It cost me money and forty-one years' labor that was hard to en-
dure.
Of that I have only given you a sketch, a glance, a bird's-eye view
Just enough to lay down principles to tell you this work how to do,
For in that way I do not want my time to spend.
I am getting old now, of course my time here must soon end.
To perfect a great work experience has taught me it takes a long
time,
And after it is done, to introduce it, it is the same I find.
This is the reason I do not want my time to fool away,
For I well know this great science cannot be introduced in a day.
This science is far in advance of the age, that I well know.
Of course I understand that it must spread very slow;
Ignorance is the great power; against that it will have to contend;

Nobody knows how long or when it will end.
It may be hundreds of years before it is well understood,
Or it may go very fast; if it does it will do a power of good.
I do not want any man to think, after they have read this work
    through,
To make money out of this work is all I want to do.
Of course for this work I shall have to charge now a little fee,
Or I never can introduce this science, you can easy see.
The last dollar is going now in this work that I have got,
Excepting a few blacksmith tools and my little red shop.
Before I quit there is a little more to you I want to say,
The principles in this work are right; there is no other way;
And if they are not adhered to, you had better beware,
Your horses will all be better off with their feet bare.
Now I will in this work bid you all adieu;
I do not want you to think I have given up and got through;
I have not, I am going to follow this work around,
And teach and introduce this science I am bound.

Adieu, your humble servant,

GERARD DOAN.

No. 1.

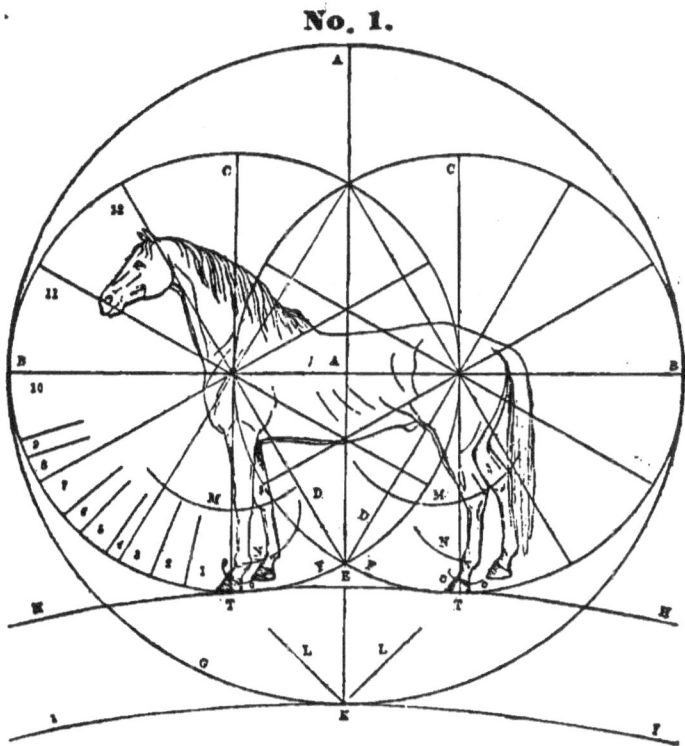

Cut No. 1 represents the natural horse before he has been changed
from natural by having his feet ironed. There are other causes,
which are often the case. The causes that change the horse from
natural are very slight compared with the many and great changes
and many degrees of change about which I have written, caused by
ironing their feet. I have told you in this work that the horse is a
machine, and must be in harmony of action or he will run badly.
These cuts are to show you scientifically, to give you an idea, or to try
to, of the suffering condition your horses are thrown in. Cut No. 1
shows the horse natural, inside of his circle, all in harmony of action
—no leverage, no runover feet, no contraction. The center perpendicular line, A, horizontal center line, B; it crosses at A in the center
of the horse. If the horse is not drawn out of shape or off his base,
he is balanced in the center. He can place his feet at fulcrum, E,
where the two circles, F F, cross lines; place the hind foot to D line

forming fulcrum with E; place the forward foot to D line. When this is done, you can see there is another center and fulcrum of levers formed if the horse is as he should be. When his feet are all placed in the center at fulcrum, E, he can rotate both ways from points B B to K, or he can rear up until point B of horizontal line in front comes to A, perpendicular line. If he is natural, he can kick up in the same way. He can rotate both ways, horizontal line B B to A and K, without hurting him in any way, if he is natural and inside of his circle. When the horse is going through this exercise, changing ends, every time he changes he will place both his hind feet when he comes down at fulcrum, E; his forward feet the same. If you will watch him, you can see this. The horse has four drive-wheels. These cuts only show one side. The drive-wheels are all of one size if the horse is natural; I mean he rolls four of a size, and the size is according to his own length and size; and the size of wheel he rolls is governed by the harmony of action he is in or out. This cut shows him all in harmony of action. See how accurate all works out. The two perpendicular, C C, lines crossing horizontal, B B, line to T T, forming two fulcrum of levers, or centers. Here is where the horse gets his pro-pelling power and balance of leverage that enable him to draw heavy loads up heavy hills. Throw him off his base, or out of his circle, and he loses his power according to the degree. The great circle, G, will show you the lever power the horse has if he is in his circle and natural. From B to B and from A to K he has that length of lever power, turn him any way you may on this globe. The line H H, I drew to show you a rest for the drive-wheels. It is made on a circle to represent the globe or earth—to convey principles that are not seen and yet exist. The lower line, I I, is the real line to show the earth and the leverage power the horse has, and lines L L are placed there to show another center or fulcrum of levers. No matter what part of the globe the horse is on, he is always on the summit. If he stands up, his feet and legs point to the center of the earth; the same with man. The horse is quite a machine; he has a gearing running hori-zontal; his feet are a circle of leverages, all acting from a center at every step the horse takes, if they are not fixed so they cannot. He has a very complicated perpendicular circular gearing, which I have not put all on in full, it not being necessary to convey what I wish to. I thought it would complicate it too much. It will be easier to under-stand and explain all the better as it is. He has too, withal, a folding crank motion, which I will explain. That crank can be affected

badly and be made to vary in length by botch-work done on the feet
In order to show the principles the horse moves on I have lined the
drive-wheels something like spokes in a wagon wheel; put the horse
in motion, each spoke as the wheel rolls will take its place at the point
T T; all become in their turn perpendicular lines, C C; the horse
changes when in motion, feet at the point T T at the same time, if he
is all in harmony both forward and behind.   When he is trotting fast
if you see when he changes if he is all right, you will have to see
quick or you will not see when he does change.   I do not pretend he
spaces off as he rolls along his strides, or steps regular as they are
spaced in this cut.   I have marked some degrees on the forward drive-
wheel to show something of the action of the horse; these degrees I
did not put on the hind drive-wheel.   The principle is the same on all
and on all horses, both before and behind ; and after you have experimented on horses forty-one years, I am right, you will find.   The
horse when natural can place his forward foot to No. 12, and even
higher, the other foot remaining on the ground; he can do the same
with his hind feet; he can place his hind feet where F F circles cross
lines and form fulcrum at the top.   I have marked off degrees, and
numbered them from 1 up to 12.   They are not regularly spaced off.
These lines are to show the irregular change and degrees of change on
the same horse.   Do not forget it is the same on the horse's hind feet.
This will be more fully explained in other cuts.   You can see I have
struck circles from the two centers of drive-wheels at the gambrel and
at the knee, M M.   Look, then you can see at the fetlock there are
circles from the gambrel and knee, N N.   Look; these two you can
see.   From the fetlock there is another circle from O O; and if you
destroy the structure in my foot, or feet, you will find I cannot go.
When the horse is put in motion he changes at point T T, and leg
folds toward the center of drive-wheel at the knee and fetlock and
heel.   They fold the same on the hind drive-wheel, and these folding
cranks all fold toward the great center, A, and he gets the balance of
lever power in this way.   When he reaches out his feet to put himself
in motion one half of his legs folds toward three centers, the other
half unfolds; he gets the balance of power.   In this way the cranks
fold and unfold, striking half circles rotatory motion.   The principles
are there just as much as they would be if this machine was made
with cog-gearing.   He has   got a   power   on   those drive-wheels.
When he is even with himself and in his circle, all natural as his creator made him, he can straighten out his legs from A to K, and whirl

around and around very easy. You can see all working in harmony from the great center.

No. 2.

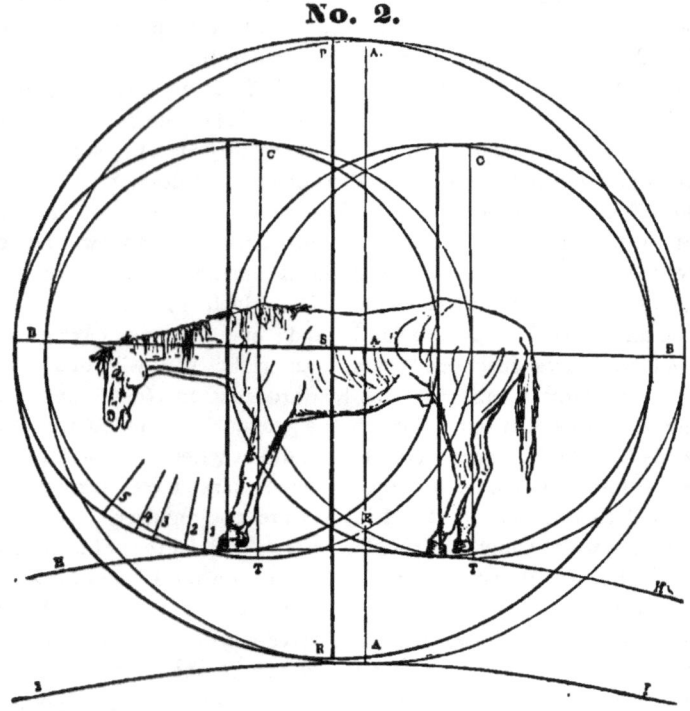

Cut No. 2 shows the horse off his base, both forward and behind; it shows him out of his circle; it shows two sets of circles and perpendicular lines. This cut will show you something of the first stages of the horse's change from natural. Do not forget there are all degrees of this change, and his suffering commences at the first change. As this horse now is, he is in a bad fix. Now I will ask some wise man to tell me how this horse can be got out of his trouble, burning, blistering, rowels, and all kinds of mutilating. You may fasten his feet where they now are, hitch tackles to his neck, and draw him in his circle, or roll him in, or pry him in, or blister him, or burn him in, he will not stay; and you cannot get him in his circle and put him in harmony in any such way. I put him in his circle with a lever, and it is all lever principle I work on to do it. It is all done working on the feet. There is the cause. I have explained that

about as well as I can. The light perpendicular lines, A and C C, are
the natural lines; the space between A and C, center perpendicular
lines. The horse is out of his circle and off his base that much. You
will find that throws all out of harmony of action; the same degree
the horse is all out of his balance. Look; there are two sets of circles and lines, you can see. This only shows in this small cut a small
degree. The horse is off his base or behind himself. Take a full-
sized horse and line him as this cut is lined; you can find lots of horses
off their base eighteen inches, and some more. I have marked and
figured a few degrees. The horse in this condition cannot step far, he
has not got much action. He has lost his lever power, caused by contraction; he is sick; all is out of mash. The machine will not run
much, and heats badly when put in motion. He cannot rotate from
B B to A; he cannot rear up or kick up either way; neither can he
any better turn around. It all works the same when he gets up or
lies down. Roll him back until A line comes to P, then there will be
only one set of circles and lines, you can see. If it is done right a
will in harmoy of action be. I have left this cut as little complicated
as I could and convey what I wanted to. If I had laid out two sets
of gearing, and put all in these cuts which I could, it would about
spoilt them to convey the principles that I well understand to others.
Look where fulcrum E is; it should be where the forward circles cross
lines on heavy perpendicular, P, line, then A would take the place of
S and in the center be; and T T would move forward with C C.
There are six centers now. If that was done there would be only
three. Take hold of circle at the top at point and line A, move it forward; the circle would at that point travel a large degree, while it
would hardly move at R and A. That you could see all would come
in one line, then all in harmony would be. This poor horse's body
must all move forward and his feet remain where they are. This may
look like a hard job to do without medicine of any kind, and yet it can
be done, and it is a very simple job to do when once understood. As the
horse's body moves forward, no matter what degree, if it is done
right, his back will straighten across the loin, and his head will rise as
his body moves forward, no matter what degree, until all is in
harmony.

No. 3.

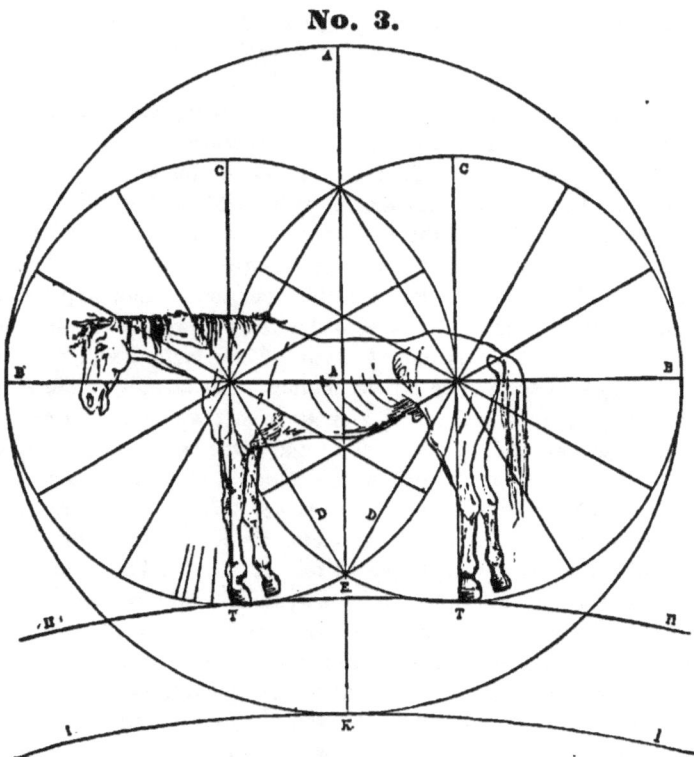

This cut No. 3, shows the horse in his circle and balanced in the center, and yet he is badly out of harmony of action, caused by improper care of his feet and contraction. This is what I call balancing the horse between runover feet, contraction, and leverage. This is what I call a bad job. It has balanced him over forward, tipped his ankles forward, and his knee; that is caused by leaving the heel too high, or toe too low, or both. Sometimes the fault is all in the shoe by dressing the foot; it can be done in that way, and often is, and in many and many degrees of this and on the same horse. This horse is not so liable to fall over backwards as the horse shown in cut No. 2; but he is liable to lose the use of his feet and legs, and has, nearly. He has but very little action, and is liable to fall at every step if he is hurried. His feet are bad, both internally and externally. He is a great sufferer, and the cause is located in his feet. Reader, you may think this picture overdrawn, some of you, but I assure you it is not.

I can produce thousands of horses that are worse off than this horse is shown to be. This horse has more ailments than are shown in cut No. 2. He has been kept in his circle, or, other words, tried to be kept on his base and balance and failed, as all do that try to do it in this way. Cut No. 2 shows the horse thrown off his base by the soles of his feet rising up. Do not forget it can be done many other ways, about which I have written. If the sole had been lowered on the principles laid down in this work, he or his body would have gone back on his base. This horse (cut No. 3) has had his feet dressed in such a way it has added more to his trouble, and the first cause still remains, and has grown worse. It is of longer standing. The coffin-joints are badly affected, and all is bad internally. He is sick all over, and not fit to work. Now, I want some man to tell me, if he can, how he is going to get his poor horse out of this trouble with medicine of any kind, or any treatment excepting the principles laid down in this work. I mean the ailments the horse has at the present day that I treat and write about. I well know this is the right and only way out of this trouble, and the horse should never be in it. But this is the way it is; how long it will be so I know not.

The horse shown in cut No. 2 thrown off his base I left in the fore-part of this work; at that time I could do no better. Such as he go over backwards often. And this horse (cut No. 3) I left in this work after balancing him as well as I could. Him I came around to see. I found him cocked on his ankles and tipped on his knees. I have no recollection of ever serving a horse in this way in my life; but I have straightened thousands of them, and shod them to prevent them from balancing over in the way this is shown in this cut. Some horses can stand and work many years in this condition. They suffer greatly; they are weak; they cannot draw but a small load compared with a horse that is all sound and natural. I have marked a few lines or de-grees pointing toward the center of the forward drive-wheel. His steps are short; he does not get much balance of power on leverages; the folding cranks do not work; he is stiff; no knee action; no action in any way; he stubbs and pegs; blunders along; swaying right and left. He has all he can do to stand on his feet. He can stand hitched to a load or by the side of another sound horse better than in any other way. This horse is harder to cure than the one shown in cut No. 2, and yet it can be done. In the condition this horse is now in he has but very little action; you place his forward feet to line D, forming fulcrum at E. How long do you think he could stand cocked on his ankles and tipped on his knees? Place his hind feet at the same fulcrum E. In the condition he is now in he would fall very quickly, you would see. If he was put in his circle by working on the right principle on his feet he could rotate both ways until H H

No. 4.

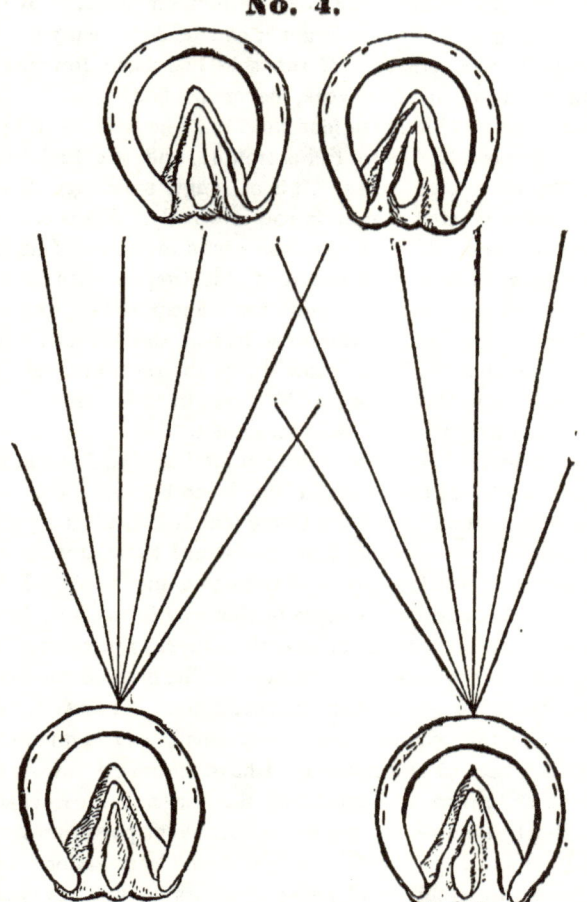

line and B B would meet, and he could rotate from A to K just in the same way, and that would be, of course, to line I. The condition he now is in he cannot do it if he should try, although A in the center seems to be, and so is the perpendicular lines C C, and the feet seem to be in about their proper place at T T; but it is all done wrong; he cannot move well botched in this way, for this reason, it is not done in the right way. Compare this horse with the one in cut No. 1, and you can easy see why his machinery he cannot run. And after working on the horse forty-one years I found out how all this mischief was done after I got control and master of the horse's feet. If I do say it, balancing up horses I was and now am hard to beat. The opposition I meet with I do not mind. I can balance these horses and put them in harmony of action very nicely both before and behind.

Cut No. 4, or plate of cuts, is to show the base, or foundation, of the horse. This is to be looked at as though the horse had walked off and left the bottom of his feet with shoes on, the sole and frog all there. The object of this is to more clearly show and convey the condition—the foundation—of the most of horses are in, caused by unequal weight on the double heel, and showing what shape they will assume, caused by that and not being properly dressed and cared for. You can see there is not a true foot there; they are all imperfect and untrue in some way, and in many and different, no two alike. The two feet that the lines start from at the toe are to represent the hind feet. The drive-wheels on the horse's hind feet are intended to run on the outside of the forward wheels if he is natural, and nature has made him so. If nature has a chance they will run in that way. If his feet are run over it will change these lines from a straight line in degrees according to how much his feet are run over. The top of heel is the place to look. There will be all degrees on the same horse from the same cause; the weight will turn the toe in or out, the same on all the feet. And this is a very important point to look to if you want your horse to move well. Equalizing the weight on the feet is one of the most important things to be looked to in dressing and ironing a horse's feet. If it is not done properly it will turn the toe one way or the other. In driving twenty miles, and some feet in less, it throws the ankle in or out. If it should throw the ankles out, the toe would go in. If both feet should go in that way (I mean a pair), they would cross lines, as shown in this plate, and there are all degrees of that. Sometimes, when not very bad in that way, these lines would cross some rods ahead of the horse. When the horse is in this way he will grab his shoes and heels and constantly be running over himself. Sometimes he is run over in pairs, both forward feet one way and both hind feet the opposite. When he is in that way there is danger of his falling if he is hurried, and liable to if not. The fact is his feet are all turned one way or the other.

If he is run in on his feet he will knock his ankles until he is straightened. This is not seen by many. It racks the horse's ankles bad.

There is another point to be looked to where this run-over-feet business exists. Stand behind your horse and see if his legs are on a perpendicular line; that is, see if the hind drive-wheels do not stand under too much; that is, his feet huddled together In case they should by being runover, or from want of proper work done on his feet, the effect would be bad in many ways. Look up to the center of the drive-wheel; there is a fulcrum of levers up there. If his leg stood under from a perpendicular line his weight would act at that center or fulcrum of levers. These levers act both ways. They are all right when they all act together, as nature intended they should. When thrown out of harmony they work against the horse and his owner badly. These principles work the same on the forward part of the horse. Sometimes one wheel is badly out of order, sometimes all; sometimes two; sometimes three. Go and look your horse all over, put him in motion, and if you have got an eye for a horse you can see.

No. 5.

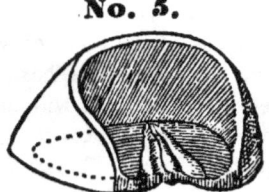

Cut No. 5 shows the foot natural; that is, the covering of the sensitive part. It shows the surface of the sole and frog internally; the heels are low and wide apart; the foot nearly round in shape; the sole nearly flat down; the double heels and frog all rest on the ground, or floor equal, and this is the way it always should be.

No. 6.

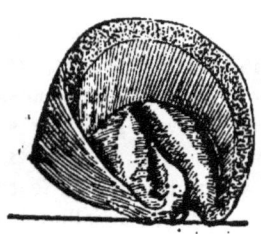

Cut No. 6 shows the foot badly changed from natural, it is badly contracted. You can see the heels are closed together. In doing this it raises the sole up. The mischief it does I have written about. To cure these horses my work treats on. I expand the foot, let the sole down, and make cut No. 6 have the appearance of cut No. 5. It does not tear the foot apart, as many would suppose; it simply lets the sole down to its natural and proper place, as it originally was. In doing this every degree, no matter how small you change or expand the foot, the circle of the foot grows larger. There are three ways to do this: The first is to pull the shoes off, dress the feet, so as to let the horse's body go back on the base if he is off, so the weight will be in center of feet; dress the feet, all slanting toward the point of frog; keep the frog cut away, so it will not touch the ground; drive with no shoes. The second is in expanding with shoes, and the principles are all laid down. The third is in expanding with shoe. The last does the work in a few days. The other two processes are slow. They cannot all be cured in that way. The second process is in expanding the foot by the horse's weight with shoes; and the last is by spreading, as shown in cuts No. 7 and 8.

No. 7.

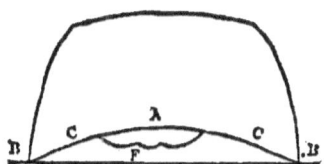

Cut No. 7 shows the arch-shape the bottom of the foot will assume when contraction takes place. This little simple skeleton-cut is to show you the whole business of expansion and contraction. The straight line, B B, is to represent the ground. Arched line, A, and C C, shows the sole of, or bottom of, the foot raised up. A is supposed to be in the center of the foot at point of frog, but it is not, and there are few that are perfectly true. F is to show the frog under A. Now I want to expand the foot and settle the frog down to straight line, B B. Suppose I put weight (no matter what kind) on this arched line, A, and the arched line above was not made fast at points, B B, where arch-line, A, forms fulcrum, arch-line, A, would be likely to settle; and if it did it would spread the foot and continue to do so until the frog came to a rest on the ground. In case the foot had shoes on that raised the frog up it would be likely to dish the wrong way.

In shoeing to expand the foot or to expand it in any other way, it should be prepared in the same way as shown in this cut—work from the center. At point, C C, an arched line, A, is to show how the foot should be dressed when shoeing to let the sole come down to flat rest on shoe. When the frog came to rest on the ground all would be right. Putting on a spreading shoe, the foot must be prepared the same.

No. 8.

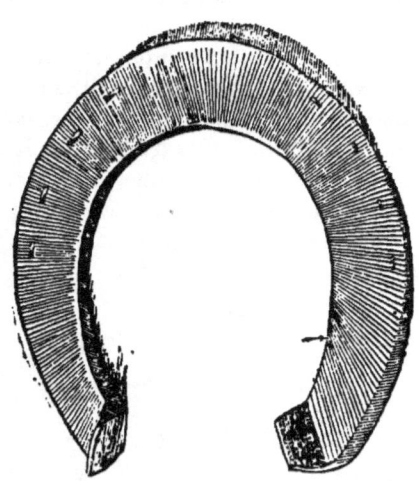

Cut No. 8 shows a very good shoe for expanding a foot and holding it. This is the best way to work on contracted feet. I can put them where I want them and hold them until they settle and grow. This shoe is concave, clear out to the edge, so as to let the sole down, except a little flat rest at the heels. This shoe is only for a temporary use. The lips raised at the heels are to

No. 9.

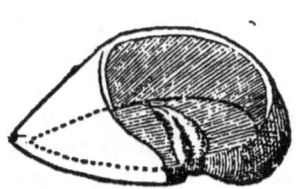

fit inside of heel, so as to spread right at the heels. After the horse has worn these shoes a few months, and had his feet spread, other shoes can be used. There are many kinds of shoes to expand horse's feet. This shoe I like the best.

Cut No. 9 shows the runover-foot, caused by unequal weight on the double heel. One is higher than the other, and, rolled under, that turns the toe in and out. The best place to see how that is is to look at the horses; there you can see it ten times better. And if you want to see how this expansion and contraction works, take a piece of stiff paper, strike circle the size of the horse's foot, cut out a goring-piece running to point in the center, about the size of the frog, then close up the space, you will see it will raise in the center in the form of a cone; let it down a small degree, mark around the circle; do that way several times until it comes down to a flat rest; you can see the circle is growing larger every time you let it down. This is the way this works on all feet. It is all summed up in leverage. To illustrate this a little more, in order to make all as clear as I can, I will take one leg and foot of the horse. The foot is the base, or foundation, figuratively. We will say the leg is a column. If you want it to stand perpendicular you must make the bottom of the base true and work from the center. There must be a center perpendicular line pointing to the center of this earth, and you must do your work so your column will balance, if you want it to stand, and it must balance all around the center. This is the way the dressing on the bottom of a horse's foot must be done. Remember, you are working around a center; when you are paring the bottom of the foot of the horse you can throw him off of balance all around the center of his foot by cutting away the bottom of the base, and it is all leverage-balancing in all ways over a center or fulcrum of leverages.

Now I will try to convey to you how these fulcrums of levers work, and what shape they throw the horse in has already been told many times. There is a horizontal fulcrum at the center of the foot raising and lowering in the center. There are three fulcrums of levers at the toe of the foot, caused by contraction and improper work done on the feet, throwing the horse off of balance in many ways, and there should be none to hold him there. If all is in harmony he will be balanced in the centers all over; then he can take the advantage of this lever-power at will and balance and throw his weight back and forward, and in all ways, around the great

fulcrum of levers shown in cut No. 10. At point C he can throw his
weight forward and back of fulcrum, A; and if he is balanced in
the center he can turn on the great center and fulcrum and roll
himself in all ways; and, doing this, he rolls a great drive-wheel
and a circle of them; and in his turnings and changing he rolls a
ball of circles around him.   If he wants to hold a load that is
crowding him, and stop it going down a hill, he throws his weight
back of the center, A, by bracing forward all of his legs.   The more
the load crowds the more he will get the balance of leverage by
throwing his weight back of center, A, as is shown in cut No. 2.
If he is all right he must be so he can throw his weight always
around the great fulcrum, C, and perpendicular center-line. B.   The
levers must be equal. as shown in cut No. 10 from center, A, to

No. 10.

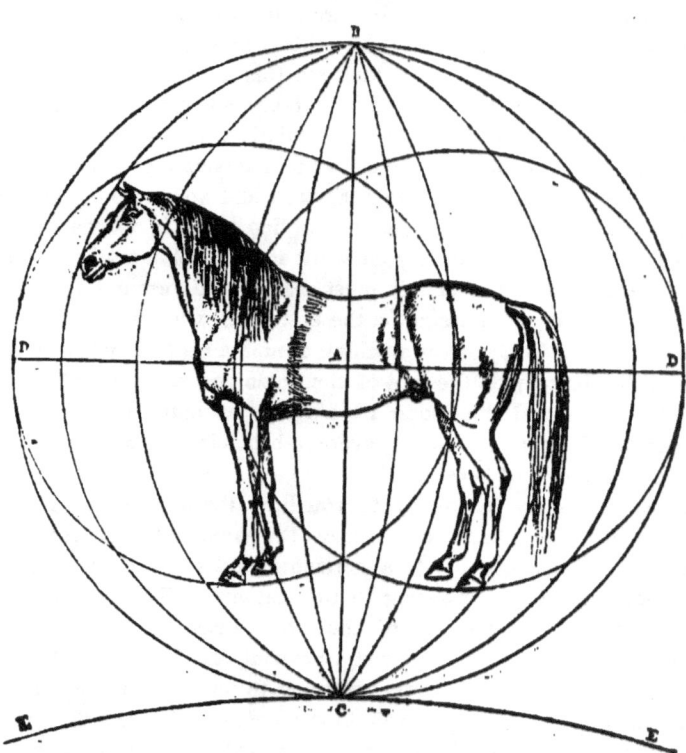

D D.   If they are he can rotate (D D line) both ways and all
ways to line, E E, around the great center, C.   This whole busi-

ness is summed up in leverage, the balance around a center of lever-power.

We will go to work on the foot, or base, again. The heel is double. If you cut those heels one lower than the other, or cork or make your shoe of unequal thickness in any way, you will throw the weight of the horse unequal on the double heel by throwing weight past the center. Throw it either way, you set a fulcrum of levers to work at the toe of the foot. That ought not to be there. By constantly throwing and changing the weight from one heel to the other past the center, that causes the double heel to work up and down. Those levers form fulcrum at the toe of the foot, constantly expanding or contracting at the heel, and these levers form fulcrum at the toe. They act horizontal, the end of lever growing on the toe of foot, the sole raising in the center. There is another fulcrum of levers, all working together, with the one on the end of toe forming fulcrum with another at the center of foot, right over the coffin-joint, one lifting, one pulling down, throwing the horse off his base, as shown in cut No. 2. This tip-back and pull-down lever has a double action: it works both ways from its fulcrums; it tips the horse over on his nose sometimes. I can prepare and iron any horse's feet and throw him over backward, and no power can make him stand, and I will do it with a lever. I can do it in this way: Cup out the feet, iron them, take a pair of tongs, and close the shoes together. That is done with lever-power. It will raise the sole of the foot in the center, throw the horse off of balance, and hold him. I can throw him over back, and down. The Creator of him cannot raise him. I will not put anything on him only the shoes He must lie there until I use the lever again. This time I expand the foot (that is done with a lever), let him go back on the base, and the shoes are levers forming fulcrums at the toe. These principles all work the same on all feet and all horses and mules.

To close up this long story, I will tell you how many centers and fulcrums of leverages there are in the horse to be thrown out of center and in center, caused by expansion and contraction, leverage, runover-feet, improper dressing of the four bases or foundation of the horse, throwing the horse off his four bases, throwing him off of balance, in many degrees and ways. There are thirty-five, one at whirlbone, stifle, gambrel, ankle, pastern, and coffin-joint. These are the hind-centers on one leg. There is the same number forward. And there are four legs, six on each, twenty-four in all, one in the center at A, one at fulcrum, E, one at R. These are perpendicular-centers. There are eight horizontal-centers to be kept in harmony—the center of the sole of the foot at point of frog, one at the toe of foot; four feet, eight in all. In nearly all of these centers there is a double action of levers both ways, thrown out of center by contraction and other causes, which I have explained enough. And I will close this long story, and the result of my forty-one, and most forty-two, years' labor has simmered this whole business down to a very simple process, curing all the ailments I treat on in this work; and that little process on the bases of the horse throws the whole entire machinery out of center and harmony of action; and all are, by working on the feet on the principle laid down in this work, thrown in harmony of action, and no medicin is required to do this wonderful work. The difficulty these poor horses has been in (I know not how long) has puzzled the brains of millions of men for hundreds of years, and yet the process is very simple. All that is required to do this work is warm water, a little cow manure (ox manure will do as well), a reasonable amount of good brains and good judgment, physical force, courage, and patience. If there is any man, or men, teaching curing horses (that are troubled with the ailments that I have mentioned in this work) on any other principles than are laid down in this book, they are not right, and I know it, and I will be qualified before any magistrate and before a multitude of people that the principles to work on the horses to cure them of the ailments that I treat on, laid down in this book, are all right if they are done right and carried out. Now just think a little and you will see you have got the prevention, and that is worth more than the cure.

Your humble servant,

GERARD DOAN.